THE FINNISH GIRL

Also by Dennis Frahmann

Tales From the Loon Town Café

The Finnish Girl

A Novel

Dennis Frahmann

Although portions of *The Finnish Girl* were inspired by real events, it is a work of fiction. Names, characters, organizations and incidents portrayed are either products of the author's imagination or used fictitiously.

Loon Town Books
www.loontown.com

ISBN: 0692236481
ISBN-13: 9780692236482

To my mother and the stories she inspired

CONTENTS

"Life can only be understood backwards;
but it must be lived forwards."

— Søren Kierkegaard

DANNY
1983
THREAD, WISCONSIN

Danny Lahti was certain that he'd failed his ninth-grade history exam. Riding on the school bus, its windows framing the leafless trees like the flashcards of autumn, he felt his stomach churn. What did a stupid test matter?

His mother, she loved that stuff, history and politics and old men in wigs. But she never helped him to study, so she couldn't harp if he flunked a pop quiz. But underlying that pit of anxiety he called his belly, or maybe lodged inside his mind that couldn't keep dates straight, Danny felt something else, like the ESP his mother always claimed to have, but really didn't. If she had a sixth sense, she would know how alone he felt. And she would do something about it.

Just before lunch and the unexpected quiz, Danny suddenly felt truly alone. Often, he sensed a bit of his mom's presence, as though her mind could reach through all his troubles and hold his soul steady. But in that moment it was as though his mom suddenly dissolved into the ether. All afternoon, he shifted uneasily in his desk chair, twitched in dread for the school bus ride to end, and rushed more than usual up the gravel driveway. He sped by the mailbox, raced rapidly past the piles of raked autumn leaves awaiting a dry day for burning, and thrust through the kitchen door. On Fridays, his mom made her famous raised doughnuts. The room smelled dead. No yeasty smell of freshly fried pastries lingered.

No murmurs of afternoon talk shows came from the television, sitting cold in its corner. No meat thawed on the linoleum-topped cupboard counters. No glazed doughnuts, no frosted sweet rolls, no freshly baked breads. Late fall light created shadowy corners in a chilly kitchen.

He couldn't force himself to call out for his mom. Perhaps she was visiting a neighbor or taking a stroll. He lingered in the kitchen. An extra chill on the back of his neck whispered to him of a story ending he didn't want to read. He would stay put and not check on his parents' bedroom. But he moved on.

He found her. And he was alone. Because she was gone. For the barest of moments when Danny walked into her room, saw her sprawled on the bed with the empty pill bottle on the nightstand, for just that fleetest of moments, he felt her presence. Lempi, his mom and the woman whose Finnish name meant 'love', was still there for him. He knew her lively eyes would open to gaze on him and that she would say everything will be all right. And he would pretend to believe her because she was after all his mother.

No eyes opened. That spark blew out. It was only him, alone in a room, and feeling colder than ever.

Danny sat there quietly, because that avoided the need to act. He would wait for the return of his father Toivo. Danny was fourteen, old enough to know he should call the sheriff or an ambulance, or at least take some action that pretended the possibility of hope. Rules existed and steps needed to be taken. But doing nothing let the past linger a bit longer.

In a room growing dimmer as the October sun set into the shadows of a cold fall night, Danny Lahti sat motionless, until the end of the workday, waiting for Toivo Lahti. That's when the Finnish timberjack walked into an unexpected emptiness that he feared he had caused and could never correct.

Danny's emptiness continued in the days that followed. He endured the funeral in the old Lutheran church and the Ladies' Aid dinner in its basement. The womenfolk in Thread sought to comfort them—the fourteen-year-old boy and the widower father barely into his forties. Danny ignored the chipper adolescent girls in the pews, who looked at him with a little too much eagerness. Despite wanting to show support, they stayed mute in their seats.

Danny wanted an explanation. His mother's suicide was an ache within him like nothing he had ever suffered. It wasn't the hunger for dinner after a long day fishing, or the curiosity of why the sky was blue, or the puzzlement about a magic trick, or the intellectual challenge of completing a logic puzzle. The yearning came from somewhere within him that he didn't even know existed. His mom had left with no explanation.

Danny wondered if his father even cared. At first, Toivo lingered in the funeral home to keep vigil over his wife's coffin, and Danny sat with him. Their dark moods shared no intersecting ripples. After Lempi's burial, Toivo seemed lost. He visited the grave plot each day, but sought true solace in the woods, where the world still seemed fresh, where the scent of life remained in the quickening wind, where bird sounds echoed through the empty branches and the fallen leaves were dampened by rains.

At fourteen, Danny was left alone in the old house. A week after the funeral, Toivo fled once again to the woods, forgetting even to stoke a fire in the wood furnace. Everything in the house still carried the scent of Danny's mother. How long would that last? He couldn't be certain if he wanted it to end immediately or to last forever. Lempi's lingering perfume swirled her presence into being for just an instant, creating a mirage of memories before they dissolved back into the past. Danny was tortured by a recent image of Lempi sitting in the basement, next to a large steamer trunk, crying into her apron. He had chanced upon his mother when he went down the basement stairs to feed more logs into the wood furnace. She hadn't heard him. Her pain seemed so great that he stopped on the stairs, quickly averted his eyes and backed stocking-feet-quiet up the stairs. She never looked up. Their eyes never met. Now this memory spoke only of her grief. Where was the comfort of her eyes bathing him in love?

What in that trunk had made his mother so unhappy? Danny still believed in simple answers, and he was convinced the trunk held one. Sitting in the basement as long as he could remember, it once belonged to his mother's old friend named Pauline, who had died long before Danny could remember.

Danny discovered the trunk lodged between the furnace and the door to the root cellar. Behind it, wooden shelves were filled with his mom's canned goods: the jars of peas, beets, carrots, and beans; the preserved peaches, pears and apple sauce; the maple syrup from the neighbor down the road; and berry jams of all sorts. His mom loved picking any kind of berry, from the first wild strawberries of late May through the raspberries and blackcaps that grew wild in their woods to the tiny blueberries from the marshy bogs nearby. On the opposite wall, cords of firewood were stacked into ramparts, just waiting their turn to burn in the farmhouse's wood furnace.

The black steamer trunk had brass corners and a large brass lock. As far as Danny knew, there was no key and the trunk had never been locked. His mom often stepped into the cool stone cellar on hot summer days and took a break from her chores by rustling through the trunk's contents.

She called it Pauline's hope chest. Pauline's mother arrived from Germany with the trunk; it carried all of her worldly goods on the American Hamburg line to America. The old immigrant gave it to her daughter

Pauline and helped her fill it with items required for a happy marriage. There was a delicate bedspread crocheted in pinks and blue pastels against an ecru base. Stacks of embroidered dishtowels, one for each day of the week, intermingled with pillowcase linens adorned with handmade lace. Porcelain from Germany sat beside bowls of iridescent carnival glass won by Pauline at the local movie house during the Depression.

In the past, when Toivo and Lempi entertained company from Clover (the town where both Lempi and Pauline grew up), Lempi liked to talk about the wonders of the chest. If a visitor showed any interest, Lempi sent Danny down to the basement to rummage through the trunk and carry back specific items for 'show and tell.' The company always responded with the obligatory oohs and aahs. To Danny, each item in the trunk was a treasure.

Although Danny hadn't looked inside the trunk for months, he knew every item and every story: who made which linens, which pieces of carnival glass were now collector items that the wily antique dealer in Timberton tried to buy and which heirlooms his mother most loved.

The basement was cold. Danny opened the heavy iron door to the old cast-iron furnace. Following what his father taught him, he built a proper base, stacked the logs to allow the initial flames to get the oxygen they needed and struck the safety match against the rough iron exterior. The flare of the match transformed the tinder into a dancing jig of yellow and orange. The blaze began.

He stood before the open furnace door for a moment, feeling the heat of the first flickers of fire, sensing the shadows of light and dark that now danced across his face. Satisfied, he closed the door with a clank and turned back to his mother's special trunk.

He lifted the lid and looked at all the familiar mementos. He removed the items, one by one, and placed them on the floor. It was like traveling back in time. The basement floor became their living room, the potato bin became the sofa for his mother and the jars of cannery were all her visitors over the years. For a moment, his emptiness receded.

Then he found something new. At the bottom of the trunk there was a thick manila envelope. Touching it filled him with a premonition. Danny wondered if his mother left behind an explanation. Would opening this envelope make it all clear and give him the strength to go on?

Inside were clippings and photos, yellowed with age and curling. Many seemed brittle. He was almost afraid to touch them. There weren't many, and he fanned them out in front of him. Any fear vanished. What remained was the slightest whiff of his mom's perfume. Danny was certain that she had very recently handled this same envelope, and he saw the papers and photos now as the tarot cards predicting his future or disclosing his mother's past. He reached for the first item.

It was a yellowing copy of *The Milwaukee Sentinel*, dated July 31, 1967. The headline read "Area of Riot Tense, Sniper Fire Goes On." Harsh black type blazoned across the page and framed a dramatic photo of a young white couple fleeing. A building blazed behind them. Danny sought to make sense of the image. Were those his parents? He read the caption, but no names were given. Who could it be but his parents? Why else would his mother have kept a sixteen-year-old paper?

TOIVO
1967
MILWAUKEE, WISCONSIN

When Toivo Lahti unrolled the morning paper and saw the front page, he was shaken. Either he was seeing some unexpected miracle or a terrible curse. He quickly stepped back into his small apartment in a 1920s walkup on the near north side of Milwaukee. He still held the paper. Acrid smoke lingered in the air. Outside, the street was unnaturally quiet. After listening to shouts from the street all night, he hadn't expected to find a copy of *The Milwaukee Sentinel* lying outside his door, neatly folded by the delivery kid, as though it were an ordinary morning.

Why be surprised that the world still continued? Like every other morning, the Golden Guernsey milkman delivered milk to the mother with three kids across the hall. The surprise was the paper's front-page photo. Toivo leaned back against his apartment door and stared at the black and white newsprint in front of him. Displayed for the million-plus scared citizens of the greater Milwaukee area was a beautiful and dramatic picture. A picture of him. A picture of the woman he loved, but a woman who didn't know his name. Caught together, fleeing from danger, two strangers, but one in love with the other. Just seeing the photo returned him to the chaos of the night before. In that madness he saw only angry young black men surging forward in a damaging froth and, adrift in their waves, the woman he loved, Lempi Makinen. He had seen no newspaper photographer.

But this morning's paper proved that there had been one. Toivo Lahti was highlighted on the front page of the morning daily for the state's largest city. He wondered if the photo made the state edition, which was printed early and shipped to places further north like his hometown of Thread. Would old neighbors see his picture on the stacked morning papers at the Trueheart Piggly Wiggly in Thread? Would his Ma and Pa see it? And would they think he was brave or a fool?

And would they wonder about the girl? The photo made the two seem lovers fleeing, holding hands for safety. Such a photo would only fan his Ma's flickers of hope that, maybe at last, her nearly thirty-year-old son had found someone. No one back in Thread would worry about Toivo being ambushed in a city gone crazy with race riots. They'd want to gossip about his love life. And if they learned that the frightened-looking woman had never spoken a word to Toivo, they would quickly move on. Even in his little hometown in northern Wisconsin with its fewer than a thousand people, there was as little interest in Toivo Lahti as there was among the more than seven-hundred-thousand souls packed into Milwaukee proper, the seventh largest city in the United States of America.

On this day in 1967, among those thousands, with a few ready to burn the city and most cowering in their homes, only one person mattered to Toivo. Last night, stuck on that same northside block, caught in the same impending frenzy, he had the chance to finally meet Lempi Makinen. He blew it. He wanted Lempi to be Jackie to his John Kennedy, Elizabeth Taylor to his Richard Burton, Guinevere to his Lancelot. It could have been. After all, whose hand did he hold in the news photo? It belonged to Lempi Makinen.

She had appeared on his street late last night. He already sensed the growing furor of his racially divided neighborhood and somehow knew that emotions were about to break out in a spasm of looting, shooting and fire—like that time back home in high school when he had been in the woods during an unexpected heavy storm and the waters had rushed down the creek above the Lattigeaux river and built up in waves behind the hurdle of the beaver dam. Just before there was too much weight for that wooden dam to bear, he sensed the danger. The dam burst. Still, the froth of water gushed down the channel and nearly dragged him into the river just above the point when the falls drop into the Lattigeaux Gorge. That's what the street felt like last night. Only last night the danger also involved Lempi, who stood in his street, an outsider in enemy territory, scouting for God knows what.

Toivo looked again at the paper. He longed to really get to know Lempi, not just help her flee wordlessly from a mob of looters and arsonists. In the movies, which Toivo loved, last night would have been a cute meet. In the movies, people always met in unexpected ways. There would be that jolting moment of awareness when two young lovers realize everything led to their moment. Here was his moment, captured by a photographer and shown to the entire world. Toivo wasn't a journalist, but even he could see that there was a reason the editors downtown had selected it to illustrate the night's craziness. Silhouetted by angry flames, the flight of Toivo and Lempi conveyed a tenderness, caring and innocence that accentuated the horror of the riots.

But in the drama of the night, after two blocks of running and with the craziness receding into the background, Lempi simply dropped his hand and said, "Thanks, I left my car this way" and she was gone. He had no chance to say his name, or even explain how they were already connected.

Toivo threw the paper so hard onto the scuffed chrome and laminate dinette table that coffee splashed from his morning mug. He wasn't being honest with himself, pretending that this was somehow a romantic movie meeting. The facts were that he was in love with Lempi Makinen. He saw her almost every working day, and she didn't even know he existed. He thought about her constantly, but couldn't find the courage to introduce himself—not even when saving her life in a riot. It was pathetic.

Lempi was the sole reason he still worked as a groundskeeper at Bremen College, whose campus was located on the east side of Milwaukee and bordered Lake Michigan. If it weren't for her, he would have already gone back to Thread to work on his parents' farm or in the woods. He had spent ten years moving from odd job to odd job after high school. Working at the fancy college for snobby kids had been intended to only last a few months as he built up some cash.

But then one day clipping the hedges outside the Shindler Hall and the Institute of Computing Mathematics, he saw her walking across the campus. He could still picture that Indian summer day in early October. The leaves of the maples and elms had started to turn, but the air was warm and still. A few high clouds punctuated the skies. The double doors to the Humanities building opened. Since it wasn't the normal hourly break between classes, he glanced with mild curiosity to see who was exiting. The first thing that caught his attention was the fabric of the young woman's dress: a geometric pattern of interlocking squares in various fall colors of browns, golds and russet reds. The lines of the dress were simple and flared outward to end about four inches above her knees. Her long blonde hair seemed to float around her and shimmered against the fall colors. But then he was struck by her purpose. She walked, no, she marched toward the administration building with confidence and assurance. He didn't know why exactly, but that stride assured him of the comfort and guidance and protection that he had wanted all his life. As she paused to open the heavy doors to Shindler Hall, she looked in his direction and smiled. Her face, which had seemed so serious, suddenly was animated with a beauty he didn't expect. The door closed and she was gone. He didn't yet know her name, but he had fallen in love.

After months of occasional glimpses, of fashions changing with the seasons, of questioning other workers, Toivo eventually gathered all the key details. His mystery woman's name was Lempi Makinen, a Finnish girl. She worked as a secretary to the chairman of the philosophy department, Dr. Cohen. She visited Shindler Hall frequently because she was a great friend with the Dean of Women, Pauline Newmann. Supposedly, they loved to engage in great debates. Most people found Lempi too forceful. No one seemed to know if she had any men in her life. He was surprised to discover she was thirty-four since she looked far younger. Each fact uncovered made her more interesting and alluring. He was uncertain why he never spoke to her, but he never found meeting new people easy. He also feared he lacked any attribute to interest her. She was a professional, spent time with the collegiate set and parried with a quick mind and wit. What would he say to her?

He looked again at the photo in the *Sentinel.* He thought of Ma on their threadbare farm. If she were to see this picture, she would be quick to imagine a romance. But how could she know how unlikely that was.

Toivo lived in a rough part of Milwaukee's Inner City, but it was all he could afford on the salary of a college gardener and handyman. He supposed that with a roommate he could have found a better place in a nicer part of town, in an area that would have been more German and less African. But he didn't really mind living where he did. He didn't need a lot of space, and it wasn't as though he received a lot company. Besides, he preferred being alone.

Still, he often would turn off the TV when the local ten o'clock news began, and instead sit by the window to gather his own report of the world near Third and North. Most nights there wasn't that much traffic in his corner of Milwaukee, but on that last Sunday in July, the evening still sported a bit of the weekend crowd, with locals getting a few final drinks before facing the Monday return to work. Often the St. Francis Social Center a block over held Sunday night dances. After living over a year on this street, he felt an outsider's sort of belonging.

Being white, he stood out. Even though he wasn't the only such person in the neighborhood, he immediately noticed that evening when a young white woman walked up the street from the south. Maybe he first noticed her because of her color, but her purposeful stride captured his full attention. Only one woman he knew walked like that. What was Lempi Makinen doing in his neighborhood? He imagined a lot of reasons. Sometimes, gardening outside Shindler Hall, he heard snippets of conversation between Pauline and Lempi. Both were liberal firebrands. Lempi was against the war and questioned why the college let its Institute of Computing Mathematics do work for the Defense Department and why the school still supported ROTC. Civil rights truly energized the young woman. In particular, Lempi defended the causes of a local Catholic priest named Father Groppi, who had been all over the local news. With the many urban race riots skipping across major cities that summer (only earlier in the month, nearly seventy had died in the Detroit riots), Lempi was convinced that the same would happen in Milwaukee. She felt the city deserved whatever happened. Pauline, who once worked for the mayor's office, argued otherwise.

Maybe someone like Groppi was making trouble and luring Lempi to the area. On the other hand, he liked to imagine Lempi as a free spirit in all things. Maybe she was in the neighborhood to take in some black music at the St. Francis Center.

Thinking later how the night was transformed, Toivo wished he had left his apartment and followed Lempi out of a sense of protective duty. In his heart, he knew that wasn't the case. He wanted a new opportunity to watch. It was night; it was his part of town; and he could easily follow her without being noticed. In his mind, he might pretend to bump into her and finally talk to her. But even he couldn't keep that fantasy up. He knew he would lack the boldness.

When he stepped out on the wide porch of his old frame building, he was glad he had forgotten to replace the burned-out entry light. Lempi couldn't easily see him. She stopped at the corner and appeared to examine a note in her hand, momentarily unsure on directions. He took advantage of her pause to step lightly across the creaking boards and jump down onto the lawn. Should he stay in the shadows and watch from a distance or should he head out to the sidewalk and walk up to her? Why, he could even say "Hello" or ask if she needed help with directions.

Toivo considered for a moment about what his work friend Dick would say. Calling Dick a friend was a bit of a stretch. Toivo didn't have many real friends, at least not since Jeremy, and he hadn't seen Jeremy after moving to Milwaukee. No, in truth, Dick was just a work acquaintance from the maintenance department at Bremen. Dick showed Toivo the ropes when he was first hired. They got along well enough, ate lunch together and laughed at jokes they heard on the *Smothers Brothers* show. Dick was a fanatic over *Bonanza*, and for that matter any Western, and so usually he wanted to talk about those shows. They didn't chat about much else, although Toivo had tried to learn as much as he could about Lempi from Dick. Dick considered Lempi a bitter old maid, and didn't understand why anyone would find her interesting. Having worked nearly twenty years at Bremen, Dick remembered when Lempi first appeared on campus. He claimed there had been some scandal about why she wasn't admitted, and that her friend Dean Newmann had pulled strings to get her a job at the school instead. She audited a lot of classes, so by now, she probably had the equivalent of a Bremen degree, not that any woman to his mind needed a college degree.

Toivo made a decision and strode westward toward Fourth. He decided to see if he could catch up with Lempi. Tonight could be the night when he finally talked to her.

As they turned on Fourth, he saw a large crowd of blacks near the St. Francis Center. A cordon of police surrounded them. Surely, he thought, Lempi will see there was danger ahead and turn around. But she continued striding forward in her way. Just then a car backed into a fire hydrant in front of the Center. A geyser burst into the muggy air, streaming droplets down on the assembled crowd. Everybody shifted, as thought seeking a better ground for what may lay ahead. More police rolled up, now in full riot gear.

That stopped Lempi. But from the streets around them, people were beginning to pour out of their houses. Not the old or the children, and probably not those with jobs in the morning. But then a lot of people in this part of town didn't have jobs to go to in the morning. They were moving toward the center of action. Even with the hydrant's water raining down, their mood seemed hotter. In the light of the street lamp, he could clearly see Lempi's face. It was frozen with an intensity that somehow made her seem younger. She inched forward, like a small kitten that might dare to stalk a mangy coyote invading the yard.

A shot rang out. It seemed to come from the rooftop across the street. The police tensed into formation. Cries of "pigs" rang out. Someone yelled, "burn, baby, burn." That propelled the police into breaking up the crowd and arresting whomever they considered the ringleaders. A flash of a Molotov cocktail flew across the sky and landed on the rickety porch of an abandoned century-old home. The flames caught in the weeds around the porch and quickly flared up the dried-out flooring planks, blazed through the carpenter-ant-ridden pilasters and leaped into the eaves. Toivo was fifty feet behind Lempi. She hadn't noticed him. She was too transfixed by the flames. Just like the mob. No one moved to try to extinguish the fire. The police line lunged forward.

"Burn, baby, burn" and another Molotov cocktail was flung from the roof. It rolled beneath a police car. Another shot rang out. Was it a sniper or was it the police? He didn't know. And then someone began shooting out the streetlights, which only made the flames of the burning house seem brighter. The sound of the crowd had shifted, becoming deeper and more ominous.

He stepped up behind Lempi, and grabbed her hand. "We gotta get out of here," he shouted. The sound of the mob was growing louder, the heat of the fire could already be felt, and smoke was welling up beneath the cop cruiser. An explosion could occur at any moment. Lempi didn't even look at Toivo. She just stared at the scene unfolding before her with the fascination of solving a puzzle. He tugged harder at her hand. She seemed to shift. He began to run, and by refusing to release her hand, commanded her to follow. The police car exploded. And there were more shots. The sirens of responding police cars raced up the streets. And Toivo and Lempi were fleeing.

Toivo said nothing, not even after two blocks when Lempi released his hand, said her car was nearby and slipped into the darkness. Not even then did he manage to say "hello" or "goodbye."

Pauline Newmann, dean of women, laughed as she stepped down the broad steps of Shindler Hall. Lempi Makinen followed her without a smile. The campus was nearly empty on a hot August day. The start of the fall semester was still weeks away. After eight days of curfew and headlines of violence and arson, normalcy seemed ready to return to Milwaukee. Optimism, or maybe just relief, was apparent in the bounce of Pauline's step.

Toivo mowed the quadrangle that faced Shindler Hall. Scorching heat from the early afternoon sun and mugginess from Lake Michigan prompted him to strip off his work shirt. Although his pale Finnish skin was prone to a quick burn, he wasn't worried. This late in the summer, he was bronzed—at least on the arms—even if a lighter ghost image of the tee shirts he normally wore lingered on his torso. Bare-chested, he felt a bit exposed. When he looked in the mirror all he could see was a skinny man with little hair on his chest. At the same time, on a day like this one, with the smell of freshly-mown grass under blues skies, and the low-level buzz of insects and the singing calls of birds, you had to let the sun shine down.

Pauline's laugh surprised him. Toivo saw the two women walking down the sidewalk directly to where he stood. Lempi in her sleeveless shift displayed well-tanned and well-toned arms. But her face was expressionless, and he was reminded of the night the city riots started. Lempi was not sharing Pauline's pleasure. They stopped just feet away beneath the boughs of an old oak tree. Pauline looked at him expectantly. He turned off the lawn mower. Scanning his face and his half-naked body, which was drenched with sweat, Pauline seemed quite pleased with the situation.

"This is the man," she said definitively to Lempi. "This is the man who saved your life last week. I told you when I saw that photograph in the *Sentinel* that we had seen him before. Today, hearing that mower, I finally realized where." She turned to Toivo, "It was you, wasn't it?"

"Yes, ma'am," he replied, uncertain whether he should look at his grass-flecked boots or at the two of them. He decided to look at Pauline, since she was talking to him, but he sneaked sideway glances at Lempi. It was his first opportunity to look at her up close in daylight. Even though he knew that this woman wasn't one that most men would find beautiful, he loved the strength he saw in her almost-boyish body with its small breasts, tiny waist, but wide hips. Energy emanated, not from her body, but from her stance and eyes. He dared to look straight at those blue eyes snapping with impatience.

"Well, then," Lempi said, "I suppose I must thank you." She held out her hand to shake his, and continued. "My name is Lempi Makinen."

So sweaty from the mowing that even his palms felt wet, he wiped them against his dirty jeans. He shook her proffered hand rather robustly. "I'm Toivo Lahti, and you're welcome. It was nothing."

Pauline clapped her hands together, and exclaimed, "Oh, you're both Finnish! This is really most wonderful. And you both work here at the college. Have you never really met? It must truly be kismet that you should encounter one another at such a dangerous time. Really, it's most remarkable."

Pauline was like a mother hen fussing over her chicks. It was rather annoying, and Toivo was more than a little afraid that she would ask him a penetrating question. Dean Newmann had a reputation on campus as an effective, even ruthless, administrator. She once worked for that old Socialist mayor of Milwaukee, Frank Zeidler, and she was the person he turned to for implementing tough decisions. Now in her fifties, the dean's very German look was still a beauty in a city with more than its share of German beauties. Toivo stole another glance at Lempi, whose face, more Finnish in its breadth, shifted from flashing impatience to annoyance.

"Must you carry on so?" asked Lempi. "If only that newspaper photographer hadn't snapped that stupid picture."

"But he did, didn't he?" Pauline turned her attention back to Toivo. He wondered briefly if he should restart his lawn mower. It would be one way to end a conversation he wasn't eager to have. On the other hand, he thought it rude to yank the mower cord in the middle of someone talking. Pauline, recognizing none of his angst, jumped into her questions. "So, Toivo, what were you doing in that area of town? Were you one of those idealists like Lempi trying to show solidarity with the oppressed?"

Toivo, while recognizing the affection in Pauline's mocking tone, wasn't sure he wanted to answer. But he had always been polite to his elders. "I live in that area. Can't really afford much more."

"Oh," Pauline seemed momentarily nonplussed, "why wouldn't you live there? Many lovely old homes and it's close to so many things. I lived in that area when I first came to Milwaukee from Clover. But why venture out on the street at that time of night? A sensible person stays in bed." Her last comment was clearly aimed at Lempi. Toivo, feeling uneasy about why he followed Lempi that evening, tried to think of an escape.

"I could hear something was going on. I walked up the street out of curiosity." His answer sounded reasonable. Toivo didn't worry they would ever visit his place and realize that he was too far from the flashpoint to hear anything. The lawn mower cord seemed alluring. But Lempi was looking at him with some sort of interest, and Pauline noticed.

"Well, you're a very handsome young man, and I'm just happy that you were there to whisk my Lempi away to safety. I've known her and her family for years. I would never be forgiven if I had allowed her to get in trouble in this big city. As much as she might want to." She smiled at Toivo, "I suppose we should let you get back to work. You were quite sweaty when we walked up, and although it is quite becoming on you, still I suspect the break we provided is appreciated."

Toivo was relieved and elated. The women were about to leave. Unlike the night of the riot, at least now Lempi knew him.

"I'm just curious, not that it matters," Pauline said as she turned her gaze to encompass Toivo and Pauline, "but did either of you recognize each other that night? Surely, you've seen one another before. Such a coincidence you would be in the same place." Toivo, so close to escape, felt impaled. A hot flush moved up his entire body, across the weaker tan of his torso, darkened the already bronzed tones of his arms and swiftly rose up until it threatened to turn his blonde hair red. The more he tried to dampen it, the more he felt aflame.

"No, of course not," said Lempi.

Toivo bent down to grab the whipcord. Starting that mower would drown out any further conversation. He felt the intensity of Pauline's gaze on his flushed back. He wished they both would go away. Then she spoke.

"Lempi, we're really being rude. This young man might have saved your life. We should find a way to thank him. Let's have him over for dinner. I can cook for both of you."

The idea terrified him. He only wanted to admire Lempi from afar. If he actually had to spend time with her, she would soon realize he was nothing. He needed to stop it this very moment.

"That's not necessary," he said.

"Don't be silly," Pauline responded. "We'll have you over on Saturday night. Lempi's father is in town, and he can really be unbearable at times. It would be a tremendous favor to both of us if you were there to add something new to the mix, derail his mind from his usual rants."

Now it seemed as though Lempi had been shaken free of her studied indifference. "That's a stupid idea, Pauline."

"Nonsense, you'll just be three old Finns from upstate. You'll have tons to talk about. I'll make all the old favorites. I happen to know your father likes my blitz torte a great deal." She paused, and then added as an aside to Toivo, "You'll find that her father is surprisingly old. Lempi was definitely a second crop on their farm. I grew up in the same town and have known the old man forever, and I am quite confident he will find you definitely interesting.

"It's all set then for Saturday at six. I won't take no for an answer from either of you." Toivo and Lempi looked at each other full in the eye. Each saw a resignation to their shared, if mutually undesired, fate.

For the fifth time that evening, Toivo did a self-inspection. By the cracked glass of his medicine cabinet mirror, he judged himself presentable for the dinner ahead. Every day since his encounter with Pauline and Lempi, he agonized over the impending meal. He even brought it up with Dick, breaking out of the usual chatter of television and weather.

"Don't go mixing up with those artsy-fartsy types," cautioned Dick. "The women who work in the offices at this college, they ain't for people like you or me. Too full of themselves, you know, and always dreaming up those big ideas, talking nonsense. Come down by Red's Tap with me and have a few beers instead. You'd have a better time and you could meet some fun girls."

But Toivo didn't listened to Dick. He took the bus downtown to the big Gimbel's store, so he could buy the right kind of clothes. He wandered through the huge men's department, but couldn't picture what he was seeking. Then he thought of those East Coast prep school boys who attended Bremen, not the Wisconsin farm kids with good grades, but the soft kids from out of state who pretended to know something the others didn't. Maybe he could go for their look with their plaid madras shirts and tan chino pants.

He wanted to explain to Dick what excited him about this dinner. Curiously, it was the same thing that frightened him. Always a loner, ever since he could remember, he liked tramping solo through the woods or taking care of the farm cows. After high school, he drifted from job to job hoping to find something that might excite him. But the years merged into a dull blur. On the rare occasion that he found something or someone he actually liked, he didn't know how to pursue it.

If only it could be as easy as his love of movies. Back in Thread, he attended the Saturday matinees by himself, never part of that rowdy crowd in the back rows that hooted and hollered at the westerns or later made out with the girls. In Milwaukee, he discovered the Downer Theater on the east side and immersed himself in foreign films and old movies. It opened his eyes to new worlds where people cared, acted out of commitment and took stances. While others might aspire to the fairy-tale romance of ruling kingdoms or fighting heroic battles, he connected with the shimmering allure of emotional complexity, finding pleasure in feelings that drove action and in behavior that combined both mind and body. Cinema opened him to the possibility of there being more.

Lempi tantalized him with that same possibility. How could he explain that to Dick—Dick whose favorite activity was taking the free tour and drinking himself silly at the Pabst brewery, who was still mad two years later that the Braves had decamped for Atlanta, and who spent every Sunday night watching *Bonanza*? How could Dick ever understand a woman who emanated energy and purpose? Lempi was a proclamation one had to follow.

Most women bored Toivo. It didn't matter if they were pretty or not, whether they were big-breasted or small, dark-haired or fair. They seemed vapid and too eager for him to lead. But from the first moment he saw her, he knew that Lempi was somehow different.

But did he really know that? Staring at himself in the mirror, Toivo had more than a twinge of doubt. What could Lempi see in a fellow like him? He studied the face that stared back at him. It was tanned, almost sun-burned from a season of grounds keeping, his hair nearly bleached white by the sun and grown long like some British rock band. His blue eyes were clear and well set in a broad face, but he felt his chin was weak. And as for the rest of the body, well, it was just long, lanky and uninspired.

And what would they talk about? He never paid much attention to any topic in high school; he just wanted to get back to the farm and his solitude. Neither his Ma nor his Pa did much in the way of reading or talking. Silence gave him time to think and to enjoy the routine of work. But you couldn't talk about that with college women. Toivo had wandered through many jobs: working fishing boats on Lake Superior, raising barns in Central Wisconsin, lumbering in the north woods and picking cherries in Door

County. That summer in the orchards of Door County had been a good one. That was where he met Jeremy, who was a little like Lempi. He was driven and smart. Toivo never had trouble talking to Jeremy. Maybe it would be the same with Lempi.

"Stop it," he said to himself. "You don't even know what you want. Stop judging yourself."

Toivo couldn't express what he hoped for or what he feared. Feeling like he was about to walk into a lion's den, he didn't know whether he wanted to slay the lions, be eaten by them, or for that matter who the lions even were.

Toivo had imagined Pauline's home to be a big foursquare house sheltered by giant elms. Instead, it was a modern, one-story rambler in the suburbs of Wauwatosa. It faced a quiet street where the trees were little more than saplings on the parkway. Inside, her house was tasteful and modern. A low-slung, tweed sofa was placed perpendicular to the fieldstone fireplace. Opposite it were two rather uncomfortable looking chairs upholstered in leather. A large abstract painting over the sofa made no sense to Toivo.

Neither did the dining room table. The wood was polished teak, and he held his hand against it, as though to absorb the beauty of the wood grain. He liked the feel of wood. But that table's carpentry seemed insubstantial, and he was concerned that his weight would break the matching chair. On the table were more china, glassware and silver than his parents even owned. He sat next to Lempi who was wearing a perfume that made him want to lean over and inhale deeply. Across the table were Pauline and Eero Makinen, Lempi's father. The old coot looked as displeased to be sitting at this table as Toivo felt uncomfortable. Before them was a plate festooned with salad greens, sliced almonds, mandarin orange segments and some odd-green wedge that Pauline called an avocado. It seemed slimy.

When Toivo first arrived, Lempi and her father were on the sofa. So he had been forced to sit on one of those uncomfortable leather chairs and face that incomprehensible painting with its squiggles of yellow and green. Even as Pauline attempted to converse, he found himself distracted trying to make meaning of the painting's spaghetti lines.

At the dinner table, Pauline repeated for Eero the tale of Lempi and

Toivo's first meeting. Clearly, she had told the story more than a few times by now, and Toivo recognized how it had been honed. He almost felt like a hero in hearing the retelling. But Eero was having none of it. The old man looked to be nearly eighty, and he carried himself with the assurance of an old lion overseeing his pack of lionesses. But he didn't view Toivo as anything other than a small rodent on the periphery. He interjected, "I don't understand why my daughter needed to be in the middle of all those people."

"Pa, their cause is our cause. Our country has been so unfair to the black people. That's why there's unrest in the streets. I need to understand it and I need to support it. If we don't do something, the whole country could be destroyed. I heard something might be happening, and I wanted to be there." Lempi did not allow for the possibility that her father or the others in the room might view her zeal as a misguided opinion.

"It's not your problem."

"Of all people, Pa, how could you say that? You left your home country to flee oppression. Your son, my brother I never met, gave up his life to fight for a better world. How can I not do the same?"

"Don't bring up Risto."

"Why not Pa? You don't ever want to talk about Risto. You don't want to talk about Ma. You don't want to talk about the way this country treated you. You know you've been treated wrong."

"That's enough. You don't know what you're talking about."

Throughout this conversation, Pauline grew tenser. With his last statement, Eero threw Pauline a look that demanded she put a stop to this conversation. Toivo was surprised when the always confident dean quickly complied.

"Enough, Lempi. Tonight was meant to be a pleasant visit, not a replay of your frequent family arguments. We have a guest, and we should find out more about him." Toivo wasn't happy to hear those words, but as Pauline asked him questions about his past, he surprised himself by relaying more details than usual. The truth was that he seldom had a chance to reminisce, and there were more than a few happy moments to his nearly thirty years. He described his favorite chickens, rabbits and cows of childhood. He roamed through the woods of his memory and brought to life the oddities of the small farm. He practically bloomed as he spoke of the pleasures in picking cherries

"Boy," began Eero, and the word came across as a friendly overture, "your stories make me think of when I first bought my land from the railroad agent in Clover. It was hard work clearing that land, the way we had to blast out the stumps, but my Marja and I loved what we were building."

Lempi laughed, "Oh, Pa, don't bring up your stump stories again. He just loves talking about how daring he was with explosives."

At that moment, a timer went off in the kitchen and Pauline rose to attend to the next course. As Toivo poked at his green wedge of avocado, the conversation continued in a looser tone. Toivo forgot his nervousness. Lempi even laughed once or twice.

After the salad (and Toivo found that he didn't mind the avocado after all), Pauline served a rolled-up German steak dish called roladen with spaetzle noodles. Everyone at the table ate eagerly. Soon the plates were cleared, and Pauline brought in her blitz torte—a layer cake of meringue, yellow cake and custard. Eero visibly beamed and said, "You're too kind to this old man." Everyone was relaxed.

"What are you doing with your father while he's here?" Toivo asked Lempi. By now, Toivo no longer feared discovering who Lempi was or vice versa. In fact, he realized she was exactly the kind of driven personality that he admired from afar. She also had other quite likeable aspects. She truly cared about both Pauline and Eero, and somehow that made him quite glad.

"I'm thinking we should go to a movie. The theater in Clover has closed down, and Pa hasn't been to a movie since last year when we saw *The Russians Are Coming, The Russians Are Coming.*"

"Stupid movie," muttered Eero.

"I thought it was funny," replied Toivo, feeling a little daring in contradicting the old man, "but it wasn't my favorite."

"Do you see a lot of movies?" asked Pauline. "What are some of your favorites?"

With that, Toivo began recounting those films from the past year that he particularly liked. Once he noticed that this conversation created a different level of interest in Lempi's eyes, something beyond the mere politeness or easy amusement with which she had responded to his earlier stories, he grew more expansive. Since he went to a lot of movies, he pulled memories like Christmas names from a hat. He spoke of *Fahrenheit 451* and how he liked Julie Christie and sometimes worried that powerful people could be quick to take away freedoms. And then he jumped to *Blow Up*, which he had just seen and didn't really understand, but he always liked Vanessa Redgrave, ever since *Camelot*. After that, he mentioned *Hawaii*, because he seemed to be talking about British actresses, and Julie Andrews was another fine one. He thought the native Hawaiians didn't get a fair shake when the Americans marched in. He was pleased that both Pauline and Lempi closely listened to him.

For the first time that entire evening, Lempi asked him a question. In fact, it may have been the first time she directly addressed him. "And of all those films you seen in the past twelve months or so, what was your favorite?"

He quickly replied, "*A Man and a Woman*. It's a French film."

"Yes, I know," she replied with some amusement, "I've seen it as well, but don't you think it's a bit sentimental and romantic?"

"How can you say that?" said Pauline, "After all, the two lovers meet in that movie by accident. It could almost be the story of you and Toivo. A chance affair."

At that moment, some burst of honesty overtook Toivo. In the years that followed, he never understood why he suddenly acted like a totally different person. "Not totally by chance," he said. "I've worked at Bremen for nearly two years, and I've seen Lempi before. You have to notice a woman like Lempi. When I saw her walk by my house that Sunday night, and I knew how wild emotions were in my neighborhood, I figured I had to follow her and make sure she didn't get into trouble. Even though I knew you didn't know me from Adam." He said this to Lempi almost as an apology. "And when everything went crazy, instinct just took over, and I came up from behind you, grabbed your hand, and made you leave. I didn't want you getting hurt." With his admission public, he suddenly felt so good that he sat there quietly without danger of blushing or feeling out of place. In fact, it was Lempi who looked at him now with amazement. Her own face reddened. Eero seemed amused and bewildered at the same time. But Pauline was aglow.

"Lempi, you see, you really did have a knight in shining armor at your side. We must never let this one go!"

As summer wound its way through a colorful fall that flowed into the first snowflakes of winter, Pauline was determined to keep Toivo around. Without her matchmaking, it's unlikely Toivo would have remained a constant presence. But whether it was because Lempi didn't care enough to resist, or that Pauline saw this as her last chance to connect Lempi to love, or maybe that Toivo was happy to recast his life as a movie scene, Toivo and Lempi saw each other with increasing frequency.

At first, Pauline's favorite maneuver was to walk across the quadrangle and lure Lempi out of the humanities building. Then she would casually invite Toivo to join them to picnic on the lawn. Although Toivo was often quiet during those noontime breaks, that didn't matter. Pauline and Lempi were free at sharing their many opinions. As the new school year gained ground, Toivo learned to predict what each might say. Lempi was like the more radical Bremen students: against the war, for civil rights, and in love with new music. Pauline found this fervor for leftist causes endearing. She neither endorsed them nor disagreed, but rather drifted to the safe middle. Her emotions were reserved for local causes, especially a concern that Milwaukee wasn't living up to its potential. The two sharply disagreed over the summer riots. Lempi claimed the country's black citizens had a righteous anger forged by oppression. Pauline was dismayed that her city failed to take advantage of opportunities made possible by her old boss, Frank Zeidler. Pauline saw Zeidler as a man who had been prepared to make the right investments, but the suburbs opposed him out of a fear of higher taxes. Often, Toivo would get lost in their arcane arguments. Still their noontime meals gave him a chance to be close to Lempi, and he found the women's affection and respect for one another relaxing.

The trio fell into sharing lunch once or twice a week. At times, he felt the tolerated little brother of Lempi, and at other times, the favored son of Pauline. As he became more comfortable, he made the occasional contribution to their debates, all of which invariably brought a smile from Pauline and a questioning look from Lempi.

It was a warm fall. The campus lawns were always filled with students. Bremen was a small residential college with fewer than 1500 students, and the eighteen-year-old freshmen came from across the country. Pauline amusingly pointed out the awkward pairings of young love. But by mid-October, it was clear that their outdoor lunches would soon be forced to end.

On the Friday of Homecoming the three sat on a bench facing the library with its domed roof. The conversation lulled. Pauline brushed a few crumbs from her skirt. Lempi turned unexpectedly to Toivo and said, "You know, she'll never give up dragging us to these al fresco lunches until you ask me out. Since I don't intend to keep sitting here when the snow starts falling, just tell me a movie you'd like to see and we'll go."

"How about *Bonnie and Clyde*?" Toivo surprised himself by discovering he wasn't the least bit nervous in suggesting it.

"Sure," she replied.

Their relationship entered a new phase. The routine included seeing a movie each weekend, followed by a pizza pie. Their time together included long stretches of silence, but it never felt boring to Toivo. Over pizza, they explored their common background of growing up as first-generation Americans, born to Finnish immigrant parents and staked out in small Wisconsin towns. They learned they both shopped in co-op stores, could count up to ten in Finnish, and relished dishes that others might find odd—like a baked milk pancake that could only be properly cooked with milk rich in colostrum from a cow that had just recently given birth. Both agreed that this traditional Finnish dish called *pannukokku* was delicious.

While Toivo began to think of Lempi as 'his girl,' he wasn't certain what word she would call him. But he didn't dwell on that. His growing confidence moved their relationship forward physically, even though Lempi found his slow trot around the bases amusing at times. She joked that they had met during the summer of love, and they'd better live up that name before winter froze everything over.

Toivo hadn't told Lempi this, although he was fairly certain she realized that he was still a virgin on their first night together. The experience was a bit disappointing. He had expected some great display of bodily fireworks. He consoled himself that Lempi seemed to enjoy it, and he was relieved to have passed another milestone. After their first time, the evening activities moved to a different place. Lempi paid more attention to him, and the second time left him feeling completely emptied, exhausted and glowing. Toivo would have liked to talk to someone about his feelings, but he knew his friend Dick would make it a joke, so he tried to tell Lempi how their sex gave him a new sense of contentment.

Opening up was never easy for Toivo. He knew that the Finns' reputation for being humorless and devoid of emotion wasn't true. It was just that his parents never displayed physical affection for one another.

Feelings were left to dwell beneath the surface. They could be constantly in motion, swirling and beating, without disturbing everyone else. As a Finn, Lempi should understand that.

But when the time came to have an honest conversation about how each of them felt, it didn't work out. Somehow his initial comments invited Lempi to talk about her first love. Toivo couldn't imagine how she could interpret his fumbling attempt to open up as an inducement to talk about her first lover. But once she started, what could he do?

He listened to how she had just been out of high school and angry by being rejected by Bremen College. In an act of rebellion against her parents, she arranged a baby-sitting job with neighbors who were taking a driving trip to the West Coast. They wanted someone along to mind their two boys. Lempi thought it a reasonable trade to be able to see the country. In the course of a month, the family planned to visit all the major national parks, drive the coastal route from San Francisco to Los Angeles and return to Wisconsin on Route 66.

In the Dakotas, they picked up a hitchhiker named Peter. A student at the University of Wisconsin in Madison, Peter painted abstract paintings. He had plans to spend the summer in San Francisco. Lempi found him amazing. Well-read and funny, he kept the car in stitches with his tales. As the family camped near the Badlands, Peter and Lempi stayed up late. Peter heard all about Lempi's family, how her father left Finland at the turn of the century, how her older brother disappeared in Russia and why Bremen rejected her. She told him what she thought was right and wrong with the world. He learned she hated Communist-baiting politicians like Nixon and Joe McCarthy. In turn, he told her of his dreams, of the possibilities of great art and why she was beautiful.

Two nights later, camping in Yellowstone, Lempi walked through the meadows to meet him in the gloaming of the evening. With the moon rising and Venus shining brightly overhead, they braved the potential of nearby bears to mate in the grass. Lempi shocked Toivo as she described her first time. She used language so raw, but so casually, that it bruised him. But what could he say? It was as though he asked for it, even though he knew he hadn't.

Lempi and Peter had three more nights of sex before the travelers reached San Francisco. Peter thanked everyone for the generosity of a cross-country ride, and headed to the Tenderloin to meet his friends for the summer. Lempi prepared herself mentally to ride the cable cars without him.

Both promised to stay in touch. Which they did. Lempi looked forward to reconnecting when Peter returned to Wisconsin. Clover wasn't that far from Madison. She anticipated a future life together. But Peter was drafted, went to Korea and never returned.

While this tale was recounted, Toivo and Lempi were in bed, nude. The first snows of November flitted outside the windows of Lempi's bedroom. The couple pulled the patchwork quilt made by Lempi's mother up tight. Toivo wanted to leave the bed, go into the living room, pick up his clothes, get dressed and drive home. Instead he forced himself to look at Lempi. Pale beams from the street lamp streamed through the window. Lempi was almost ghost-like. She looked straight up at the ceiling, oddly silent. Even in the dim light, he could see tears on her face.

In that moment, he knew that she might not ever be fully his. But he also felt confident for the first time that he meant something to her. Somehow, he had given her the security to confront her past and share it. He was convinced that no one else knew this story, not even Pauline. This gave him comfort. Lempi was as trapped by her Finnish emotions as he was. Rather than chilling him, this realization made him more secure.

Beneath the covers he reached out his hand to grab hold of her fingers. They lay there in the darkness, hands clasped, staring upward in silence.

By winter, Toivo and Lempi were the odd couple of the campus: the woman from the office and the man from the grounds. The academic folk always saw Lempi Makinen as a bit of an odd duck, and they took her romance in stride. Back in the maintenance sheds, the men in their overalls decided that the shy Finnish kid must have more depth to him than they had thought. Linking up with a pretty office girl gave him bragging points.

Pauline spent less time with both of them, giving time to let her little recipe for romance rise. Sometimes she stopped to chat with Toivo when she saw him shoveling the sidewalks. Occasionally, she ate lunch with Lempi in the staff lounge. She invited the couple to her house for Christmas Eve, and surprised Toivo with a hand-made woolen scarf, imperfectly knitted in the school colors.

In January, Lempi found a new cause: Senator Eugene McCarthy announced his candidacy for president as the candidate against the Vietnam War. At Pauline's Sunday dinner, Lempi argued President Johnson must be denied another term. Pauline agreed that the Vietnam War was immoral and illegal, but suggested that Governor Romney of Michigan would be a more likely candidate to unseat the current president. Lempi set down her knife and fork and calmly finished chewing, but Toivo saw the flash in Lempi's eyes.

"Next thing I'll hear is that we should hope Richard Nixon wins the race," Lempi said.

"I'm serious," Pauline responded. "Governor Romney did a good job after the Detroit riots. And you have to admit that he recognizes the Vietnam War is futile. Remember last fall he said the military brainwashed him."

Lempi dismissed the older woman. "You're hopeless. Always willing to settle for the halfway path that never gets you anywhere. Even if a Republican ended the war, they'd make everything else worse. You worked for a Socialist mayor How could you even consider not getting behind a Democrat on the right side of history? I'm volunteering for the McCarthy campaign, and so will Toivo."

With one remark, never discussed between Lempi and him, Toivo was drafted as a foot soldier in the "Clean for Gene" march, a cause he barely understood. He liked leaving weightier decisions to others. He didn't understand why the United States was fighting for South Vietnam, nor how the war escalated every month into an ever uglier wound. He paid attention to the arguments only because of his friend, Jeremy, who he had met picking cherries. Jeremy was about to graduate from college, and was likely to be drafted. As an anthropology major, Jeremy understood what happened to men in battle, and he desperately wanted to avoid a cause he found wrong. Jeremy had once disclosed a secret to Toivo: he liked men. If Jeremy declared to his draft board that he was a homosexual, he would be categorized IV-F and wouldn't be drafted. But Jeremy feared destroying his life; he would end up jobless and disowned by his family.

Toivo couldn't discuss Jeremy's plight with Lempi, but knowledge of his friend's quandary committed Toivo to Lempi's crusade. They volunteered frequently at the McCarthy offices on the North Side—recruiting college students to work on the upcoming Wisconsin primary, doing ward research and engaging in emotional debates on the immorality of the war.

March 12th was a high point. Election returns came in from the New Hampshire primary, the first of the season, and President Johnson stumbled badly, receiving less than 50 percent of the Democratic vote. McCarthy earned over 40 per cent. Lempi was transcendent. "See," she said to Pauline, "even in a conservative, staid place like New Hampshire, common people know the war is wrong and we need a different president. It's a turning point. America is ready to do the right thing."

On primary night, Toivo stayed at Lempi's walkup, where she attacked him with a fierce joy. And he responded, because he too was happy. He really believed the war could be ended. Maybe people like Jeremy wouldn't have to bare their souls to escape fighting.

A few days later, Lempi's high skidded to a new low. Senator Robert Kennedy announced his run for the presidency. McCarthy's performance paved the road by proving the current president was vulnerable. Toivo, who had been devastated by Jack Kennedy's assassination five years earlier, was confident that anyone in the fabled Kennedy family had to be good for America. Wasn't it good if someone as beloved as Bobby Kennedy was willing to take on the president? Surely LBJ was doomed.

Lempi would have none of it. "Bobby Kennedy enters the stage like he's a prince, ready to play a role to seduce us all. But don't trust him. He used to be on the staff for Senator Joe McCarthy. That lying senator with his Red baiting destroyed my family in the fifties. I can't ever forgive anyone who was part of it."

"I don't understand you. Bobby Kennedy's done so much for the blacks in America. You're so fervent on civil rights."

"But I want a man and a family I trust. Joe McCarthy was the godfather to one of Kennedy's children. Did you know that? And do you know that Kennedy's sister Rose is institutionalized in a home in Eau Claire, up by Clover? What kind of family sends their mentally retarded daughter a thousand miles away? I don't trust that man. Eugene McCarthy's a man of honor. The complete opposite of Joe McCarthy! And Robert Kennedy!"

Lempi's bitterness to Senator Kennedy was irrational. For the first time Toivo sat back to wonder who she really was. All he knew was that he loved her. He wasn't sure if Lempi felt the same about him. Even though he increasingly spent most nights with her, they maintained separate places. But when it came to marriage, Lempi was a bit of a hippie. She was quick to revel in sex but wary of formal commitment. Toivo knew only one thing for certain. When they walked together, holding hands, Lempi remained centered in some calming sea of simple motion. And if they didn't talk, if he didn't excite some cause or another, then in those moments she was happy. In those calming minutes, he too was happy.

If he could have walked with Lempi every moment of his life and remained fixed to the ground, sheltered by blue skies with a smattering of clouds and the feel of the hot sun on their faces, smelling the fresh breeze from Lake Michigan blowing across their skin . . . if he could have done that, he would have been in heaven.

Toivo was grounded enough to realize that Lempi was unlikely to want such a future. She probably was never as calm as she seemed in their walks. She was always planning her next step. She quickly gained credibility in the Wisconsin primary campaign for McCarthy. She rounded up scores of young men and women from campuses across the city: Bremen, Marquette, Alverno, and the UW at Milwaukee. She convinced guys to shave and cut their hair, girls to put on make-up, all to wear more conventional clothes and become the young collegiates their parents wanted them to be. She energized her college kids to walk the streets, ring doorbells and make the pitch for change. She reminded them that their hands held the keys to their future: they could convince an older generation to select the candidate who would lead all Americans to a better tomorrow.

On the Sunday before the Wisconsin primary, she met with her troops in a conference room at the Schroeder Hotel. Senator McCarthy was upstairs conducting strategy sessions. Lempi needed to energize her kids for a successful last push. Tuesday's election would give the farmers, the mechanics, the brewers, the teachers and the parents of Wisconsin an opportunity not only to say "no" to the current president but also to ensure that an intelligent, caring man moved them forward on the road to victory.

"I am more than ten years older than most of you," she began. "I've had the opportunity to see many changes in this country. We fought back the evil Joe McCarthyism of the fifties. We resisted those who would divide us by fear. We battled for the civil rights of our brothers in the fields of the south and the cities of the north. But now there is something we must fight for even harder—and that is to end this unjust war that is killing our sons, our brothers, our friends. It is a war with no hope of success and no purpose in being fought, a war that has already killed thousands of American youth, a war for which General Westmoreland just demanded more than two hundred thousand additional troops.

"It is time to say no to this killing machine. This war is not morally justified. It must be ended. And you, the college students of America, can make that difference. Nearly seven million of you are enrolled in American colleges and universities. You are the difference. You will be the army for change. You are the tidal wave who will lift Senator Eugene McCarthy to be the next president and end this war. Make your parents proud. Do what is right for America. Make yourselves proud. Tomorrow, when we generate our final push to the voters of Wisconsin, when you walk door to door, remember what we fight for. Remember what we can do. Know that Senator Eugene McCarthy is the man who will lead us forward."

The kids looked at Lempi with fervor, ready to swing into action. Toivo was proud of his girl. A door swung open. Another volunteer ran into the room, "He's not running. He's not running!" And everyone knew in an instant that President Johnson had withdrawn from the race.

No churchgoer ever displayed as strong a look of redemption mixed with pleasure as Toivo saw on Lempi's face. It was as though her rally speech had been the straw that broke the incumbent president's back. Pleasure, satisfaction and ecstasy swirled to create a Lempi barely recognizable to Toivo.

A student turned on his transistor radio to play at full volume. The room could hear the words being repeated on the radio network. Toivo pictured Johnson's lumpy nose and doughy cheeks as he listened to the unexpected words:

"I will not seek, and I will not accept the nomination of my party for another term as your president."

Lempi sunk into a folding chair. The students around her crowed and danced with pleasure. She scanned the room until she caught Toivo's eye, and her intense smile of satisfaction chilled him to the bone.

Two days later, on April 2, 1968, the citizens of Wisconsin voted. Eugene McCarthy received 56 per cent of the Democratic vote. Lempi and her legions had delivered for the Senator. She was so happy that Pauline said

Lempi glowed.

"I made a difference," Lempi crowed. "People in power can't just do whatever they want. Johnson's own party rejected a sitting president. When has that happened before?"

"Don't you think McCarthy had something to do with the win?" Toivo kidded. Over the months, he learned to show less awe of this woman. Pauline just smiled, because like many of those she knew in the academic world, she was delighted by the Wisconsin vote. But even more, she was overjoyed that Lempi found something to energize her.

But two days later on April 4, Lempi descended to a new low. Martin Luther King Jr. was assassinated in Memphis. Unwilling to believe it was a lone gunman, Lempi was convinced there were interests who wanted to keep the attention away from the war by reigniting racial tensions. A new wave of violence swept across the United States. Over 39 people were killed in the riots following King's assassination, but Lempi was even more disturbed that more than 20,000 people had been arrested around the country. The evening news showed U.S. troops deployed in the nation's capital. Lempi gave the silent glare to anyone who suggested Kennedy could heal such vivid wounds.

Her gloom deepened as the political season went on. Kennedy gained political traction in one state primary after another. Lempi debated taking a leave of absence to travel for the campaign. Pauline reminded Lempi that she, along with several others from academia, had already been named as a McCarthy-pledged delegate to attend the Democratic Convention that summer. When had that happened before? Surely there was a limit to what could be expected of her. But Lempi, convinced that the Oregon primary on May 28 was key to McCarthy's success, wanted to go west. She never asked Toivo whether he would travel too. She just assumed he would. But like many of Lempi's grand plans, this one never came to fruition.

In early May, Eero appeared from Clover for a visit. During the weeklong stay, Toivo spent the nights back at his place since Eero had the only bed in Lempi's apartment, while Lempi used the sofa. But Toivo realized he left some of his shaving equipment behind, and he was pretty certain that Eero found it. But the old man never mentioned it. On the other hand, Eero was quick to share opinions of his daughter's behavior.

"Her Ma and I love her dearly, but that don't mean that we know what to make of her. She's a child unto herself, you know, the way she grew up all alone, with Ma and me already old people by the time she came to us," he said to Toivo.

"Weren't you happy though to have a child at last?" asked Toivo.

"Well, she wasn't our first. Actually three came before. We had ourselves three boys, one right after the other. Two of them, they died when they were young. Risto, he was our youngest, and he left the country a long time ago. Lempi, she never knew any of them. Risto was already gone nearly a year, when she came along. Never saw his little Lempi. By then, Ma and I were already in our forties, and it was the heart of the Depression. We weren't the best family to come into.

"But we always loved that little girl. Maybe we spoiled her, but it's hard to spoil children too much when you're making a living off a farm in the clover belt. The best parts of the state were all settled a century ago. By the time I came along from Finland, the railroads and lumber companies were just selling off what they had no more use for. But the land was mine, mine and Ma's.

"Of course, it wasn't as bad as those scrub brush woods your Pa settled up there in Thread. At least in Clover, the soil drains well, and the season's long enough for growing corn, so it wasn't a bad life that Lempi had, as long as you don't mind living with a couple of old farmers who don't have a lot of time for play."

Toivo wished that his father would talk as openly as Eero. He knew little about his own parents' lives, and never thought about whether their small farm was on good land or not. "What was Lempi like as a girl?" he asked.

"She was one who always knew what she wanted. Didn't make no difference what was going on, she had an opinion. A little bit like me I suppose. I've always thought I knew what was right, and what was wrong, and what people should do next. I've pushed some people pretty hard at times. I guess Lempi learned that from me. She's never fearful to state her case. She can be funny at times, but she's never trying to be, and she doesn't really want to be. She knows she's right, and she has no patience to wait around until the rest of us come to agree.

"Luckily, she was pretty and that took the edge off all those opinions. Took after her Ma in regard to those looks," he said and paused.

"I never saw a picture of your wife. Was she pretty too?" asked Toivo.

Eero seemed momentarily confused. He stumbled a bit. "Well, they're different. They each have their own look. Lempi, now she had really fair skin and that lovely blonde hair. She was the golden one in school. But she always took up the cause of the underdog. Back during the war, we're talking about World War Two, not this Vietnam War, she got mad when some of the others harassed the German kids in town. She said they're all Americans. Course most of us parents weren't really Americans, especially those of us who didn't become American citizens when we came over, but just stayed what they call alien residents. Have to register at the post office every year. But to Lempi, our neighbors were all Americans, all loyal and ready to serve. Maybe that's why what came later was so hard on her. She's never been good at accepting the fact that everyone don't think the same."

"What happened later?" Toivo asked

Eero grimaced. "That's a long story, and if Lempi hasn't told you yet about what happened to our family in the fifties, then I best leave it alone. She'll tell you someday, and it don't really matter no more. It's done with." The man dropped into silence, his rheumy eyes fixed on Toivo, evaluating him. He seemed to be trying to find some answer to a question he needed resolved. Finally, he spoke again, "Do you love my daughter?"

Now Toivo was momentarily confused. Lempi and he had never really discussed this question, although he knew his answer. He just hadn't ever said it aloud, and it seemed wrong to first voice his emotions to this old man. But he had no good reason to avoid the question. "Yes, I love her."

"And no secrets?" the old man pressed.

"No. No secrets."

"Because that girl can't have any more secrets in her life."

Lempi didn't take leave from Bremen College; she and Toivo didn't travel to Oregon; and Eugene McCarthy won the primary without them. Suddenly, Kennedy's forward momentum seemed blocked and Eugene McCarthy still might win the Democratic Party nomination. Pauline, Eero and Toivo all thought that this news would reinvigorate Lempi's mood. But it didn't. Not being in Oregon, she didn't feel as though the victory had much to do with her. Instead, she dwelled on the negatives reported nightly on the national news. There was no end in sight for the war. Racial tensions were thicker than ever. Governor Wallace—the man who had stood at the university doors in Alabama to block black students from entering—was riding Southern white bigotry with a third party run for president. But Lempi's main concern was the upcoming California primary.

"Maybe I should go to California and help out. McCarthy has to win California or he won't get the nomination," Lempi mused. Toivo listened, but in his mind, he dwelled on the last time Lempi traveled west—back when she was a teenager and had a road trip affair with the artist. No way was he letting her go.

When the California polls closed on June 5, they were both in her apartment listening to the news. Bobby Kennedy was projected to win. All the early polls agreed. Indeed as the first results came in, it seemed almost certain.

"I can't listen to this," Lempi said, "so I'm going to bed. Morning is soon enough to find out if Kennedy blocked McCarthy and ruined our chances." Toivo, having learned not to argue, thought Kennedy carried a better chance to actually win the overall race. Certainly, he could beat Richard Nixon, the likely Republican nominee.

Toivo stayed up, feeling restless, and listened to late night radio. Lempi's living room provided a good view down the quiet residential street. At this late hour, there was very little traffic. Only the streetlights and the buzz of June bugs flying around the light bulb on the porch landing disturbed the darkness; none of it was loud enough to interrupt his thoughts or block out the low murmur of the radio. He may have dozed off, because it was after two when there was a change in tone from the radio. "Kennedy has been shot."

He was hit with a sickening mental return to an afternoon five years earlier. He had been working odd jobs and painting a neighbor's living room in Thread for a few dollars. The neighbor's television has been on, but Toivo had been alone in the house when the first reports came in from Dallas. President Kennedy had been assassinated. As he listened to Walter Cronkite on that damp November day, he felt abandoned and afraid. He kept painting because he didn't know what else to do. Now on this night, he was again alone in an empty room listening to his world fall apart. What was there left to believe in? Riots in the cities? Senseless deaths halfway around the world? Civil rights leaders gunned down? And now this? He shivered, even though the night was warm. He continued to sit there alone. Seeing no value in waking Lempi, he let her sleep. She could find out in the morning, he thought. Behind his logical thoughts, he was afraid she would be happy. He couldn't deal with that.

But his fears proved misplaced. Awake all night, he plugged in the coffee percolator at six am. Perhaps it was the perking sound or the whiffs of fresh-brewed coffee that roused her, but Lempi soon stepped into the kitchen. Her bed hair seemed endearing, and her short pajamas might have been sexy in another moment. She yawned, and then noticed his face. "What's wrong?" she immediately asked.

"Someone shot Kennedy, and it doesn't look good for him," Toivo replied.

She just stood there for the longest time and said nothing. Toivo had grown accustomed to reading Lempi's emotions. This morning, though he confronted a foreign language. Something shifted and adjusted, but whether it was slow or fast, whether excited or appalled, he really couldn't tell. Her eyes slightly widened; her cheeks flushed, and she said simply, "Oh." She stepped into the bathroom and he heard the water running in the tub.

Only that evening in bed did she open up. After listening all day to the radio updates, watching the evening news and learning what had transpired in the kitchen of the Ambassador Hotel in Los Angeles, they knew the senator was still alive, but wasn't expected to live. It was almost overlooked that Kennedy severely beat McCarthy in the California primary.

Lempi confessed, "My first reaction was glee, because I thought that this would give McCarthy a real chance at winning the nomination. And then I felt revenge, because I hated Kennedy for jumping into the race after McCarthy had the courage and initiative to prove Johnson's weakness. Then I was mortified. How could I react this way? How can I be such an awful person? I'm worse than a child."

Toivo, not knowing whether Lempi was awful or not, simply kissed her slowly and lovingly. She kissed him back. Somehow in some way, it became different than any earlier night. They made love that night within her guilt, and the act became more precious because of the emotions beneath them. For the first time ever, Toivo believe that Lempi actually did love him.

When they awoke in the morning, they turned on the radio and learned that Robert. F. Kennedy was dead.

Mid-August, just a year since Toivo first grabbed Lempi's hand to guide her escape from the Milwaukee riots, the two of them sat in Lempi's apartment on a Sunday afternoon. Modeling outfits she bought at Gimbels to wear at the Democratic Convention in Chicago, Lempi sought compliments from Toivo. He found them easy to give. Lempi chose her clothing well. Their bright colors and patterns, more akin to the summer of love than a political gathering, accentuated Lempi's fair skin and blond hair and minimized her overly broad hips. Better yet, the new outfits lifted her mood, which made Toivo happier.

"No one could accuse you of being the Establishment in that dress," teased Toivo.

Lempi smiled indulgently. "Maybe I'm acting silly, taking all this time to think about how I will look at the convention. But there's still a chance that McCarthy could pull it off, and I'm part of a historic delegation. There's only nine of us in the Wisconsin delegation from the academic world, and I'm the only one who's not a college professor. I'm representing women. I need to look my best."

"And here I thought you were doing this all for the Yippies and their Festival of Life," joked Toivo. At least, he hoped Lempi thought he was joking. Truthfully, he didn't want his girlfriend in Chicago this week. He didn't care how groundbreaking it was for a college secretary to be a delegate. He was afraid Chicago wouldn't be safe. In particular, he didn't like what he was reading about these left-wing radical Yippies. What kind of name was that anyway? Just yesterday, their leader Jerry Rubin hosted the Yippie convention to nominate a pig called Pigasus for president. After parading the animal around town, a bunch of the protestors had been arrested. When he read the story in the morning's paper, he wanted to push the front page in front of Lempi's face and say, "See this. I told you Chicago wasn't a sane place to go. Please stay home."

But he knew he wouldn't succeed. At least the pig looked cute, unlike the raggedy Yippies. Toivo's friend Dick was full of stories about Yippie threats to the Windy City. Maybe they would throw nails onto the freeway to block traffic, or pile cars into barricades to keep out the police and National Guard. There was even a wild rumor they would dump LSD into the city water supply and send the entire Democratic Party on a mind trip.

Toivo wasn't naive. He knew trouble could also come from Mayor Daley who ran Chicago as a law and order guy. Chicago police, in training for months, were on twelve-hour shifts. The *Sentinel* reported Daley was promising "law and order will be maintained." To Toivo, all the bravado seemed like spraying briquettes with lighter fluid.

Even though Lempi liked to claim she had ESP, Toivo felt he was the one with an extra sense. Last year before the riot, he knew Lempi was walking into trouble. This August he felt a similar premonition about Chicago. Lempi would claim that Toivo fell victim to fears spread by the military industrial complex, or suffered the repressive tolerance that kept this country locked into an immoral war. Lempi liked her jargon, and Toivo didn't feel smart enough to argue. Instead he admired her outfits. Tomorrow he would drive her to the station to catch the southbound Chicago and Northwestern train. And he would worry.

The next day, as commanded by Lempi, he pulled up to the modern train station, stopped the car to let her exit, and watched as she struggled through the doors with her rather large suitcase. She refused to let him help, and she didn't look back to wave goodbye. That evening Toivo met up with Pauline at her house to catch the convention coverage (both of them secretly hoping that the cameras would pan across the Wisconsin delegation to offer a glimpse of Lempi). He didn't tell Pauline of Lempi's cursory farewell; he knew she was all too familiar with Lempi's ways. Besides, he didn't want Pauline to worry, even as he fretted. They sat in their separate and uncomfortable chairs in Pauline's suburban rambler. They listened to Aretha Franklin sing "The Star Spangled Banner." They kept eyes focused on the black and white tube in its teak credenza. Neither said a word about the violence being reported between the police and the Yippies in Grant Park.

In the days that followed, their concern deepened. Long-distance calls were expensive and Lempi had warned them she wouldn't be calling. They only knew what they saw on television or read in the papers. It seemed as though the Democratic Party was falling apart in front of their eyes. In their unspoken decision not to worry one another, Toivo remained silent when police roughed up on camera a television reporter named Dan Rather, who was seeking an interview with a Georgia delegate. Toivo idolized Walter Cronkite, and he agreed with the anchorman who said on air, "I think we've got a bunch of thugs here, Dan." Toivo wished deeply that he had put his foot down and not allowed Lempi to attend the convention. Vice President Humphrey was sure to be the nominee. Supporting McCarthy in Chicago was a waste of time.

Wednesday's news worsened. Both Toivo and Pauline were now watching TV together from her slightly more comfortable modern sofa. Violence around the Hilton Hotel, where McCarthy's operations were based and where Lempi was staying, was escalating. Police were being injured, demonstrators chased down and tear gas dispersed. On the podium before the TV cameras, a senior senator decried the police use of "Gestapo tactics." At that denunciation, the cameras zoomed in on Mayor Daley who, caught up in rage, clearly cursed. No sound mike picked up his voice, but the words seemed clear.

Pauline was appalled. "Did he just say 'fuck you, you Jew' to Senator Ribicoff?"

"I can't watch anymore. I'm going home," said Toivo. He feared some future camera movement, inside or outside the convention, would pan and capture Lempi in trouble. Since Lempi's passions lay more with the protesters on the street than the suited-up pols inside, Toivo couldn't predict what Lempi might do in such a charged city. But he knew a helpless feeling would engulf him if he somehow discovered her recklessness while watching television coverage. He found temporary comfort in solitude as he drove home and turned off the radio.

Nearly midnight when he got home, he trudged up the steps to his second-floor apartment. He did not turn on the television. Unable to sleep, he sat up all night in his old ratty armchair. If he dozed off for a few minutes, he was always jolted back awake by the underlying sense of danger. After hours of this, the early light of dawn washed through his blinds.

The phone rang. In its peal, he felt the reverberations of fear and hope. Hope that it was Lempi calling, even though she had warned that it would be too expensive and that he would have to wait her return. Fear that it would be Pauline, Eero or some nameless police officer in Chicago with unwelcome news that Lempi was in a jail cell, a hospital bed or on a slab in the morgue. The sense of impending disaster, which had had been hanging over his head for days, ratcheted up as he let the phone ring four times before he made a dash to pick up the receiver.

"Hello."

"Toivo, it's Lempi." She sounded out of breath. A lot of noise in the background suggested she was in a room full of people. Toivo nearly collapsed in a release of tension.

"Thank God, you're okay."

"Of course, I'm okay. Were you worried? There was no need. I've been working all night on the fifteenth floor in the operations center. I was never down on the street."

"Thank God."

"Others were, so I know what's been happening. Kids from the campaign fled up to our suite, beaten by the police, covered in blood. Toivo, this country is rotten. It won't do what's right, and only defends what's wrong."

"But you're okay."

"Yes, I told you I'm okay. Why are you so worried? Nothing's wrong with me. But the Yippies were right; the police are pigs. The Chicago cops raided our floor in the middle of the night. They tried to force us out of our own rooms! Out of the campaign center of a United State Senator! This is a man running for the presidency of our country. And they treat us like criminals. They accused us of throwing things out of the windows.

"But luckily the Senator showed up. He faced down the cops and demanded to know who's in control. And no one dared to answer. And Senator McCarthy said, 'Just as I thought. No one's in charge.' And that ended it. They left us alone, and we're all okay."

"You don't know how happy I am to hear that, but if everything's okay, why call me at six in the morning?"

Lempi was momentarily quiet. The earlier sounds of ruckus in the background were dissipating. He sensed that she had chased her colleagues away. "My eyes were opened tonight. Somehow seeing the Senator behave so purposefully, taking control of a difficult situation, facing down his foes, I was inspired. I was energized. And I knew there was something I had to tell you."

A little flutter of joy began to beat within him. The drama of the night had moved Lempi to confirm her love. Then the fluttering turned to seem more a presentiment of danger.

"Toivo, I'm pregnant, and I'm going to keep the baby."

It was good to be home. There was so much in Thread that Toivo wanted to show Lempi—lakes and dells that he loved as a boy, woods he explored as a teenager and landscapes he hoped one day to show his child. He could hardly wait until March when Lempi would make them both parents.

He never dared to ask Lempi what she meant on her Chicago phone call when she said she would keep the baby. Had she considered an abortion or adoption? Surely she knew he wanted to be a father? Didn't she understand how this signified good things? In the late September splendor of a northern Wisconsin autumn day, watching Lempi and his own mother, Ida, walk ahead of him in the quiet town square, he felt a great warmth and sense of well-being.

It took so much effort to convince Lempi to drive north to meet his parents and see his hometown. What would it take to convince her to marry him? With her showing signs of pregnancy and agreeing to meet his parents, his sixth sense hinted at the answer he wanted.

"She's a pretty girl," his father Erik said. "Never would have thought she was older than you. Looks so young, but she's getting some weight to her, that one." Toivo looked sharply at his father, who blushed. "I don't mean it that way. She's got a good figure, and she'd make a good farm wife. I mean there's a lot of worries on her back that weigh her down. I knew women like that from the old country. Something always wearing them down. It's those long nights in Finland. But still that don't mean Finns have to be downbeat."

"Lempi's not down beaten," protested Toivo.

"Didn't mean to say she was," Erik said and focused on relighting his pipe. The father and son lapsed into more comfortable silence.

Toivo wanted Lempi to impress his father, and he wanted this beautiful part of the country to excite her. His secret hope was that she would leave Milwaukee and move north. Something about Big and Little Sapphire Lakes, with their clear, deep blue waters, gave him joy. It was the same belonging he felt deep in the woods, surrounded by trees reaching to the skies, hearing the cries of birds and feeling the slight whisper of the breeze encircling him. In the shelter of the stone walls of the dairy barn, all the milk cows patiently chewing their cud and waiting to be relieved of their heavy loads of milk, he felt the same moments of peace. It happened when he worked on the fishing boat with its day-to-day routine on the water. Hand picking of cherries with Jeremy was like that too. He never found that peace on the manicured grounds of Bremen University or the busy streets of Milwaukee.

Up ahead, Ida and Lempi stood near the somewhat dilapidated gazebo in the town square. He couldn't hear the words between his mother and

Lempi, but he could tell that his mother was pointing out landmarks. This little town was the whole world to his mother. She had arrived in America as a young girl with her parents. She remembered little about Finland, certainly not its major cities like Helsinki or Turku, or even of passing through Ellis Island and New York. Her world had always been the farm, this little town of Thread and the county seat of Timberton in Penokee County.

He tried to picture the town through Lempi's eyes. Red's Piggly Wiggly on the north side was a modern up-to-date supermarket built two years earlier. Toivo admired its plate glass front and the fluorescent brightness that flooded onto the street. On the square's opposite side, the Great Northern Highlands Express was pulling into the small train station. It was traveling south from Timberton to Green Bay and then on to Milwaukee and Chicago. Train travel was a little old-fashioned, but he liked the rails. He momentarily regretted he hadn't suggested the train to Lempi, instead of the long drive up Highway 17.

Next to the station was the movie theater where *True Grit* was playing. For a moment he considered suggesting they take his parents to the afternoon matinee. But then he recalled that Lempi and he had seen it in Milwaukee earlier in the summer and Lempi railed over the right wing politics of John Wayne. He didn't need to subject his parents to that. In fact, he hoped to keep Lempi off politics the entire weekend. Since Chicago and facing the reality that the election would be between Nixon and Humphrey, Lempi usually ignored politics. Occasionally, a news item about George Wallace's third-party run would inflame her. Instead, she was becoming more interested in the campus anti-war groups. Even Pauline warned her that she was behaving inappropriately for a staff member of the college. Lempi countered that the kids were the only ones trying to improve the world.

"Well, what's Lempi rushing off to?" Erik's sudden comment broke through Toivo's musings. "It looks like she's going to talk to that old coot, Mr. Packer. Why'd she want to do that?"

Mr. Packer was the town hermit and pack rat. He moved to town years ago, was friendly to everyone and looked like a hobo. He sported a long beard, was missing an arm and was at least seventy. Toivo had a quick answer, "She's always looking for someone to help."

Ida walked back toward Toivo. "Does she know him?" Ida asked.

Lempi and Mr. Packer hugged and then engaged in an animated conversation. Toivo shrugged. He had no explanation.

After a few minutes, Lempi rejoined the three. "An old friend," she said in explanation.

"You know that old man?" asked Erik in surprise.

"He used to work at Bremen."

"Really," said Ida with incredulity.

"Actually, he was once a professor there."

Even Toivo found that hard to believe and said, "That oddball. How can that be?"

"I guess everyonc has secrets," replied Lempi and she didn't say more. Ida suggested lunch, and the four of them walked across the square and entered the old Thread Tavern for fish fries. They didn't speak again of Mr. Packer.

Later in the weekend, after attending services at the Lutheran church with his parents (Lempi stayed at the house) and eating his mother's oven-fried chicken for Sunday dinner, Toivo alone sat in the living room. In the kitchen, Ida and Lempi washed and dried the dishes. It was a small farmhouse. Pretty much anywhere Toivo sat would have allowed eavesdropping on the conversation happening by the sink. On the other hand, he could have chosen to join his father who was smoking on the front porch.

"So what do you think of our little town?" his mother asked Lempi.

"It's quite interesting in its own way," Lempi responded. Toivo's heart sank a little. Lempi and Pauline described things as interesting only when they could think of nothing nicer to say.

"Maybe after Toivo and you get married, and have the little one, you might think about coming up here and living. You know, his Pa and I are getting kind of old. This farm would be Toivo's if he wanted it. It's time we moved into town. This old place is not that much, but it let us raise that good boy out there." Toivo sensed his mother knew he was listening in. As a little boy, he always lurked around the visiting ladies to hear their gossip.

"I don't think that's likely."

"And why not? A big city like Milwaukee is no place to raise a child."

Toivo wondered if Lempi looked away from his mother before replying. He pictured her standing at the sink, with a dishtowel in one hand and a wet glass in the other, her eyes staring out the window toward the small wooden barn with its flaking red paint. "Toy would never want to come back here for good. He loves city life."

He bristled when she called him "Toy" to his mother. Her new pet name made him seem small and unimportant. But he was even more annoyed that she thought he loved the city. He only tolerated Milwaukee because of her.

"And I can't imagine living again in a little village like this," Lempi continued. "Are there even a thousand people here? It's so far from everything. You don't even get television reception. It's 1968, but in a town like this, I feel like it's still the 1930s. I grew up in a little town in the center of the state. That town wasn't kind to me, and I don't see how I could ever be happy in a place like Thread."

"What about that old professor you met in town today? Mr. Packer seems very happy to live here. I see him all the time, and he always has a kind word to say."

Lempi was quick to reply. "Mr. Packer, as you call him, already had his life ruined, and he was brought down to the very bottom. I knew him when that happened, and I will never forgive the forces that did it. Unlike him though, I can still fight, and I will. Thread is too far away from the site of the battles I need to fight."

After returning from Thread, Lempi and Toivo skirmished frequently about their future lives. Toivo wanted to marry immediately. Lempi found reasons to delay. By New Year's she was embarrassingly large with child, and they still lacked an agreed-upon date. Their other battleground involved Lempi's working. Toivo thought Lempi should quit her job once the baby came. They could get by. Lempi branded the idea ridiculous. The city was far too expensive to get by on one small income. Toivo knew there was a way to solve that problem. They could return to Thread where he could easily support a family of three on the small farm. But the hometown option wasn't even on the table.

Lempi was raised as an only child. This upbringing bestowed on her a total inability to balance the competing emotions of others. She felt it was her due to get whatever she requested, and she resented it deeply when she did not. As a result, others seldom found Lempi as appealing as Toivo did

Earlier in the fall, Toivo's old friend Jeremy showed up. As feared,

Jeremy had been drafted and was about to be inducted. Toivo wanted Lempi to meet his old friend, and so the trio tromped to a small bar down the street to have beers and burgers. But after less than an hour, Lempi left them. The men continued talking over a couple of boilermakers.

"She's a pretty woman," Jeremy said. "What makes you love her?"

Toivo wondered why Jeremy asked that question. He often thought Jeremy had a crush on him. It first occurred to Toivo the night Jeremy confessed to being a homosexual. Toivo didn't understand men who liked men and called themselves gay. He thought such behavior was queer, although he would never say that to Jeremy, because Jeremy really was the best friend he ever had. So when his friend asked him why he loved Lempi, Toivo truly stopped to think about it. He was afraid that Jeremy found Lempi dismissive and disagreeable earlier in the evening.

He gazed down at the table and his shot glass of brandy and the bottle of Pabst, looked past the men drinking at the bar and the lighted signs for Hamm's and Miller beers and tried to articulate a driving emotion that wasn't even clear to him. How could he say he was in love because of the way Lempi walked, or that he felt secure in her determination and self-assurance? Could Jeremy appreciate the way he admired Lempi's willingness to say what she thought and to pour her heart and soul into causes? He knew people like his coworker Dick thought Lempi pretty, maybe even a little beautiful, but dismissed her as too aggressive. He loved her initially because he created an imaginary version that lived so long in his mind that it wore in a comfortable groove. But then he met her. And he learned he loved her in a deeper, truer way because she made him content. And because she accepted his quiet ways. With her, he could be who he was. That acceptance gave him the courage to strive to be a little bit more. Which pleased him. But how could he say all that, even to someone who knew him as well as Jeremy?

"I just do," he replied, and Jeremy accepted the answer.

The truth was he loved Lempi when she behaved badly, when she ignored what he wanted and even when she trampled over those around her.

Eero was visiting from Clover. He was joining Lempi and Toivo to welcome in 1969 at a New Year's Day dinner at Pauline's place. Toivo feared it would be a night of trampling.

For the first time since Toivo met her, Pauline invited another guest—a FBI agent she had met. He had been sent to Milwaukee to investigate a series of bomb threats. During his investigation, he met Pauline and they became friends. Now Pauline wanted the young couple to meet this new man in her life, but Pauline, knowing Lempi, extracted a promise that Lempi would be on her best behavior.

The afternoon started out promisingly. A blaze burned brightly in Pauline's stone fireplace. Her Christmas tree in the corner of the room was bedecked with the miniature lights that had lately become the rage. The hi-fi played Frank Sinatra. Toivo might have preferred Credence Clearwater Revival, but he knew that Lempi never paid any attention to background music and that Pauline was strictly old school. Pauline introduced them to John Tuzzi, her FBI agent friend.

"His real name is Edgar John Tuzzi," laughed Pauline. "But he's dropped the "Edgar."

"No one's used it since I was a little kid, but I have to admit I don't want to share a first name with the Director," said John.

Lempi broke in. "His name is actually J. Edgar Hoover, isn't it? So you're not really sharing first names at all. Actually, you're both hiding your first names it seems to me. I wonder what that means." To Toivo, Lempi's words came across as a blustering warning.

Tuzzi just laughed. Soon Pauline poured them all glass of Mateus, a Portuguese rose wine. Eero looked at his glass with a slight grimace of dismay. Toivo was a kindred spirit. He preferred drinks that didn't require stemware. But the alcohol loosened everyone's spirits. Seated around the table laden with roast beef, many vegetables and a steaming bowl of whipped potatoes, it seemed a good year was beginning.

Pauline described her favorite floats from the Rose Parade earlier in the day. She recently bought a color television, so this was the first year she saw the floats in all their glory. To Toivo, it seemed a good moment to ask how she and Tuzzi met, even though he already knew the story.

Tuzzi answered, "As you know, there's been radical threats on different college campuses, even a fire bombing of the bookstore by Marquette University. Over Thanksgiving, someone dropped a bomb made with ammonium nitrate from an airplane. It landed on a field near New Berlin. Luckily it didn't go off."

"I saw that in the paper," Lempi said quickly.

"We think these events may all be connected to one of the radical student groups. My team was sent here to try to stop them before they do some real damage," added John.

"John was making the rounds of the colleges talking to various deans and officials. I was on his list. We sort of hit it off," Pauline was smiling and slightly red-faced as she said this.

"I was supposed to be checking on student groups at Bremen, but throughout the interview, I just kept thinking how beautiful Pauline was. When you're in your fifties and single, like me, and you meet someone that takes your breath away, you can't wait," John said.

"Well, you waited until later in the day . . ."

"I needed to be off duty before I could ask you out. There are protocols after all."

"Wait a minute," Lempi broke in. She didn't display any sign of being charmed by this middle-aged romance or any reticence in interrupting. "I know you. But you don't remember me at all, do you?" Even for Lempi, the tone seemed cold and unyielding.

Tuzzi's confusion was apparent.

"Over fifteen years ago. Here in Wisconsin. In Clover. Pa, don't you remember this man?"

Toivo felt quite confused, even as he saw some level of comprehension work its way across the faces of Tuzzi, Eero and Pauline. For Tuzzi, it was tinged with discomfort, in Pauline fear and with Eero anger.

"I did work in Wisconsin then."

Lempi stood up at the table, "And you were sent to investigate my parents. Don't tell me you don't remember them? Eero and Marja Makinen? Suspected spies, or some such nonsense. One of them is still here, sitting across from you."

Tuzzi was calm. It was clear he knew what Lempi was referencing. "It was a different time. We were checking immigration status, and I don't remember all the people we were asked to investigate. But I remember those we deported as un-American, and you weren't among them. It was just a questioning, I'm sure." John looked toward Pauline as though wondering whether she wanted him to leave, although he showed no shame about whatever had happened.

"That's so long ago," Pauline said. "Surely you can forgive John for doing his job, even if it did hurt you at the time. It wasn't personal. Can't we forget about what's done, and focus on the future? Like your wedding and the baby."

In her desire to blockade an uncomfortable route, Pauline deliberately baited Lempi with a question that was sure to anger her. In Lempi's mind, Pauline had no right to meddle in any of their marriage or baby plans.

For whatever reason, Lempi didn't react. She took Pauline's lead and dropped her interrogation of Tuzzi. But her glare clearly indicated she wasn't totally finished with the topic, and her voice switched to being bizarrely playful. "Toy and I have decided to get married well in advance of the baby's birth. After all, we wouldn't want him to be a little bastard."

Pauline did not find the use of this word amusing. Toivo sat amazed at hearing the details to a plan never discussed with him. Lempi didn't notice or care. "So I was thinking we will make it official near the end of the month. Pa, do you think you could come back in a few weeks for a wedding?"

"Of course," he replied.

"Since Toy and I are already living together, we will keep it simple. I think just a private ceremony, and I don't want it to be religious. Pauline, I was thinking we might ask your friend, the Mayor, to preside. Do you think he would do it?"

"I'm sure Mr. Zeidler would be happy to do that."

"Then it's all settled. You won't need to ask your favorite question anymore." Lempi reached across and took Toivo's hand. "I know Toy would have done this back in the summer. Then wanted to marry on my Finnish name day. Wouldn't that have been sweet? But I was waiting for some sign. I know that's just foolish. We need to move on."

Pauline smiled broadly, "I am so happy to hear that. And what have you decided about working?"

"Who do you think you are? My mother? Of course, I'm going to keep my job. We can't afford to live on Toy's salary." For a moment, Toivo considered reminding Lempi they could move to Thread. "Besides," Lempi continued, "I need to stay at Bremen and remain close to the students. We need to effect change in the world. They are the only ones who can make it happen. The people in this country have been so disappointing in the way they elected Richard Nixon president. They've completely forgotten the violence that Mayor Daley's pigs poured onto the people who tried to make a difference. When our own government turns on us with such violence, is it any wonder that the moral side retreats into its own violence? When we're led into a war in Vietnam by lies, it is only moral to resist. And if it is moral to resist, then surely it is moral to resist with force." Her last statement was almost spat at Tuzzi.

Tuzzi wasn't sure whether he should be amused or disturbed, "You do know that I work for the FBI, don't you?"

"Indeed, I do," Lempi replied, "and you do know that you're the reason my mother is dead. Yet, we both continue to sit at the same table."

Their child, Daniel, arrived March 7, 1969. Seeing his beautiful son being rocked to sleep in the cradling arms of his wife prompted Toivo to forgive Lempi's mood. She dove into motherhood with the enthusiasm that accompanied all of her manias. In the last weeks before birth, she scavenged a cornucopia of books and guides from the women's center. A bookshelf in the living room was lined with the new titles. She proceeded to systematically study each of them. Secretly, Toivo was relieved that that feminist books didn't convince Lempi to use a midwife, who instead opted for a hospital delivery and an epidural.

Lempi suffered no post-partum depression. She emerged from the hospital with her new son and a new emotional buzz. At first, Toivo speculated the doctors put Lempi on some mood stabilizer. But he quickly accepted that her mood wasn't chemical. Maybe it was hormonal or genetics, but at age 35, a mother for the first time, Lempi transformed: reasonable, optimistic and solicitous of Toivo's opinions. She even stopped calling him "Toy." Daniel's name was quickly shortened to Danny, but Toivo was okay with that. He rather liked the breeziness of it. The sound rolled off his tongue pleasantly. He smiled just watching his son's face, whether asleep, awake or blowing tiny bubbles.

Lempi's anger over Pauline's FBI boyfriend also vanished into the wind. After meeting Tuzzi, Lempi called Pauline to say he would not be welcome at their civil ceremony. Toivo could never pry from Pauline, Lempi or Eero what happened back in the Fifties. But in Lempi's motherhood mood, she no longer seemed concerned with her political blacklist, became tolerant of Pauline's hovering and eventually allowed John on the occasional visit.

One day, in the midst of this new mood of reconciliation, Pauline appeared with a key and an astounding offer. The older woman was overjoyed and not at all dampened by the late spring blizzard forming outside their apartment.

"I have something to suggest," Pauline said, "and I want you to promise to listen to me all the way through. Don't be tempted to say 'no' before you've heard me out."

Lempi smiled tolerantly. Danny was in her plump arms. Lempi had kept on some of her weight from the pregnancy, and Toivo thought it made her look more endearing. "Okay, I promise," she said.

"You may not know this about me," Pauline said, "but I've been saving up over the years. I know I won't be working at the college forever. I'm already 54."

"I know how old you are," Lempi replied, still smiling. Just then, Danny burped unexpectedly. All three smiled reflexively.

"My financial advisor recommends that one of my investments should be in real estate, in addition to my home. So I just bought a fourplex for the rental income and appreciation. It's in Wauwatosa, just blocks from my house." Pauline paused, uncertain how to move on.

"Okay?" Lempi said.

"The thing is, I know I'm going to have challenges as a landlord. Look at me; I don't know how to fix anything. You know I always have to call in handymen for any job. And Toivo has been so good helping me on the odd repair. Well, here's what I want to propose. One of those four apartments is for the super to live in, and I want that super to be Toivo.

"You'd be helping me out so much. It wouldn't take a lot of extra time, just collecting rents and handling the on-going maintenance. The apartments are all in good shape. The existing tenants have been there a long time. They're all really good people. And here's the thing, you'd live there rent-free. Lempi, you could stay home and take care of Danny.

"I don't want you to worry about finding some babysitter you don't even know, or have you drop Danny off with her every morning. You'd be working all day at the college and missing everything about your baby as he grows up. His first words, his first steps. I know you don't want to miss that. You can't let yourself miss it."

Pauline pushed her argument forward so rapidly that a few minutes passed before she realized she wasn't getting any resistance. Lempi's smile only broadened. It was not sardonic or skeptical, but a true smile that sparkled in her blue eyes and transformed her broad face into one Toivo wanted to remember forever.

"What do you say, Toy?"

So awestruck by the generosity of Pauline's offer and Lempi's response, Toivo didn't even notice Lempi used his diminutive name. "Of course. Absolutely."

With those words he rushed over to Pauline to hug her with a fervor and thankfulness never given before to his mother or father or, for that matter, anyone in his past.

The fourplex was built in the early Fifties: two stories, brick exterior, and two side-by-side apartments on each floor separated by a staircase. Toivo's duties were light and easily handled in addition to his job at Bremen. He never regretted that extra effort. Not only did it give freedom to Lempi, but Toivo loved the way the morning light streamed through the building's front windows, which in turned framed a decorative stand of white birch in the small front yard. Each morning, looking at the silvery bark of those trees, he felt more confident that it would be okay to stay in the city.

Then things changed. Lempi's old moods returned. If Toivo thought much about why things changed, which he preferred not to do, he suspected he planted those seeds of change. Lempi had been fine until the day she found him in their bedroom reading a letter and crying. Jeremy's mother had written to say that Jeremy, who had never wanted to be a soldier, had been deployed to Vietnam and was killed in action within the first month. Toivo certainly knew Jeremy was only one of tens of thousands who had died. But Jeremy was the first dead soldier he really knew. He sat dully on the edge of the bed, and was filled with a profound sadness. He didn't even feel the tears streaking his cheeks.

It was in that moment of abandonment that Lempi walked in. He handed her the letter. Although she had only met Jeremy once and didn't really like him, he had died in a senseless war that she had tried to stop. She handed back the letter. "The evil never ends," and she sat next to Toivo and hugged him.

Maybe that letter had nothing to do with the return of her old moods.

The timing could have been a coincidence, but the beatific Lempi dissolved into a wilder one, who swirled in the currents of anti-war fervor and reconnected with longhaired, denim-clad activists from the campus. After work, Toivo would enter the apartment to find the front room filled with grungy, but earnest, boys and girls sitting around Lempi in the living room. There would be a pungent wisp in the air. Lempi would wave a weak hello at him, as he would walk back into the kitchen. Her friends weren't people he could like. Even when he tried to participate, he didn't fully connect with the conversation. They dropped names of people, like Marcuse, and spoke of initials and organizations, like the SDS or Black Panthers, that made little sense to him.

He grasped one thread of hope—Lempi's clear love for Danny. Maybe Lempi's involvement with these student radicals provided her a counter-balance to being a stay-at-home mother. Life was filled with compromise and adjustments. Did he want a beautiful son growing up under the careful eye of his mother? Did he like coming home to a clean house and a well-cooked supper? If he did—and he did—then was it too much to listen to Lempi's occasional rants against Vietnam and the government?

Pauline reacted quite differently. She argued for sensible moderation, but Lempi would counterattack by accusing Pauline of having abandoned her own youthful ideals. Pauline would remind Lempi how she had pulled herself out of the small town of Clover to work in city government for a Socialist mayor. That storyline enraged Lempi. She interpreted such remarks as grading her political endeavors of the past year a failure. Eventually, the two women negotiated an uneasy truce. Pauline acted the spinster aunt who doted on the baby relative; they avoided more serious conversation; Pauline's visits grew a little less frequent and she usually left Tuzzi behind.

When the spring term ended and the Bremen campus emptied out, Lempi's ad hoc living room students continued to meet. Toivo suspected most of the longhairs were actually student dropouts or hangers-on. He didn't like the looks of any of them, and he mistrusted their motives. Toivo had a prickling worry that these kids were the kind of left wing activists that most interested the FBI and agents like Tuzzi. He harbored a secret hope that somehow Tuzzi had recruited Lempi as a double agent to infiltrate these groups.

In late July, Toivo left work early because he was excited that the crew of Apollo 11 was scheduled to land on the moon. A camera was with the crew and transmitting back to earth, and he wanted to see it live on TV. As he came through the apartment door, eager to turn on the TV, the crowd was different than usual, creepier somehow. Lempi looked up startled, "You're home early!"

"I want to watch the moon landing. Why don't you guys focus on the exciting things going on, instead of the evils of government?"

It seemed as though the crowd, especially the New York-looking leader, rolled their eyes as one. With a flurry of "yeah, mans" the group took his arrival as a cue to disperse. Within minutes, all were gone. Lempi looked at him quizzically.

"You should get Danny out of the crib and let him sit on your lap while we watch this," Toivo suggested. "When he's older, we can tell him he saw man land on the moon."

Lempi smiled sadly, "You're just a romantic fool."

As he sat down on the sofa, he noticed a pamphlet that had fallen between the seat cushions. It was from the University of Wisconsin and was about creating an explosive called ANFO out of common farm items like ammonium nitrate and fuel oil.

"What's this doing here?" he asked Lempi. The pamphlet triggered a fear in Toivo that he couldn't even name.

"That's just a publication I got from the University."

"But why? It's about explosives."

"Actually farmers use the stuff to excavate watering holes."

"I know what ANFO is. We used it in the iron mines when I worked in the Upper Peninsula. Why would you want a pamphlet on it? What are your friends up to?"

"They have nothing to do with it. I told Pa I might help him write up his early farming years, and I thought this might be how they blew up the stumps when they cleared the land. You know how he likes to talk about those old days."

Toivo was uneasy, sensing Lempi was lying, even though he knew his own father cleared ten acres of stumps in Thread using ANFO. He couldn't let the subject drop, but he didn't know what he wanted to ask. "Who would want to read about your father's early years? Why write it up?"

"Well, maybe it's about me then. You know I am a Red diaper baby, one of those second-generation Communists. I'm sure Tuzzi would love to read it, although he's probably already written the ending." Lempi meant it as a joke, but it was one of her frequent jokes that only sounded bitter. He thought he should ask more. But the TV was on, and the lunar module was preparing to open hundreds of thousands of miles away. Toivo dropped the subject. He wanted to celebrate the moment of discovery instead.

Pauline stormed into their apartment. She had walked the block from her house in subfreezing temperatures without a hat or gloves. "What are you getting involved with?" she demanded.

Toivo was in the bedroom changing Danny's diaper. He chose to remain behind closed doors. Since the Christmas break, Lempi had been in one of her sourest moods. What had she done to anger Pauline? Whatever it was, the timing was unfortunate. Pauline and Tuzzi were scheduled to come over later for a Christmas Eve dinner. Their presents were already wrapped and under the small tree.

"I don't know what you're talking about," Lempi responded.

"Don't play games with me. I've known you since you were a little girl in Clover. I've watched you grow up. I've been by your side ever since you moved to Milwaukee. I can read you like a book. You're obsessive again. But you really must be more sensible. It's not just you anymore. It's Toivo and Danny too. Don't mount your silly horse of righteousness."

"You're being ridiculous," Lempi retorted. Lempi's tone changed. It was edgy, too intense—a voice that came out whenever she felt backed into a corner and became incapable of listening.

"You know I'm not wrong. Look at these photos I uncovered when I was straightening up papers on John's desk. I recognize these people. I've seen them on campus, and I've seen them sitting on that sofa, talking to you. Why would the FBI be interested in your friends?"

"Ask John."

"I will not let him know that I looked at his government papers."

"But you did!" A note of keening triumph in Lempi's accusation chilled Toivo. He knew he should enter the living room to moderate this argument and so he settled Danny back into the crib.

"And when you ask them about 'my friends,' ask John what's going on at your precious Bremen College. Does the school think we don't know about its secret government contracts and how it works for the Department of Defense? Bremen's math geniuses are improving the targeting programs against innocent people in Vietnam. Ask John about those bombings. Ask him which of your colleagues are war criminals."

Toivo entered the room. Pauline sunk into their one oversized upholstered chair and was white with fear.

"Your precious John. He's just an agent of an oppressive government engaged in an illegal war. He always has been, and I guess he always will be. And you're worried about the people I know. The people I know are the good people who oppose the wrongdoers."

"Lempi," Toivo said her name softly, trying to pull her back from the edge of the cliff.

"And what about *your* friend?" Lempi turned on Toivo. "Jeremy would not be lying in a grave now if it weren't for this damn war. What do we need to do to honor that sacrifice?"

"Lempi, you know I love you," began Pauline. "You haven't been yourself these past few months. You've become too emotional . . ."

Lempi stopped her. "Who are you? My mother? I don't think so. You aren't our saviorr or protector. Why get so involved with our lives? Who asked you to buy this building and have Toivo be the super? Did I ask you years ago to find me my first job? Have I asked you to interfere constantly with everything I do? Did I ask you to push Toivo and me together at every opportunity? So fine, you did it. And now we're here. With a baby, and a cheap apartment, and a husband who has no ambitions. And you begrudge me my friends."

Pauline's face was wet with tears. "Lempi, I don't know what to say."

Toivo stood still. Lempi's harsh characterization branded him. He avoided Pauline's eyes, not wanting to see anyone or have anyone see him. Lempi just rewrote their history into a tale he didn't want anyone to read. Danny whimpered in the bedroom. Each person could hear Danny, but no one stepped back to soothe the baby.

Lempi was even, controlled and so cold, "I think it would be better if you didn't come back for the Christmas Eve dinner, Pauline. I don't think I could sit across the table from you."

"Lempi, what are you saying?" Toivo pleaded.

Pauline stood up and straightened her coat. "Lempi is right. We can talk again in a few days, when we've had time to think about what we've said. Good-bye." She walked out the door.

***

That evening was spent in silence. Toivo and Lempi opened their wrapped presents for one another on Christmas Eve instead of waiting until Christmas morning. After the gifts, they dined on a small smorgasbord of Swedish meatballs, pickled herring, cheese, holiday stollen and plenty of decorated cookies. Even though they unwrapped their gifts in a rather desultory manner, glittery paper remained strewn about the room in a gay mimicry of happy times. As they quietly handed one another their few gifts, they managed to murmur "thank you" and "just what I wanted" but the words were without feeling. The presence of the two unwrapped gifts still under the tree—a new purse for Pauline and an elegant cigarette lighter for John—loomed large.

Toivo was determined to stay mute and never acknowledge what Lempi said about him to Pauline. He excused Lempi; she got trapped in an emotional argument. She just built on statements until she stood on a dangerous ledge with no path for retreat. But Toivo couldn't forgive her for maltreating Pauline. The older woman thought of Lempi as the daughter she never had. Such love should not be treated lightly.

As they settled into bed, Toivo leaned over to touch Lempi's lips. He believed couples should never go to bed angry. Even though they both remained furious, he at least wanted to demonstrate the symbols of reconciliation. Lempi didn't resist the slight peck. Toivo had hopes that the morning's light might show a path forward.

In the midnight gloom, with Christmas Day only minutes away, a distant boom reverberated. The muffled sound prompted Toivo to speculate, "Fireworks?" Lempi didn't respond, but seemed almost amused by his question.

In the morning, they were awakened by a strong knock shortly before seven am. Tuzzi was standing at the door looking tired and shaken.

"I have some bad news," he began and just started talking to the two of them, still in their pajamas. "Pauline was very upset when she returned from your apartment yesterday. She wouldn't tell me why, but she said she needed to work. So even though it was Christmas Eve, she went to her office at Bremen."

Wild fear engulfed Lempi's face. Toivo didn't understand why. Surely, John would tell them that Pauline stayed out all evening or decided to drive back to her brother's place in Clover.

"Someone bombed the campus last night. It destroyed Shindler Hall, including her office. We believe Pauline is dead, killed in the blast." Tuzzi shuddered and sought for a moment to speak without his voice breaking. "A group called the Radical Anti-War Front phoned the *Sentinel* to claim responsibility for destroying the Institute of Computing Mathematics."

"No, no, no," Lempi muttered. "She shouldn't have been there; no one should have been there on a holiday. I made her angry. It's all my fault." Toivo wrapped his arms around his wife. Together, they faced Tuzzi.

"Maybe she left early," Toivo said, seeking to land on the faintest of hopes. At the same time, he wondered if the loud sound they had heard during the night had been the explosion from so many miles away.

"I want to think so, but her car is still in the administration parking lot. The blast was enormous. Blew out windows in almost every building on campus. The whole town could hear it. I want to believe she is still alive, but . . ." and Tuzzi couldn't finish the sentence. Then he found support in his FBI training. "We think this is the same group that has been responsible for the earlier smaller bombings I've been investigating. It looks like they used ammonium nitrate and fuel oil. They probably didn't realize how powerful the blast would be."

Seated on the sofa with her head in her hands, Lempi cried softly. Toivo thought of the pamphlet he had found months ago between the seats of that very sofa. He looked at Lempi as though she was someone he had never seen before. He felt he didn't know the woman before him, nor why she was crying.

They were planning Danny's first birthday party the day Galen visited them. He was Pauline's brother and now the executor of her estate.

"Sorry to stop by without calling, but I wanted to take advantage of being in Milwaukee to tell you this personally."

"What's that?" asked Toivo. Since Pauline's death, he took more initiative in day-to-day interactions. Lempi responded very hard to Pauline's passing. It completely washed away her anti-war fanaticism. Toivo chose not to ask any questions about her friends, now disappeared. From Tuzzi, he knew the FBI believed the bombing ringleaders had fled to Toronto.

Galen began, "I'm sure you know, Lempi, that you were very important to my sister. She always saw you as her closest friend, and only wanted success and happiness for both of you. You probably don't know all the ways she sought to help you over the years, and for that matter neither do I. She was that kind of person, and she always thought that Lempi needed to be out of Clover. Just like Pauline herself needed to escape. Pauline was very proud of you, Lempi."

Lempi listened to this ashen-faced.

"Knowing that, I'm sure you won't be surprised to learn Pauline named Lempi as her primary heir. Our parents are gone, and I'm her only sibling. You were the most important person in her life, so I think Pauline did the right thing. Other than a small bequest to Bremen, you get everything that belonged to Pauline."

"That's quite a surprise," said Toivo.

"Unfortunately, Pauline had very little and she was quite stretched financially."

"That doesn't make sense," said Toivo. "She told us how she had been making careful investments. She even bought this building for her retirement."

"I don't know why she bought this fourplex," said her brother, "but the truth is she couldn't afford it. She mortgaged her house and scraped everything she had to buy it, and it remains heavily mortgaged. The building doesn't pay for itself, not even close. You will likely have to sell both Pauline's house and this apartment building to settle the estate's debts. Unfortunately, Toivo, I don't think you make enough to be able to cover the monthly costs the way Pauline did."

Through all of this, Lempi said nothing, looking only at her hands, and rubbing them nervously.

"There is one other thing," Galen said. "Pauline specifically wanted you to have her hope chest. It's in the back of my truck now. I didn't want it to end up being sold with other furniture in the estate sale. While Pauline never got married, when she was young, our mother gave her the old steamer trunk as Pauline's hope chest. Ma had used it when she emigrated from Germany. There are a lot of family artifacts in this trunk, and more than a few things that Pauline planned for her married life. For my sister's memory, please treasure these things. Would you promise me that?"

Lempi looked straight into Galen's eyes and solemnly nodded. Toivo wondered what was really going through her mind, but he knew better than to ask.

After reviewing and signing a few documents for Galen, Toivo helped Galen move the aged steamer trunk from the truck into their apartment. Sitting in the middle of the room, it exerted an unexpected presence. Of course, Toivo recognized it. It had always sat at the foot of Pauline's bed. Seeing it now without Pauline unnerved him. It was as though the trunk had become a mirror reflecting their lives already lived, and offering a glimpse into the chasm of the years ahead.

Finally, after minutes of silently regarding the trunk, he made a decision. He didn't care what Lempi thought; he knew what was needed. "I guess we will have to move. Can't stay here if the building's going to be sold. It's time to leave the city. Let's go to Thread and take over the farm."

"Whatever you think's best," said Lempi.

Her agreement was said with her old force of absolute resolution, but it was uttered neither with a sense of promise nor of happiness. There was only penance. Toivo could only hope that in the quiet north woods both Lempi and he would find whatever they needed.

Danny put down the newspaper clipping, and wondered if he should ask his father about the photo when Toivo got home that night. But he didn't think he would. He reached for the next item in the stack. It was a poorly mimeographed program for the 1951 graduation ceremonies at Clover High School. Its purple color was fading away. Inside he found an old postcard as well as well as a color-tinted photo of his mother as a teenager, posed along side another older woman. Lempi looked happier in this photo than Danny ever remembered her. Danny read the commencement program and was surprised to see his mother listed as delivering the valedictorian's remarks. Why had she never mentioned that?

PAULINE
1952
CLOVER, WISCONSIN

Pauline Newmann was in a place she didn't belong.

A huge American flag hung from the rafters. Below the flag was a stage with three rows of empty chairs on risers. Before it all was a simple podium flanked by pots of red and gold chrysanthemums. The Clover 1952 commencement ceremonies were about to begin.

Pauline Newmann sat in the next to last row of folding chairs on the floor of the gymnasium. Built in the flush of optimism of post World War Two, the brand new Clover High School was hosting its first graduation. Pauline could almost smell the drying varnish on the beautifully finished maple floors. The bleachers along the side of the gymnasium were pulled out in anticipation of an overflow audience. Earlier in the basketball season the stands overflowed with Clover Redskin fans. For the first time in decades, the town's team advanced to the state finals, falling just short of winning the 1952 Level III conference title. But tonight the stands were nearly empty.

Pauline followed her alma mater's sporting progress from afar. Her preferred afternoon paper, *The Milwaukee Journal,* did an adequate job at covering statewide high school athletics. She didn't know what the *Sentinel,* a Hearst rag, covered. But in the end, it really didn't matter. While Pauline grew up in Clover, she wasn't a graduate of Clover High School. There was only one reason she was in Clover that night.

The band, described as an orchestra in the program, played the initial measures of *Pomp and Circumstance.* The band seemed larger, and the brass instruments shinier, than during her days at school. Her high school days, such as they were, occurred during the Depression. The town had been smaller and poorer then. Only after the end of the war did the plumbing fixture factory expand its plant in town.

The high school seniors looked smart, all in their black gowns and mortarboards with hanging red-and-gold tassels, as they marched up the aisle. Back in Milwaukee on a Thursday night, she would probably be watching *You Bet Your Life* on her new television set. But no television program would have kept Pauline away from this night. Marching into the gymnasium in alphabetical order, the 79 seniors were about halfway through their march. Then Pauline saw her: Lempi Makinen. Her baby. Her secret. Her reason for being.

Earlier, Pauline vowed that she would not get emotional. Yet here she was with tears brimming in her eyes. She forced the tears away before they could attract attention. Eero and Marja didn't know she was here, and if they found out, they would be angry. But already she had missed so much of Lempi's life, she couldn't miss this night.

A man slid into an empty grey metal chair behind her. "What are you doing here, sis?" he whispered.

Lempi walked by, neither looking for nor noticing Pauline. Pauline wanted to watch Lempi march forward with her wonderfully endearing and purposeful walk; instead she wearily turned to face her little brother, Galen.

"I came up to see the folks," Pauline said. "And I thought I'd come watch my brother hand out the diplomas. I hear you're head of the school board. However did that happen, Galen?" She smiled broadly to keep at bay other emotions.

"I know you too well, Pauline," Galen replied. "I know when you're lying. But I gotta hurry backstage because I have a purpose here tonight. You don't. But we're going to talk about this later."

"Whatever you say, little brother." The final students walked up the steps to take their seats. "You better get going, Galen. The invocation is about to begin."

Lempi looked lovely. Such passion in her eyes. Energy in every movement. There was so much of Pauline's spirit in this young woman mixed with the idealism of her father. Of course, Lempi thought Eero and Marja were her parents, and Lempi's birth needed to remain a secret. She would gain nothing from suddenly discovering that an old maid in Milwaukee was her true mother. Besides, what did a "true mother" even mean? Eero and Marja had always been the mother and father who celebrated Lempi's triumphs as they occurred and consoled her failures. Pauline seldom even knew of such events, yet surely there was a meaning to "true mother" that mattered.

Luckily, Pauline's parents still owned Newmann's General Merchandise. Visiting her parents gave her a reason to be in Clover; helping in the store provided an occasional interaction with Lempi. Although she would never admit it to her parents, Lempi was the only reason Pauline returned home so often and stayed so long. Clover was a small town, and until the IGA supermarket opened in 1949, Newmann's was the only grocery store. Sooner or later, everyone came into her parents' store, and Lempi often ran in for last minute items. Because Lempi was bright, ambitious and curious about the larger world, she quickly gravitated to Pauline as a sympathetic, big-city woman who shared helpful advice and insights. As Lempi handed her the shopping list, or as Pauline brought out some of her dad's famous summer sausage, or bagged a dozen cookies from the bakery bins, they found time to gossip about the world outside of Clover and build a small friendship.

Pauline was quite certain Lempi would be pleased if she knew Pauline was attending her graduation. If not for Pauline, Lempi would never have applied to Bremen College where she was almost certain to receive a full Shindler scholarship. Pauline reasoned she was making amends for giving her daughter up for adoption and disappearing. Tonight was a milestone for Lempi that Pauline was not going to miss—no matter what Galen thought.

On stage, the principal introduced Lempi as the 1952 class valedictorian. No other student had been a close second. How had such intelligence emerged from her loins? Pauline was anxious to hear what her daughter—yes, her daughter, even if almost no one in the room knew it—would say in her valedictory speech. The microphone system was clear, loud and as new as the school's gym.

Lempi began, "Ours is a strange era, an era which can be summed up in one word: fear. Story headlines and newspapers offer the world little hope. They tell us that our country is filled with danger and that we are surrounded by people seeking to destroy our American way of life, with Communists and radicals infiltrating our government and schools and institutions. Our citizens seem to have no trust today that people are good, and that there can be different ways to approach the same problem . . . "

Oh, what was her girl doing? It wasn't safe for anyone, especially Lempi, to take issue with the current anti-Communist fervor. Senator Joe McCarthy practically lived down the road from Clover. Pauline knew all too well that the Makinen family had more than a few skeletons in their closet. But as Pauline looked around the room, she realized few townspeople were paying attention. The farmers and their wives, the shopkeepers with their families, the factory laborers and their friends were all here to see their sons or daughters, friends or relatives walk across that stage and exit with a diploma. They had their Kodak Brownies ready to capture an important family moment. An earnest girl, no matter how clear her tone or emphatic her phrasing or incendiary her comments, wasn't interfering with their celebrations. Like the invocation or benediction, Lempi's speech was just another river of words.

Lempi closed, "If you are taking the effort to really think critically, then I congratulate you. If you are not, all I can ask is that you try to find a way to examine what is really true for you. Don't be satisfied with merely listening to others. Learn. Think. Judge. When people begin to listen and think, instead of merely accept, then it will be a better world. Thank you, ladies and gentlemen."

Polite applause followed. Soon another student was recounting favorite memories of school days together. Pauline daydreamed through the rest of the ceremony. She had come to hear Lempi speak and that was over. She thought of how proud Lempi's real father would have been and wondered why she thought of that man so seldom. She daydreamed about what would happen when Lempi attended Bremen. Even though Eero and Marja might feat that Pauline would somehow compromise the years of silence, she was certain they would want someone to look over their daughter in the big city.

Pauline snapped back to attention. The diplomas were being handed out. She stood with the rest of the audience. The smiling graduates streamed by, oblivious to being out of step with the recessional music. By accident, she caught Lempi's eye. Lempi's broad face broke into a surprised but pleased smile. Pauline knew she would relive the look over and over again when she took the train home to Milwaukee.

When the rest of the townspeople walked out to shake the hands of their graduates, Pauline remained seated. She wanted to retain for a moment that unexpected smile. She also wanted to avoid explaining to the Makinens why she was in Clover.

Galen Newmann walked out from behind the stage and noticed that his sister was still there. He came over to sit beside her. "So . . ." he said.

"So," she replied, "I'm glad I came."

"You know, half the town already thinks that Lempi is the result of an affair between that old man Eero and you. He was quite the rake in his day, and Marja was awfully old when their blessed baby came."

"Oh, you can't believe that nonsense," Pauline said.

Galen smiled like the goofy younger brother she remembered. "Well, I was only eleven when you disappeared for that summer. I knew enough to figure out you were pregnant, but Mom and Dad never let on who the father was."

"I can assure you it was not Eero Makinen," said Pauline decisively. "Let the town gossip. You can't stop them, and Lempi's never going to know the truth. It was the Depression. What would a single mother have done? I'm just grateful that Eero and Marja wanted another child, and that all of us were able to go on with our lives. And as to the father's identity, that's my secret alone."

Galen smiled, "I guess it's a new world anyway. Look at you now: a career woman in the big city. Wouldn't have happened if you had married some dumb farmer in Clover. And that girl. There's more than a bit of you in her."

"Whatever do you mean?" Pauline was more than a little pleased.

"Did you listen to her speech? She has no fear and she wants to right wrongs. She's Clover's young radical."

Pauline shook her head, "Those old Finns, they were all Communists or Wobblies or some such thing. Growing up among them, how could Lempi not lash out at today's fear-mongering?"

"Speaking of that, you should watch your back," said Galen, more serious again.

"Why?"

"Don't you read *The Milwaukee Sentinel*? They call your boss, Mayor Zeidler, a Stalinist stooge." Galen looked worried.

Pauline worked for Frank Zeidler, a Socialist elected as Mayor of Milwaukee. He was the third Socialist mayor in Milwaukee's history, so his political affiliation wasn't exactly a novelty. "Everyone knows Frank Zeidler is a Socialist, and Socialists have been mayors of Milwaukee for the majority of this century. Like every Hearst paper, the *Sentinel* feeds on scandal."

"Still, be careful. People are crazy these days."

"Let them be crazy. Tonight, I won't think about that. I came here to share at least one happy moment with my secret daughter. And I did." Pauline stood up. "See you at the folks."

***

When Pauline discovered she was pregnant at 17, her mother devised the solution. That's what mothers do: find a way to surmount their children's problems. The answer proved to be both simple and elegant, and was right in front of their faces. But in the Thirties, as a girl who was carried away on a pleasant summer evening into pleasing a departing boy and as a daughter who never before disobeyed her old-world father, Pauline would never have imagined such a way out.

Her pregnancy was so unfair. Until that enthusiastic night with the local boy, Pauline had been a virgin. The two of them weren't even dating. But the fact that the boy was about to leave for Europe to fight for a cause was so romantic. Who knew if he would ever come back? A few drinks, which she wasn't used to, the warm spring night and apple trees in bloom under a full moon all argued in the boy's favor. How could one say "stop" to all that? In the morning, he boarded his train to New York where he would catch a ship to cross the Atlantic. After the first few moments of waving good-bye to his train, Pauline seldom missed him and never regretted their night together. She thought their lovemaking made her a little worldlier than the other girls in Clover.

But less than two months later she realized her period was late, and she knew what that meant. Suddenly she didn't feel so worldly. Even if she would have wanted to forge a life forever with the cocky idealist off to Europe, he wasn't there to marry. She recalled vague stories of a way to end a pregnancy, but it sounded dangerous and certainly illegal—not something that old Doctor Koch would do. And how could she raise a baby unmarried? Everyone in town would despise her, and it would block all plans to escape Clover, attend college and live in a big city. Her father Walther Newmann was a smart, successful businessman who had squirreled away the cash to support his promise that she could go to college. Even in the Depression, her escape was tantalizingly possible.

The only place to turn was her mother. Gertrude Newmann took the news in stride. "We figure out the plans, and then we tell your father. Not one moment sooner," the German immigrant said to her daughter. "I don't want you feeling shame, and there's no reason to go tell Father Schmidt at the church. You can confess this sin directly to God. In the end, God helps those who help themselves."

Less than a week later, her mother had a plan. For the first time, Pauline really understood the perseverance and strength of Gertrude. As a poor girl from north of Hamburg, Gertrude journeyed alone to the United States, traveled half way across the continent and found her distant cousin in central Wisconsin. Her battered steamer trunk was always with her, and Gertrude gave it to Pauline for her bridal hope chest.

Gertrude's solution folded two audacious lies around one another. The first falsehood was Pauline's cover: Pauline needed a better education than Clover offered; and Gertrude's cousin would let Pauline spend her senior year in Milwaukee so she could attend a more challenging city school. Because everyone in Clover knew how clever Pauline was, everyone accepted the story—although many privately thought Walther Newmann was foolish to waste good money on sending a girl to college.

The second lie was more complicated, and resulted from Gertrude knowing so many of the townsfolk's secret desires and hopes. Pauline and Gertrude were home alone preparing the evening supper when Gertrude asked, "Do you know Marja Makinen?" Pauline was peeling fresh beets from their garden and the question was so unexpected that she nearly cut herself with the paring knife.

"Yes, she can be a bit strange," Pauline said.

"When your father isn't working the counter, Marja often sneaks into our store. Those Finns mostly shop at their own coop store, but Marja can't get what she really wants there, so she comes to me. Anyway, we talk, and I know some things about her. And what do you know? She's very sad about not being a mother."

"But she has a son named Risto," Pauline pointed out, knowing this fact very well.

"Yes, but he's gone and left, and who's to know if he's ever to come back. Her other two young ones died when they were just little boys, right after World War One. Marja was very kind to us Germans in those days. Not everyone in this town was. The truth is that now she's all alone with her husband Eero and she wants to be a mother again. But she's over forty, and that's not very likely."

"No, I guess not," Pauline replied.

"So she and I talked, and we figured it out. In a few months, Marja's going to go stay with her sister up to Duluth. She'll be complaining about not feeling well and wanting to see a specialist. Lots of Finns up in Duluth, and she'll want to see a Finnish doctor, not a local German like Dr. Koch. But it's going to turn out she weren't sick at all, but pregnant. Imagine that, at her age!" Gertrude put on a false facade of jollity. "She'll have her baby up there. And she'll come home with that baby, but it'll be your baby. They'll adopt it and never tell no one that it didn't come from their own bed."

"And her husband Eero agreed?"

"Marja will take care of that."

"What about our family?"

"Don't worry. I can handle your father."

And that's what happened. There were a few angry flare-ups in the Newmann household when Gertrude informed Walther of the fait accompli, but being in shock at his daughter's condition and having no better approach, he eventually agreed—as Gertrude knew he would. However, he never fully accepted the outcome since he always referred to Lempi as "the Finnish girl," never wanting to give the newborn credence as a real, live being.

Pauline could only imagine what went on in the Makinen household when Marja informed Eero of the plot. Perhaps he just accepted the elaborate role. Over time, Pauline learned that Eero felt deeply about certain causes, but crossing his often-mercurial wife was not one of them.

As for the town, Clover was struggling, and there were better things to concern oneself with than Pauline's fate in Milwaukee, or that strange birth of Lempi Makinen in Superior. A few years later, the world was at war again, and worries shifted to whether the town's sons would make it back from hard-to-pronounce battlefronts in Europe or the Pacific. Time passed. With victory came prosperity. Farms did well, local factories expanded, the town's boys went to college with the GI Bill and Lempi Makinen grew up.

Despite what her little brother said, Pauline was quite certain only Galen ever pondered whether Lempi was the love child of Eero and Pauline. As an eleven-year-old who had not been told why his sister suddenly moved away, he had always tried to solve the puzzle. Everyone else was too busy to connect eighteen-year-old dots.

Gertrude's plan worked as devised, with one exception: Pauline's college plans hit a roadblock. She couldn't finish high school while carrying Lempi, and despite the rationale of moving to Milwaukee to get ready for university life, Pauline was forced to postpone college.

Because she didn't know how to explain that postponement to Clover, Pauline simply remained in Milwaukee. At first, unfairly bitter about her mother's plan keeping her out of college, Pauline struck out on her own. She found a job as a maid at the home of a rich banker on Milwaukee's east side, and finished her high school senior year through night classes. As the drudgery of that life weighed her down, Pauline recognized her foolishness.

She reconciled with her parents and returned to Clover for a summer to work in her parent's store. Everything changed the day Marja Makinen walked into the store with her small two-year-old girl. Lempi was beautiful and precious. Pauline wanted to leap forward and grab the child out of her adopted mother's arms. Marja eyed Pauline warily. Both knew the truth, but both also knew that it could not be said aloud. Pauline reverted to "isn't she adorable" and made faces to encourage the small child to smile. Marja watched with wary pride. Internally, a change came over Pauline. She recognized an eternal connection between herself and this child. She decided that she would need to do more so she could be there in the future should Lempi ever need her.

Pauline convinced her father to fund college as originally intended. Gertrude was again her ally, although Pauline suspected her mother simply wanted to increase the distance between Pauline and Lempi. Pauline returned to Milwaukee to enroll at Bremen College where she studied English and education with a goal of becoming a teacher. She met interesting people, including a Milwaukee boy named Darryl Banks. He came from a good family and was soon a constant friend. But something always held her back from committing to him. Then World War Two began, and by the time Darryl Banks came back from the War, both Pauline and Darryl had moved on with their lives. Pauline knew that marriage between them would not happen.

She taught English after graduating Bremen, became active in the teacher's union, met Frank Zeidler (a member of the Board of Education) and volunteered to work on his campaign when he ran for Mayor. When he was elected, she accepted a position in city administration.

Through it all, she returned frequently to Clover. Her parents suspected the real point of her visits was to keep an eye on the progress and growth of Lempi. Eero and Marja developed a wary acceptance of Pauline's interest. No one encouraged her to become devoted to Lempi. But in the end, that didn't matter.

Pauline stayed over commencement weekend and helped out in her parents' store. Saturday, stepping off the porch to head to the store, she pinched a large sprig of blooming lilac from the bush that bordered their neighbor's sidewalk. Pinned to her dress, the flower's fragrance pleased her more than any perfume. She loved the early summer with its blooming bushes of lilac and the light breezes of June mornings.

The store was quiet, and the increasingly dwindling clientele was a worrisome sign. The new IGA store at the town entrance was a self-service supermarket, where people trolled their shopping carts up and down the aisles grabbing whatever items they wanted. At Newmann's, goods were still largely kept behind the counter on tall shelves. Obtaining them required the help of a clerk like Pauline. Also, Newmann's carried many bulk goods, and modern housewives wanted their products fully wrapped and sanitized. But Pauline's father said he was too old to convert to new ideas.

"I was hoping you would be here," a young perky voice said. Pauline knew the voice belonged to Lempi. "I thought I saw you at the graduation. Why didn't you say hello?"

Pauline thought about all the potential answers: Your mother and father are afraid to have me spend time with you. I fear being too close because I might not bear to draw away. You might discover you don't really like me.

Pauline didn't say any of that. Instead she answered, "My trip was a last-minute decision to visit my parents. I thought it would be fun to see the new gym. By the way, I enjoyed your speech. Congratulations on making valedictorian."

Lempi blushed, "Thanks, not that my speech made much of an impression on anyone else. I don't know why. Half this town, at least most of the Finns, were once radicals themselves. Some of them were even Communists. You know that American Communist guy they just arrested at the border, trying to sneak in from Mexico. Gus Hall? He used to come to this town. He's been in our house."

"Probably not a good idea to promote that these days," warned Pauline.

"Oh, I know. Everyone's afraid there's a Communist under every table and bed. Senator McCarthy's the worst. I'm embarrassed he's from Wisconsin. Well, I don't need to tell you that. You work for a Socialist."

"Not the same thing as a Communist," Pauline pointed out.

"Practically the same. At least it seems that way from the way people talk these days. Did you know I have a big brother that I've never seen? He went to Russia in the Thirties."

Pauline remembered Risto well. "Yes, a whole group of kids left Clover together. They wanted to build a better world. Do your parents ever hear from Risto?"

"No, he hasn't written in years, but there is a picture of him on their bedroom bureau, so I know what he looks like. I think I take after him. Did you know him when you were young? Ma and Pa think he died during the war, but I can't ever say that aloud. There's still a hope he might show up. But you know if he did, this country wouldn't let him back in." Lempi looked quite dismissive, and for some reason, Pauline found her political innocence endearing. Had she ever had such energy and spirit?

Lempi veered onto another track. "Did you hear? Bremen accepted me, and I'm in the running to be a Shindler Scholar. I have to go to Milwaukee for an interview. Oh, maybe I could come and see you then. Would that be okay?"

"I'd like that," Pauline replied, trying not to smile too much.

"It's really important, because without the scholarship, I could never afford to go to a school like Bremen. Actually, I can't afford to go to any college without a scholarship. Ma and Pa don't have very much, and they don't even want me to leave town. Maybe they worry I'd be like my brother and never come back. But I know I'm destined to do something wonderful, something important. Don't you think so?"

"I am sure you are," responded Pauline with a fierceness that combined her conviction, belief and hope.

Lempi looked at her with a bit of surprise, but continued. "I'm so glad I met you. What would I do if you never came to town? My mother never listens to me the way you do. Imagine if I get that scholarship. We would be in the same town! We could talk all the time."

"I would like that, and I feel confident you will win it."

Pauline was quite certain of that statement. She was pulling every imaginable string to influence both Lempi's acceptance at Bremen and her consideration for the Shindler award. Pauline felt no guilt about her actions; clearly, Lempi deserved it. The girl was smart and articulate. For years Pauline planted seeds about the wonders of Bremen, because when it came to Bremen, Pauline felt she could be the fairy godmother. In their earlier occasional store chats, Pauline was dismayed to discover that Lempi aspired no higher than the state college in Eau Claire. Even the prospect of the University of Wisconsin in Madison seemed out of reach to Lempi. But Pauline schemed to raise Lempi's vision.

Pauline was a Bremen alumna and talked about the school with passion. Even though many other schools might be as good or better than Bremen, Pauline pushed the small Milwaukee college because she had connections both to Bremen and the Shindler Scholar program.

Lempi would likely be accepted at any great school, but paying for it would be the challenge. Each year, a high school valedictorian from Wisconsin received a full scholarship as a Shindler Scholar. There were always many applicants, but Pauline was going to make sure Lempi was this year's winner. She had a plan. Endowed by the Shindler family, the scholarship's selection committee was chaired by Berndt Shindler, who just happened to be the boss of Pauline's good friend Darryl Banks. Tom Ferber, Pauline's old professor of history, was the faculty member on the selection committee. And Mayor Frank Zeidler, her boss, was a trustee for Bremen College. Pauline was employing every one of those connections to grease the skids.

Exerting influence proved more challenging than Pauline expected. She started early in the spring and first approached her boss. Although Pauline had trouble picturing the socialist Zeidler mingling with the Milwaukee and East Coast Brahmins who made up the bulk of the Bremen trustees, he was the city's mayor and certainly had a voice on that board.

Having known Zeidler for years, Pauline expected him to agree quickly to help a poor girl with no connections. But when asked, he said no. Pauline's face dropped. She hadn't even considered that possibility. Zeidler said he couldn't endorse someone he didn't even know. Pauline should have foreseen how her boss would stick to his ethics. Unwilling to give her up on her daughter's future, she cajoled him into at least meeting Lempi.

He agreed that if she impressed him as predicted he would agree to recommend her consideration.

Persuading Darryl to intervene with Berndt Shindler proved more challenging, but Pauline was ready to leverage their long past together. When she first met Darryl fifteen years earlier, Pauline was attracted to the college boy's slender, dark physique and his thin debonair mustache. After the war, she realized he looked a bit like the English actor David Niven.

Darryl befriended Pauline during her freshman year at a moment she really needed a friend. Being a few years older than the rest of the girls and a shopkeeper's daughter from rural Wisconsin didn't make her the perfect fit at Bremen. The sorority set barely acknowledged her existence. Darryl, a local wealthy boy, didn't mind. He found Pauline beautiful, smart, outgoing and focused, and frequently told her so.

As sophomores, Darryl first invited Pauline to dine at his parent's brooding eastside mansion. Their furniture was heavy and rather Teutonic, which Pauline found amusing, since the Bankses were of English descent. But they completely relished the German atmosphere of the city in which they lived, and they equally welcomed the young country girl. They were gracious, in the way it is easy for the rich to be. Their candy factory made them wealthy—Banks Bars could be found across the country—and they didn't worry over who their son might marry.

By the time Pauline graduated, magna cum laude, her small handful of girlfriends all expected Darryl would soon propose. For that matter, so did Pauline. Certainly his parents expected to welcome her into the family. Maybe even Darryl planned such an outcome. But a part of Pauline felt unworthy. It was easy to use Darryl's attendance at the law school of the University of Chicago as an excuse to delay things. Meanwhile, each time she visited her parents in Clover, she found a way to see Lempi. She might walk by the elementary school, work in her parents' store or take a Sunday stroll timed to the end of the Finnish Lutheran Church services. Foolish as it seemed, a little girl on whom she had no legal claim held more importance than a potential marriage into wealth.

The start of the Second World War put everything firmly on hold. As soon as the war began, Darryl moved to Washington. Pauline was never quite certain what he did. She suspected he worked for the newly formed Office of Strategic Services, the secretive spy agency. But if he did, he never told her. By the time the war ended, the two of them had evolved in quite different directions: she was now a confident teacher, working in the union and interacting with a more varied set of people; he was back in Milwaukee and eager to go into any business other than his parents'. Old family friends hired him as the new vice president of advertising for Shindler Brewery. Pauline and Darryl remained in touch, even friends, but bounded more by the past than the future.

Pauline suggested they catch up with a weekend dinner at Karl Ratzch's, an old German restaurant that Darryl liked. Back in the Thirties, the two had eaten there on the occasional date. Since the restaurant had recently won a major travel magazine award, its current popularity would appeal to Darryl, and nostalgia should make it easier to touch his heart.

The room was much as she remembered: the tall, vaulted ceiling with its wooden beams; leaded pane windows surrounding stained glass inserts; and booths with wooden tables and red leather banquettes. An elderly waiter handed them the heavy menus. Darryl said, "Reminds me of our younger selves."

He quickly ordered a martini. They reviewed the menu. Pauline ordered her favorite, beef roladen with spaetzle. Darryl asked for the roast goose shank. The waiter left. For a moment, they both looked at each other without speaking. Pauline wondered when the movie-star allure of Darryl had disappeared. They gossiped about old friends. Each asked about the other's parents. After talking about Walther and Gertrude, Pauline felt the moment right.

"Darryl, I've become very fond of a young student I met while working at my parent's store. She's very talented, about to graduate from high school, and I'd really like to help her escape Clover."

"Okay." Darryl's voice shifted as though he suspected he was being lured into a trap, which in a way he was.

"She's extremely bright, the daughter of Finnish immigrants, and a person who I know would just do wonderfully well at Bremen, if she only received the chance."

"And how do you think you could help her?" Darryl asked. It seemed to Pauline as though he was suddenly fascinated in the remaining bits of goose flesh on his plate.

"I am hoping it could be 'we' who help her. The girl's name is Lempi Makinen and I've known her parents a very long time. They were already in Clover when I was born, and they sometimes shop at my parents' store. I know they don't have a lot of money, but Lempi is so smart and clever. She's going to be the class valedictorian, and Bremen would be just a wonderful place for her. Close enough to home for everyone to be comfortable, but challenging in a way that would really let her spread her wings." Pauline sensed she wasn't being very persuasive.

"All very interesting, but again how do you think we could help?" He waved to the waiter to clear their plates and bring the after-dinner menu. "I'm sure the college would love to have her, but isn't that their decision?"

Pauline drilled in. "There's no question she will be accepted. She's brilliant, and I know it will show in her grades and essays. The problem is money, but there's a solution there as well. Your friends, the Shindlers, underwrote that wonderful scholarship fund to pay for a deserving valedictorian each year. I know there's a lot of competition with smart kids seeking the award, but this girl really deserves it. Mr. Shindler chairs the review committee. They meet with the applicants, and I think a good word from you in advance could do so much to ensure that he really saw Lempi in her best light. He respects you so, the way you've done so much for his brewery, like creating that that successful TV show they sponsor. Everyone in the country knows Shindler beer. He has to see that you can recognize talent." Pauline stopped, afraid she was becoming sycophantic, even though she meant every word of what she said.

Darryl shifted in his chair. At that moment, the server whipped out the after-dinner menus. Darryl studied the desserts and coffees with unusual scrutiny. Since Darryl always ordered the Viennese apple strudel, Pauline knew he was stalling for time, but she waited. Finally, Darryl called back the waiter and requested apple strudel for each of them, as well as two coffees.

"What do you say?" Pauline asked, downplaying her anxiety.

"Clover is right in that Red Belt isn't it?" he began. "Isn't it mostly Finns and Russians in that county? They've always been so radical up there, promoting farmer co-ops and voting for oddball parties. As I recall, Henry Wallace and the Progressive Party got a few votes up there in the '48 election. Not surprising really, even though the Progressives were just a front for the Communist Party."

Pauline found this tack astounding. Darryl was a solid Republican but he never seemed concerned about her work for a Socialist mayor. What was all this talk of radicals? "Everything you say is true, but what has that got to do with this young girl? She's an American citizen, loyal as can be." There was a small twinge of guilt in saying this, as she recalled some of her conversations with Lempi. She would have to counsel Lempi before the Shindler interview.

"Pauline, you are so naive." Darryl spoke as though he were correcting a little child's arithmetic error. "Don't you read the papers? This is no time to allow anyone with questionable pasts into our lives. Do you have any idea the lengths I go to ensure we have only the right people appearing on the *Shindler Talent Train*? I don't let anyone with any connection to the Communist Party or questionable unions on that TV program . . . not to sing, not to write, not to tell jokes, not even to work behind the camera. This is not a time we can let our guard down."

Everyone in town knew Berndt Shindler was fiercely anti-Communist, and more than a few colleagues at City Hall thought Shindler would have been happy if the Nazis had won the war. Was this man across from her—a man she had once considered marrying—simply aping his boss' extreme views? Or did he really believe that there were Communist sleeper agents in a burg like Clover?

"You sound a bit ridiculous. Clover is a little spot in the middle of nowhere. Lempi is an eighteen-year-old girl."

"But is she clean? Can you honestly tell me she has no sympathies for anti-American movements? What can you tell me that about her father? Her mother? Her family? Her friends? I wouldn't recommend anyone to Mr. Shindler that isn't one hundred percent clean. I have a duty to apply the same standards I use to guard the reputation of Shindler Brewery. Do you know for certain she is clean?"

"Dear God, is this a Congressional committee? What kind of questions are these?" Pauline felt she needed to take her own form of the Fifth as her mind reeled out a long list of condemning facts: Lempi's own opinions, the emigration of Risto Makinen to Russia in the Thirties, Eero's support for the cooperative movement and who knows what else. She eyed her apple strudel with its watery whipped cream. She recognized that pushing Lempi any further was more likely to create an enemy for Lempi than a friend. She retreated. "You're right of course. It's silly to become so concerned for a neighbor's daughter. I'm so sorry to have brought it up."

She lifted her coffee cup to her lips to watch how Darryl responded. There was a bit of puffing up that made her relieved to have escaped marrying this man, and all discussion of the Finnish girl was dropped.

***

Sitting in the cluttered but sunny office of Professor Tom Ferber always gave Pauline a boost, which she needed as she was about to tackle her third attempt to promote Lempi's cause. Even when she was a student, she found Ferber's near-toppling stacks of books and the shelves overflowing with travel souvenirs strangely comforting. She looked at the middle-aged scholar with a sense of pleasure. He was tall, thin, and almost gangly. His missing arm always served as her reminder that Ferber had fought for the country during World War One. This man, more than anyone else, successfully challenged her to think critically. Yet he remained an enigma. While she knew he was almost an extended member of the lumbering baron family of the Oxfords who owned half the timberlands in northern Wisconsin, at the same time he walked easily among the laborers and union men who kept Milwaukee's factories humming.

The first time they really talked had been after she aced his American history class, some fifteen years earlier. They sat in this very office, on a spring day not so different than the one gaily blazing outside. At the time, she sought to thank him for being such a good teacher. She admired his probing questions that prompted them to dig deep. He brushed aside her compliments and shifted the focus to her aspirations. When she casually mentioned her hometown of Clover, he recalled a visit of his in 1933. That quite startled her. "Whatever for?" she asked. He told her of a group of local farm lads about to depart Clover and infected with what he called the Karelian Fever. This was his joking way of referring to the idealistic children of Midwestern Finns who fled the Depression and sought to build a just society in the Soviet Karelia region, north of Leningrad and bordering Finland.

Pauline was nervous. Ferber smiled. She could feel the afternoon sunlight glinting off her auburn hair, and she felt a bit flushed. "You look worried," he said paternally.

"I came to ask a favor," she began, "I thought it would be an easy one to ask. But Darryl made me realize otherwise."

"What did that tightly-wound-up young man do now?" asked Ferber. Her former professor never cared much for her old beau. Darryl was fond of argument for argument's sake in Ferber's classes.

"It's more in the way he thinks than what he does. Darryl sees Communists around every corner, and he's deathly afraid they'll touch him and make him 'it' or some such thing."

Ferber leaned back in chair, "A lot of that going around these days."

Pauline felt a flicker of concern cross her face. "That could be. But it hardly seems warranted, and so often, it's clearly unfair. Times change, and what you did in the past, or what your family may have done in the past, shouldn't brand you forever. We don't live in Old Testament times."

Ferber looked out the window, and then returned his gaze to Pauline, "Is there someone specific we're talking about?"

"Yes," said Pauline. This was her moment. "It's a young woman I've come to admire in Clover, a brilliant girl who's just graduated and been accepted at Bremen. Lempi belongs here. You would find her a marvelous student, and I am sure in another time she would easily win the Shindler grant. But there may be a problem."

"And what is that?" he asked.

"Remember you told me you once went to Clover to interview those young men headed off to Russia."

"Yes."

"Her older brother was one of those silly idealists. Risto Makinen was an ardent Communist even when we were in high school. He's probably dead now, at least he's never come back. But I'm afraid that won't keep him from hurting Lempi. Darryl thinks such connections are poisonous. Poisonous to him is what I mean. He won't even consider speaking well of Lempi to his boss, Mr. Shindler. That old man would listen to him, after all he has done for the brewery."

"And you come to me, knowing that I represent the faculty on the Shindler scholarship committee. You want me to speak well of her."

"I am just trying to ensure she gets a fair shot. Doesn't a girl deserve that?"

He stood up and turned to the window to stare toward Shindler Hall. The streaming afternoon light gave him an almost heroic aura. Pauline reflected that he must have been a handsome young man. Campus lore claimed he had fallen in love with an Oxford heiress, but that she, loving another, left him a perpetual bachelor.

Still looking out the window, Ferber spoke with a tinge of sadness. "I will do what I can, but be aware that I may hurt her cause more than I help."

"What do you mean? You're the most respected scholar at this school."

"Kind of you to say, but Pauline, you place me on an undeserved pedestal. If you were to look at this through Shindler's eyes, you would conclude that my being in Clover when those boys left twenty years ago makes me as dangerous as Alger Hiss or the Rosenbergs. People like Shindler are always quick to see a conspiracy. With people like him, you can never escape your past, however accidental it might be."

"You make it sound like everyone in this country has joined a witch hunt. This is America."

Ferber sighed. He turned to face her, his smile almost a grimace. He sat down heavily in his chair. "Thirty-five years ago, I nearly gave my life for this country on the Western front. Sometimes, I think the arm was only a down payment, and that maybe my sacrifice will end up being my honor, not my life.

"Dear Pauline, I love history. Truly I hope we can learn from past mistakes and that one day my skills will right at least one wrong. But my study of the past is like listening to a record that skips over and over, forcing us to hear the same unpleasant sins."

"Professor Ferber, maybe helping Lempi is a way to right a potential wrong before it is even done." Pauline felt unexpectedly uncomfortable. Asking Darryl for his help exposed him as deeply tarnished; she feared her quest might undermine another bulwark of her life.

Ferber went on, "Forgive these frosty musings, but sometimes I can't bear to see this modern paranoid strain in American life. We all fled from somewhere to establish a world suited for us, leaving behind binding ties. Whether for economic or religious reasons, or maybe mere reasons of boredom, our ancestors came here for a better life, all swirling together in a grand experiment. But it's as though we always demand the catalyst of hate and fear to keep some of us apart. In the early years, it was the Indians, and after the Civil War, we added Negros to the mix. But perhaps they proved not to be enough, because we always seem to be gravitating to a new fearful enemy.

"When I was fighting for freedom in 1917, do you know how American citizens of German descent were treated here at home? With hatred, even though they chose the U.S. as their country. Ask your parents how it felt to be German during that war. My great despair is that there are always leaders ready to stoke that hatred. We seem to have already forgotten how President Wilson enacted the Espionage Act of 1917 and the Sedition Act. That law, despite our Constitution, claimed thought, not actions, was sufficient reason for deportation. You were just a little girl in 1919 when the Palmer raids deported thousands unfairly.

"I can see in your eyes that you think this old man is rambling, and that this history lesson has little to do with the young girl you seek to place under your aegis, but, Pauline, it never stops. Americans always need an enemy, even when it's our own populace seeking to make things fairer. Remember the strikers at the Allis-Chalmers plant in 1937? The way the Hearst papers and most of Milwaukee went on and on, imagining it was all a Communist plot, instead of the common man just seeking a fair life. Yes, when we were at war and Stalin was our ally, the country found someone new to hate in the Nazis. But the war is over, and the Nazis have disappeared.

"So it's back to the Communists. People like Joe McCarthy and Senator McCarran are fear-mongers. Frightful things like the atom bomb only help to fan the flames. And Truman isn't seeking to douse a one of them. Maybe the fall elections will give us a man of character."

Pauline looked around the room overflowing with Ferber's collections. She tried to imagine all the knowledge contained in the stacks of books piled to and fro. Why study all of that if it only led to dismay and cynicism? Maybe she should allow Lempi to remain a small-town girl.

Pauline's work made her optimistic. She was truly inspired by her boss, Mayor Zeidler. Although he would have nothing to do with the extremes of the Soviet Union, he was a believer in the brotherhood of man working in cooperation for the betterment of all. He believed it was possible, at the civic level, to achieve practical and meaningful steps forward. His vision inspired her each day on the job—the perspective that it was possible to build a better Milwaukee, to link the suburbs and city core with new high-speed roads, to feed the soul of the city with new museums and zoos, to unite citizens and to open up opportunities for the Negros who had come from the south. He stood up for socialism. Didn't Milwaukee's own experience show that Ferber was too pessimistic? Couldn't she stand up for Lempi and help her thrive in a modern world? Isn't that what everyone wanted for themselves and their family?

"Is today's world really so depressing, Professor Ferber?" she asked her mentor. She could not believe it was.

"I hope not, but I fear your talk of this young girl has brought out the cynic in me. Perhaps I read too much. The paper today talks of this proposed Immigration and Nationality Act, the so-called McCarran bill. The proposal mocks American rights. It allows anyone to be deported if there is the flimsiest of connections to Communism. Don't be too harsh on Darryl. I don't ask you to forgive him or adopt his beliefs. It's hard not to collaborate when you're surrounded by people calling for conformity and betrayal.

"Perhaps there will always be the 'other,' the person we hate, the stranger we suspect, and the difference we distrust. Maybe someday if we triumph over Communism, there will be a new enemy to monitor and deport, like the French or maybe a religious group such as the Buddhists or Muslims. There are always so many people who aren't us.

"But don't worry, Pauline, I will speak for your young lady, if that's what you want. Bring her by so I can meet her before the interview. You are right. This could be my chance to prevent a wrong from happening."

Ferber paused for a minute, then added, "And Pauline, another thing, you need new interests. You've closed too many doors in your life."

The phone rang on a late June morning. After seeing the morning headline about the Senate passing the McCarran Act, Pauline was in a disagreeable mood. The world was making Pauline feel so unpleasant. She didn't like the fact that whatever she wanted to do for Lempi was swept up into political maelstroms she neither comprehended nor cared to navigate. The passage of the new immigration act reminded her of Darryl and his ilk. Why couldn't everyone focus on important day-to-day issues like water or roads and get something done that actually mattered to people? That was what her job at the city was all about. Better yet, why couldn't she celebrate a smart and beautiful daughter's achievement?

The phone kept ringing in its insistent way. She picked up the receiver. There was an operator's impersonal voice, "I have a collect call from Miss Lempi Makinen of Clover, Wisconsin. Will you accept?"

Pauline felt so confused. Why would Lempi call? The girl never even wrote a letter. A sudden flash of both hope and fear crossed her mind; Marja and Eero had told their daughter their secret. "Of course, I will accept."

Lempi's voice was panicked. "Pauline, I didn't know who else to call. Things are falling apart, and I need someone to talk to. You're so smart, and you have friends who are important . . . "

"Lempi, slow down and take a breath. Start from the beginning."

"Yesterday, like every day lately, I was waiting for the mail. Invitations from the Shindler committee should come in late June. And finally that piece of mail was there, an envelope with the big blue Bremen crest. I opened it immediately, and I couldn't believe it. The school didn't ask me to interview for the scholarship. Instead, they revoked my acceptance letter."

"What?"

"It doesn't make any sense, does it? And the day got worse. The FBI showed up. They questioned Ma and Pa about coming into the country and what they reported on their last alien registration forms. They asked the same questions over and over, trying to trip them up. I couldn't sleep worrying, not knowing what to do. Then this morning, I walked over to the Muellers so I could use their phone to call you."

"Lempi, listen to me. I'll take the afternoon train and be at your house tomorrow morning. Before I go, I'll visit Bremen and see what I can find out, but don't tell anyone else about the FBI. Just wait for me."

Pauline returned the black receiver to the cradle of the heavy phone base. The dial's circle of numbers and letters reminded her of a roulette game with its aimless ball whirling about and landing wherever chance might take it. How could an elderly farm couple interest the FBI? For that matter, why would Bremen rescind acceptance to a promising young student? A suspicion chilled her. She feared she had caused this. She collected her hat and handbag. This morning, she wasn't going to City Hall or Bremen. Darryl Banks was about to get a visit.

Darryl's secretary Arlene said Mr. Banks was in a meeting. Pauline didn't care. She whisked by the woman, mustering all the authority she acquired from being a city official. Arlene was not lying. Darryl, sitting across a low coffee table from another shorter, swarthy fellow, was engaged in a business conversation. Pauline interrupted. "Darryl, I need to ask you a question."

"Pauline, please, not now. Step out and work with Arlene to schedule another time. Jerry Sommers and I are in the middle of something important."

The name "Jerry Sommers" seemed so familiar. Should she know it? Hadn't it been discussed the other day in the Mayor's meeting? Wasn't he the fellow leveraging an American Legion position to ferret out suspected Communists? She remembered now. Sommers had been sniffing around City Hall. She turned toward the pudgy-faced man, "Aren't you the publisher of *Midwest Monitor*?"

"In all its glory," he responded.

The *Midwest Monitor* was an index that named individuals who failed to pass Jerry Sommers' suspicions and innuendo. Subscriptions were sold for a high price to those forced to prove loyalty. Around City Hall, rumor said that Sommers sold, for an even higher price, an opportunity for the accused to offer evidence that could remove their inclusion. There were others in this racket, many on the national level, but that didn't keep Pauline from viewing Sommers as scum.

"Darryl, why would you meet with this man?" Even though Pauline doubted the value of advertising, she once viewed Darryl as a heroic fighter for all that's right in America. He had fought for America in his own way. She didn't want to discover he was just another conformist bending to the weight of the Red Scare.

"Pauline, you don't know what you're talking about. I can't let *Shindler Talent Train* employ the wrong kind of people. Do you think Mr. Shindler would want millions of American Legion members to write letters and boycott his beer because the show employed Communists? Good Lord, there's a Shindler tap in nearly every American Legion bar in this country. I have to listen to Mr. Sommers and all those others whose work helps ensure we only clear the good people to work for us."

Sommers broke in, "And don't forget that we make sure the bad people are visible. We protect America from being undermined. Soviet agents are clever, with long arms and seeds planted years ago. We can't let provocateurs or propagandists usurp this wonderful medium of television to warp young minds. And these folk are dangerous people who would. You know they would.

"It's not just New York or Los Angeles. Here in the Midwest, we have a long history of Communist sympathizers. That Gus Hall guy they just arrested at the Mexican border. Our government found him guilty along with rest of the American Communist Party leaders five years ago. But he skipped bail and fled to Mexico. What does that say about his mettle? Did you know he grew up in Minnesota's Mesabi Iron Range? Hall has a lot of friends in the Wisconsin woods and mines and farms; heck, there are probably some people who even think he should run for President. Oh, that man has planted more than a few seeds. Well, we got Hall now where he belongs, but we still need to find those seeds he planted and yank them out."

"You're ridiculous, seeing Communists everywhere," Pauline protested. "You actually placed the president of the University of Wisconsin on your list."

"And he belongs there. Darryl has mentioned you, young lady. I think he called you feisty. Told me that you worked for that socialist Frank Zeidler down in City Hall. I sometimes wonder about your boss."

Pauline ignored Arlene, who had walked in from the vestibule and now stood primed to guide Pauline away. Pauline remained motionless in her sensible black heels, her austere business suit, embodying the image of the perfect career woman. College-educated and part of the city's management. Yet she was speechless. Somehow, and she didn't know why or how, this smug young businessman named Darryl—who over the years joked with her, plied her with compliments and worried over her first impressions at his family dinner table—this man engineered the withdrawal of Lempi's acceptance letter and the surprise appearance of FBI agents. She just couldn't imagine a reason why: did he hate her or did he fear for his own reputation? She turned, nodded to Arlene and walked out without another word.

After taking the Wisconsin Central afternoon train to Clover, the next morning she borrowed her Dad's oversized 1952 Chrysler, with its automatic transmission and other modern wonders, to drive to the Makinen farm. Walther Newmann liked to buy the newest model each fall, and his latest car was harder to steer than Pauline expected. Even though it had been in the family nine months, the auto still seemed new and Pauline felt nervous approaching the Makinen homestead. Since Lempi's birth eighteen years earlier, Pauline had never visited the family or been to their house.

She drove slowly. The farm was two miles east of town on a gravel road. A heavy cloud of dust trailed her sedan. The flat countryside was marked by fields, occasional woods and marshlands. Pauline often walked such country roads in the June days of her childhood, searching out patches of wild strawberries or tracking tasty stalks of asparagus gone feral. When she noticed lacy fronds of asparagus close to going to seed, she nearly braked. Her mother added such greenery to her vases of garden-grown gladioli. But Pauline had a mission. Unable to alert the phoneless Makinen house to tell them she was on the way, she knew Lempi was waiting. There was no time to search for wild asparagus. Lempi's college dreams had been torpedoed.

The farm was directly ahead: she saw the red barn with its wooden silo, the small bungalow-style house with its hip roof so popular forty years earlier and the many small buildings that always dotted Finnish farms. She suspected one of the outbuildings was a sauna. A large maple tree, thick with green leaves, stood near the corner of the house's deeply recessed front porch. A rope swing hung from a thick branch of that tree. Pauline imagined for a second watching a youthful, tow-headed Lempi pumping herself to the sky in that swing. How she would have loved to have seen that!

She pulled in, her car wheels spinning a bit of the loose gravel of the driveway. A large collie bounded to the car. Eero stepped out of the kitchen door at the side. Strange how no one ever used the front doors of these farmhouses. Pauline couldn't tell if the old man was happy or angry that she was there. Pauline's car had an upper-middle-class luxury that seemed somehow out of place on this small farm, but as Pauline walked toward Marja and Lempi who had joined Eero on the kitchen landing, no one paid attention to the auto. The parents were wary, but Lempi was clearly relieved by Pauline's presence.

"Thanks so much for coming," Lempi said, motioning Pauline into the house. "Let's go into the front room. Mama, can we have ten o'clock coffee and offer Miss Newmann some of your sweet cardamom bread?"

Marja said nothing, but moved toward the counter, where the electric percolator was already plugged in, and opened the breadbox. Eero, however, spoke, "It was very kind of you to come all this way, but Lempi shouldn't have asked for your help. This shouldn't be your problem." There seemed a veiled threat in his words.

Pauline felt uncomfortable. Each of the adults shared a secret they didn't want the child to know. Pauline replied, "But I feel I must help. Over these past few years, whenever I've talked to your daughter in our store, I've so extolled Bremen College. It's my alma mater, and I don't understand why they would do this. And then the visit from the FBI. I know they're not connected, but Lempi is right to find this disturbing. I want to help, if at all possible."

The bread and coffee were ready. It proved more comfortable for the four to sit at the kitchen's round wooden table. From her chair, Pauline peered into the parlor with its uncomfortable-looking horsehair sofa and a large fern on a wooden pedestal by the window. The room was of another era; she was certain their conversation in such a place would have been all too formal. At the kitchen table, with the sun shining in and with hot coffee cups in their hands, they seemed almost a family. Eero picked a sugar cube from the bowl, stuck it between his teeth and sipped the coffee through it. In Clover's cafes, Pauline had seen many a Finnish farmer drink his coffee the same way. She drank her coffee black.

"Tell me about the FBI visit," she said. She would look at the Bremen letter later. Already she was considering various ways to investigate the change in admission status. With Frank Zeidler or Professor Ferber's help, she could certainly find some way to correct that matter.

Lempi looked at both parents for permission to tell the story. They gave small nods. "The day before yesterday, late in the afternoon, this big black car drove into the yard. Actually seeing you drive up in Mr. Newmann's car gave me a chill, because the other day started the same way. A black car rumbled through the gravel, and Perdu ran out to bark at them. But it wasn't a friendly face that stepped out of the car. There were two agents wearing dark suits and hats. They didn't smile. Pa was in the fields. It's haying season, and he was out raking the mown hay. So I met them first.

"One asked, 'Is this the home of Eero and Marja Makinen?' and I told them it was. They showed me their identification badges. I'll always remember their names: Edgar Tuzzi and Greg Nolan. They said they needed to talk to my parents. I asked them why, and they said it was a routine follow-up on alien registrations. Ma and Pa have to register every year at the post office as alien residents, since they never became citizens, but no one's asked questions before.

"By that time, Pa was driving his tractor in from the fields because he saw the car arrive. Ma came out too, and she was worked up because she could see this wasn't any door-to-door salesman. Ma's English has gotten so bad, especially when she gets nervous or excited, so I decided to lie to the agents and told them my parents didn't speak English, and that I would have to be their translator. I don't know why I did that, but once I said it, what could I do? They believed me. They asked to go in the house and sit down, which we did. In the front room. Ma and Pa sat on that sofa. The two agents stood."

Pauline listened closely to Lempi, occasionally checking the faces of Marja and Eero. It was clear they both understood English well enough, despite their daughter's impromptu lie to the FBI. There even seemed an element of pride in Marja's face as she listened to Lempi's recounting of the FBI interview. The two agents asked questions related to Marja's and Eero's immigration almost forty years earlier: were they already married in Finland or did they marry here, what year did they arrive, why did they emigrate, which city was their gateway into the country?

Lempi said, "Ma got so rattled by the questions. I knew I would have to answer for her. I don't think Ma's always answered the questions the same way on her alien registration. I know that she actually first arrived in Montreal, and then came to the United States to live in Wisconsin. And Pa came through Ellis Island in New York. But who knows what Ma's said on her various registrations. I never reviewed them. Anyway, these agents acted like she was lying, and I just knew I had to help out. So when they asked, I told them what they wanted to hear. No, I said what they needed to hear. I said Ma came through New York. And that seemed to be it and they left, smiling and thanking us for our time. It's only because of the letter from Bremen that I got so worked up and called."

Pauline wanted to shake some sense into Lempi. Why didn't she just tell the agents that her mother sometimes got confused? Misstatements like this had been used before to damage people, and with this new McCarran Act that was just passed . . . well, Pauline just didn't want to think about it.

Maybe the real issue was Bremen, and she talked with the family about what she would try to do about that matter.

Pauline stood to leave. "Mr. and Mrs. Makinen," she said, "I will do everything I can to see Bremen changes its mind and invites Lempi to be interviewed as a Shindler Scholar." Lempi smiled her thanks.

Pauline returned to her father's large car, drove the gravel roads back to Clover, and in the dust of the road, wondered whether she had done any good.

Sitting on the hard train seat back to Milwaukee, watching the Wisconsin countryside go by—the gently rolling hills, the copses of hardwoods along the small creeks and rivers, the weathered barns and white farmhouses, the farmers gathering hay in the sunlit fields, the small towns facing the rectangular stations with their Railway Express office signs and the dented pickups next to the feed mills—amid that rolling cavalcade of the rural life she knew so well, Pauline felt hopeless. Nearly twenty years earlier, she took this same route to Milwaukee. The season had been a bit later: the farmers were harvesting corn, many still working the fields with horses not tractors. In those Depression years, the buildings were usually weather beaten and sorely in need of paint. Today, some farms boasted concrete silos beside their wooden ones. More buildings sported a fresh coat of paint. Closer to Milwaukee, she spotted the occasional new-fangled television antenna on a farmhouse roof. Yet the passing of two decades hadn't changed Pauline all that much. Emotionally, she was as out of control today as back in 1933. The thread that weaved the decades together was a brightly colored line woven from her obligation and love for the new life she created. As a teenager, Pauline blamed no one but herself for how it happened. She gave in to the pleasant smile, a joking way and the summery promise of pleasure. But like her mother, Pauline had always faced facts straightforwardly. She still did.

When she first looked upon her little girl, in the first minutes after birth, holding her baby, she knew that she couldn't even give this beautiful life a name. That had been part of her promise to Marja and Eero. But she bestowed an unvoiced name that only she knew. In her mind, Pauline called the small baby Sonja. The talents and achievements of the Scandinavian skater, Sonja Henje, inspired Pauline. She hoped that the spirit of the athlete might look over this girl. The name Sonja also reminded her of a German word her mother used when she saw something breathtakingly beautiful, *schöne*. To Pauline her small, bawling baby was truly *schöne*. She vowed that she would always protect her little Sonja.

If only her little Sonja, a woman really, could skate away from the thin ice now beneath her. Pauline couldn't imagine the deed or statement that angered Darryl into such hurtful actions. But rhythmic hours on the train between Clover and Milwaukee reinforced Pauline's conviction that Darryl instigated this disaster. His ties to the Shindler family gave him the means to prompt Bremen officials to reconsider their admissions. Shindler's recent gift of a million dollars to fund the building of a lavish new administration building was surely entry enough. Darryl also knew Jerry Sommers. Another subscription or two to his *Midwest Monitor* might be all it would take to convince such a man to plant names with the FBI. The scenario she imagined seemed so possible and at the same time so unlikely. Why would Darryl hate her so much? She rewound the years of their relationship, trying to ferret out any action or statement that could have kindled a smoldering rage. She could think of nothing, but she was determined to summon Darryl to her offices in City Hall.

Darryl came as requested. His face revealed no lines of worry. Relaxed in a grey flannel suit, he walked into Pauline's office. "What's so important?" he asked.

"Why did you do it," she demanded. "Why ruin a young girl's life?"

Confusion crossed his face. Without asking, he took the chair facing her desk. Twirling the hat in his hands, he said. "Pauline, I really don't know what you're talking about."

She reminded herself that he might have been a spy during the war. He would know how to dissemble, but she would remain clear, direct and unemotional. "I asked you to support a young woman's candidacy for the Shindler scholarship. What happens? Suddenly, Bremen not only fails to invite her for an interview, which is routine for any accepted Wisconsin valedictorian, but instead Bremen revokes her acceptance. And, out of the blue, the FBI investigates her law-abiding parents, U.S. residents since the early 1900s. When I visited you last, you were talking to that despicable Jerry Sommers. I know you could make this happen, and I don't believe in coincidences. I can't imagine why you would do this, and I don't need to know the reason, but I need you to fix it."

Darryl reached for the toy globe Pauline kept on her desk. He pulled it forward and lifted it toward his lap. He spun the orb. For a moment, he stared at the continents spinning about. He looked up at her. She saw the tenderness from their school days. "Pauline, it is a small world, but that doesn't mean everything is connected. I had nothing to do with your friend's issues."

She wanted to believe him. They had too long a history to let it simply twirl away. "Okay, I will accept that, but then will you help me make things right?"

"Pauline, don't you read the papers or watch television? People like Senator McCarthy aren't making this all up. There are bad people around us. We need to ensure we work with loyal people. Everyone on *Shindler Talent Train* is required to sign a loyalty oath. I am not unique in enforcing that pledge. Most businesses and government agencies do. Look how we're fighting the Red Chinese in Korea. And the Soviets have the atom bomb. The world has become a dangerous place.

"I don't know about the individuals you're trying to help. But they're not my concern. I worry about you. Remember how when we first met and you bragged about those idealistic boys who left Clover to work in the Soviet Union. You were so ardent then, I wondered if you weren't a Communist. And then at Bremen you idolized Professor Ferber. What do you still see in that old man? He's written so many left-wing books. Then there's this place." He moved his hand to encompass the entire Milwaukee municipal building. "Oh, I know our mayor is a Socialist, not a Communist, and Zeidler is very quick to condemn the Soviets. Henry Wallace and the Progressive Party in '48 weren't Communists either, but the Communists took them over.

"Pauline, you live in a fairy land if you don't see the enemy around us. Don't get so close to them. Quit this job. Come work for me. You'd be great in advertising. And for God's sake, forget about this kid from Clover. What is she to you? Nothing. Look out for yourself."

Billowing white cumulous clouds drifted slowly westward, dragging shadows across the Bremen campus. Pauline sat on a bench on the quadrangle's lawns, waiting for Professor Ferber to meet her for lunch. After yesterday's confrontation with Darryl, she needed to talk to someone she trusted. Despite the lovely day, the college lawn wasn't an ideal spot for a meeting. The construction of the administration hall funded by Shindler family made the setting noisier than expected. The door for the Humanities building opened. Her tall, one-armed friend walked out. She noticed that Ferber was growing a goatee. She waved and began to unpack the small picnic lunch. She laid out liverwurst sandwiches on rye bread, potato salad richly yellow with chopped eggs, and two nicely ripened peaches.

"Hello, dear," Ferber sat down. "To what do I owe this delight?"

"I need your advice," Pauline replied. Since meeting with Darryl, she stewed over what to do. Asking for any further help from the Mayor was out of the question: it would be abusing their working relationship. But the old professor was as trustworthy as her father.

"Is it about this young girl named Lempi?" he asked. "I've been told the school did a loyalty review of this year's class and cast out some students. I'm told it was Shindler's idea. What the tycoon wants, the tycoon gets." Ferber waved dismissively at the large building under construction across the lawns.

"Her acceptance letter was rescinded," Pauline said.

"I'm sorry, but it's not just students being reviewed. They're also looking at staff. My spies tell me Shindler was quite upset to read that the president of the University of Wisconsin was listed in one of these questionable loyalty publications. He vowed that there would be no such issue at Bremen. He is the head of the Board of Trustees, and that does give him a great ability to get his way."

Pauline was now worried about Professor Ferber. "Are you in trouble?"

"How would you define 'trouble?'" He chuckled, but it wasn't with amusement. "The school decreed a loyalty oath is required of all staff. I refused to sign."

"Why? You're a loyal American. Why wouldn't you sign?"

"When one gets old, one sometimes feels the necessity to cling to one's principles. As waterlogged as they may become, they do seem the only way to cross stormy waters."

"What happens if you don't sign? You have tenure. They can't fire you."

"I do have tenure, although I suppose they might find a way to destroy even that. There are morals clauses, which are always subject to debate. In any case, earlier this week, I was called into a special review to face Shindler, the college president and a few hand-selected college faculty members. Of course, they wanted to know why I wouldn't sign. I said I considered it antithetical to the expression of free minds and an institution of higher learning.

"That only led to the inquisition. I am a historian. I shouldn't exaggerate. But they did fixate on an odd set of questions. They wanted to know about my book on the Spanish Civil War. Didn't my thesis in that work, they asked, sympathize with the aims and ambitions of Soviet Russia? Well, it doesn't, as they surely would have known if they had taken the time to actually read the book, which of course they hadn't. But at least that question dealt with my scholarship.

"They switched to probing what I believed: was Henry Wallace a reasonable candidate for president? What about Norman Thomas? What did I think about the Progressive movement? Did I advocate for the United Nations? Did I support religious education? Do workers get a fair shake in this country?

"Forget about freedom of speech. They don't even agree with freedom of thought. As for logic, they have none. Because I wrote a book about the Spanish Civil War, they wanted to know if I knew leaders in the Communist movement in Spain and if so then surely I must know the U.S. Communist party heads, and did that in turn mean I interacted with convicted Communists likes Gus Hall and, ipso facto, I was certainly part of some group he rallied in Wisconsin years ago. In short, through their tortuous logic, I was deemed untrustworthy."

"That's like some silly children's story," Pauline protested.

"Perhaps, but I no longer care. I've had enough of it."

"What do you mean?"

Ferber reached out to take one of Pauline's hands. He clasped it tightly like an old friend about to say farewell, "I've resigned."

Pauline felt deflated. "Don't give in like that."

He held her hand tighter. "I'm not giving in. I am being true to myself. I've long had a book in me that needs completion. Regina and Casimir Rabinowicz, the owners of Midwest Meatpacking, are old friends. They seldom use their huge country camp in northern Wisconsin, near a small town called Thread. They've offered me a cabin on that estate, along with a little bit of money to pursue this book.

"I don't want to abandon you and many other students, past and present. But I will take my books and my ideas to pursue other interests for the moment.

"And, dear, if you want to help your Lempi, now is not the time to fight these forces. Allow a year or two go by. Have her reapply to Bremen later, or suggest she go to a state school. The important thing is that you don't give up on her and that you don't let her be ensnared in this madness."

Pauline was adrift. She avoided wondering whether the mayor she so admired would be on her side if he knew her story. She vowed not to see Darryl. She couldn't ask for advice from her parents. Walther and Gertrude would have no sympathy for Pauline's lobbying on behalf of Lempi. There was no way to even hint to the Makinens of her dilemma and the potential way she had damaged them. She alone bore her frustration and anger.

Professor Ferber quickly decamped for the northern woods. Pauline hoped he was happy there. He had been her only close friend and the sole person to whom she could disclose anything. One afternoon at a civic event, she encountered Mrs. Rabinowicz and asked about Ferber. She reported he was making great progress with his book, and Pauline replied she looked forward to reading it. In reality, she hoped a massive case of writer's block would return the older man nearer to her.

Lempi, however, rebounded quickly. From her mother, Gertrude, Pauline learned Lempi volunteered to babysit and travel with a local couple as they took an extended western vacation. Having recently sold their farm, the couple planned to travel until they could settle into their new place that fall. Gertrude didn't know when the family would be back, and Pauline suspected her mother hoped Lempi would stay behind on the West Coast.

Weeks later, Pauline was surprised to receive a postcard from San Francisco. It was her first piece of mail from Lempi. The girl's handwriting was clean, well formed and the up-and-down loops all ended precisely where they should. The hand-tinted scene of Coit Tower in San Francisco seemed like a postcard from an era twenty years earlier, with none of the current day's Kodachrome color photography. Lempi's tone was wildly positive, or perhaps Pauline read too much into a couple of sentences. But after that she heard no further news from Lempi

At Thanksgiving, a holiday that in past years always lured her back to Clover, Pauline nearly chose to stay in Milwaukee. But Thanksgiving dinner was the only time during the year that a turkey dinner would draw out most of her father's nearby relatives. Deciding not to miss all that, she drove her recently acquired car home for the holiday. Her parents and her brother's family, her aunts and uncles and the network of cousins brightened her mood. Many of the younger ones treated her like a rare bird that flew in from the big city. They found her smoking scandalous, and the farming cousins were appalled when she accidentally mentioned that she sometimes bought oleomargarine instead of butter. Even her father gave her a dismissing look.

On Friday morning, buoyed by the family holiday mood, she went to the store with her father. That morning, the door above the bell tinkled frequently. Many in town ran out of key provisions after their big family dinners. They popped in and out of the store all day long. She stopped paying attention until she heard that familiar voice, "Pauline, how nice to see you."

She looked up. "Lempi, what a surprise. I thought maybe you decided to stay in California."

"It was tempting to remain behind. It's so beautiful out there. And I'm so glad I went. I had such a wonderful time."

"Thank you for sending me the postcard. You look good," Pauline said. "I'm sorry about what happened with Bremen. It turned out there was nothing I could do."

"Stop thinking about that," Lempi said. "I couldn't have left Ma and Pa anyway, and what would I have done in a big city? I've been so busy here."

"What are you doing?" Pauline asked.

Lempi said she sold tickets at the Clover Theater, a small bit of Andalusian-themed cinematic elegance, whose walls were flanked with fake bougainvillea-lined balconies underneath a ceiling painted with a starlit Spanish sky. Pauline's imagination always blossomed when she went into that theater as a child. Someday she hoped to visit Europe and have adventures as grand as those promised by the interior of her small-town movie palace. But she was disappointed to learn Lempi worked there; a small-town job was not the fate she imagined for a girl with such intelligence and wit, not to mention the fate that she would want for her own daughter. Lempi could be a nurse or a teacher or who knows what might be possible in the years ahead. During the war, women proved they could do anything. They still could. She mustn't accept a lifetime chained to this town. That's when the idea came to Pauline. She would invite Lempi to visit her in Milwaukee before Christmas.

"I'm glad you're happy," Pauline began. "But you know I always regretted that I didn't get to show you Milwaukee when you were going to travel to the Bremen interview. But we could still do that. Would the theater get by without you for a few days? So you could visit?"

"Cool," said Lempi. Pauline wondered where the girl picked up such slang. Lempi seemed different, worldlier; perhaps that came from watching every movie that passed through the theater. Then Lempi asked, "Could I invite a friend to meet us while I'm there? He's an art student in Madison named Peter." Too startled to say no, Pauline agreed, and soon the details of the visit were in place.

Lempi's stay turned out better than Pauline envisioned. When she visited Pauline's office in City Hall, the young woman twirled gaily in the wooden desk chair and listened intently when Mayor Zeidler stopped by to say hello. The mayor encouraged her to shoot for the stars. The two went shopping at both Shusters and Gimbels. Pauline acted like an indulgent mother outfitting her charming daughter, encouraging Lempi to try on all sorts of dresses, determined to help Lempi create a personal style that went beyond mail deliveries from Sears and Roebuck. Pauline liked the way Lempi moved in a swing skirt; somehow, it charmingly tempered the girl's forceful walk. Pauline was surprised by how well Lempi took to a pencil style-dress. She didn't know how Lempi inherited those wide hips, but the slim silhouette of a pencil dress combined with the right girdle and bra gave Lempi a lovely hourglass figure. Pauline didn't care for the popular Peter Pan collars, which seemed to broaden Lempi's already wide face. While Pauline had little spare cash, she reasoned she had no need to glamorize herself—she was practically a middle-aged woman. Treating Lempi was a great pleasure.

They saw the city sights. Lempi particularly enjoyed walks along Lake Michigan and slow drives through the mansion-lined streets of the North Point area with its fairy-like water tower. Pauline rattled off the fortunes that built the neighborhood: lumber mills of northern Wisconsin, railroads and shipping companies, breweries, newspapers, the meat packer and heavy manufacturing plants that dotted the city. Milwaukee wasn't dominated by one industry like Detroit with its car factories or Hollywood with its movie studios. Pauline also introduced Lempi to the real Milwaukee—a city filled with hard-working, middle-class people who built things and came home each night to modest homes that were well kept and near leafy parks. Milwaukee was a town that embraced the townsfolk from Clovers all over the state, and Pauline hoped the city would lure Lempi to stay.

Lempi was entranced. Pauline was delighted. They decided to visit the Bremen campus. Maybe one day, she suggested, Lempi might apply again. Even in the muted light of the short days of December, the campus exerted its charms. Sandstone buildings dating from the latter part of the nineteenth century looked radiant in the sunny afternoon. The sun shone through bare branches of maples and elms to create whispery shadows on the blue-white snow. As they walked toward Shindler Hall, nearing completion, Pauline felt no need to mention that its funder blocked Lempi's college days.

In walking, dining and shopping, they became friends. Pauline shared her inner thoughts. Lempi talked of her dreams. Pauline, who never traveled herself, was quite impressed by Lempi's ability to recount sights from her summer trip across America. Pauline could imagine the otherworldly landscape of the Badlands in South Dakota, the majesty of the Yellowstone geysers and the vertigo-inducing drops to the Pacific along the Big Sur highway. Lempi disclosed details of her fling with Peter Epstein, the young art student from Madison, which made Pauline glad that she had agreed to invite him for dinner. She was looking forward to meeting a boy who was willing to take a bus from the university in Madison just to see them for the night.

Lempi recounted first meeting Peter. The family Lempi traveled with picked up the hitchhiking boy in the Dakotas. He stayed with the family all the way to San Francisco. Lempi had a silly glow whenever discussing this boy. Pauline hoped that Lempi had shown good sense on the road, but then reflected that good sense on a summer night many years earlier would have prevented Lempi's very existence.

Peter was to meet them on a Saturday night, and the following morning Pauline would bring Lempi to the train station to return to Clover. For Lempi's last night in the city, Pauline decided the dinner should be something special. They would dine at Karl Ratsch's. Such a famous Milwaukee restaurant would impress the boy, but as the evening grew closer, she regretted her choice. She didn't want to be reminded of her last visit to that restaurant when she had requested Darryl's help.

A young man waited by the reception desk when they walked in. Lempi took the lead, "Pauline, this is Peter Epstein. Peter, this is my good friend Pauline."

Each looked over the other. Pauline could see the surface charm of this fellow. He wasn't tall, but quite thin, with a very New York Jewish look to him. Suddenly, she worried about suggesting a German restaurant. But this was Milwaukee, where else would they eat? He had intelligent eyes. She liked that.

"Cool to meet you, Pauline," Instead of shaking her hand, Peter stepped over to Lempi, nuzzled her ear with a strange kind of kiss and said, "How's my baby?" Lempi smiled indulgently.

Pauline looked for the maître d'. They were seated, and the waiter brought the menus. "The roladen's very good here," Pauline said, "and this will all be my treat."

"That's good," laughed Peter, "because places like this aren't really my beat, you know, don't have that kind of bread."

Lempi stared at the young man with a ravenous look. Pauline was questioning whether she thought much of the boy. At least he had worn a jacket and tie, although they were hardly well cared for. But then she only had to look at his gnawed-at fingernails to understand the state of his clothing. His nails were dirty, with bits of paint at the cuticle. He was a painter, maybe that was to be expected.

"Lempi tells me you're studying art. What kind of artist do you hope to be?" she asked.

"Abstract Expressionist."

Pauline looked at him blankly.

"Have you heard of Jackson Pollack? No? Well, he's big on the New York scene. There are some real characters out there. You know it's all about capturing the inner state, letting the paint and the color blow your mind."

Pauline sometimes really liked a cover on the *Saturday Evening Post*, but otherwise held no interest in painting or sculpture, and certainly not in abstract paintings. Perhaps it was a failing of hers, but she much preferred reading to almost anything else. She didn't quite know where to go next with the conversation, but that wasn't a problem. Lempi and Peter surged forward, carried by an enthusiastic interest in one other.

By the time the last coffee was drunk and the bill was presented, Pauline's head throbbed. She understood little of the conversation, disliked the constant slang and couldn't imagine how Lempi knew so much about so many things. Clearly the two of them wrote one another frequently, and were already fluent in a language of personal jokes and interests. The three neared the restaurant's front door, picked up their coats from the coat check girl and Lempi leaned into Peter for a more traditional kiss. "So good to see you again," she said.

"I'm a lucky guy to know this chick. Don't you think so, Pauline? Good to meet you. Sorry, but I gotta split. Catching a late bus back to Madison. Baby, come and see me sometime." He looked up at Pauline. "That was for Lempi, but you can come too." He leaned forward to kiss Lempi again.

Pauline offered him a ride to the bus station, but he said not to worry and he started walking in the direction of the station. A light snow was falling. The temperature hovered around the freezing point.

Lempi turned to Pauline, "Thank you so much for dinner and being nice to Peter. I don't worry about college anymore. You know why? Because some day, I just know that I am going to marry that man."

Christmas, then New Year's, came and went. It was 1953. For Pauline, life was better now that she had forged an actual relationship with her daughter, although she wouldn't let herself think in those familial terms. She had to be realistic in her expectations. The relationship was with a girl named Lempi, not her daughter. Lempi's mother was an old woman in Clover.

Each Monday the mailman delivered a letter postmarked Clover and addressed in Lempi's splendid handwriting. Pauline soared for a moment; Lempi's letters were amusing and detailed in their observations, and far too brief. Although Pauline didn't understand what prompted the weekly notes, she reveled in their arrival. A few written phrases would whisk her back in time to remind her of her own youthful moods and emotions. But had she ever been so young? Leaving home pregnant, giving birth alone in a hospital room, living with a relative who might as well have been a stranger and harboring no innate optimism that life would turn out wonderful—that had been Pauline at seventeen.

Admittedly she grew up in a depressed world. But today remained far from rosy. Many of Pauline's circle welcomed the inauguration of General Eisenhower. Her Republican acquaintances were eager to see Truman gone. Her Democrat friends were relieved that a reasonable Republican had prevailed. Belonging to the Socialist party, Mayor Zeidler hoped the new president would prove a pragmatist and support strong cities. Pauline was uncertain. When she read the previous summer's *New York Times* piece on Eisenhower editing a campaign speech in Green Bay to kowtow to McCarthy and dropping defense of his own mentor George Marshall, she grew wary. Just because she worked in government didn't mean she trusted politicians.

Look at how Truman mired them in a war without even getting Congressional approval. Everything seemed a stalemate in Korea. The U.S. wasn't losing, but it didn't seem to be winning. Young men were still being drafted. The Russians continued to test the bomb. The Supreme Court refused to intervene in the Rosenberg case. Everyone was afraid of hidden traitors. And now the Supreme Court ruled that the McCarran Act was legal, which would certainly make it easier to deport suspect immigrants. Maybe Professor Ferber had spiked her suspicions, but Pauline was finding it hard to be optimistic.

Pauline disliked being melancholy. She wouldn't be feeling this way if it weren't for Lempi and the redbaiting that kept the girl from studying at Bremen. At times, Pauline was tempted to write again to Lempi's real father, as though that would somehow change things.

Lempi's weekly letters often discussed Peter, his talents and his cleverness. Lempi, who had yet to lay eyes on a single painting by Peter and who had spent only a few days with him on the road, was planning an entire life with Peter. Pauline distrusted the callow youth. Look at the sloppy way he dressed, his poor personal grooming and his absurd vocabulary. Perhaps love gave a special lens to see things others didn't, but she doubted that Lempi meant much to Peter.

Lempi also worried about her mother in these letters. If Pauline had known years ago how mercurial this Finnish farm wife could be, Marja would not have been the first choice for an adoptive mother. In those days, Marja showed none of the highs and lows that now caused her daughter to worry about suicide. When Pauline mentioned Lempi's concerns to Gertrude, her mother quickly dismissed it as trivial. "The woman lost her children when they were young. It changes you," her mother said. "Besides you spend too much time with Lempi. She's not yours. You need to work on your own life."

On Valentine's Day, Pauline returned to Clover. She casually mentioned her planned visit in a letter to Lempi. Pauline walked a fine line when in Clover because she knew that Gertrude disapproved of her interactions with Lempi. "No good can come of it," she would say.

Outside her parent's house on that Valentine weekend, the snow was hard and crystalline. Inside thc family kitchen, everything sparkled warm and snug. Gertrude and Pauline rolled out sugar cookie dough, cut out hearts, baked the cookies and decorated them with red and white powdered sugar icings. Galen and his two boys were coming over; the nephews loved sugar cookies.

In the midst of this baking, Lempi knocked at the door. "Your father said you would be here. Pauline, I need your help again."

Gertrude gathered up the bowls, spatula and knives to carry them to the deep farm sink. She ran hot water, avoiding the need to join any conversation the other two might have. Lempi didn't notice the German woman's cold shoulder.

"It's Ma," Lempi said. "This letter came for her. It says she may be charged under the Immigration and Nationality Act of 1952 for falsely registering and for perjury. It warns she could be deported."

Several months later, Pauline sat on the hard benches on the Federal Court House in Milwaukee beneath bright fluorescent lights. The linoleum tile floors and heavy oak paneling made for an echoing silence. The judge had not yet arrived, but Marja and her lawyer were sitting at the defense table. The prosecutor and his assistant were taking their chairs. The court stenographer was in position. The bailiff looked around the room as though about to announce the judge. The courtroom had no windows, but outside, Pauline knew the skies shone blue, trees hinted of red and orange and Indian summer hovered.

She reached for the slightly shaking hand of Lempi, who sat between Pauline and her father Eero. Eero held his spine unnaturally straight as though the crisply starched white shirt and the old black woolen suit, which had seen better days, gave no leeway to slouch. A broad band of color in his tie hinted at a spirit that could not otherwise be found in his uneasy apprehension. Lempi, unnaturally pale, appeared lost in a simple dress that looked a size too large. Pauline thought back to the previous December when the two of them flitted from store to store to seek fashionable outfits. The innocence of those days was now a wispy memory.

In retrospect, the letter from the Feds was like a cat teasing with the bird it would devour. Months after the letter's arrival, four FBI agents, two to a car, spun into the gravel driveway of Makinen farm. At work selling movie matinee tickets, Lempi was unaware of their arrival. Eero was in the field harvesting the first of the oats. Only Marja was in the house. She was canning. Bowls of peeled tomatoes were on the kitchen table, each fruit just dipped in boiling water to enable the peeling of its skin. The first tomatoes had already been pushed through the chinaman's hat to extract their juice. A bit of red pulp was splattered on the table.

In the field, Eero pushed his tractor into top gear. He sped in from the back forty, but by the time he arrived, the uninvited cars were gone. Before he crossed the porch to enter the kitchen, he knew Marja was gone. As he had gunned up the farm path between his hay fields, Eero saw the agents pushing Marja into one of the black cars. Her hands were clearly handcuffed. Two of the agents seemed to be the same ones who questioned Marja nearly a year earlier. He walked into a kitchen marked by the hot acidic smell of tomatoes. A ladle lay on the floors, its red contents spewed against the icebox door. The kitchen held no other answers. The agents left no papers to explain the taking of his wife.

He drove his old Ford pickup down the gravel roads at a speed too high for the rough roads. He bounced wildly about. Tracking the agents' route was easy—a murky, but dissipating, cloud of dust churned by the heavy government cars was slow to descend to earth. Where the gravel road intersected with the paved highway, the dust cloud ended.

Eero knew the government cars would have turned south toward the big cities of southern Wisconsin—maybe Madison, or more likely Milwaukee. Eero turned north toward Clover. The town was not large. Its main street ran parallel with the railroad tracks. The only hotel, with its front porch lined with large pillars, looked more like a Southern plantation than a Wisconsin inn. It was a remnant of long ago lumbering days and a time when Eero first brought Marja to Clover. Across the street stood the movie house, with its interior promising an escape to southern Spain. Even a small town had its illusions, but at that moment, Eero needed the reality of finding his daughter. She would know what to do. For the first time in his over forty years in America, Eero felt alien.

Pauline learned all of this in the weeks that followed the arrest. The first muted alarm arrived in her mother's weekly letter. Gertrude felt no sympathy for the Makinens, was suspicious of all Finns in town and preferred to believe that the government made no mistakes. Outside of the Finnish community, the whole town shared Gertrude's views.

Lempi did not call for Pauline's help. Instead, she tried to go it alone. Perhaps she felt she had cried wolf once too often in the past, summoning Pauline when there was no real cause. Perhaps, Pauline fretted, Lempi lost hope that her city friend could even make a difference.

But Pauline was determined to protect her daughter and the girl's parents. Pauline read Gertrude's letter twice the morning she received it and then called the Makinen's neighbors since there was no phone at Lempi's house. She harangued Mrs. Mueller until the farmwife agreed to walk the quarter mile to bring Lempi to the phone and have the girl place a return collect call. When the call came, Pauline did not ask for details. Too many of the farmers still used party lines. Nosy neighbors were apt to listen in on the call, and she had no desire to add new grist to the rumor mill. She asked only for the key detail: a local lawyer hired by Eero couldn't even find out where Marja was being held. Pauline begged Lempi not to give up hope and assured her that she would find a way to help.

Pauline turned to Zeidler for advice. Milwaukee was rich in different heritages, and the Mayor spoke to any local ethnic group that invited him. After enduring his own years of red baiting, he had the right contacts. A small-town lawyer willing to risk his own reputation for a neighbor labeled a radical would get nowhere against the Federal government. But with Zeidler's help, Pauline identified the American Committee for the Protection of the Foreign Born.

Eero and Lempi engaged Jakob Zimmermann, a lawyer at the Committee, who made quick sense of the situation. He confirmed Marja was being held in Milwaukee. He established the rights that should have existed all along: a lawyer could accompany Marja when being interviewed; she had the right to refuse to answer a question and she could terminate an interview. Zimmerman shook his head when he heard the details of the first FBI visit. He sternly informed Lempi that they could have denied the FBI agents entry into their home since they showed no warrant. But that was hindsight: The FBI agents were given access to their home. The family did answer all of the questions that were asked. And Lempi did serve as an interpreter, even if not completely accurately. Zimmerman was not happy about those facts, but he assured them his group knew what it was doing. The Committee represented hundreds of aliens facing deportation as well as scores of naturalized citizens threatened with revocation of that citizenship.

Lempi and Eero felt some hope, and, for the first time, Pauline believed that her help would make a positive difference.

However, Pauline chose not to disclose to Lempi and her father that Zeidler warned the Committee itself was under a great deal of observation. In 1948, the U.S. Attorney General listed it as a Communist front, and just the year before, in 1952, the head of the nearby Michigan chapter was forced to exercise his Fifth Amendment rights after being subpoenaed before the House Un-American Activities Committee. It was the group's only way to avoid handing over sensitive case files involving the persons they were defending.

Nevertheless, sitting in the courtroom on the day of the trial and seeing Zimmerman beside Marja, Pauline felt a flicker of hope. The elderly Finnish woman was nearly sixty, and had seldom left Clover after settling there as a young bride. She was certainly no subversive. Any judge, guided by a sensible defense attorney like Mr. Zimmerman, would realize the prosecutor's case was nonsense. Pauline squeezed Lempi's hand a little tighter. She looked at the young woman's face hoping to find some sign of confidence. Behind them, the door to the courtroom opened and closed. Lempi's eyes widened in recognition.

Jerry Sommers walked in. What was he doing here, and why would Lempi recognize him? Pauline felt again that prick of conscience that somehow she sparked this trouble when she asked Darryl for help. Darryl could be the only connection between Jerry Sommers, Lempi and her family.

"That's Greg Nolan," hissed Lempi, pointing to the man who walked behind Jerry. "I'll never forget his face, nor that of Agent Tuzzi. They're the FBI guys who first questioned Mama."

"Please rise for the Honorable John Hedges. Court is in session."

Later, Pauline realized she had romantically anticipated drama and justice to play out that day. Always fond of Perry Mason mysteries, Pauline anticipated the proceedings to bear some resemblance to an Erle Stanley Gardner plot. Ideally, Zimmerman's cross-examination would brilliantly expose a corrupt plot to falsely indict an innocent farmwife. The day proved to be nothing like that.

First on the stand was Jerry Sommers. The stocky, dark-haired man was sworn in. Even at ten in the morning, he seemed to need a shave.

"Mr. Sommers, do you publish the *Midwest Monitor*"

"Yes"

"And would you describe its purpose?"

"We review public records and private information to identify individuals who may not be trustworthy because of their association with subversive organizations. And we provide those lists to employers and agencies to help them ensure the loyalty of their staffs."

"And in this capacity, you became aware of the defendant, Mrs. Marja Makinen. Can you tell us how that came about?"

Sommers enjoyed testifying. "I was reviewing the Karelian Technical Aid group and its members. They were once headquartered in Superior, Wisconsin, and this group unwisely encouraged young Midwesterners twenty years ago to abandon this great country to support our enemy, the Soviet Union. In reviewing the list of agents they sent overseas, I came across the name of Risto Makinen, the son of Marja Makinen."

Of course, Pauline remembered Risto. In high school, the Finns and Germans usually stuck to their own. But it was hard for her or any of her classmates not to pay attention to the lad. He wasn't movie star handsome, although he did have dark and luxuriant hair. He was tall enough not to be short, but perhaps not actually tall. But that didn't matter. He was confident, a little bit cocksure, and always ready to strut the halls of the old brick high school. Risto was full of life, optimistic and quick to convince you that the world could be a wonderful one, if one only did the right things. He almost bridged the gap between the Germans and Finns. She often wondered what happened to Risto's Panglossian view of the world once he got to Leningrad. Unlike some of the boys who left, he didn't return home in a year or two from the Soviet experiment. Risto was one of nearly a dozen who left the Clover area at the same time, all in high spirits to do good. Pauline found it disturbing that Sommers described these idealistic, adventure-seeking youths as agents against the United States. Risto only wanted to make the world better. He thought he could make a difference in Karelia, a Soviet territory that was once part of Risto's Finnish homeland.

"In your professional opinion, Mr. Sommers, would you say that the Karelian Technical Aid group was a Communist front, and that anyone who participated in its activities was, therefore, also a subversive?"

"Absolutely,"

"In your capacity, have you also gained access to regional listings of American Communist Party members?"

"I have."

"And on those listings, did you ever see the name of Marja Makinen?"

"Yes, she is listed as a member of the party from 1933 to 1939."

The trial was going fast. Zimmerman was saying little. Pauline wanted to ask why he didn't object, but she needed to trust him. Eero and Lempi watched intently. Marja stared down at the table, not looking at the judge or the prosecutors. She had glanced briefly at Pauline, Lempi and Eero when she first entered the courtroom. She attempted a reassuring smile, but the lines of despair were deep on her face. Now, she looked up briefly when Greg Nolan was called to the stand.

Nolan was sworn in and identified as the FBI agent who interviewed the defendant the year before. The prosecutor asked, "In the course of your questioning, did you ask the defendant for her point of entry into the United States?"

"I did, and she said New York."

"Objection." For the first time, Zimmerman raised a concern. "The agent was speaking to Mrs. Makinen through an interpreter. He can't be certain what she said."

"Overruled."

"So, Mr. Nolan, prior to this visit, you also had an opportunity to review Mrs. Makinen's alien registration forms, which have been submitted annually since 1948, and what did those forms say?"

"Sometimes she listed New York, and sometime she said Montreal."

"And what is your professional opinion as to the matter of where she arrived?"

"It doesn't matter where she arrived. One way or the other, Mrs. Makinen has perjured herself on an official government declaration."

"Objection!"

Pauline looked at Lempi, and thought back to the day she first learned of the FBI visit. It wasn't Marja who lied that day; it was Lempi. Zimmerman, who also knew of Lempi's improvised translation, allowed the testimony to continue.

When a break was called, Zimmerman joined them for a quick lunch of a sandwich and cup of coffee at the corner diner. "I must put Marja on the stand," the lawyer said. "She needs to explain her confusion, and why she was a member of the Party. More importantly, she has to become a real person to the judge. He needs to see that this elderly woman poses no danger. It would be outrageous to deport Marja to a country she hasn't seen since being a small child. Without her on the stand, we have nothing to refute the government's claims. Under the McCarran act, they've proven all that is needed to deport her."

Back in session, Marja looked pale as she took the stand. Her hands shook slightly as they held tightly to a lace hanky. Marja's nervousness visibly increased as Zimmerman approached. The translator, an elderly man with a thick mustache, was so close as to be intimidating. Marja's voice was low while his translation boomed, which put Pauline on edge. She needed to be here for Lempi's sake, but she would be much more comfortable back in City Hall, immersed in the minutiae of suburban annexation plans and proposals for sensible water rates.

Zimmerman's tone was soothing. "Marja, it's important that we simply tell your story now. Just listen to my questions and answer them fully and truthfully, as you have pledged to do. Marja, are you a Communist?

"*Ei, en ole.*" she said in Finnish, and the translator boomed out, "No, I am not."

"Then why did your name appear on the American Communist party listing?"

Marja looked over at her husband, embarrassed, as though she was about to reveal a secret she planned never to tell. The translation came quickly, "When my little boy left for Russia, I was so sad. All my children were gone. My beautiful love there was not yet born, but my first two boys had died as little children. And now Risto was gone too. And I needed to know what happened to him. I needed a way to stay in touch, even if Papa didn't. And you know youngsters. They don't think to write."

"And the American Communist Party," her lawyer prompted.

"I joined it because the Party man told me they could help me keep track of Risto if I was a member. What mother wouldn't do that? What mother wouldn't do whatever she could to stay close to her baby?" Marja suddenly stopped as though surprised by her own words. Pauline felt compelled to look to the floor.

"And are you still a member?"

"No, I quit. I made them take my name off when Russia invaded Finland in 1939. I knew I could not trust them anymore, and anyway ever since 1937, they didn't even know what had happened to my Risto. I only had love left." The translator suddenly realized that Marja was using the word Lempi as a name, not the emotion, and corrected himself. "I only had Lempi left."

"One more question, Marja. Why have you given different answers regarding your point of entry?"

"I came to this country by landing in Montreal and then traveling to Wisconsin. But Eero, he came through New York, and sometimes I was confused whether the question was being about me or us. I can be easily confused, but I came to Montreal."

Our lawyer sat down, and the prosecutor stood up. He did not smile, and his tone seemed dismissive. "Mrs. Makinen, I can understand you might be confused at times, but do you expect us to believe you were confused in your own home, with your own daughter as translator, while talking in person to two agents of the United States Government. Why at that moment did you still claim to arrive in New York?"

Marja looked trapped. To the judge, it probably made her seem guilty. But to Pauline, it was the anguish of a mother. Marja knew she had not been confused and that she provided her daughter an accurate answer. She knew that Lempi independently chose to provide the FBI with an answer that Lempi thought better. But how could she disclose that in front of the entire court? It was a crazy country and a crazy time. Even an old immigrant woman could see that. Lempi had already been denied attending college for reasons that remained murky. Who could say what would happen to her if the government knew how she misled the FBI?

Marja hesitated only for a moment. "I was confused. I don't know why."

"All, right, fair enough, Mrs. Makinen. But let's give this next question close attention and be sure you are not confused in the way you answer it.

Are you now, or have your ever been, a member of an organization subversive to the United States?'

"No," she quickly responded.

"Really, you have admitted that you systematically associated with members of an organization known to be subversive. You have admitted lying by giving contradictory answers on a Federal form. Why should we believe you now?

"Objection."

Little more was said. The case was soon over. The government's position was straightforward. Marja had been a member of the American Communist Party, an organization that was legal when she belonged but was now tainted as subversive. She had perjured herself on official government forms. Under the Immigration and Nationality Act of 1952, either fact—and certainly both—was sufficient cause to deport her. Zimmerman's defense was a plea for decency and mercy: this was an elderly farm wife, who filled out a few forms inconsistently, a mother who tried to stay in touch with a wayward son and a woman who was not actively involved in any way with subversive groups. Certainly she was no threat to the United States and certainly no decent society would discard her so heartlessly.

During the recess while the judge deliberated, Zimmerman warned Eero and Lempi that the case might not go their way. But it was only the first day of a potentially longer struggle. If the case went badly today, they should not give up hope. The Committee had much experience in appeals. Zimmerman was confident they would eventually prevail. The sentiment was noble, Pauline supposed, unless you were the family whose mother was caught in the trap. The morning, which began with some promise of resolution, was followed by an afternoon growing heavy with despair. The judge returned to his courtroom.

The judge cleared his voice to speak clearly and unemotionally. "I find in favor of the Government's case, and hereby order Marja Ida Makinen to be detained at Ellis Island in New York until such time as she can be deported to her native state of Finland."

Despite the judge's initial ruling, Marja stayed in a Milwaukee federal cell and was not sent to Ellis Island in New York.—Zimmerman's only clear victory. Lempi refused to stay on the farm (which was over a hundred and fifty miles from Milwaukee), quit her job and moved into Pauline's small apartment—all so she could be close to her mother. Eero was forced to stay on the farm since cows must be milked twice a day, regardless of legal troubles. Without Marja's help with the milking each morning and evening, Eero was always running late. An automatic milking machine would have helped, but there was no cash. Instead, he sold a few cows both to reduce the workload and to help pay part of the legal bills.

Under other circumstances, Lempi's stay with her would have elated Pauline. It was her chance to learn what her daughter liked, to see the breakfast light play through Lempi's blonde hair and to smile a secret smile at the girl's too earnest ways. But she found these moments impossible to enjoy. Marja's possible deportation loomed over them. Pauline accompanied Lempi on her first two trips to the jail's visiting room, but then begged off. She claimed that she couldn't get away from work. In reality, she found the visits a slow, caustic drip. Despair and hopelessness fluttered about Marja like a tattered cloak, and her eyes also saw all. In Marja's sad, hooded eyes, Pauline saw anger and fear over Pauline's bonding with Lempi. It was easier not to visit.

Each day, Lempi went to the Federal building and talked to her mother in Finnish for as much time as the guards would allow. Each week, she met with Mr. Zimmerman, hoping to hear good news but instead leaving burdened by the frustrating slowness of appeals. Each Friday, she penned a long letter to her father, usually in English, but sometimes with an occasional Finnish postscript. She described in detail her mother's feeling and thoughts. Each minute, she lived in hope that things would return to the old normal.

Eero wrote back sporadically, always in Finnish. Pauline was unable to read the letters, so Lempi shared their updates about the farm and neighbors. Pauline, who received her own weekly letters from her mother, knew the German part of town largely ignored the Makinen plight; the Finnish group was afraid to get involved since each of the Finns had their own skeletons. There was always the neighbor, friend or relative who had been a Wobbly, a Communist or one of those crazy kids who caught Karelian fever.

Pauline tried to interest Lempi in life beyond Marja. One weekend, she even suggested they drive to Madison to surprise Peter. Even though

Pauline hadn't cared for the young man during their dinner together, she hoped he would be a distraction.

"Peter's been drafted," said Lempi. "He's no longer at the University."

"When did that happen?" Pauline asked. The boy sent frequent letters, but Pauline didn't pay attention to the postmarks. She didn't want to spy on Lempi's life.

"A while back. He's nearly finished basic training. He's afraid he'll get sent to Korea," Lempi said. "We never even got to say good-bye in person."

Just as well, thought Pauline, who didn't really trust a boy who had so little grounding. Still, wanting Lempi to experience more than a daily jail visit, Pauline suggested Lempi join her on a visit to Tom Ferber.

"He's my old professor from Bremen," Pauline explained. "He's writing a book but usually works at a cabin up north. He's in Milwaukee for a week or so, and wants to get together. I think you would enjoy meeting him."

On Sunday afternoon, they drove to the North Point mansion where Ferber was staying. Casimir and Regina Rabinowicz, the wealthy meatpackers who also owned the camp where Ferber was writing, lived in a three-story limestone mansion with a circular drive. Pauline worried Lempi would feel intimidated. But Regina, a buxom and perky woman in her fifties, proved a friendly hostess and the opposite of how Pauline imagined a millionaire's wife.

Ferber was totally at home among the rich furnishings of the well-appointed house. Unlike Lempi, he didn't seem to worry about servants serving him afternoon coffee and pastries.

"How did the two of you get to know each other?" Pauline asked Tom and Mrs. Rabinowicz.

Regina laughed, "We were servants together."

"I was not a servant," said Tom.

"Well, I was. It was never quite clear what you were to the Oxfords. You see, Pauline, before I met Casimir and before he made all this money, I lived a much simpler life. But when I was straight off the boat from the old country, I was lucky I could find a job. The Oxfords were so wealthy, all that money from the forests they despoiled, and they needed many, many servants in that big mansion of theirs. But Tom, he was like their confidant, a regular Cardinal Richelieu to old man Oxford, always lurking about. But I think it was because you loved that Oxford girl." Regina smiled indulgently.

"That was another era," Tom said. "I was awfully young, and more than a little naive. Seeing Lempi reminds me of those days. It was a time when I still thought the world offered great promise, and that all things were possible. It's a feeling unique to the young, available only until the world slams you into reality. Speaking of which, Lempi, Pauline told me about your mother's case. Is there anything new?"

Lempi seldom talked about her mother's case with others, and she hesitated for a moment. "Our lawyer asked that the deportation be suspended due to hardship. But the government has ignored him. I guess governments do that. The Finnish government hasn't even acknowledged that the United States is trying to send Ma back. We're all in limbo, with Pa still back in Clover taking care of the farm. Ma is just worrying herself near to death."

The professor nodded in understanding. "Pauline, did I ever tell about the time I was in Clover? This was back in the Thirties when I was researching immigrant groups in the state. It was early summer, and a bunch of boys were about to head for the Soviet Union. As I recall, there was a small riot at the train station."

"That's when my brother left America. Maybe you met him?" Lempi perked up at the idea. Pauline remembered that day—and not just because Ferber had told the story before. Her father had quickly locked down their store during the melee, but Pauline stayed by the window, straining to see the boys that were leaving.

"This was nearly twenty years ago now, with many books and articles and students since then. I don't remember any of those boys. Now, some things you don't forget, like your friend Pauline. I still remember the day she showed up in my class. There, I thought, is a smart and beautiful young lady."

"And then you discovered the truth," Pauline joked.

"Don't deny your talents, my dear. This old teacher is very proud of you and your work. It's tough for a woman to have a career, and I admire what you do, working in the Zeidler administration. I like to have people around me who can make a difference, to know people who stay centered."

"What do you mean?" Lempi asked.

"Most people flock to the extremes. Maybe it is something found in all humans, and all the institutions we create. Take this great state of Wisconsin," he said. "It generates enormous riches in people like the Oxfords and the Shindlers and," he nodded to Regina, "the Rabinowiczs. It creates great movements like Bob LaFollette and the Progressive Movement or even the innovative farmer cooperatives of the Finns and the farmers with Land O'Lakes butter. But then there are the extremes. Sometimes, it's petty tyrants like our own Senator Joe McCarthy. Sometimes it's the ruthless destruction of the very things that made us what we are, like the wasted cutover lands that were once our great northern forest. Sometimes, it's just men who find a way to extort others by pretending to do good.

"Oh, I've been close to this tipping point, seeing good men turn bad, sitting at the right hand of an old lumber baron like Barney Oxford. There's something about power and idealism that leads to greed and fanaticism. And after years of study, I can't say I have the smallest clue as to what will become the catalyst or the damper."

"Oh, Tommy, you're so gloomy these days." Regina poured him another cup of coffee. "If that's what comes from working on your books in Thread, I need to take our cabin back and evict both you and all the stuff you're collecting. When we were last at the camp, that meddling grocer man, Big John Trueheart, told us he's taken to calling you Mr. Packer. He says you squirrel away everything that crosses your path. But I say stop your packing. Stop collecting dire thoughts. Look at this young woman visiting us today. I am sure she will prove to be a wonderful influence on the world."

Lempi blushed.

"Yes," Ferber said, "I am sure Lempi will bring great things into this world and prove this old man unnecessarily gloomy."

Limbo persisted. Marja remained imprisoned awaiting deportation; the Finnish government ignored the U.S. deportation orders; the American government rejected Zimmerman's appeals and Marja's depression deepened. Eero worked the farm by himself; he rarely trekked to Milwaukee to visit his wife. Lempi still stayed with Pauline and visited her mother each day possible. To occupy the long hours between the daily visits, she enrolled part time at a secretarial college. Letters flowed in and out of the household: Lempi's weekly note to her father, the occasional reply from Eero, the increasingly infrequent exchanges between Peter and Lempi. The old friends from Clover became more distant. Unsettled as it was, life fell into a routine that flowed through the fall and into 1954.

Pauline sometimes wondered if this would be the new script for her life. The old familiar characters dropped away. Ferber returned to Thread and his writing. She missed their conversations and always having a person at hand in whom she could confide. She banished Darryl from her life, or perhaps he simply avoided her. There were times she imagined what life might have been if they had married before the war. By now, she would probably have children who would call her "mommy" and they would be growing up in some lovely house in the suburbs, playing tennis or swimming at the country club, while she entertained Darryl's work friends. Instead each day Pauline traveled downtown to her large, but always chilly, office. She sat at her massive oak desk and worked through the frustration of suburban leaders determined to fight every positive step the Mayor attempted. They only wanted lower taxes for themselves, with no concern for the overall health of the city that made their riches possible.

But at least there was Lempi. The girl had such energy and commitment to doing what was right. But that was slowly vanishing. Her mother's plight was making Lempi cynical, and Pauline worried that she was forgetting to enjoy life. Pauline actually looked forward to Peter's return from Korea, where he was among those safeguarding the armistice and exchange of prisoners. In person, Lempi would likely decide if he was the one or let herself open up to others. The girl was pretty and smart, many boys noticed her and yet she never went on dates. Pauline wanted that to change.

March was wet and dreary. Zimmerman said the U.S. government, frustrated by both Finland and Canada's refusals to accept Marja, was filing new charges against Marja. This time the government claimed her crime was that she had not applied for travel documents for self-deportation. The lawyer called the claim ridiculous. Yet Marja was not the only one in this quandary. Supposedly, the government was doing the same thing to another Finn, Knut Heikkinenen, who wrote for the Finnish paper *Työmies*. He too faced deportation for once being a member of the Communist party. Zimmerman reported stories from around the country of elderly immigrants in their sixties or seventies who were being forced from their homes for the loosest of Communist connections.

Classes in shorthand, typing and filing did not distract Lempi from worrying about her mother. But then the unexpected letter from New York arrived. Peter's mother informed Lempi that Peter had been killed in a truck accident in Korea. His body was being shipped back to the East Coast; there would be a funeral in two days. Pauline held Lempi for what seemed like hours as her daughter cried—whether for Peter or for Marja or for the general turmoil of her own life, Pauline couldn't tell.

"I was so worried," Lempi said, "when Peter was drafted. It was just after that terrible battle at Pork Chop Hill, and the war had been going on so long. But by the time he finished basic training, the Armistice was signed, so I thought he would be safe. I knew that over fifty thousand American boys had already died, but I thought Peter would be safe.

"I know you think we hardly knew each other. Just a few nights together on a road trip out west, a dinner and many letters. But he meant something to me, and maybe some day I can talk about how wonderful our time was in Yellowstone." Those words confirmed for Pauline that Lempi fell to the seduction of a handsome boy in the moonlight just as she had done so many years ago. But that's what made life life. Pauline couldn't regret her decision, because if it had been different, she wouldn't have Lempi.

"Lempi, I don't know if this will help, but I want to share a secret. When I was your age, I met a boy who I really liked and we made love. I know I seem an old woman to you, and my secret may seem scandalous. But for that night, that boy was the wonder of my life. He left the next day and I never saw him again. But there is a part of that man who still lives within me, and a memory that I will never let go. And I cherish that memory and always will. Love, however fleeting or short lived, makes the world better. It makes a person better. I really believe that.

"Lempi, I don't know how or why you fell in love with Peter. And I don't need to know the whys to know this: you are richer because of him, and you should treasure whatever he gave you. Don't let go of it. Grieve for him, but celebrate what lives on. Can you do that?" She drew her daughter close to her, a daughter who would never know just how much she meant to her true mother, and held Lempi quietly as the night closed in around them.

***

In late April, with Marja's case still unresolved, Lempi found a new passion in watching the live broadcasts of the Army-McCarthy hearings on the local ABC station. The Army accused the Wisconsin Senator of bringing undue pressure to favor a former aide now in the ranks. The broadcast clearly portrayed the bullying and abusive nature of the Senator. Lempi always felt that McCarthy's anti-Communist campaign directly caused her mother's troubles, so she was pleased at seeing the media quickly fleeing the Senator's cause.

The month after the completion of those hearings, Marja's case took an unexpected but positive turn. Marja was freed to go home on bail. Out of the blue, the government took a new tack as the case awaited a Supreme Court appeal. Zimmerman was ecstatic. Pauline, knowing a bit about government finances, cynically thought the Feds were tired of paying the jailor's bill. Lempi thought somehow that McCarthy's disgrace had broken the logjam. Regardless, Marja was scheduled to return to Clover by Independence Day. At last, she could sleep in her own bed.

After convincing a local neighbor to milk his cows, Eero drove to Milwaukee so he could take his wife home. Lempi decided to return with them.

Pauline couldn't convince Lempi to remain. She met the family at the Federal building when Marja was released. For over a year, Pauline had found excuses to avoid visiting Marja and was astounded to see how the woman had aged. She was jumpy, furtive and spoke non-stop Finnish. Pauline didn't know what Marja was saying, but she could tell the woman was repeating the same things. Lempi looked at Pauline briefly and said, "Ma's saying everything is all her fault, and that we should leave her be. She's convinced she's ruined my life."

As Eero, Marja and Lempi drove off in Eero's old pick-up truck, Pauline waved enthusiastically. The three travelers were tightly packed on the bench seat with a fidgety Marja bookended by the smiling Eero and Lempi. Pauline kept waving until the truck was out of sight, and then she dropped both her smile and her wave. She turned to return to City Hall and work, already dreading her empty apartment at day's end.

Lempi fell back into the practice of sending a weekly letter to Pauline. The letters spoke of Marja's continued despondency and obsession over the damage she caused the family. Pauline's mother wrote that most of Clover shunned the old woman, but it was clear from Gertrude's letters that she saw nothing wrong in that.

As the summer went on, Pauline pushed all thoughts of Marja out of her mind. Marja only reminded her of Lempi, which in turn made Pauline long for the months the girl had been her roommate.

One day at work Pauline was playing the radio low in the background. She could work better with a bit of sound. She seldom paid attention to specific songs or the programming in between. At the top of the hour, the news came on. For some reason, she turned up the volume.

It was a series of news items from around the state. But then came the unexpected blow. "A fiery tragedy today in the small town of Clover. Accused Communist Marja Makinen found dead outside the family barn by her daughter. The older woman, facing a deportation order, committed suicide by setting herself afire. Authorities provided no further details."

Less than thirty seconds. One small news bit from the radio's roundup. To most listeners, a momentary and perhaps gruesome story. To some, maybe to many in Clover, it was good riddance to an accused Communist. But to Pauline, it was a horror. After months of sharing her home with Lempi, she knew how the girl thought and reacted. But how would any person barely an adult handle discovering her mother dead in such a horrific way? To see a blackened body knowing the pain that it endured?

Dreading her daughter would be engulfed by emotion, Pauline decided to save her. She didn't stop to plan her next steps. She simply acted: took the elevator down, retrieved her car, started driving to Clover, committed to rescuing Lempi and bringing her to a safe haven in Milwaukee. Eero would not stand in her way. Lempi's young mind could not be reminded each day of Marja's painful escape from living. Pauline needed to free Lempi from guilt. Without that salvation, Pauline knew the girl would grow bitter and angry. She would close in on herself and give up. She would blame herself.

Pauline could not let that happen. Pauline had to save her Sonja, her love, her Lempi. And she would.

Danny turned over the San Francisco postcard he found inside the old commencement program. It read, "I have seen such wonderful things on the trip. So much seems possible. Not going to Bremen no longer seems important. Wish me luck. Always, Lempi." The card was addressed to Pauline Newmann. He wondered about the relationship between his mother and Pauline, when his mother had been in San Francisco and why Pauline left a trunk filled with mementos for his mother.

He picked up another newspaper clipping. This one was in Finnish; he recognized the unusual mixture of letters, all the i's and k's and double vowels. The masthead of the paper read Työmies, *and the clipping pictured a group of young men on the front page. They didn't look all that much older than he. While he couldn't read the text, he scanned the names in the caption beneath the photo. He noticed "Makinen" which he knew was his mother's maiden name. But he couldn't figure out which person in the poorly reproduced photo went with which name. His grandfather, Eero Makinen, died when Danny was still a small boy. But the people in the paper seemed to be dressed in Depression-era garb. His grandfather would have been middle-aged by then. There must have been another Makinen in the family. Maybe he had a cousin.*

RISTO MAKINEN
1933
EN ROUTE TO LENINGRAD

Round and round, the train wheels clicketty-clacked, as noisy as the tumbled thoughts of Risto Makinen. He was on a great adventure. Each new revolution of the wheels, each telephone pole against the horizon, was another step forward. Just nineteen, on his own and heading east, Risto was barreling down those iron tracks, heading to New York and beyond, prepared to make his stamp on history.

His Pa had taken the reverse route years earlier, leaving Finland when he was just nineteen. But the old man had been out for himself. Risto was different. He could see clearly how the common man was oppressed. The Depression was sucking the blood out of all workers. Risto couldn't stand the way Ma and Pa worked every minute of every day just to survive on that sad piece of land they called a farm. The railroads and lumber companies cheated every Finn they ever connived into buying their leftover lands. No one could make that poor land pay off, especially when the big money tycoons in Chicago and New York refused to pay a fair price for milk. But Risto knew the world could be different. It was up to him to make it so. He looked over at his pals Charlie and Art, and then at all the other guys who had left Clover that afternoon. This was the group with the vision. They had the courage to take a stand.

What a day already. When he awoke that morning, Ma lured him from bed with his favorite breakfast: fried eggs, bacon and toasted cardamom bread spread thick with Ma's homemade jellies. Ma seemed so teary-eyed when they drank their morning coffee together. It was sad to think it might be their last shared drink for who knew how long. He figured Ma knew that if things went well in Karelia, he might never come back. After all, Pa had left his own parents years ago to come to America. But she had to know how exciting this all was. He wished she wouldn't try so hard to keep from crying. She could be so moody, and he didn't want to think about that. He looked instead at Pa, who just stared back stolidly. The old man slurped his coffee through one of those damned sugar cubes he always put between his lips. Pa was going to act the Finn today, wasn't he, pretending like he didn't have any emotion. But Risto knew the old man was proud of him. Pa taught him to think about the common man throughout his growing up years. Pa sent him to the Young Pioneers camp up to Houghton. He knew that there was a noble experiment going on with the Soviets, and that Soviet Karelia, which practically was the same as Finland, needed the help of smart, able Americans. Pa knew that Risto was doing the right thing by volunteering.

Across from him on the train, Charlie Niemenen spoke, "Hey, Risto, what do you think we should do the first thing we get to New York?" Charlie, a year younger than Risto, was always smiling and following Risto. It had started in grade school, continued through high school and, now, Charlie was following him to Russia. It was good to have a best friend along.

"Why, we're going to find ourselves some women," replied Art Wepling. Art dropped out of school after eighth grade to help his parents on their farm. When they lost it, Art hitched out on the rails. For the last couple of years, he had been hoboing across the country. He preened as though his experiences made him wise about the world, but Risto still considered Art the dull kid in class. Just the opposite of Risto himself. Risto was a quick learner. He barely spoke a word of English when Pa and Ma dropped him off in first grade. And that teacher, if she knew a word of Finnish, certainly never spoke it. Ma heard teachers liked apples and forced him to give his teacher that fruit. But she ignored it, and Risto knew that damn well every German in town knew enough to tell a Finn *kiitos* as 'thank you.' Acknowledging him would have been a simple thing. But Risto outsmarted that spinster teacher. He caught on to English fast. He learned his numbers and letters quicker than any other boy or girl in that one-room school. By the time he went to high school in town, everyone in Clover knew him as the clever Finnish boy. That's why when he joined the Karelian Technical Aid campaign, other Finnish boys followed.

Risto replied to both Charlie and Art. "I reckon we'll head to Finn Hall first. In a place as big as New York, the Finns ought to have a pretty fine meeting hall. And there should be girls there to say goodbye to brave heroes like us." He smiled, feeling sure of his insight.

Risto knew a thing or two about how young women responded to noble intentions. Throughout high school, he was aware of how the girls viewed him. When he looked in a mirror, he didn't see someone who was handsome. He had dark hair, hazel eyes, and was five foot ten, but he knew he wasn't tall, dark and handsome. On the other hand, he could smile and make his eyes twinkle. He improvised clever talk that made girls giggle. Such talents were not easily dismissed. Other boys, more attractive than him, couldn't do any of those things and weren't as lucky with the girls. Still, Risto wasn't going to teach them his tricks. Let them find their own talents. Charlie and Art, who had been hanging around him for years, had yet to pick up a thing.

He looked at his two friends, sitting in the seat across from him, each still excited by the sendoff in Clover. He wanted to disclose the details of the farewell he experienced the night before, but determined it was nobler to be discreet. He hadn't been planning anything special for his final night in Clover, but if he had, he couldn't imagine a better girl for it than Pauline Newmann. It wasn't fair that a girl could both be beautiful and smart. Even though she was two years behind him in school, he always knew she had a little crush on him. But she was one of those sensible German souls who didn't get carried away with emotion. She thought things through and considered the import of every statement and action. No one ever accused her of impetuous action. Everyone knew she planned to go to college, and since her father was a successful grocer, she wasn't likely to stay in Clover, no matter how long the Depression lingered.

Given all of that, he hadn't expected to see her outside Clover's Finn Hall last night. When he stepped outside for a quick cigarette and a break from the noise, he noticed her. Back inside, the building was filled with Finns from Clover, its surrounding farms and all the nearby Finnish communities. A farewell dance honored the eleven local youth who would leave the next day. All eleven were heading to Russia and the woods of its Karelia district. They were investing their lives to create a more just world, one that would rise above the Depression and its poverty. These boys believed Communism could work. Local Finns, always a radical lot, were proud of their boys. On the other hand, the local Germans dismissed the boys as naive. That's why Risto was so surprised to see one of those German girls outside the hall.

It was a warm May evening with a full moon and the hint of fragrant apple blossoms in the air. Risto suspected Pauline was like a naturally curious cat. She wanted to understand people willing to upend their lives, travel thousands of miles and live by their convictions. Pauline was too sensible to do any of that, but that didn't mean those emotions didn't intrigue her. He walked over to her, and they struck up a conversation. He offered a cigarette. Surprisingly, she accepted and smoked with a practiced air. She asked him unexpected questions about his motives and expectations. He wondered why he hadn't spoken to her more often. Neither of them suggested they take a walk. They simply found themselves strolling away from Finn Hall, down Main Street, past the hotel with its white-pillared porch and along the banks of the millpond. The full moon reflected off its surface. In the bright moonlight, their shadows seemed both substantial and ephemeral.

"Do you think the moon will be as beautiful in Karelia?" Pauline asked. Until that moment he hadn't considered their encounter romantic, but that question compelled him to kiss her. She didn't seem surprised, and she didn't try to stop him. None of it was planned. In that way, it was totally unlike Risto's previous encounters with local girls, which had always been elaborately thought through. Their impromptu pairing was heated and intense, but also warm and gentle. For many minutes afterward, they lay against the green grass in each other's arms. On the moon shining down on them, the lunar craters seeming to create a happier face than either remembered. Risto realized during their lovemaking that he was taking Pauline's virginity, but he didn't mention it. Pauline certainly knew Risto would be leaving the next day and that she was unlikely to ever see him again. She didn't mention that.

On the rocking train, all these memories of the previous night made Risto squirm.

"What's with you?" Art asked. "It's like you can't sit still."

"Ah, it's this new suit," Risto responded. "First suit I ever had. Been mostly jeans and overalls until now. But all dressed up in a suit and tie, sitting on a train to Chicago. Makes me feel kind of important."

Charlie broke in, "And in Chicago we'll change for the overnight train to New York. And then a boat to Stockholm. And another to Leningrad. I can tell you now I'm not wearing my suit all the way there."

They laughed. Risto returned to thoughts of Pauline. While his parents drove him to the train station, he thought about the unexpected nighttime romance and hoped Pauline would be at the station to wave him good-bye. He imagined her running up to the train window and thrusting a lace handkerchief at him, as though providing a pennant for her knight-errant heading off to the Crusades.

But the scene at the train station was wild. There was quite a crowd, more people than had probably gathered at any time since Fighting Bob LaFollette had stopped in Clover during his 1916 presidential run. Pa still liked to talk about that day. But this crowd might be bigger. Everyone who had been at Finn Hall the night before was there, because the whole Finnish community showed up to wish good luck to their eleven boys. There were the Communists, the socialists, the Wobblies, the co-op gang and even the Apostolic Lutherans who never had anything good to say about the Soviets. Over six thousand people from across the Midwest, mostly Finns, had already journeyed to Russia as part of Karelian Technical Aid. Today, though, was the departure of the first group from the Clover area. Even the local Finnish band was ready to serenade them.

The other ten boys elected Risto to make a farewell speech to the crowd. Risto, always comfortable at making spur-of-the-moment talks, timed his cadence to pull in the crowd. He switched between Finnish and English, both to please the old-timers and to excite the young. He decried that local farmers were toiling endlessly to fill the coffers of the heartless rich in the big cities. He promised that he and his comrades would do great good in a land where the workers had taken power into their own hands. At that point, a bright flash from a camera illuminated the group of eleven. Later, one of the men told him that a reporter from *Työmies*, the Finnish paper in Superior, snapped their photo. Throughout his short talk, he scanned the crowd trying to spot the auburn-haired, blue-eyed Pauline. He didn't find her. The crowd gave a huge cheer as he finished his remarks, but he felt deflated.

The band struck up the "Internationale," the anthem of the Communist movement. The cheers grew louder. Unexpectedly, a loud whistle blew. Clover's four policemen pushed into the crowd, yelling "Break it up, enough of that." At the same time, the train pulled into the station and the boys quickly boarded it. The town cops were driving away the crowd, preventing parents and friends from making their final farewells. Many in the crowd resisted. The religious Finns quickly scattered. Some local Germans appeared to join the police. Fisticuffs broke out.

As the train pulled out, Risto looked out over and above the scuffle. For a moment he had a straight view down Main Street. He could see the front of Newmann's General Merchandise. During the few brief seconds of that perspective, he was convinced he saw a young woman appear in the store window and wave her handkerchief. He stowed that image into his mind for the battles ahead.

"Where should we go first?" asked Charlie excitedly. The Broadway Limited had just pulled into Penn Central, and the Clover boys' overnight trip to New York was over. Uncharacteristically, Risto looked to Art for guidance, since the guy had traveled all over the country during his tramping days. He should know what to recommend. One of the other kids said, "We gotta see the Empire State Building. It's the tallest thing in the world." Risto remembered when it was dedicated two years ago. He thought then how great it would be someday to survey the world from such a high platform. Today he didn't want to seem an eager rube, so he ignored the suggestion. The surrounding bustle of people put him out of sorts. Folks just streamed around him and his friends. The frenzy in the grand concourse of the train station made him feel small. When they changed trains in Chicago, he first felt that way, but he was distracted then by needing to find a fast lunch and locating the track number for the New York connection.

"Isn't someone supposed to be meeting us?" asked Art. He held tight to his suitcase. The eleven guys instinctively formed a small circle in the middle of Penn Central's grand hall of glass, steel and marble. Risto read once that the Baths of Caracalla inspired the station. He liked knowing obscure facts, and he figured this would be about as close to Italy as he would ever get. Above the glass ceiling, the sky seemed muted and dirty but morning sunlight streamed in.

Art was right. Someone was supposed to meet them and where was he? Risto was annoyed that the greeter wasn't already there. Here were eleven guys, ready to travel thousands of miles to a country they had never seen, prepared to work for a year or two, or maybe more, in the untamed wilderness of a Russian forest, after shelling out several hundred dollars a piece for the honor, and what did it get them? Stranded in the middle of a train station. He knew their four hundred dollar payments were meant to cover the train and ship tickets—and there were a lot of tickets to this journey—as well as to cover initial living expenses. Ma and Pa really scrimped to help him raise the funds. In that regard, he was no different than anyone else on this trip. He didn't think that after paying so much, they should be abandoned in Manhattan.

"Maybe we look for the main exit," suggested Art. "Does anyone know who's supposed to be meeting us?" His voice dropped to a whisper, "Hey, look at her."

A slender, petite blonde girl was walking straight to them. "Looks like one of those Norwegian farmer's daughters over Minnesota way," said another boy.

"I'm in love," said Charlie. Art slapped him on the back. The boys laughed.

The girl stopped directly in front of the eleven. "What are you boys looking at?" Her icy-blue eyes looked them over. "You're a day late. You were told to arrive yesterday. You know you're not the only gang we have to herd."

Charlie looked abashed, but Risto smiled. He couldn't help himself. He liked take-charge girls. For a moment, he thought of Pauline back in Clover. He could imagine her with such a tough exterior. But his experience told him hard shells usually required only the lightest of taps to crack open.

"You're late, too," he said, "We've been standing here nearly half an hour. If we knew a pretty girl was meeting us, we might have used that time more wisely to freshen up." He mimed a little bath.

"A regular little Charlie Chaplin, aren't you? Well, you look more like W. C. Fields." The girl's words stopped Risto in his tracks and he blushed. "Listen, guys, this is serious business. Nearly three hundred of us will leave on the Swedish American Lines in two days. There's a lot of stuff you need to learn before we ship out. I'm here to be your guide."

"Are you going to Karelia too?" asked Charlie. Risto picked up on his friend's tone of hope.

"Of course, I am. So pay attention, we're in this together. My name is Lydia Amundson. I grew up here in Brooklyn. My job today is to get the eleven of you to Finn Hall in Harlem. There're places for you to stay there and we'll brief you on the project. So take these tokens and follow me. We're using the subway."

Like little ducklings, Risto and the others followed Lydia. She led them down into the catacombs below the modern day temple of Penn Station. They dropped their tokens into the turnstiles, stepped onto the subway platform and boarded a BMT train heading toward Brooklyn. Risto enjoyed the rocking of the train from Chicago to New York, but the darkened tunnels of New York's underground spooked him. The screeching wheels and the flashing lights were oppressive. He felt small and powerless against the incessant pushing of the crowds. At 42nd street, they switched to an IRT train heading north. He fought a crazy urge to grab the hands of Charlie and Art. He was afraid they would get separated. Mentally, he turned to picturing the heroic nation building ahead in Karelia. He imagined himself sweating in the summer sun, with his shirt off and his muscled chest bronzed by the sun. He visualized his expert use of the cross saw to fell a tree, while being watched by that cute Norwegian girl Lydia. The train jerked and he looked up. Across the car Lydia, hanging onto a strap, watched him unsmiling. He blushed for the second time that day.

He really wanted off the train. At each station stop as new hordes streamed on and off, he considered bolting. He wanted to be free of the press of people. The train began moving upward; hints of light came into the tunnel. The train broke free of the tunnel and pressed forward on elevated tracks, unleashing views of the city. For the first time, Risto saw Manhattan, the rush of buildings packed tightly together, the streams of people on the street below, the high buildings in the distance and all of it clogged with more people than he had ever seen. It was amazing.

The train stopped at 125th street. "We walk from here," Lydia said. She gathered her troops, left the train, descended the stairs, turned north toward 126th Street and walked west. "We're heading to the Finnish Progressive Society Hall. You'll see that it's a grand building, constructed entirely with donations from Finns. All brick, four stories high, with a gymnasium and swimming pool. Even a sauna. I'm sure you Finns are missing that after two days on the train."

The broad door of the Hall was framed by a tall stone lintel and flanked by two tall arched windows. The facade made Risto proud to be a Finn. No building in Clover was so grand. After giving them a detailed tour of the hall, Lydia introduced them to others who would be part of the Karelian contingent. They stopped near the pool, and Risto was amazed to see that black men were swimming along side the whites. Charlie muttered something about Negroes.

Lydia was offended. "We're all in this together, all men fighting for the common good. Two years ago, one of our janitors tried to prevent Negroes from attending a dance here. We put him in a mock trial, found him guilty and expelled him from the Party. We Communists have to stand for all that's good."

"What happened to the janitor?" Risto asked.

"The government deported him for other reasons," Lydia responded and said nothing more.

In the day and half that followed, Lydia guided them around the city. Art fulfilled his wish to see the world from the top of the Empire State Building. While standing on the observation deck with the Clover boys, Lydia pointed out all the great sights of the city. To the southeast was the Brooklyn Bridge. To the southwest was the Statue of Liberty, a scene they would see up close when they sailed away the following day. Off to the west was Times Square. (Later that evening, Risto walked around the theaters and imagined the stories being told inside.) To the northwest was a large green square. Lydia said that land was Central Park. Beyond that in the distance was the great Columbia University and near it were St. John's Cathedral and Riverside Church. Lydia asked if they had brought along their wallets stuffed with their fortunes. If so, perhaps they should shop on Fifth Avenue before they headed to the Soviet Union. Everyone wears diamonds in the People's Republic, she joked. They laughed, uneasily, thinking of the unemployed and homeless in America. The Great Depression was not improving. Neither Risto nor his friends had real prospects back in Clover. Going to Karelia was about more than helping the Soviets succeed; it was also about their own survival.

During this time, Risto's melancholy ebbed and flowed. He caught Lydia staring at him while they were atop the Empire State building. Instead of admiring the sights, Risto thought of the enormous wealth the city represented and the enormous poverty hidden within it. As Lydia watched him, her lips seemed softened by a tender smile. Although he was sure he imagined that, he still filed it away.

The big day arrived. Nearly three hundred volunteers arrived at the docks of the Swedish American Lines. They were ready to board their ship for the long journey to Gothenburg, Sweden. Representatives of the Finnish Labor Club lined the wharf to wish the travelers well. They handed over a large red flag that was fringed with gold thread. On it, a sickle and star were embroidered with the same gold thread. Over the docks flapped the stars and stripes, but in their hands they carried the flag of the Union of Soviet Socialist Republics. This flag represented the country that would soon be their new home. Because the other volunteers quickly determined that Risto was well spoken, they asked him to accept the flag on behalf of the group. Lydia seemed pleased with the remarks he made.

In addition to the flag, they were handed a large box of mail to deliver to those already in Karelia from previous Technical Aid trips. Since the group already in Karelia numbered several thousand, the box contained quite a large packet of letters and packages.

All were on board. The ocean liner sounded its loud whistle. The Karelian-bound lined the outer decks. They let loose a series of loud cheers. On the wharf, the members of the Finnish Labor Club waved red handkerchiefs. Slowly the steamer backed away from the dock. The cheers continued but slowly grew softer. Risto watched the skyline of Manhattan recede. Until this moment, he had never been away from the Midwest. Now he was about to cross an ocean. But Risto knew he was journeying to a new Russia and to a world being built for the benefit of all. The ship picked up a little speed as it headed out of New York's Harbor.

Off to the right were Ellis Island and the Statue of Liberty. Risto stood at the rail watching the tall green lady, her arm holding aloft the light of freedom, as she fell behind them. He and the other volunteers steamed to a new destiny.

Risto found the ocean fascinating. He liked to walk the promenade deck, intrigued by the way the teak deck seemed to rise and fall with the waves of the sea, as though nothing beneath his feet could be firm. He was energized by the way the vastness of the north Atlantic horizon merged with the summer sky. It prompted daydreams of the possibilities ahead. On the first few days out of New York, Charlie and Art seldom ventured far from the tiny room that the three shared. It was deep in the bowels of the ship's third class. While Risto was certain that crisp air would have fortified their spirits, they preferred to damn their seasick-sorry selves to the privacy of the cabin.

Perhaps their maladies were fortuitous. Unlike Risto's pals, Lydia suffered no such illness. She too liked to promenade, and occasionally walked with Risto. By talking above the rush of the sea, he discovered how different each was from the other. Until this trip, Risto never considered his life restricted. No one around Clover, especially the Finnish farmers, had much money. To him, the linens on the bed and the food in the third class dining room were small luxuries. Lydia rated things differently and expressed her disappointments in many items. This only raised Risto's view of her worldliness and value, similar to the way she became more desirable when she didn't respond quickly to his wit.

Alone at night, in the quiet of his bunk, he would think of Lydia and what they might do in privacy. Annoyingly, her face would merge with that of Pauline, and that would always jerk him back into reality. He would lie in bed frustrated. He had no desire to reflect on Pauline. Whether in daily life or nighttime fantasies, he focused on the future. What was past was gone. It couldn't be retrieved. There was no merit in nostalgia. Lydia represented the prize ahead. She was a future he could grab with both hands and make the most of. He never wondered what Art or Charlie might be contemplating in their bunks. Maybe they just fell asleep, eager for an escape from their seasickness. No one ever mentioned any furtive rustlings heard.

As they neared England and their short stop there, either the seas calmed or the recruits grew more accustomed to life on water. In any case, Charlie and Art were in good spirits when they joined Risto and Lydia on deck as the ship steamed through the English Channel on its final days before reaching the North Sea and Gothenburg, Sweden.

"Ain't it amazing," said Art. "There's England on one side and France on the other. Never thought I'd see this."

"But when you were tramping across America, you saw so much of the country," said Lydia. "Wasn't that amazing too?"

Art seemed disturbed by the question. "I saw a lot of shit, that's what I saw. Sorry about the language Lydia, but riding the rails wasn't romantic. There were some good people, quick to offer a helping hand or hire you for a job that maybe didn't need doing, all to make sure you had a hot meal in your stomach or a haymow to shelter you on a rainy night. But you see a lot of bad people. They got theirs, whatever that may be, and they don't care what you got or don't got. Then there's men who want to be your friends in a way you don't want no friend. And cops who just like to hurt people." Art trailed off.

Charlie jumped in, "Forget about all that. Now, we're doing something good. You and Risto and me. We're like the Three Musketeers." Risto figured Charlie had seen some movie, because he knew his pal never read the novel.

Lydia laughed. It was like a clear bell that made England and France seem shinier. Charlie beamed at making her laugh.

On this boatload of Karelian Technical Aid emigrants, Paavo Karvala was the leader. As the ship approached Gothenburg, he pulled everyone into the dining salon between lunch and supper. Karvala was a short, wiry man in his forties who had remained to himself during much of the voyage. But when he spoke, he grew in stature. Clearly, he believed in what they were doing, and the volunteers recognized the reality ahead. The man impressed Risto.

"We're almost there," he said. "Soon, in Leningrad, we will be true comrades. We will be working together to support a common goal. All of us left a lot behind in the States. There's family and friends. Some of us had good jobs. Others of us knew hard times all too well. But now we've left that behind to face Karelia—an untamed wilderness. It has beautiful timber ready to help build a stronger Soviet, but it needs someone to lumber it. It has vast lakes and rivers teeming with fish, but it needs someone to catch them. It begs for labor to tap into its riches, and our hands are the hands that will make the difference. What we do in the days and months ahead will not just benefit you or me, but it will help all of the Soviets. We will prove to the world that there is a better way than capitalism."

Risto reveled in the power of this mission. At home, he felt Ma and Pa constantly judged him, wondering why he had survived, when his two brothers had died. They never suggested it, but he often thought they considered him the wrong one to live. Well, he would show them that there was a reason he beat the odds.

Paavo explained the logistics ahead. "This ship goes as far as Gothenburg. There it will pick up passengers for a return trip to New York and Montreal. That's its regular run. We booked a smaller ship to take us to Leningrad, but there's not room for all of us. So I need some of you to stay behind for a week, travel to Stockholm and take a different ship. If anyone's interested, let me know."

Eager to have dry land under them and to undertake a new adventure, Art, Charlie and Risto all volunteered for the later boat. Paavo entrusted

Risto with the packet of tickets and documents. Risto's pleasure at being picked as the leader grew when he learned that Lydia would also wait for the second ship. All of them would take the train across Sweden to Stockholm. That evening they stayed at a hotel that serviced passengers of the Swedish American Line, and when they went down for supper in the dining room, they encountered a group of Americans (all of them earlier volunteers for Karelian Technical Aid) who were sailing home the next morning. The eight men, all similar in age, not one older than twenty-five, looked a little thin and weather-beaten. But eating and drinking a lot of beer put them in excellent spirits.

"Why go back to America?" Risto wanted to know.

"Oh, you'll find out soon enough," said one of the men.

"But there's no work and no hope in America," persisted Risto. "And you were on the front lines making Communism work."

Three of the diners laughed out aloud. One even spit out beer in astonishment. The person who first spoke continued. "I was like you once. I wanted to believe. But they don't really want us, or appreciate what we could do. Don't think of Karelians as real Finns. And if you don't learn Karelian, they aren't about to speak Finn to you. And believe me it's no worker's paradise. Things are even tougher in the Soviet than back in the States. They don't know what they're doing, and they just waste your good work. You'll see."

Lydia whispered to her three friends, "Let's get out of here. We don't want to be like them"

But the next morning when they boarded the train to Stockholm, Risto felt shattered. He never considered the possibility that there wouldn't be a pot of gold at the end of this traveling rainbow. All his years growing up, he listened to Pa talk about political systems and why Communism was the best. When a Finn from Minnesota named Gus Hall came through town a year earlier organizing the movement, Risto found the fellow invigorating. That man had an answer to every question or objection that anyone raised. Risto left the rally convinced that the Russians and all of the Soviet Republics were the vanguard of the future. They just needed time. The working men on the front lines in Russia were the noble ones to respect, not rich capitalists in Chicago or New York.

'What are you thinking?" Lydia asked. He didn't answer, not knowing what he would say. Looking out the window, he noticed the fences bordering the fields on either side of the train tracks. Back in Wisconsin, they would be barbed wire, but here they were entirely of wood. Otherwise the lakes, forests and fields didn't seem all that different from home. But he still felt homesick. There was no way he could even acknowledge the question that Lydia asked. How could he admit that he was questioning his reason for being here? Too late to turn back, he had no choice but to travel forward.

In Stockholm, his worries disappeared. Lydia's many contacts resulted in dances to attend, youth meetings at which to speak and be admired and so many sights to see. The city was filled with young idealists ready to have fun. The elegant hotels along the waterfront were beautiful, and the old section of town called Gamla Stan, just past the Royal Palace, was Risto's first introduction to the weight of history. He marveled at buildings hundreds of years old. In Clover, where the forest hadn't been cleared until the 1880s, nothing was over fifty years old. Even in New York, which Risto knew was founded in the 1600s, everything seemed up-to-date. Here in Stockholm, he wanted to linger on the old cobblestone streets. But Art and Charlie were always quick to search out the next hot spot.

Their hotel wasn't one of the elegant ones facing the waterfront. Rather it was located up a side street. Their rooms were on the sixth floor of a building that already seemed tired. While Risto felt no qualms when their sightseeing group boarded elevators to travel to the 102nd floor of the Empire State Building, in this worn building he said a silent prayer each time they packed into the small compartment. After the second day when the elevator stalled for a few minutes between floors, he claimed a need for exercise. From that moment forward, he always took the stairs up and down six flights.

The days passed quickly. Soon it was their final evening in Stockholm. In her room, Lydia held a party for everyone who would travel to Leningrad in the morning. That list quickly expanded to include all the friends made over the past few days. Her room was quite large, faced the front of the building and sported a small balcony overlooking the narrow street below.

Several guests brought bottles of vodka. Other carried in smoked herring and favorite Swedish dishes. A bottle of aquavit appeared. Soon a Swedish smorgasbord and bar were in full swing. The radio was turned up; people began dancing. Amid the hubbub, Charlie raised his hand and shouted, "To the USSR!" He raised his shot of vodka and downed it. The crowd cheered. One of the girls said to Lydia, "Get the flag.' Lydia was responsible for the large red banner given by the Finnish Labor Organization in New York.

Soon it was pulled out of its storage box, and several partygoers were parading about the room. Charlie had a bright idea, "Let's hang it from the balcony."

Before Lydia could say no, the banner was draped over the balcony and securely tied to the railing. It fluttered in the light breeze. Although it was already nine o'clock in the evening, it was also June and Stockholm was far north. The sun still shone brightly. The group crowded around the window and began to sing the "Internationale." Most didn't seem to know the words or even much of the tune, and from those who did, it emerged as a babbled mixture of Swedish, Finnish and English lyrics.

"Hey, look down there," shouted Art. On the narrow street below, a small crowd was forming. As the revelers stared down, passersby pointed up toward the window. They were clearly agitated.

"What's going on?" Risto wondered.

Two pedestrians appeared, pulling along a police officer from around the corner. The cop looked up at their window, and then headed straight to the front door of the hotel. Someone turned off the radio in the room, and they all quieted down. The heavy machinery of the elevator turned across the hall. The elevator doors dinged. Then a knock on the door.

Outside in the hall, a small crowd pushed a police offer forward. He began to speak in Swedish, which few of the recruits knew. One of the locals stepped forward to translate.

"He says you can't fly a Soviet flag in Stockholm. He says you must it take it down so he can confiscate it."

"But he can't do that," Lydia said. "We have to take it to Leningrad."

After more back and forth with Lydia showing off both her Swedish and her persuasive charms, the policeman finally smiled. The Swedish-speaking guests also smiled. The millers-about frowned. Lydia reported to the rest, "He says we can keep the flag, but only if we take it down now."

The party was over. The flag was stowed away. Guests left quickly, along with any bottle not already emptied. Everything quieted quickly. Risto was among the last to leave. The room he shared with Art and Charlie was just down the hall. As he walked out the door, he turned back planning to say one final goodnight to Lydia. That's when he saw Lydia and Charlie kissing. They were in an embrace that didn't seem like a first time kiss. Risto said nothing at that moment, or a few minutes later, when Charlie returned to their hotel room.

The next day they all traveled to the pier to catch the overnight ferry to Leningrad. For a few minutes it seemed as though they might miss their boat. An unexpected dockworkers strike had started overnight. The police lined the docks but they allowed paying passengers through. A small brass band from the local Communist club had planned a farewell concert on the dock, but the musicians weren't allowed to pass. Instead they set up an impromptu concert among the strikers. Tubas and trumpets seemed half hidden behind the strikers' placards. All in all, as the music began and the Karelian Technical Aid volunteers pressed through the strikers, carrying their own luggage to the boat, it became more festive than their departure from New York or from Clover.

On the Baltic Sea voyage, Risto reflected on the scene in Lydia's room. Were Charlie and Lydia romantic? When did that happen? A girl as serious as Lydia shouldn't have any interest in a goofball like Charlie, and Risto didn't like the possibility that she might. She would end up hurting Charlie. Things felt unsettled. Risto didn't know what would happen when they reached Leningrad. The recruiters promised that he and his friends would be assigned to the same village, but since the brief conversation with those returning home, Risto worried that he too eagerly believed everything promised.

In the morning, the sun, already high in the sky, sharply illuminated the waters of the Baltic Sea and Leningrad in the distance. The island of Kronstadt, the entry to the city, lay ahead. At last, they were in the Soviet Union. Their mission was about to start. Risto determined to put aside his worries about promises and his memories about his final night in Clover. This morning, he was a Communist pioneer, ready to do his best for mankind. It was a new world.

Arriving in Leningrad reminded Risto of *Juhannus*, the traditional midsummer night festival that the Finns in Wisconsin celebrated. On the longest day of the year, everyone's spirits were high. Neighbors took breaks from the haying to party on beer and cake. With ice and rock salt stowed in the ice cream makers, the men took turns at churning pints of fresh cream into frozen custard studded with wild berries. Little boys and girls ran around the house, playing childish games that were so important to win. Wives clustered to gossip. All was done in an atmosphere of goodwill and hope. Even after the sun set and the men smoked their final cigars, Risto never felt a desire to go to bed. It was his favorite day of the year.

Reaching Leningrad was like that. The city teemed with possibilities. He, Art and Charlie—along with the other Clover boys, like Essa-Pekka, Otto, Samuel, Misha, Kai, Heikki, Eric and John—Finnish names and American names—were now all in Russia. After clearing customs, Lydia shouted to the whole gang of them. "Follow me to the cafeteria. All the locals insist the only way to start your Russian life is with a bowl of *ukha*. They promise me it's the best thing one can possibly eat in Russia."

The boys eagerly followed Lydia to the immense cafeteria filled with delightful aromas. Lydia spoke Russian to order bowls of *ukha* for each of them. The rich aromas of the fish broth filled Risto's nostrils, and his stomach growled. Charlie heard the rumblings and playfully punched Risto in the arm. Big chunks of bream, cubes of potatoes and circles of green leek floated in the bowl. Risto tasted his first Russian dish. It was wonderful. By god, it was the best soup he had ever had. If this defined Russia, why had he waited so long to come?

"We need to see everything that's beautiful in the city before we leave for Karelia," Lydia exclaimed. "I made a long list before we left New York. I want to see so much: The Hermitage. The Winter Palace. St. Isaacs. Oh, and we need to find the Smolnin district where the peasants and Lenin planned the Revolution."

The setting was unlike anything Risto had ever experienced. Admittedly, the skyscrapers of Manhattan were impressive and the old stone buildings of Stockholm streaked with history. But now he was in the center of a universe that mattered—in a galaxy of the future—and he and all his Clover friends would be the stars helping to light the way.

Back in Clover, Risto could never have imagined that he and his friends would willingly walk palace halls for hours to stare at fussy old paintings. Names like Titian and Raphael were just topics in dusty books that bored him; art meant little more than the litho covers to *Colliers Magazine*. But in Leningrad he loved to watch the way Lydia pondered the intricacies of a painting. He laughed silently at the silly comments that

Charlie would make, especially when Lydia awarded his naive utterances with respect.

There was one dark spot. He overheard a guide at the Hermitage telling an American tourist that the government supposedly sold twenty-one of the museum's most important paintings to Andrew Mellon. According to rumor, the masterpieces were on their way to Washington, DC. Even though the art in question was no longer on display, Risto dismissed the story as ridiculous. The thought of an American plutocrat stealing the country's patrimony was too depressing, and he chose not to repeat what he heard, certain that it was a lie manufactured by capitalists.

One day, the three guys struck out on their own, leaving Lydia behind even though she was the only one of the four who spoke Russian. Risto, however, was determined to learn. The day was hot and they found an ice cream vendor who willingly sold them cones for their American dollars and returned several kopecks in change. Summer produce filled other stands at the street market, and Art decided to buy some fresh berries. Since the merchant spoke neither Finnish nor English, bargaining proved a challenge. But through pointing and smiling, they made clear what they wanted to buy. The smiling merchant prepared the berries. As their leader, Risto collected all of the coins from his friends and held them out for the merchant to pick out what was needed. But the merchant seeing their coins pulled back the berries. He waved his hand to signal the deal was off. Not knowing what went wrong, the boys only laughed. The day was too beautiful to worry about any misunderstandings.

That evening they returned to the hotel where the volunteers were boarding, and they recounted their day to Lydia. She asked to see their coins, and then laughed. "What you have is practically worthless. No wonder the berry man turned you away. Where did you even get those coins?"

"We bought some ice cream with our dollars, and this was our change," Charlie said.

"Don't do that again," Lydia counseled. "Someone took advantage of you. An American dollar goes very far here. You should use them only in a Torgsin store, which requires hard currency and never takes Russian rubles. You'll find they're the only place that sells many necessities. Keep your dollars for such stores."

Again, Risto felt a twinge like when he overheard the Hermitage guide gossip about the missing paintings. Why wouldn't Russian authorities let their own people buy the best? Why have special stores for foreigners? He would bring that question up with Paavo at the upcoming general meeting. But the next night, there was no opportunity for any such questions. Paavo Karvala took the stage at a small hall nearby and briefed the volunteers.

"Here's the general plan," he told them. "We do this with each new contingent of volunteers. We'll talk to you individually to identify your special skills and aptitude, since we want to deploy you in the best possible way. We've talked to the officials in the Soviet Karelo-Finland Republic. We have identified their most pressing needs and will seek to assign you in ways that best meet them. Many of you brought with you personal property connected to your trades or skills. We will consider such assets when we make our assignments. But we will also be realistic and sensible. Supporting the common good and seeking to help each of us make the biggest contribution possible will guide every decision.

"In three days, we will go by train to Petrozavodsk. For those who haven't been paying attention to my talks, that's the capital of the Karelian Republic. But don't expect a Washington or New York. Petrozavodsk is still very much a frontier town. But the region's real challenges aren't in the capital. They're in the small town and villages dotting the forest north of the city. Most of you, especially those without special skills or education, will be asked to work in the lumber camps."

Paavo's approach seemed sensible. Risto always expected a posting in the woods. His Pa talked about working in the lumber camps of northern Wisconsin and Risto felt he knew what to expect. Also, Risto frequently helped clear woods on their back acres. He had experience in tree felling and sawing. Both Charlie and Art worked in the woods before, so Paavo would probably keep them together—the three musketeers of the woods. When the meeting ended, Lydia asked the boys where they hoped to be posted. Risto immediately answered for his friends. "In the woods."

Charlie squirmed a bit and said, "I don't know. Lydia, where do you expect to be?"

"They will ask me to remain in Petrozavodsk to teach. This was arranged before we left New York. Since I speak English, Russian, Swedish and Finnish, I can help manage the overall Technical Aid resources."

"Then I hope I'll stay in the capital as well," proclaimed Charlie.

"Somebody has a girlfriend," teased Art.

Risto was annoyed. "Don't be daft. We all signed up together and we agreed it would be in the woods. Charlie can travel into town whenever he wants, but we work where the need is."

"Risto, you're so certain of yourself, but how did you get that way?" asked Lydia. "Where did you get that fervor? Are you running away from something?"

Risto could have answered that in so many different ways. Pa and Ma's life—the way everything they did was consumed by that handful of cows, swine and chickens they called a farm—was simply numb-inducing boredom. Who wouldn't run from that, and who wouldn't flee a nation mired in a Depression that was sucking all hope from everyone he knew? Staying in Wisconsin would have forced him to define his future. It was simpler to hand that mission over to Karelian Technical Aid. And yet there were things he regretted leaving behind. His parents loved him, and he in turn loved them. And there were many pretty girls in Clover. He'd miss them. He surprised himself that he even missed Pauline Newmann.

He looked at Lydia. She was really quite lovely and so strong, not at all the right match for a guy like Charlie. She was just humoring Charlie by letting him moon over her. And why had she left New York?

"I could ask you the same thing," Risto said to Lydia. "Are you running away from something?"

"Not at all. I'm racing toward making a difference. I studied both Russian and Finnish for the last two years because I knew the region needed someone like me. When you grow up in New York, you see the way people are oppressed. Why accept life as it is when you can make it better? To do that, I had to jump in and do what it takes. Maybe someday I will go back to New York, but while I'm here, I intend to give it my all."

Risto liked what Lydia said. He too might stay only a few years. Someday, he could go back to Clover and to his family, but for now he had a mission to complete.

The train trip to Petrozavodsk was just a hundred miles or so, but in other ways it was Risto's longest journey. Traveling from Clover to New York moved him across the only nation he knew. The Swedish jaunt seemed a holiday. Now, in the flat, marshy lands north of Leningrad, he headed to a life he chose. As in Sweden, the Karelian fences along the way were made of wood, but the bridges were rockier, the towns sparser and the sense of being foreign far greater. He was no longer home.

Petrozavodsk wasn't a large city, maybe twenty thousand people at most. Admittedly, that was far larger than Clover, but the place seemed less sophisticated. The buildings were mostly of unpainted wood, seldom more than one story high. The streets were dusty and unpaved. Having studied the region in advance, Lydia informed them that before the fall of the late Czar, many liberal political exiles fled to this far northern town. They made little progress in creating a city. A few sawmills and brickworks were all that suggested this town was a center of industry.

"This is the capital of a Republic?" mocked Art. Risto recalled how Art had tramped across most of the western United States. Unlike Risto, he had experienced many cities.

"Don't look so bad," said Charlie.

When they got off the train, guides from previous volunteer groups divided the newly arrived, and they led each subgroup to their assigned ramshackle apartment building. Along with five others from the Clover contingent, Risto, Art and Charlie were crammed into a single room apartment.

"Don't worry," said the guide. His Finnish was poor, and Risto wondered why he didn't speak in English. "Paavo says you will only be here for a few days. You're heading toward the town of Kem to work in the woods. Welcome to Petrozavodsk and the Soviet Republic of Karelia."

In nearly twenty years of living, Risto never felt as cold as the first winter days he encountered in Karelia. Nothing compared to it, not the time he fell through the ice when skating on the Niemenen pond and not the January afternoon when he was eager to get home from school but took a wrong turn when taking a shortcut through the woods. That day he didn't find his way home until dark, but his Ma was waiting with hot chocolate in a warm kitchen. Karelia was an unforgiving place, and the camp west of Kem offered no maternal elements.

When the recruits arrived at the camp's site back in the heat of late June, nothing existed. Only trees lined the steep bankside to the lake. A sputtering motorboat delivered some two dozen of them to the designated spot on Upper Kjuto Lake. The journey took hours across a series of three lakes to reach that point, and the guys were eager to disembark. During the entire boat ride, Risto saw no sign of a working forestry. Evergreens stretched endlessly to the flat horizon. Although the spires of the trees somehow hinted at a more impressive landscape, the land was remarkably flat, more likely to dip into a bog than to rise into a hill. Clear blue skies were unmarred by any distant smoke of civilization. Except for the splash of the waves, the drone of the boat's motor and the occasional call of a water bird, all was silent. Even the recruits said nothing, not sure of what waited at the end of the trip. In the sunlight of the long days of June, the expanse of green trees and the blue, nearly black, water seemed idyllic. But even in those first hours, Risto worried about the long nights of winter ahead. The lakeside location for the new lumber camp appeared chosen for it high banks, which were visible from some distance. They knew where the boat was headed long before the craft reached wading distance.

Jumping out of the boat on arrival, Risto and the others were happy. The suspense was over. Charlie started to hoot and holler. Everyone eagerly became stevedores to unload the camp supplies: saws, mallets, hammers, nails and a pot-bellied stove. Pounds and pounds of initial provisions for their new beachhead. In the direct summer sun, the work made them sweat, and their perspiration attracted swarms of mosquitos. Charlie voiced the crazy idea to go skinny-dipping. Before long, all the guys stripped and jumped into the cold waters. The local Karelian boat pilot looked at them as though they were fools, but the boys felt alive. It was too soon for these Americans to wonder what would happen to them in this distant wilderness, separated from home, country and even women.

Paavo Karvala stood on shore watching his younger recruits cavort. The older man, having crafted the longer-term plan for the camp, would establish the daily rules and routines. But at that moment, he didn't stop the younger men from their play nor did he say anything; Risto, however, sensed some disapproval. He walked out of the lake, grabbed his shirt to wipe off the water, pulled on his pants and stepped over to Paavo. He wasn't sure he cared much for this person. The fellow seemed unfriendly and lacking in passion. But he was the boss. "So where do we start?" Risto asked.

Paavo looked at Risto appraisingly. "We'll let your pals splash around. Not much still possible today, so maybe a little fun helps everyone gets a good night's sleep. In the morning, we start cutting trees and building shelter. Summers don't last long up here," he said.

"So we'll start with the sauna?" said Risto. Back in Wisconsin, traditionally every Finn first built a sauna on their homestead. The bathhouse was essential to the Finnish way of life. Building the sauna first was also practical. Because the building was small, it could be built quickly. Until larger buildings were in place, it provided initial shelter. Besides, Finns favored building many small, specialized buildings. Every Finnish farm was a miniature village with a multitude of outbuildings.

"Don't be foolish," said Paavo. Like Lydia, he had grown up in metropolitan New York and didn't concern himself with rural traditions. "We need a sleeping hall first. There's only one iron stove in our shipments. We need to plan to bunk together in a single dorm."

Risto looked down at the lads in the water: Olli-Pekka and Eric, Kai and Otto, and all the rest, all of them friends after the long voyage from New York. They were all variations of Risto. Most were in their late teens or early twenties, unmarried farm boys and first-generation American. They were motivated as much by adventure as by idealism. Paavo's criteria on assigning roles hadn't been shared with the volunteers. Still anyone could discern that married couples were usually assigned to city jobs or at least placed in the larger villages. Perhaps that made sense. Being older, such volunteers usually had more established trades useful to larger communities. The few single women, like Lydia, were all given assignments in Petrozavodsk. That left the rest of the recruits—the strong Midwestern farm boys with no attachments—sleeping on the forested banks of cold lakes, close to the stars but distant from city lights.

Charlie came running up from the shore. He had no concern about being naked nor did he wonder what Risto and Paavo were discussing. "What's for supper?" he asked.

"Ham and beans tonight," said Paavo. "But tomorrow some of you boys have to go fishing, and others out in the wood to gather berries. We need to live off more than just the supplies we brought in."

In the heat of June, it seemed a fun adventure. These farm boys knew the basics of carpentry from building on their parents' homesteaded farms. They weren't deterred by the task ahead. How hard could it be to build a couple of cabins, stock up on local provisions and lumberjack the giant pines?

Back in the States, with the right tools and surrounded by a modern world, it might have been easy. There were merchants and trains, tradesmen and bankers. By God, you could order almost anything from Sears and Roebuck. But in Karelia they had almost nothing. A few days after their initial arrival, the motorboat returned. It tugged along two barges low in the water, loaded high with provisions. The delivery included several workhorses, steel runners to build timber sledges, high-quality handsaws, clothing and stocks of food. By then, the dormitory, built of logs and notched in the Finnish way, was nearing completion. Risto once read that the Finns in the initial Swedish colony of the Delaware Valley were the settlers who introduced the log cabin to America. While he was proud of anything any Finn had done, Risto couldn't help but be dejected when he looked at his group's first building. The roofline seemed a bit lopsided and the gaps between the logs were poorly caulked. They would have to fix that before winter, or their one pot-bellied stove wouldn't have a chance at keeping them warm.

Now months later in December, Risto realized that it required more than caulking and a cast iron stove to keep everyone warm. He was glad they finally had a sauna. At least once a week, they felt warm from the rush of hot steam as water was splashed on super-heated rocks. It was so much better than this constant draft. As it was, months had passed before Paavo finally decided a sauna was required. Maybe it was to fight the lice, although he had heard Paavo had a scheme to use the sauna's steam to shape saplings into some kind of tool for the spring transport.

Art sidled up to Risto one evening. It was only five o'clock, but it had been dark for hours. "I hate it here."

"Why?" Risto asked.

"I ain't never been in one place so long before. And the work is hard, the food is awful and I ain't never warm." Art replied.

"We knew it would be tough. You gotta remember what we're here for. We're trying to improve things."

"These Karelians don't want improving. They don't even want us here. Won't speak proper Finnish even though they know how."

Risto wanted to argue the point, but he was doomed to lose. He remembered earlier in the fall when they took the motorboat into Kem, the nearest town of any size. Situated at the end of the series of three lakes and north of Petrozavodsk, the town wasn't a very large place, but because of the number of Karelian Technical Aid volunteers in the surrounding forests, it did have one store for people with foreign currency. Risto was shocked by the nasty looks from locals when he shopped in that store. But that trip had its fun moments. Thanks to a few local Karelians who had moved into camp in late summer, Risto had picked up a bit of the local dialect. It wasn't all that different from Finnish. Now in Kem, with women around, he put his imperfect Karelian to the test.

One thing was familiar. Like any Finn, the locals kept their emotions close to the vest. But Risto knew how to break through that. With a bottle of good vodka from the Torgsin store, his smattering of Karelian and a quick smile, he made the rounds at a Saturday night party and managed to dance with more than a few cute Karelian girls. One woman, Irina Rovio, was particularly special. She studied English, and wanted to practice it with Risto. She was a passionate believer in the Party and the future of Karelia; her second cousin was Kustaa Rovio, one of the Karelian leaders who first organized the Karelian Technical Aid. Naturally, Risto made sure Irina realized how much he had given up to help her (and her cousin's) dreams come true.

He looked forward to his next visit in Kem, because he was pretty certain Irina would be looking for him. Risto wasn't going to be like Charlie, who always mooned over the letters he wrote to and received from Lydia. Risto read most of those of notes, whether Charlie offered them or not. Risto was pretty sure Lydia thought of Charlie as a little brother, and he would never be so foolish as to pin his hopes on some cold New Yorker. A pretty local girl with connections sounded better. Unfortunately, with the lakes frozen, there was no way to return to Kem until after the spring thaw. But Risto could wait.

And Risto could adapt. He fell into the rhythms of the short, dark days of winter. Each morning, the work crews bundled up, marched through snow to reach the day's targeted trees and saw them down. Pairs of workers, with each on either side of a cross saw, cut through the wood. There was something enormously satisfying in that final crack as the tree, weakened by an incised cut, toppled from its own weight.

But Risto proved imperfect at foretelling his future. Unexpectedly, Paavo moved him to another assignment in January. Risto suspected Paavo didn't like any two workers becoming overly comfortable in a routine. In the woods, there was a lot of time to talk and plot. Not that people did. The work was too strenuous, and silence better supported success. But Paavo never worked in the woods himself, so how would he know? Besides Risto suspected Paavo didn't like him, even though Risto was always asking him questions and trying to suggest better ways to do things.

"We should caulk the logs on the sleeping shack."

"Why don't we plan to build a road to Kem?

"You should build your own office for the camp."

Paavo ignored Risto's recommendations, but he did reassign Risto again, this time to the transport team. Each night after the camp went to bed, he and Olli-Pekka took a sledge equipped with a large container and heavy hand pump to the frozen lake. They cut a hole through the ice and pumped near-freezing water into the sledge's container, used the horses to drag the sledge into the woods and then worked their way back to the camp flooding water over the flattened path. The resulting sheet of ice created a frozen road that eased moving logs during daylight. Each night, they reconstructed this icy road, because each day the sledges of logs pulled by the horses hammered the ice road apart, and the sun—as weak as it might be for its few hours of shining—would further destroy it.

Day by day, the log piles on the lake's edge grew larger. In spring when the ice cracked and broke, the logs would be ready to be tumbled into the water, tied and floated through the lakes to Kem's sawmills.

Risto hated ice road duty. While Art and he had been a great lumberjacking pair, Risto had no talents for the ice patrol, as simple as it was. With Art, he could drop a tree faster than any other duo in the camp. Their trees always landed exactly where intended. Risto was also annoyed to work all night and sleep during the day, while Art got to tackle trees with a new partner. What Risto disliked most of all was how the reassignment affected Art. His old friend grew more bitter. Each day he became more committed to return to the States. Risto, having no such urge to return, looked forward to the spring, seeing Irina in Kem and making sense of Karelia.

Risto saw Irina sooner than expected. After less than a month on icing duty, Risto had a new assignment. "We're running out of hay for the horses," Paavo said. "I want you and Charlie to take a couple of horses to a large marsh about halfway between here and Kem. Some folks from the town will meet you there. They'll help you load some of their swamp grass harvested last fall."

"Why do you keep giving me these crappy jobs?" asked Risto. "Why don't you let me stick with what I'm good at?"

Paavo looked at him and just smiled. "You better dress warm. It's a long trip, but the horses need the fodder."

Risto put on a double set of long underwear and an extra sweater before bundling up in his normal winter gear. Charlie and he had been to the haying area in the late fall before the first snows. He knew several larges piles of dried grass were stored for later pickup, but he also recalled that site was a hard trip even without feet of snow impeding the way. Now, in January, there would be wolves out and they would be hungry.

The two started at the first hints of dawn. They wanted to reach the marshes by early afternoon, before the light started waning. Overall, the trip would take three days: one day to the site, another day to load the sledges with hay and a third to return. As they started out, Charlie kept up a steady banter for the first few hours. He recounted the latest gossip received in Lydia's most recent letter. But when the sun reached its low peak, both men worried about the distance still to trek. The garrulous Charlie quieted down. The horses seemed wary. They didn't know where they were headed, and the woods seemed too quiet.

"Did you do something to Paavo?" asked Charlie.

"What do you mean?"

"You keep getting the shit jobs. And Art and I get pulled into them, because Paavo knows we're friends."

Risto pondered that. He tried to show respect to the group leader, but maybe the guy thought Risto represented competition. After all, Risto was well liked and knew how to talk in public. He was the kind of person who should be team leader.

"What was that?" asked Charlie. "Did you see it?" Risto only saw the long afternoon shadows near the forest's edge. Their destination was the rough cabin on the marsh's edge and it couldn't be much further. He wasn't letting Charlie spook him.

"See it. There's something in the woods. We're being followed."

Risto was about to say, "We're almost there." Then he heard the unmistakable howl of a wolf. The horses heard it too. They held a fevered look in their eyes, and quickened their pace. Risto saw a dashing shadow between the trees. He looked over to Charlie. Charlie seemed ready to whip the horse into moving faster.

"Don't," warned Risto. "You could overturn the sledge. The wolves won't attack if we keep moving. There're two of us and the horses. They'll be wary."

"Why didn't Paavo give us a gun?"

"I don't know."

The horses trudged forward, their heavy hooves breaking through the icy top crust of the deep snow. The gloaming skies made the shadows deeper. It was impossible to tell whether glimpses of movement represented a slight breeze or the signs of an approaching wolf. Then it was clear. Wolves. Three stood in front of their sledge. The animals' mouths were open, their tongues hanging out. The sun was dropping fast. The moon had not yet risen. Risto thought he could see the wood-shingled roof of the marsh cabin a few hundred yards ahead. They just had to get through the wolves.

A shot rang out.

The wolves scattered.

Two people came from the direction of the cabin. Both held guns and were dressed in the rough winter clothing of native Karelians. One pointed a gun into the air and fired another warning shot, even though the wolves were already out of sight.

One of them laughed. A woman's laugh.

"You boys getting in trouble?" she asked in heavily accented English. It was Irina Rovio. She was one of the locals Paavo had arranged to help Charlie and Risto gather the hay. Risto decided the journey might have some rewards to compensate for its risks.

Winter came and went. With the warmer days of spring, the thick lake ice rotted and the waters of Kjuto Lake reappeared. As clear water flowed again, energy in the lumber camp grew more restive. The rough overland road to Kem started during the previous fall could now be finished. But the narrow road being carved through the woods was not planned for transporting logs. The timber felled during the winter would be shipped to Kem utilizing the trio of Kjuto Lakes as a water highway.

Back in December, when Paavo finally allowed the men to build the sauna, it wasn't for cleanliness. While the men were permitted to use it for their steam baths on Saturdays, the rest of the week the men dragged saplings into the sauna. Softened by steam, the wood could be wrapped around stumps, and once twisted, the coiled saplings were moved to the cold water of the lake to stay supple. Now in spring these wooden loops were being used to link the logs into giant booms, which would be towed in series by the small steamboat through the chain of lakes. Even in the roughest of lake waves, the sapling ties would stay strong and yet, when needed, severed by one quick slash of an ax.

Reassigned once more by Paavo, Risto joined Art on log boom duty. Many trips across the Kjuto lake chain and up the Kem river were required to convey the harvest of logs. The transport was often boring and mindless. But Risto soon learned not to let down his guard. A storm could suddenly appear on the horizon, whip the lakes into massive swells and threaten to break up the giant log rafts. In such waters, the tugboat provided little control over its trailing train of wood. With their hooks and poles, Risto and the other men on duty were hard pressed to stay alive. Slipping and falling between the logs was an ever-present danger. In the water, one could as easily perish from the shifting weight of the enormous trunks as from the bone-chilling waters. Going through the narrow straits between each of the larger lakes was particularly tense, since they had such little room to maneuver.

On the final run of the season, while on the last of the three lakes, Risto spied an enormous storm looming on the horizon. The winds picked up, grew in ferocity and drove the lake into frenzied waves. The booms broke apart. The storm soon passed, but the damage was done. Hundreds of logs, representing weeks of the camp's labor, were dispersed, bobbing on the lake's surface. Prevailing winds forced them into into one large bay, where they jumbled up against the shore like a giant's game of pickup sticks.

Risto said what was obvious. "We can't abandon so much timber. We have to find a way to reassemble the boom."

It took days of corralling. Each log was wrestled back into position, and with the loss of their twisted saplings, the team needed to improvise binding. The work, done with little sleep, was made easier by the June sun that shone nearly around the clock. At any given time, the men hardly knew whether it was day or night. They only understood what was left to do, but they persevered to save the harvest, deliver the logs and finish the run.

The boys were on leave in Kem. Other loggers were also in town, mostly Karelian Technical Aid volunteers from other lumber camps in the area. The wild atmosphere reminded Risto of his father's tales of the lumbering days in Timberton, Wisconsin, where gambling, liquor and women ruled the day.

By now, the recruits had transformed into a new breed. Risto sometimes wondered what happened to the boy he had been. Back in Clover, he didn't understand how tough life could be nor did he appreciate all that he had. Now, he sometimes thought about Ma and Pa on the farm, and, occasionally, he daydreamed about Pauline. But such thoughts were fleeting. There was so much to do. Within their first year, the lumber camp grew to include the main dormitory and sauna, as well as a stable, kitchen, dining hall, storage shed, blacksmith shop and a separate manager's cabin for Paavo. The camp began to resemble a small village. The men voted to call it Sisu, using the Finnish word that described the fortitude and guts for which Finns were renowned. Compared to Kem, Sisu was tiny and all male.

In Kem, Risto was eager to show off his growing mastery of Karelian. He quickly accepted an invitation to speak at a youth association meeting. He spied Irina Rovio in the audience. As he spoke, he paid special attention to her. Afterwards, he convinced her to dance. She laughed easily, and they quite enjoyed their evening. No mention was made of how she had rescued him from the wolves. He jokingly asked her about her relation to the leader of the Karelian Republic, Kustaa Rovio.

"A distant cousin," she replied.

"Ah, you're a good person to know then," he joked.

"Knowing me won't win you any favors with him," she replied. "But I might have a few favors to give myself."

The next day she invited Risto to join her family for Sunday dinner. It was delicious, complete with a fish pie in a rich pastry and a Finnish barley flat bread. Dessert was forest berries. He ate heartily as this was his best meal since starting at the camp. He easily kept up with the family's conversation in Karelian. Neither he nor Irina spoke either Finnish or English the entire afternoon. Still, in a way he couldn't quite define, he felt the family's disapproval. This was the first time a Karelian girl invited him to meet her family. For all he knew, all fathers and all brothers acted with suspicion. After months in the confines of the lumber camp, Risto was just happy to be among men who weren't farting and belching.

A few days later, Charlie arrived in Kem, part of the first contingent to officially travel on the newly completed road. "We rode horses out, but plan to take a truck back. Next winter, we won't be so cut off," he said.

Civilization was coming to their part of Karelia. For some reason it made Risto a little sad, but also eager to do something new. So he jumped at Art and Charlie's suggestion that they use a month's leave they had coming to travel to Petrozavodsk. Risto suspected Charlie simply wanted to see Lydia again, an idea Risto himself found appealing, even though it meant leaving Irina's side.

Karelia's largest city didn't have many attractions, but it did include the Czar's House and a large circular market hall on Karl Marx Street where one could walk from shop to shop and never reach the end. Nearby was a restaurant in a former church building. People said it was the best in town. Lydia joined them for dinner on their first night in town. She looked lovely and as determined as ever. Charlie never stopped smiling, even when chewing his reindeer steak.

"Have you picked up your mail?" Lydia asked. "The Technical Aid headquarters has been holding everyone's mail all winter since there was no practical way to forward it to the camp."

Risto was ashamed. He hadn't once thought about letters. In fact, he hadn't taken the time to write to his parents in months, not since penning a short note when they first arrived in Leningrad. The next morning, he discovered Ma had sent several letters over the course of the past year. Even with no one watching, he blushed with embarrassment. In the stack, he was surprised to see another envelope. The return address said Pauline Newmann. Because there were so many, he decided to read his family notes first. He was also a little afraid of what Pauline might have written.

By the time he finished his Ma's most recent letter, he was shellshocked. Incredible as it was, he had a sister named Lempi. How was it possible that his parents could have a baby at their age? He didn't even want to imagine them engaging in sexual activities. The family announcement made him glad he escaped Wisconsin. Maybe now Ma would be happy. Risto was certain she never forgave him for surviving when his two brothers died. But why was he at fault? They all caught the same sickness. Shouldn't she be happy that he was strong enough to survive? But Ma only focused on the two children she lost. Maybe this new baby would change that. Maybe she would learn to let go of the past. And what was it like for Pa being a new father in his forties? Risto, now approaching twenty-one, knew he didn't want to be a parent at his young age and he certainly wouldn't want to be one as an old man.

He turned to the final letter in the stack, the one on creamy stationary from Pauline Newmann. He pictured her sitting at a desk in her bedroom after high school class with pen in hand, like a girl in a movie writing a fan letter to her favorite actor. He liked that image of him being a movie star.

He wondered about her return address being in Milwaukee. Had she left Clover to start college early? His hands shook slightly as he peeled back the flap on the envelope. He wasn't quite certain what to expect. Would she be upset that he hadn't already written back? But how could he? He was fulfilling his mission.

"*Dear Risto,*" Pauline wrote, "*I have debated greatly in my mind whether to ever write this letter. Yet it seems so unfair, in so many ways, to never let you know some very important truths. Please forgive me if after reading this letter, you wish I had never written it.*

"*I quite hope that you never forgot our last night in Clover. I know I never will. Just like that night with its beautiful moon, you and your spirit will always be an important part of my life. I don't regret what we did, but our time together had consequences. I became pregnant. You are a father.*

"*I can imagine how shocking it must be to read this. There you are, giving your time to a cause you believe in so strongly, so far from your home, and you learn this in a letter. Perhaps you will never return to Wisconsin, and if I knew that for certain, I might not have written this letter. But because I hope you will come home one day, I needed to let you know the truth.*

"*I did not keep our baby. Mother arranged another alternative. No one, including her, knows you are the father, and so when Mother identified a local family that wanted to adopt a child, she had no reason to imagine the complications. But the people she found were your parents. Yes, your sister Lempi is really our daughter.*

"*Your parents don't know any of this, nor do mine. I truly hope none of them ever find out. Your mother and mine arranged a clever plan so no one in Clover ever learned I was pregnant, and they all believe Lempi is your mother's natural child. May it ever be that way.*

"*But I felt it essential that you should know. Now you do.*

"*I've moved to Milwaukee, and Lempi will never be a part of my life. But for a few minutes before they took her away I saw her in all her glory. She is a beautiful little girl. She has your eyes. Russia is so far away, but I hope some day you might see the glory of those eyes for yourself.*

"I know I must let Lempi lead her own life, but I also sense I will always love her. I don't expect that your life and mine will be intertwined in any way other than sharing the knowledge of this girl we created. I won't write again, unless you ask me to. But I do request one thing: keep our daughter in your thoughts and pray for her health and happiness always.

"Yours, Pauline."

He was shocked. A baby. His. Ma and Pa living a lie, one lie that they knew and another that they didn't. None of it could ever be fixed, not that he knew what a fix might even look like. He tried to remember that night in Clover. Had there been apple blossoms? What color were Pauline's eyes? Why hadn't his parents sent a picture of Lempi? He would have to write and ask for one. That wouldn't be strange. A big brother would want to see a picture of his little sister.

Only earlier in the week in Kem, meeting Irina's parents, he imagined a life spent in Karelia, a marriage with a local girl, maybe raising a family some day in these cold woods. But now he was no longer certain. There was this girl named Lempi. Was it fair for him to roam around the world, and leave his parents to raise her?

He looked around the reading room of the Technical Aid offices. Several of the other men were reading mail from their hometowns. He was quite certain that no one received news as astounding as what he learned. But he could never share the contents of Pauline's letter with any of these men. He might joke in the Sisu camp about his parent's surprising new daughter, but he would always hold the real truth secret.

Across the room, Art opened his single piece of mail. It was a book, which Art was intently examining. Risto had never known Art to read anything, even when they were both still in school. He walked over to see why this one held his attention.

"Why did someone send you a book?" he asked.

Art held up the front. It said *Children Tramps in America* by Dr. Thomas Ferber. "I'm in it," Art said with a curious sense of modesty, "I met this professor guy once while at a train camp near Omaha and he interviewed me and the other kids in the hobo camp. I guess he was writing this book about how we're getting by on the road."

Art opened the book to an interior page and pointed to a photo, "Look, that's me. I'm in a book."

Risto read the caption, "At fifteen, Art is already one of the most hardened of the boy tramps I met." Risto looked from the photo to the real life subject in front of him, a person who seemed far harder than the innocent youth pictured in the book. He wondered about himself, how he might appear at that moment compared to his earnest giddiness on the eve of leaving America. What would this Dr. Ferber make of him? Because he was afraid he looked even harder than Art.

With the road completed between the Sisu camp and Kem, Risto found more opportunities to visit Irina and her family. The young woman was clever and smart. Between the two of them, each found a way to enhance their respective use of English and Karelian. While Risto also studied Russian, few seemed interested in speaking it.

When the Czar was deposed nearly twenty years earlier, modern views crept into the northern woods. Irina Rovio was an up-to-date Communist girl, but her family remained rooted in the traditions of Karelia and the now-closed Russian Orthdox Church. Alone, Irina and Risto debated all matters concerning the common interests of man, yet Risto soon learned to keep his views to himself when Irina's parents and three brothers were about.

Despite the need for self-censoring, it was a pleasure to be immersed in family dinners. Irina's mother was an excellent cook. Food on the family table was plentiful, if plain. Mealtimes were raucous with laughter, and Risto's Karelian quickly improved as he learned to reuse his old storytelling tricks to make Irina's mother smile and her brothers laugh.

The Sisu camp itself prospered. Paavo moved to a house in Kem. It was time to plan the site of a new camp and await the next batch of stateside volunteers. Before leaving, he asked to meet with Risto.

"I am going to ask you to take over running the camp for me," he said smiling. "I think you have the respect of the men, and understand the work."

Risto was astounded, "But you always gave me the shit jobs."

"I just wanted you to understand all the aspects of the camp, and to rotate among the men, to see how you get along. The thing is, you're a thinker. Always looking for ways to do things better. And people like you. I saw that from the first days in Leningrad. So what do you say?"

Of course, he said yes. Only twenty-one, Risto knew he would never have reached such heights so soon in Wisconsin. Charlie was overjoyed. "Hey, now you can look out for me," he said.

The cash from the camp's initial production of lumber was fed back into strengthening Sisu for the second season. Buildings were improved, better stoves were imported, and a sturdy truck made a weekly supply run into Kem. Mail arrived on a regular basis, including a once-a-month letter from Risto's Ma. Her letters obsessively detailed Lempi's young life. In a way, Risto felt he was getting to know the little girl. The last letter included a photo of the one-year-old. He could see her resemblance to him, but little of Pauline.

As for Pauline, he chose not to write back to her. His life was here in this forested corner of Russian Karelia. He was making a difference. His fellow men looked up to him. A local woman and her family welcomed him into their midst. He had found a place in life.

Art wasn't so happy. "I work harder here than I ever did back in the States. And for what? These Karelian girls won't have nothing to do with me."

Once in a while, Risto caught Art just staring at his own photo in the book by the American professor. He looked at his image so intently, as though aching to be back in that scene. Risto borrowed the book to read during one of the coldest weeks of their second winter. As harsh as the weather was outside at that moment, Risto thought it better than the dangers the book described: teenage kids jumping from rail car to rail car, evading the bull cops in the train yards, scrounging for some way to be fed, sometimes victimized by older men who had unnatural desires. The tramp life contained nothing glamorous. In Karelia, they had a cause—strengthening a country and ensuring everyone was treated fairly. Why didn't Art see that? Maybe, at times, the locals weren't that friendly. Maybe elements of life back in America were easier, but what kind of future awaited any of them in America? The rich were bleeding the country dry. There were no jobs. Everyone was out for themselves and a quick buck. His Pa had left Finland thirty years earlier to escape the tyranny of the Czar. If he had stayed and fought on his home ground, maybe Finland and Karelia would already be a better place. At some point, a person had to take a stand and work for what they believed in.

Risto was willing to take that stand, and his fervor was clear. Maybe that's why local leaders invited him to speak at meeting about the work of the Technical Aid Society. Irina too was a true believer. She read Karl Marx and Lenin. She understood what was at stake. The two were meant for each other.

Risto wasn't so sure about his friends. Art had come for the adventure, and the adventure had grown dull. Then there was Charlie, a follower and dreamer, who still longed for Lydia. Now that the Sisu camp was more or less reachable, Risto invited Lydia to visit the camp and document first hand one of the lumber camps. As the recording secretary for the Karelian Technical Aid Society, she thought it was a wonderful idea, and agreed to attend May Day celebrations. When Risto told Charlie, he thought the guy would kiss him with gratitude.

Lydia declared Sisu impressive. It helped that the weather was lovely for the beginning of May. The snow was gone, and much of the team was away from camp, guiding the timber booms through the lakes. Risto kept both Art and Charlie behind to work in the camp and to be part of the reunion. When Lydia's truck motored into the camp, its sides splattered with spring mud, she stepped out, looking lovely and purposeful. Risto was reminded of that day nearly two years earlier when they first met in Penn Station.

"The Three Musketeers welcome you back," he said. She laughed. He took her to walk the grounds, leaving Art and Charlie trailing behind. To the left was a small sawmill. While they shipped most of the felled trees to Kem, they were now sawing some into lumber for their local building needs. Sisu had become a small village: the sauna, enlarged twice since the first winter; two dormitories, now well chinked against wintry gales; a kitchen and dining hall; multiple storage sheds; stables and a machinery lean-to; a small commissary; and a large central garden plot. The growing season was short, but they had engineered a small greenhouse out of extra window panes to allow an early start on cabbages. The small seedlings would be transplanted into the main plot when the danger of frost was over. Risto was even going to give tomatoes a shot, because the boys needed the vitamin C. What he really wanted was fresh corn on the cob, but the season was far too short for that. The foursome stopped in front of a small cabin, built entirely of planed timber. Shutters were open, exposing glass-paned windows, and the door was painted a bright blue.

"This is where you'll stay," Risto said. "Charlie decided we needed to have a guest cottage. We figure we're big enough to get important guests now. But you're the first. Someday maybe you can say you were here at the beginning."

"Do you like it?" Charlie asked.

"Everything is beautiful," Lydia replied, "and a testament to the work we're doing. I am so glad I came to see it." Charlie beamed.

Since most of the men were on the lumber rafts headed to Kem, the camp's cook had plenty of time to make those left behind a tasty supper including baked cabbage rolls stuffed with ground venison and a fish pie featuring freshly caught pike. Some of the camp's last apples went into a pie. The cook was a fellow American, who felt that sometimes everyone needed a touch of the old land.

Throughout dinner, Charlie strained to tell funny stories and keep himself in front of Lydia, but she treated him like her little brother. He grew quieter as the evening wore on. She wanted to discuss local politics in the Karelian capital. Tensions were growing among the politicians. No one was quite certain what Stalin and his comrades were planning in Moscow. She talked about news from the West: of Roosevelt's actions in the United States and of the charismatic chancellor in Germany. Charlie and Art found such talk boring. In truth, Risto would rather have recounted the athletic games between Sisu and the small villages around Kem. But he could feign interest in virtually any topic. Besides he liked watching Lydia's face when she got excited. The evening ended and Lydia retired to her cottage.

Charlie moped back in the dormitory. "Go seduce her," counseled Risto with a laugh. Charlie gave him a glare and retreated to his bunk. Risto thought his own advice wasn't such a bad idea. Maybe Lydia would welcome adult company. He retrieved a bottle of vodka from his office. He walked to the guest cottage and knocked. The kerosene lamp inside was still burning. Lydia came to the door.

Risto lifted the bottle. "A nightcap?" he asked.

She smiled and motioned him in. He poured two glasses. "To the Party!" he toasted.

Lydia laughed and said, "I have to question what party you have in mind." Risto knew that his nocturnal drop-by visit was a good idea. He settled in.

Late that night, before returning to his own bunk, Risto looked through the darkness of the guest cabin to see a face peering through the window. It might have Charlie, sneaking a peek after a late night visit to the outhouse. Risto didn't give it another thought.

It was decided. The New World Finn would become part of an Old World Karelian family. Risto Makinen would marry Irina Rovio. It seemed the natural thing to do. Risto's importance was growing, not only among the Americans in the Karelian Technical Aid association, but also among members of the Communisty party in Kem and Petrovadosk. They admired his work at the Sisu camp. He charmed the brothers of Irina at every Sunday dinner. And Irina and he were both ardent believers in their duty to what Risto increasingly felt was the motherland.

Since promoting Risto to lead the Sisu lumber operations, Paavo assumed the role of his mentor. "Listen," he counseled Risto, "traditions run long and strong in this neck of the woods. I've been here since the first group of volunteers arrived in 1931. I've picked up a thing or two about customs. If you want to marry this girl, do it right. Forget that stuff concerning the equality of men and women that you hear at Party meetings. When it comes to dealing with Irina's dad, Oskar, just remember tradition."

"And what are those traditions?" Risto asked.

"Oskar thinks a woman is a thing to be given away. So ask him, not her, for permission to marry. And once you've done that, in this area, it will be as though the two of you are already married because the engagement is the real commitment. The marriage is just the party to celebrate. Of course, the engagement includes a celebration too. And don't do the asking just any time of the year. Target the fall, right after the harvest. People have more time to party, and it's less bleak than the middle of winter. Just remember. There's going to be much feasting, just as much dancing, and the whole town will come. We're not in America."

Risto, following every detail of Paavo's advice and winning the respect of Oskar, requested Irina's hand in a carefully choreographed conversation ending with half of Kem gorging in a night of food and drink. The wedding outpaced even that. Risto invited all of his friends from Sisu and the Technical Aid Society to gather at Paavo's house. In turn, friends and relatives of the bride's family went to Irina's father's house. Risto's gathering then marched grandly through Kem to Irina's home. Once there, he engaged in a playful and highly ceremonious search for Irina. Once Irina was found, her friends and relatives pretended much grief over her leaving her father's house, but in the end helped her arrange her hair and don the headdress of a young wife. Everyone shook her hand.

And the two were off, leading a procession back to Paavo's home for the rite, with the bride's friends and relatives and Risto's friends trooping behind the couple. Risto used all of his meager savings—and some of Paavo's—to stage a feast. It went on for hours and might have continued even longer, but then the music started. Men vied for the honor of dancing with Irina, offering small bits of cash. Risto watched the currency accumulate, hoping that it would pay for at least part of the wedding feast.

Weddings in Wisconsin had sometimes been quite raucous. Between the Germans and the Scandinavians, local events always involved a lot of beer and many strenuous polkas. But his Karelian wedding proved exhausting. If not for another tradition—the pre-wedding sauna, he might not have gotten through it. But the night before, as tradition demanded, both Risto and Irina stripped under the watchful eyes of her parents and went into the hot sauna together. Once the door closed, they just started to laugh, quietly at first, then loudly.

"Papa still thinks he lives in the nineteenth century," Irina laughed. "He probably thinks we've never seen each other naked before."

Of course, they had already made love with each other many times, and even gone swimming in the nude. But in the heat and steam of the sauna, Irina's skin seemed rosier and lovelier than Risto ever imagined. She took a dipper of water from the pail and poured it over the hot rocks. Steam filled the room, and the heat grew intense. Perspiration poured out. Their hair was soon dripping with sweat. Still Irina looked lovely, and he was happy that she was to be his wife.

"Should I beat you with these birch switches?" she asked. That simple question convinced Risto to stop worrying about the ceremonies of the next day, the expectations of those around him and fears about whether their life together would be happy. Everything felt right.

The day after the wedding, Risto and Irina were sleeping in Paavo's spare bedroom. Paavo, puttering about the house, gave them discreet privacy.

"Tradition says I should be giving gifts today," Irina said after they woke up and before they left for Sisu. "I am expected to provide small gifts to all family members who matter to you. Your mother, your father, your little sister. But they're so far away. I will just send them good wishes. Do you think they will get them?

"And before we leave, I know Papa will want me to do one other thing. A young boy is supposed to sit on my lap. That's to encourage us to have our own children. It's a funny time to ask, but do you want to be a father?"

Risto, reflecting that he was already a father, didn't answer Irina's actual question. Instead, he said, "Could we send one real gift? To my little sister Lempi? I want her to share our happiness."

Sisu was a real village. If not fully prosperous, it was surviving. After three years in Karelia and two years of marriage, Risto considered himself an old timer. He looked around the settlement with pride. Sisu now included two small streets of homes. Risto was the first of the volunteers to marry local girls. But many followed. Each couple built their own small home, hacked out garden areas for the short summer and started domestic life. Their wives worked with their men in the woods until they became pregnant. A few months after birth, they returned to lumbering. Invariably an older female relative from one of the smaller villages surrounding Kem took the jostling truck ride to Sisu to become the *babushka*. The village was now home to six children, but none belonged to Risto and Irina. If not for Lempi back in Wisconsin, Risto might have worried he was the cause of their childlessness. But he had already proved his virility once before.

Being childless had its perks, as did being the local manager, and while Sisu was little more than a drop of swamp water in the back woods of Karelia, he was the big fish in a small pond. The original mill now sawed the best trees into lumber year round. In the spring, giant rafts of logs destined for pulp mills further south were still towed to Kem.

Paavo helped Risto expand his influence, plan ahead and make appearances at the right kinds of places, where he always injected his remarks with patriotic fervor. Paavo taught him well, but by now, he was better at all those things than Paavo. Paavo was a sturdy workhorse, destined to live out his years on the local farm. Risto knew he could achieve more. Not yet twenty-four, yet people that mattered throughout Karelia knew who he was

Marrying Irina helped. Her cousin, the famous Kustaa Rovio, proved quite willing to introduce his new kinsman to key people. There was even talk that Risto might accompany the republic's leader on an upcoming trip to Leningrad to talk about the area's lumbering industry.

Things were good. If only he could conceive a son with Irina—and maybe help Charlie win over Lydia and stop Art from complaining—then everything would be just as he wanted it. He had no regrets about leaving Clover. Even though returning to America was no longer easy, several men in his volunteer group, fed up with what they called unappreciated work, did so. The challenge was that they had handed over their American passports when they first arrived in Leningrad, and it was difficult to get the documents returned. Karelia wanted to hold on to its men. Those truly frustrated with the system simply trekked out of Sisu at night, headed for the nearby Finnish border and tried to sneak out of the country. Art often threatened to do just that, but Risto knew he couldn't afford to lose any more workers, and always persuaded Art to stay.

Midsummer's Night was approaching. He promised Irina they would celebrate the white nights of June with her parents and relatives in Kem. As the manager, he could leave camp with Irina whenever he wanted. Lydia was also going to be in Kem that week and Lydia knew many Karelian Republic leaders. That would be a pleasant diversion from drinking vodka with his brothers-in-law.

"How are Art and Charlie?" Lydia asked the afternoon they met. "Sometimes I laugh at how the group of you stood so forlornly in Penn Station when I first spied you."

"We knew what we were doing." snapped Risto.

"Did you really?" teased Lydia. "Well, I have no doubt that you would have quickly figured everything out. You really are an artist at fitting in. Everyone acknowledges that Sisu is the most successful of any of the Karelian Technical Aid camps. Both Rovio and Skylling use it as an example. You could parlay your fame into something more, don't you think?"

Risto was uncertain how to respond. Of course, he had thought about what to do next. Irina was happy to stay in Sisu, close to her family, and doing whatever the local Communist Party leaders asked her to do. Right now, they encouraged women to have more children to help populate the frontier. So that's what she most wanted. That ensured fun nights for Risto, but during the days out in the woods, Risto considered other possibilities.

Why stay in such a small settlement? And why settle for Kem? Surely, there was some important role for him in Petrozavodsk or even Leningrad.

"So how are things in the Karelian capital?" he asked.

Lydia appeared ill at ease, and hesitated before answering. Risto found it odd. She always knew what to say. For some reason, he recalled an old dairy cow on Pa's farm. During the spring thaw, the cow would stand frightened at the edge of the little creek that became a rushing stream from the melting snow. It wanted to get across the creek and reach the barn for evening milking but it feared stepping into unfamiliar waters. Risto always prodded the reluctant cow forward.

"Is something wrong?" he asked.

Lydia shook herself slightly. "It's just rumors, stories that can't be trusted. We hear things about events in Moscow and Leningrad, mostly about Stalin and plots against him. People don't know who to trust, or what might happen next. I am afraid we're losing focus on our cause. You do believe in Communism, don't you? That is why you came to Karelia, isn't it?"

"Of course," he said dismissing Lydia's concerns as uninteresting. Rumors got in the way of getting things done; Irina would think it disloyal to even discuss such rumors.

Lydia continued, "Everything we built here in Karelia is like our baby. I'm not married; many of the volunteers remain single; and we don't have children to bind us. But we do have the work we've done for this country. I want Karelia to be strong."

"And it is," reassured Risto. At the same time he thought that clearing land could never replace having a child. In some way, children made sense of one's life. He had never even met his daughter Lempi, and no one other than Pauline even knew he was the father. Yet he took delight in knowing of her existence. Still, there were dark days when he wished Pauline had never written. If Lempi were just his little sister, he wouldn't wonder how the girl was doing or anxiously await an update. He had grown addicted to his mother's monthly dispatches and their great detail about his little sister as well as the occasional new picture. Perhaps Ma wanted to lure him home and that was the reason she filled her letters with rich details of the Clover kids who were once his friends. That was how he knew that Pauline was attending Bremen College. Someday, he would write to thank her for telling him about Lempi. He was wrong to never acknowledge her previous letter.

He could send a letter while still in Kem. Surely if he sent a note to Pauline in care of Bremen College, she would receive it.

Suddenly something Lydia said pulled him back into the present. He tried to catch up with her political gossip.

"What did you say about Kustaa Rovio?" he asked.

"Some predict that the leaders of the Karelian Republic, both Kustaa Rovio and Edvard Gylling, will be arrested for nationalism."

"I know Rovio; he's Irina's second cousin. He's loyal and committed."

"I know both men as well. I'm sure such talk is nonsense. But that's what's being rumored. Fear is infecting everyone. If Rovio's your relative, you might need to be more careful."

Risto did not mention Lydia's news to Irina that evening. When they went to bed, Irina asked for updates from Petrozavodsk. Risto responded with some of Lydia's tidbits about mutual friends. Why bother with gossip about Irina's second cousin's loyalty? It would all blow over.

A few weeks later, though, both Rovio and Gylling were arrested. When he told Irina, she was dismissive, certain that both leaders deserved whatever happened. 'Stalin does not make mistakes," she said.

She remained equally unconcerned when the NKVD, the secret police, arrived two months later to arrest Paavo Karvala. "But this man was my teacher and friend," Risto protested. "He loves this country. You know he is dedicated to the people. What could he have done wrong? For god's sake, Irina, our wedding feast was at his house. How can you not be concerned?"

"We don't know everything," she said. "We must trust our leaders who have better insight than we. Just because Paavo did good things for you, doesn't mean everything he did is good. You don't know. He's an American. He can't be trusted."

"But I'm an American. Don't you trust me?" The moment Risto asked that question he wanted to pull it back. He was afraid of Irina's answer. But she surprised him.

"How could I not trust the father of my baby?" she asked. He looked at her, not understanding. She smiled in satisfaction. Then it became clear. He would be a father again. Of a baby that he would know and raise. A true father. But he found Irina's smile disturbing. He wasn't certain whether she was happy that she would be a mother, or that she had kept her pregnancy a secret from him.

"I'm going to be a father?" he asked. Only when she nodded yes did he truly believe her. He twirled her around their small cabin. "We're having a baby," he exclaimed, and he thought no more of Paavo.

But the exhiliration lasted only a few hours. Paavo's arrest and subsequent disappearance into the NKVD prisons spread alarm among the Sisu community. Art and Charlie knocked on Risto's office door.

"This is why we should have left," Art said. "We could still head for the Finnish border. We need to do it soon. I've heard they've increased the patrols."

"Don't be dramatic." Risto responded.

"If we don't leave, then what are you going to do about Paavo?" Art pursued.

"What do you mean? There's nothing I can do."

"That's not true," Art said. "You're the leader of this camp. You've been elected to the local Soviet as our representive. Paavo was your friend. You know perfectly well he has never done anything wrong. You need to stand up for him."

"Irina and I talked, and we agree there is nothing that we can do."

"You know," Art began, "you always wonder why I look at the picture of myself in the book I got?"

"What has that got to do with any of this?" Risto said.

"I'll tell you. I see in that picture a person who is smarter than me today. I never should have listened to you and followed you to this hellhole. That author, Tom Ferber, was in Clover the week we left, doing research on people like us. He tried to talk me out of volunteering. He said that when revolutionary events happen, men can turn to the good or to the bad, and that he was certain that in the Soviet Union, they had already turned to the bad. He said it wasn't too late for me to turn to the good."

"Art, you're an idiot," snapped Risto.

"And you're a miserable son of a bitch," said Art. He walked away.

Charlie looked sadly at Risto, but followed Art. Then he looked back and said, "I know you slept with Lydia years ago. You only care about yourself. You screwed me when your screwed Lydia, and now you're screwing all of us."

Risto didn't respond. He returned to his cabin. Irina had already gone to bed. He undressed, got under the heavy quilt, pulled closer to her body and spooned his sleeping wife. His large callused hands, hardened by three years of lumbering, rested lightly on her stomach. He could feel no bump, but still he knew that beneath his hands a new life was growing. He had a duty to that boy or girl. He wouldn't abandon another child. This one he would do right by. He would not risk reputation or life to defend people like Rovio or Paavo. He must stay focused on his child.

Karelia became a land of suspicion and fear. Police knocked on doors at unexpected times. Until that door knock, people could be one's friends and neighbors, folks in which one placed complete trust, but when such people departed with the police, so did all memories of the good they had done. No one could predict who might receive the unwanted rap. Among those who abandoned America to build Karelia, many vanished into the NKVD prisons. It wasn't just a foreign birth that marked a danger sign. Old friends and neighbors of the Rovios also moved into the unmentionable category. Even true Karelians who never trusted the foreign volunteers of the Karelian Technial Aid sometimes became invisible and lost in police custody. While Irina's immediate family remained free of arrests, their relationship to the disgraced former leader clothed them in a taboo. Rumors ran like the streams of a spring thaw, twisting and merging into deeper, more dangerous flows. Different people placed their hopes in different explanations. Stalin was ridding the region of capitalist plots. Others professed that Stalin had uncovered a secret Finnish plan to reclaim Karelia, restoring a birthright from the days when both Finland and Karelia bowed to a Swedish king. Only the bravest dared to repeat other more disagreeable stories. They whispered behind closed doors of other targets disappearing into the night. Some feared that Stalin had gone mad; others were convinced Trotskyites were infiltrating the Party. There was no way to sift for the truth.

Risto vowed to remain positive and optimistic. Irina held absolute faith in the righteousness of each and every arrest. "Many are opposed to what the Soviet is doing," she said, allowing for no contrary opinions. But family dinners were no longer so raucous or good-natured. Missing childhood friends of her brothers disappeared into the back of trucks headed toward prisons in Petrozavodsk, where the people were disgorged into windowless cellars. No one ever visited, and no one ever came out. Some claimed the arrested were sent to labor camps in the Ural Mountains. Other blacker theorists said the arrested men were executed and dumped into one of the many lakes. Since no bodies ever surfaced, Risto refused to believe the theory.

Lydia still worked for the government. She never discussed what was occuring. "Let's focus on our jobs," she would say. Irina, a true believer, said there was nothing to fear; his colleagues avoided any discussion; and his childhood friends eyed him with an I-told-you-so attitude.

He was isolated. Mail delivery from outside the country was suspended. Risto no longer heard from Ma and Pa. Before things turned so bad, he mailed a letter to Pauline but he never heard back. He couldn't even be certain that the letter left Russia. It may have been intercepted by censors. Working in the open woods gave him time to wonder about all his vanishing colleages, but he couldn't worry about their fates. He needed to secure the future for Irina, the baby ahead and himself. No one else would do it. He couldn't afford to be arrested, so he couldn't afford to take risks. But in this climate, what was risky?

Irina told him he worried needlessly. She knew he was loyal and good and reminded him of all he had done for Karelia: he ran the Sisu camp so efficiently; he inspired the local Communist party groups with his vision and insight; and by having a child they were doing their duty to Mother Russia. One day, without informing Risto, she invited the local Kommisar, Ivan Gorgonovitch, to Sisu.

Ivan was boisterous and laughed heartily, helped along by the bottle of vodka he brought with him. Ivan and Risto took a long sauna together, which sweated out all of Risto's anxieties. They gossiped long into the night, and he encouraged Risto to tell him about all the camp's triumphs, and who among the volunteers was responsible for what. After sharing goodwill shots of alcohol and looking into the red, sweating face of his new-found friend, Risto felt quite certain that Sisu was safe. In the heat of the sauna, the days ahead looks promising.

But less than a week later, Risto discovered his mistake. The late autumn sun had already set, the moon not yet risen and only kerosene lanterns provided light in the village. Before Paavo was taken, he and Risto had talked about securing a small generator to power electrical lights in the camp and make the long nights more bearable. How Risto wished for lights at the moment two heavy trucks rolled into the center of their small village. The drivers, turned off the engines and extinguished their headlights. From the backs, several armed men emerged to rush in to the dormitory. Irina told him not to leave the house, but he was the manager for Sisu. He needed to be informed. Risto grabbed a lantern from his cabin, hurriedly put on a heavy jacket and strode toward the dormitory.

The police wore NKVD uniforms. They were dragging out three of the workers. His heart sank when he saw it was Art, Charlie and Olli-Pekka. "Why are you taking these men?" he demanded.

"It is none of your concern," replied the one seemingly in charge. He spoke in Russian.

Risto easily switched from Finnish to Russian. "It is my concern. These men work for me. How do I even know you have the right persons. Who are you seeking?"

"We have the right people, and you would be wise to not interfere with us. The State has its responsibilities."

"But why are you taking them."

"Your men provided incorrect information and conspired against the Soviet. There is no need for you to know more." The officer and the men were nearly in the truck. Risto's friends were not resisting, as though hope had already fled. But then Art shouted out, "Risto, we don't understand Russian. What's he saying? Where are they taking us? Can't you help?"

He shouted back to his men in English, "They won't tell me. They only say you have conspired against the country."

The officer stepped forward and slapped Risto hard across his cheek. He felt blood breaking through his skin. "Shut up. No one asked you to translate. These men are in this country illegally. Let us do our job."

The slap was like a death jolt. A whole life flashed in front of Risto, from the childhood games he once played with Art and Charlie in the dirt yard of the one-room country schoolhouse they attended, to their teenage dreams as high school students, to the excitement of the journey across the Atlantic and the camaraderie the night they flew the Soviet flag from the Stockholm hotel window, to their most recent argument about Paavo.

"You can't take them. They've done nothing wrong!" Risto said.

The officer pulled a gun. "I will shoot you if you continue to interfere with a legal order. Now step back." He motioned to his men to load Art, Charlie and Olli-Pekka onto the flatbed of the truck. He turned back to Risto, "Best be careful, Comrade Makinen. We track all Americans and no one's loyalty is above suspicion."

Then the officer jumped onto the truck's running board, and rapped on the hood. Its driver started up the engine, headlights came on and the officer entered the cab. The two trucks rumbled off, a piercing and disappearing tunnel of light through the woods. Risto stared until the red tail lights disappeared completely. He stood in place staring into darkness. The alternative was to turn around and face his remaining men. He remained frozen until he sensed the others had returned to the dormitory and that the married couples had backed away from peering through the curtains of their small cabins. Then he walked slowly back to his cabin, back to Irina and back to the reality of a country he now called home.

"What did you do that for?" Irina demanded the moment he walked through the door. "Are you insane? Risking our lives for those worthless men?"

"Those men are my friends. We've known one another since I was a little boy. There is no way they have done anything wrong."

"Don't be naive. Art is nothing but a complainer. His pessimism brings down the morale of the entire camp. Only an agent for the American goverment could be so relentless."

Risto found this impossible: his wife, the woman he slept with every night, could not believe such incredible things. Surely even she could see that Art was an innocent. He was born to roam the wild roads of the world, not engage in deep thoughts or sabatoge. If his friend ever displayed any larger motives, it was only to live up to the dreams spun by Risto. Back in Clover, the future had seemed so clear. They could create a world better than the hardscrabble life of their parents. No one needed to be enslaved to plutocrats who kept their wealth from flowing to the workers who deserved it. Finns had proven that banding together worked. Their farming co-ops improved the lot of all farmers. Their union support for the Wobblies in the ports of Washington and the mines of the midwest had forced safer conditions for all. Finns were the proof that there could be a better way than pure capitalism. Pa had told him this for nearly 20 years; Risto knew it was true. Why else volunteer to work on the Karelian Technical Aid? That's why it was so easy to convince Art and Charlie to head to a foreign land. His Pa had shown bravery fleeing Finland for the New World. It was Risto's duty to return to that homeland and make a difference, prove that people could work together for the common good and seek to improve his own life the way Pa had sought to improve his.

Charlie and Art would never have joined up if not for Risto. Charlie was a follower. He was just a person who wanted a good time and he lived for the approval of Risto. How could such a fellow say no to the adventure of following Risto to the other side of the world? Risto thought guiltily about the way in which he had repaid that devotion. Instead of helping Charlie win more attention from Lydia—and Risto knew that Lydia was the only woman Charlie truly ever wanted—Risto took her for himself. Just because he could.

As for Art, his pal was a lost boy. A tramp at heart, Art would have been happier wandering the rest of his days. There was no mystery to why the photo in that professor's book entranced Art. It spoke to his longing to hit the open road. But Risto used his pull as their childhood leader to drag Art into a Karelian madhouse, lock him up in a lumber camp, surround him by miles of wilderness among people speaking a language he couldn't quite master and with no open roads to wander. No wonder Art complained.

The clarity of the moment stunned Risto. He realized he was the north star that led to this night. He was the architect of this universe. Yet the stars had not touched him. If anything, the trail he blazed resulted in his prosperity. In Clover, he left behind old parents, an unexpected baby girl he would never see and a town of people that had nurtured him for nearly twenty years. It hadn't been so bad. There was never a night when he went hungry. His Pa and Ma's farm provided a life with beauty: summer pastures dotted with grazing cows, fields of rutabagas and hay, a small apple orchard between the sauna and the barn, all under clear skies blazing with midnight stars. That's what he left behind. That's what he forced Art and Charlie to give up.

Irina stood before him. Her anger burned clearly. "You are not doing anything to help them."

"I am not beholden to you," he said.

"Of course you are. I am your wife. I am carrying your baby. And you are an officer of the Soviet government of Karelia. Your duty is to uphold the laws, even when it involves old friends who have done wrong." She dropped her voice to a harsh whisper. The kerosene lamp flickered. Its wick was too short.

"But Art and Charlie have done nothing wrong," he countered, feeling about to be overcome by fatigue.

She looked at him with disgust. "You are a fool. You gave Ivan the information behind these arrests. The way you slavered like a drunken fool in the sauna, a gossiping old woman telling Ivan about what every one said and thought in this camp. Did you think he would do nothing with that? That's why he visited. He was looking for an informer. And he found you!"

Risto couldn't remember what was said in the steam that night. But surely not what she accused. It couldn't be true. She was infuriating. Art and Charlie were his friends. He would not have betrayed them. She was taunting him, trying to convince him of her own mistaken inferences. Grabbing her by the shoulders, Risto lifted Irina from the ground. "All lies. Take it back."

"No, all truth. I despise your weakness for not knowing it."

He flung her angrily against the log walls of the cabin. As she slammed against the rough log walls, her eyes widened in surprise, fear and then pain. She slumped to the ground. A wash basin hanging on the wall fell from its nail, clanging to the floor.

Irina began to cry. Whether it was anger or pain, Risto didn't really know. He rushed to her side. He muttered repeatedly, "I'm sorry, I'm sorry." He helped her to the bed to lie down.

"I'll be fine," she said, and then nothing more.

But in the middle of the night, Irina took a sharp intake of breath and groaned deeply. She began to breath irregularly. An acrid, iron smell hung in the air.

"Are you all right?" he asked.

Even in the dim light, he could see the hand she held up. He reached out and grabbed it. He felt its wet stickiness and knew it must be blood.

"The baby," she said, and started to cry.

"I'll get you to the doctor," he promised.

Later, Risto realized moving Irina over fifteen miles of bone-jarring bumps in an old truck with poor springs was not wise. By the time they arrived at the small hospital in Kem, his wife was very weak. In the waiting room, he replayed his horrible behavior. If only he could take it back. By the time the doctor emerged from the examining room, pale dawn light invaded the room. The doctor looked at Risto with little sympathy, but all he said was, "Your wife will be fine. But your son, the baby, was lost. We will keep Irina here for several days. She's needs bedrest. And you should get your own sleep."

Risto wandered from the hospital. What to do? Paavo's cabin remained unoccupied since the older man was taken by the NKVD. Risto had a key and could sleep there. He needed time to think, sleep and drink from a hot cup. Perhaps some coffee remained in Paavo's cupboard.

No one seemed to have visited the cabin since the arrest. It was ice cold. Some food had spoiled, but there was only a lingering hint of bad odor. He found the kindling, lit a fire in the wood range and waited for the air to warm. He looked through the cupboad for the coffee, but found only tea. He knew the old Finn had loved his coffee; he wondered sadly if the tea reflected some desire of Paavo to fit into Russia. When the water boiled, he added it and the leaves to steep in a teapot. Lost in his thoughts and drinking tea he didn't really like, Risto was startled to see Ivan walk in.

"I saw the chimney smoke," the Kommissar said, "and hearing about your wife's miscarriage, I thought perhaps you were the reason. I hope you don't mind that I stopped to check. It might have been a vagrant or somone evading the police. Even you shouldn't really be here. The house reverted to the party after Paavo's arrest. But I think we can put that aside."

"Thank you," said Risto. He didn't mean it; he despised this man.

"Actually, I am quite glad to find you. There's some good news to share. The government is taking over the Sisu camp. It's time to dissolve Karelian Technical Aid. Too many of its leaders arrested for their anti-government behavior, so one must be practical and do what's best for the people."

Risto wanted to comment, but Ivan held up his hand. "Just wait. I know you're probably wondering how that's good news. But for you, it is. The Soviet will now run the mills and lumbering operations. Certainly, we can do it better than a private group. And it will benefit the people as a whole. Good news for all.

"You should know we're all very impressed by what you've done at Sisu, as well as by your cooperation in our investigation of the unsavory elements among us. We think you're ready to take on a new assignment." Ivan spread his arms wide. "It's time to let your talents spread across wider fields. We're assigning you to Petrozavodsk to attend a newly-established management academy. There you'll learn to combine the best of our Soviet skills with what we have learned from the West. We can improve Karelian practices, but we need people like you.

"No need to go back to Sisu. Tomorrow, you can go directly to Petrozavodsk. But today, I recommend you comfort your wife. All of Karelia and the Soviets suffer whenever we lose another patriot, however small. But you and Irina are young. When she recovers, you can still have many children."

Risto felt robbed of his integrity. The assignment seemed a reward for something he hadn't done. All his friends at Sisu would see his promotion in an unsavory light, and he was being cut off from friends who might have reminded him of the person he once wanted to be.

It got worse. Irina refused to see him when he returned to the hospital. Two of her brothers stood outside her hospital room. They told Risto to move along. Irina would contact him when she was ready to talk. They spoke rapidly in Karelian, even though they knew Risto's Finnish was better, to make clear he was no longer one of them.

In Petrozavodsk, he attempted to see Lydia, but she had disappeared. She had not been arrested, but instead assigned to a secret project in an undisclosed location. The end effect was the same. She was gone, and there was no way to say any goodbye or resolve any issues.

Risto visited the NKVD prison, seeking details about Art, Charlie and Olli-Pekka. He didn't care what the ramifications might be. The officer maintained they had no records of such people, and they refused to let him into the prison check for himself. It was as though his three friends had vanished and never existed.

Madness continued. More trucks. More officers in the middle of night. Camps like Sisu were visited frequently. So was the city of Kem. As were the streets of Petrozavodsk. Not everyone disappeared into unknown fates. Lately, wives, children and some men were sent to a camp east of Kem. By now, only a handful of volunteers from the old Karelian Technical Aid Society still worked in Karelia. Between 1930 and 1933, more than six thousand men, women and children traveled there to devote their lives to the cause. Under the looser rules of the past, perhaps as many as a third returned to the United States. Later, as passports were held and Soviet restrictions put in place, a few hundred more vanished, seeking escape across the Finnish border. Still, Risto knew some three thousand American remained in the Soviet Republic of Karelia for the cause, but by 1938, Risto could count no more than 500 still free.

He was one of those five hundred. He was free in another sense as well, since Irina refused to return to their married life. To his face, she called him the murderer of her son. She would not forgive him, and instead sought happiness by working hard in the woods where she refused to give up the manager's cabin. The new supervisor was forced to build a new one. When Risto returned to the camp to try to win her back, Irina would summon one of her burly brothers to bar the door. After a few times, Risto didn't try again.

Then Irina too was sucked into the maelstrom of the purges. Ties to the former republic leader, Kustaa Rovio, caught up with her entire family. One bright and shiny morning in their small village outside Kem, the police confronted Irina and all the family members. They were loaded into the back of the truck, given little time to gather belongings and sent to a detention camp east of Kem. Or so people assumed. Even Risto with his contacts couldn't see the camp's registration lists or confirm they existed.

Ivan scoffed when Risto went the Kommissar's offer to seek help. "What kind of fool do you think I am?" he said. "Your in-laws were reactionaries, tied to the bourgeois past. Besides, everyone knows there will be war with Finland. For our own safety, we must move the Finnish population to the detention camps. It's the only way to ensure a secure Western front."

"But the Rovios are Karelian," argued Risto. "They don't even speak Finnish. There's no one who believes more in the Communist cause than Irina. She will fight to the ends of the earth against any enemy of the Soviet."

"Finnish, Karelian. It's all the same. Beside you're an American. What would you know? Can't place much trust in your opinions, can I?" Ivan smiled. His reference to America tortured Risto. How long would it be before he too was shipped away or murdered?

"Yes, I am an American. And I am a Finn. But also I am also Russian. I chose this country. I chose this life. How can the state not trust me?"

Ivan was amused. "Who says that we don't? Look at what we've done for you. Trained you. Given you responsibility. We value clever men like you. Why would we not trust you? By now you speak four languages: English, Finnish, Karelian and Russian. People listen to you; you have a way with words, whatever the language. You've a natural talent for management. Men like you are rare. Men like you are not sent to camps on frozen lakes. Unless . . ."

"Unless what," Risto demanded to know.

"I'm kidding. There is no 'unless.' Unless you try to create one. And that would be a foolish thing to do."

Throughout the summer of 1938, Risto focused on his work and studies. He seldom talked to anyone, largely because there was no one left to talk to. Around him, people whispered of the increasing tensions with Finland. The Karelian border with Finland was only miles from Sisu and not that far from Petrozavodsk. Everyone was convinced that Stalin and his surrogate Molotov planned to push the border further west into independent Finland. Despite the non-aggression pacts signed between Russia and Finland in 1932 and 1934, most expected war. Old-timers remembered how in the East Karelian uprising of 1921 Finnish volunteers fought with Karelians against the larger Soviet. No one expected the current leadership to allow that to happen again. As for those Karelian leaders who understood the historic ties of Finland and Karelia, they were executed or imprisoned—rumors claimed the same happened to tens of thousands of Red Army officers. Some called the events of the past two years Stalin's Great Purge, but none dared speak of it openly.

Unexpectedly, a letter arrived from Risto's mother. Mail with America had been blocked for years, and Risto was afraid that this envelope represented a test of his loyalties. He didn't care. The sight of his mother's penmanship was bread to a starving man. However meager the letter's contents might be, Risto needed it to survive another day.

But the letter sapped his strength. The letter's tone made clear that Ma had been writing monthly since he left. Risto could only wonder if her letters were piled in some storage bin in a Leningrad post office. She tried to explain away his silence of the past three years. She raised the possibility that the U.S. government blocked mail from the Soviet Union. She wrote that there were many anti-Communists in the American government. She even noted how she joined the U.S. Communist party to increase her ability to stay in touch. Reading between the lines, he realized she thought he chose not to write back.

Her letter covered the same details she always noted: news of Pa, the farm, Clover townsfolk and his little sister Lempi. A photograph of the four-year-old girl had tones that were a bit washed out, but Lempi stood proud in her simple dress, no doubt sewn from the fabric of empty flour bags. The girl's long blond hair hung straight, and her light-colored eyes looked forward with a gritty look. It made Risto smile. He wondered if

Pauline ever saw the girl, and what she thought of the child they created. He stared at the picture for a long time, similar to the way Art once gazed at his own photo in the book on tramps. He saw the broadness typical to most Finns' faces, and Lempi had the same blonde hair he once sported as a child. He wondered if her hair would darken when she got older. Risto tried to imagine how the child might become a woman. He realized he would likely never know. He doubted that another letter would ever get through.

The picture convinced him that he must escape this country. Maybe for a while his presence here had done good, but those days had ended. His friends were gone. His wife was imprisoned. He was alone in a land that promised brotherhood, but delivered terror.

He heard rumors that the government was training a special group of the American Finns for a radio and intelligence corp. If war were to break out, this group could provide Finnish translation and help spy on the opponent's radio transmissions. They were recruiting from the few Karelian Technical Aid volunteers still around, since those in power felt the volunteers' loyalties would remain aligned with Russia, not Finland. Rumor also claimed a smart American woman named Lydia Amundson headed the corps. Risto had found her secret mission. He had dreaded learning that Lydia had been caught in the purge, but now he realized she might be his path to escape. If only he could join the radio corps.

He broached with Ivan the possibility of volunteering for this rumored army unit. He suggested it was his patriotic duty to support the Motherland in advance of the expected war. Ivan would have none of it. "We're opening new lumbering operations east of Kem. They will be well back from the border and easily protected. When there's war, we will need the timber. You are our most experienced camp manager. Why should we risk all that just so you can play soldier?"

Risto was not deterred. If he enlisted in this special unit, he would be sent close to the Finnish front. After five years of living in the Soviet Union, he interpreted rumors well enough to be certain that the drumbeat of war would only grow louder. When the inevitable war started, the confusion at the border would surely be immense and he could find an opportunity to escape across the border and surrender to Finnish forces. With his skills in English and Finnish, he could talk his way to the American embassy in Helsinki. Even if that didn't happen, at least he would be out of the current environment of fear.

Ignoring Ivan's advice, he persevered on his quest. He learned that Lydia was at a base outside of Leningrad. Arranging a reason to travel to the giant city, he made his way to Lydia's camp. On seeing him, Lydia seemed cool and remote. He worried about what she might have heard about his actions in Sisu. "You seem to be doing well," she said. "I hear how you have become a favorite son of the Komsomol."

"They want to use me. It's the only reason I am still alive," he said.

Lydia seemed surprised by his statement, yet the resolve Risto found so attractive in her was now steel-hard. He couldn't be certain if she displayed any true emotion.

"So are you here because you want to use me?" she asked.

He couldn't help but smile. "Well, you did help me find my way around Penn Station and Manhattan," he said. "You've known me longer than anyone else in this country. But I don't want to use you; I want you to use me. Let me join up with your team. I could do more good at the front than hidden away in the woods."

"There is no front," Lydia said. "And there is no team."

"But there will be," he countered, "and my language skills have become as good as yours. If they need a person like you, then surely they could use another one. We're practically twins."

At that she laughed. For a moment, she looked at him with some of the emotions they once shared, but it was quickly shielded. "Perhaps, but my work is secret. Let's say there was a planned Karelian Radio Brigade. Even if there were, it would never be my decision to let you join. You underestimate yourself. You've gained quite some fame as a backwoods worker. The only way you could join this unit is with the direct permission of the First Secretary of the Central Committee in Karelia. It's a new fellow named Yuri Andropov, and he might not yet be biased against your cause. Maybe your clever tongue could work its magic with him." Lydia would say nothing more, and their conversation soon faltered. All the people they knew in common were gone, or at least, they had no news they dared to share of old friends.

When Risto left, he lightly brushed his lips against Lydia's. She showed no overt response, but the brief electricity of their touch remained with him. On the train back to Petrozavodsk, he pondered what life might have been like if he had pursued Lydia instead of Irina. Why hadn't he? Was he so loyal to Charlie's longings that he didn't act on his own? And where did that get either him or Charlie?

Others would not even joke about visiting the Central Committee's offices. No one knew what went on in the basement rooms, and there was the perceived danger that one might not leave the building once one entered. But Risto had nothing to lose. He would probably end up in the building's cellars soon enough. Likely sooner than later if anyone discerned his real objective in pursuing this enlistment. Yet he was confident in his ability to present any case, and he displayed no nervousness when he was ushered into the office of Yuri Andropov.

A man was looking out the window when Risto entered. He turned around and seemed no older than Risto. Risto was surprised by the relative youth of the First Secretary. The man's smile was friendly and he spoke in cultured Russian. "You seemed quite intent on meeting me," he said. "Few are so insistent."

"I am told I need your permission to enlist in the Karelian Radio Brigade and to be relieved of my current duties."

Andropov looked down at a paper on his desk, "And it says here the lumbering camp which you are to lead is critical to our defense efforts. The new camp is far from the border, ensuring you would be well protected should a war ever break out. Do you have some death wish?"

"I want to do what's best for my country," Risto replied.

"An interesting statement. I have to wonder what country you reference. You are an American citizen, are you not? Born in their Midwest? We appreciate your willingness to work in the Soviet Union on behalf of us all, but one questions to what degree the United States still streams in your blood. America after all is a country often antagonistic to our motherland. And you're not far removed from Finnish interests. Your father and mother were born there, were they not? These days, some call the Finnish government a vicious and reactionary Fascist state. It seems quite eager to harm our country.

"And this report also references your wife and her family, with their connections to the old regime. Placed in one of our settlement camps near Onega, keeping them safely on our side should there be a border war. It seems only your talents keep you above suspicion. Yet you are here asking me to move you to the Finnish front, to put you in harm's way and to keep your talents from benefiting mother Russia. Perhaps some mischief still brews in your American mind."

"There is no need to worry about any of that," assured Risto. "I am as loyal as the Brigade's leader, Lydia Amundson. We have known each other for years, share similar backgrounds and are each dedicated to the Party."

"Perhaps. It's hard to say what each of us might do one day for the Party or for the Soviet Union. We only make our choices day by day. But you are far too valuable to risk. We all know that war with Finland is inevitable. But the Finns will lose quickly to Soviet might. Such a small country is the least of our worries. But there are others who might prove more dangerous, like those in Nazi Germany, who currently feed Finland with munitions. Bigger battles will come.

"So what do I do with you and your request?

"I think the forests of Karelia are not the right place for you. But neither is the front. Soon, we will move many of the displaced Karelians to work settlements in the Ural Mountains, where Moscow has identified resources to be mined and factories to be built. Strong management skills will be needed. People like you.

"Unlike Kommissar Ivan, I do not think small. I am happy to honor your wish to do more for the Soviet Union. I will send you to work in the Ural camps. There is no place that you could do more.

"Oh, and you should be happy to know the Rovio family, including Irina, will be among those resettled in the Ural. You and your wife can be a family again."

On the train ride east, Risto was given a seat in a coach car that was well heated and stocked with provisions. He had not yet seen Irina and her family, although he was assured they were on this particular train. He suspected they were among the hundreds assigned to the cattle cars open to the wind. But he didn't really care what happened to the Rovios. He was certain Irina would refuse to live with him once they arrived in the Urals. Even if she were willing, he saw no reason to be burdened with such a family.

Most of his possessions had been left behind in Petrozavodsk, but he had saved a few mementos and photographs. One was from his youth. It showed his parents, still looking like newlyweds, along with his older twin brothers and himself. He looked about five, so it was still during the Great

War. They all looked happy that day, even his mother, who began suffering her depressions only after the twins were gone. He remembered how the family had taken the farm wagon into Clover for shopping. Pa, on the spur of the moment, decided to have their portrait captured by a photographer traveling through town.

His other photo was the more informal snapshot of Lempi sent by Ma. He suspected it would be the last picture he would ever see of his girl. There was no way Ma and Pa would ever track him down in the Urals, even if postal traffic someday restarted—even if he survived what he suspected was actually a concentration camp. In the photo, he could make out his childhood home in the background behind Lempi. His old bedroom window looked right over her head, and he longed to crawl through that window to return to his old life.

Both photos rested in his hands. His eyes moved between his childhood picture and that of his daughter. In Lempi, he saw little of Pauline or himself. Maybe Pauline had cruelly deceived him about Lempi's birth. This couldn't be his daughter.

"What do you have there?" asked a familiar voice.

He looked up. "Lydia, what are you doing on this train?" He wasn't certain whether her presence alarmed or elated him.

"They say you should be careful what you wish for. You wanted the two of us to work together. Apparently your visit to First Secretary Andropov achieved that. He determined that none of the Technical Aid volunteers were to be trusted on the front. So now here I am. With you. Sent to the Urals."

She sat down across from him, but she smiled. Maybe life wouldn't turn out so bad, he thought. Perhaps there was a new opportunity ahead. He put the photos back in his pocket. They represented lives that had no need of him.

"You have a knack" he said to Lydia, "for showing up when trains have left me in the most precarious of positions."

And the train rumbled on.

Danny found the old clippings frustrating. Why had his mother kept them hidden in this trunk, and when had they arrived?

Behind the clipping were two old photos. One was of his mother. It was a picture from where she was a little girl. She always kept a larger version of it in her bedroom and he instantly recognized it.

But the other was unfamiliar. It other showed a couple in old-styled clothes standing behind three small boys. He turned the photo over. A handwritten note said "Eero, Marja, Johani, Jaacko and Risto." He knew Eero and Marja were the names of his mother's parents, although he had never met them. His grandmother had died long before he was born, and his grandfather shortly after Danny's birth. His mother seldom talked about either, and would always grow quiet whenever Danny asked about his grandmother. She had never mentioned brothers. Were these cousins? He checked the newspaper clipping again. Risto Makinen was the name of one of the young men in the 1930s clipping. The boys must have been someone important to his mother. Could she have had three brothers? But they looked like they had been born so long ago, long before his mother. He studied their faces, wondering about this family, thinking one of the boys looked like him, looked like Danny.

EERO
CLOVER, WISCONSIN
1972

Eero Makinen knew he was old, but by God he was still going strong. His eighty-fourth birthday had been just weeks earlier. Lempi and Toivo drove down from Thread with little Danny, and spent the night with him in his old farmhouse outside Clover. After cake and coffee, Lempi once again tried to talk him into selling the farm and moving into town. But why would he ever do that? His whole life was wrapped into the very walls of this house he built himself. He knew every inch of every room, every mistake he ever made in framing, every update taken to please Marja—and she had been a hard one to please. He knew this house as well as he knew this farm. Over the decades, he had walked every bit of the pastures, fields and woods. He remembered blowing the stumps, picking the rocks and planting the apple trees. His whole life nourished this place, and now someone else leased those fields he labored so hard to clear. He might be the only person left who cared about these memories, but he wasn't about to give up his house.

He disliked falling into these nostalgic moods, but too often he couldn't restrain himself. What else was an old man to do? Watch that idiot television box? They killed too many people on those Westerns and cop shows. During his eight decades, he saw enough death that he did not need to watch it reenacted by television actors. But the old photo albums, which Marja kept so close to her heart, were another story. He could paw through them for hours. Turning the weathered paper leaves spotted with foxing was a trip back in time. The black and white old photos still shimmered brightly. There was Marja as a young woman, just as he remembered her, with her face glowing in hope and expectation. In another, Lempi, so small, standing right outside this very house. He pictured the day they took that picture. His little girl was so serious even when the photographer tried to make her smile. If only she had learned to let loose with a little joy. He paused at another page. This portrait of his first family always pained him.

Except for him, they were all gone now: Marja, Johani, Jaacko and Risto. Marja and he planted their hopes deeply in the spirits of those three boys. They were to blossom into the American dream, grow up and prosper in this adopted country that Eero fought so hard to reach. But his boys were all gone, strewn into the winds as though hit by a summer twister.

He pushed the photos aside. Lempi still represented the possibility of happiness. His sacrifices might still prove worthwhile. Eero felt a sudden pain, like he maybe needed to go, but he wasn't going to use the indoor bathroom. He added that useless room after the death of Marja. His wife begged him for years to add indoor plumbing, beginning her pleas when Roosevelt brought electricity to the farms and after Northern States Power strung power lines along the gravel roads. But he never wanted the expense. He found reasons to postpone until it was too late. Now he felt guilty that he waited until Marja was dead, but at the same time he was angry about giving in to Lempi's insistence for the superfluous addition. But just because he had indoor plumbing didn't require him to use it. The new small room off the kitchen was best reserved for company. A Saturday night in the sauna always cleaned him better than any soaking in a porcelain tub. And he liked sitting in the old outhouse, even when it was twenty below. As a kid back in Finland, he relished the time to himself—when no one bothered him and he could think what he wanted.

When he visited Lempi on the old Lahti farm outside Thread, she hated that Eero insisted on using the still standing outhouse. His son-in-law's house sported a modern bathroom, updated in harvest gold tile by Toivo's parents just before they handed over the farm. Lempi wanted Toivo to tear down the old structure some fifty yards from the house, but there were always other pressing priorities. Except for Eero's occasional visits to his daughter and family, no one ventured into the drafty, damp structure. Eero liked it all the more, knowing that he was the only one who sat on the well-worn wooden seats. A ten-year-old Sears and Roebuck catalog still hung on a hook inside the small building, its torn pages ready for duty as toilet paper. Every time Eero walked into Lempi's farmhouse kitchen after an outhouse visit, Lempi vowed Toivo would tear down the structure the very next day. But the unpainted wood hut still stood.

Eero had always spent too much time in the outhouse. It drove his mother crazy when he was a twelve-year-old on his family farm between Turku and Tampere in Finland. He realized now that his mother feared he was abusing himself in the privacy of the outhouse. But he wasn't. He just liked the quiet. Besides he knew other spots to satisfy his urgings.

His father paid little attention to Eero's doings; after all, under Finland's strict laws of primogeniture, the farm was destined to be Matti's, Eero's older brother. The fabled family farm. His father was so proud of the fact that the Makinens had lived on the same land since 1537. Given a chance, his father would display the old deed to the family farm, with its hard-to-read, old-fashioned lettering. Queen Cristina of Sweden officially granted the land in 1635, and the Makinens had been landowners for the centuries since. As prosperity went in Finland, the Makinens did well. But Eero despised the farm, even as he loved it.

Admittedly, he never knew the family farm as well as he grew to understand his own acres in Clover. The Makinen farm had been too big, and tenant farmers tended much of it. But Eero could still recall each of the buildings and the dates of their construction. The large house with its peaked eaves was built at the start of the nineteenth century. The old stables were nearly two hundred years old. The sauna from 1710 was the oldest building still surviving on the place. The dairy barn and the hay barn were nearly as old. The outhouse, he realized now, was undated. But it was a simple building, often moved to sit over a newly dug pit. In its way, it was ever changing.

His father, Heineke Makinen, allowed the outhouse to move and change. But as for the rest of the farm, and for that matter, the rest of Finland, his old man saw no reason for any change. Sweden lost the Grand Duchy of Finland to Russia about the same time the family built the farmhouse that Heineke sometimes grandly called the manor. But the Makinens didn't consider themselves Swedish or Russian. Heineke was proudly Finnish. When Eero was eleven and Czar Alexander started the Russification of Finland, his father vacillated between accepting the new orders and defending the family heritage. But Eero determined as a small boy that he would leave the country someday. There was nothing for him in the land, whether it was Swedish, Russian or Finnish. The fabled farm would never be his. At most, as second son, his brightest future would be to become an ordained Lutheran minister. But Eero never recalled having a belief in God. Now, after eight decades of living, nothing encouraged such a belief. He was pretty certain that the day he died would be the absolute end. He held no expectations of an ethereal place where he would again see his beloved Marja or their three wonderful boys.

He wished it were otherwise. He felt he had unfinished business with all of his family. As a young man, Eero vowed his sons would never deal with the indifference and scorn he faced as a child. He wanted each son to value his individual importance and to tackle personal goals. But he never told his sons how he felt. Perhaps it was forgivable with Jaacko and Johani. No one anticipated that such young boys could have their bright spirits so quickly snuffed out. But Eero knew he could not forgive himself so easily. Their death had been neither easy nor fast. They were young when stricken, but he had days in which to tell them whatever he should have told them. And what excuse could he possibly give about Risto? The boy was practically a man by the time he left Clover. In his heart, Eero knew that it was his own beliefs that inspired the boy to volunteer for Karelia. It was Eero's passions that drove the boy's fervor. Times were bad in the Thirties, but Eero should have known that things would turn around. He should have held Risto back.

Marja never forgave him for any of it. Until the day she drenched herself in gasoline, her eyes always blamed Eero for losing all three boys. So unfair. How was it his fault he let the boys go to the Muellers that summer day? How was he to blame for Risto's convictions?

Eero wondered if his own father ever regretted Eero's departure for America, and then laughed at himself for thinking such a thought. His father detested those who abandoned Finland. Many nights—around the dinner table with his mother and father, his brother Matti, and little sisters Aini and Alli—Eero heard his father rail, flinging out political rants as predictable as the food on the table.

How he still longed for some of those meals. Always there was the rye bread and the potatoes. As a boy, he grew so tired of them. But now he craved his mother's cabbage rolls — the parboiled cabbage wrapped around a mixture of barley, ground pork and egg, and then braised in a cast-iron pan on the old wood stove. The cabbage leaves cooked dark, almost charred, but the flavors melded together. He suspected now that his mother overcooked her rolls, but it didn't matter. That's what he grew to love and that was the standard by which he judged Marja's cabbage rolls.

In those old days, Matti usually prompted the start of their father's dinner rants. Several years older than Eero, Matti felt secure knowing the farm would be his. He didn't dread the possibility of preaching pabulum from a pulpit. He didn't worry about his father's moods and could enjoy the man's temper.

One night at dinner, Matti started up. "I heard the Nurmi family's left for Hanko. They're boarding the *Urania* for England where they'll catch a different ship to America." Mentioning an emigrant—one of their own tenants, no less—was a taunt to their father. Matti knew very well how Heineke would react. Even though the Nurmi tenancy had not worked out and there were no other feasible options for them, his father would disapprove their abandoning Finland.

"Good, I say," said his father. "That family was just bad blood, not real Finns. Worthless as tenant farmers. They had some of my best land, and still couldn't make a go of it."

Even though Eero was only fourteen at the time, he remembered coming to the defense of the family. That summer's growing season had been particularly short, and Eero also knew that his father had increased the "hand money," or the not-quite-legal leasing fees, to two hundred marks. His father also demanded more labor days. No one could make the land profitable under such circumstance. "But you expected too much," he said.

Heineke attacked back. "The Nurmis are not patriots. Their real duty is to stay here and improve our country. They should help preserve our uniqueness against this increasing Russification. If they're not brave enough to do that, then I say good riddance."

Surprisingly, Matti came to the family's defense. "But their oldest son is nineteen. With the Czar's new order that Finns are to be drafted into the Russian Army, they want to leave now before it's too late." Matti's greatest fear was to be stripped of his privileged place at the farm table and sent as a soldier to patrol some lonely Russian border. Sometimes when Eero sat alone in the outhouse, he imagined just such a thing happening. In his daydreams, he envisioned Matti dying in some border skirmish, and he exulted in being promoted to first son and heir.

Heineke dismissed Matti's point. "Well, that would be the son's duty. But you don't need to worry about that. Large landowners are needed where we are. We keep the economy going and protect our lands. The Czar's men won't conscript you, Matti." Eero still remembered how his father then turned to the fourteen-year-old Eero. His look made clear that such a benefit would not be passed down to the second son. That's when Eero knew for certain he would go to America.

***

Too many memories. The digestive pangs came back and jolted Eero into the present. It was only mid-morning; he had already been there once today, but he needed to visit the outhouse again. Age brought too many such visits. His bladder seemed to shrink with the passing of years. Although he would never let Lempi know this, he recently carried an old chamber pot down from the attic and kept it by his bedside. In the darkness of the night, it was a long walk to the outhouse. He lived with chamber pots when he was young, and he could do it again.

When he was a boy, his mother had a working girl named Berte whose job was to empty the chamber pots each morning. But that practice ended after his mother died and his father remarried. The new wife Inge was young and pretty, and Eero never liked her. Maybe she just felt insecure and unwanted by anyone other than Eero's father, but Eero thought Inge had a mean streak. Inge was raised in Helsinki and put on many airs. Accustomed to the life of a merchant's family, she disliked being on a farm up country. When she arrived, she bought her own maid with her—a woman who found emptying chamber pots beneath her duties. Since Inge quickly found reasons to dismiss his mother's long-term helper, and Heineke was unwilling to fund a new Berte (when he already paid for Inge's maid from Helsinki), it fell to Eero to take over emptying all the chamber pots. Eero always suspected Inge found Berte too young and pretty to keep around. And so he was stuck with carrying out the morning pots.

Dismissing Berte severed the last remaining tie between Eero and his mother. If she still lived, Eero's mother might have kept him in Finland. She understood him and appreciated the boundaries placed on his life. In the last year of her life, after his mother began to pale and weaken, Raili and Eero engaged in long conversations, sometimes in her bedroom as she rested, and other times, he joined her in the kitchen as she sat on a chair and did what she could. He stammered out his frustrations.

"I have a horrible life," he once complained.

"You don't know what awful could be," she replied.

"Really? Matti torments me, lords over everything, just because he knows the farm will be his one day. And Father doesn't honor anything I say. I can see it in his eyes that he doesn't like me."

His mother didn't contradict Eero's observation. "But you have a roof over your head and food on your plate."

"I'd give it all up to be happy!"

"Eero, you don't know what you're saying. Don't ever wish for such horrible things. When I was a little girl, so many people died of famine right here in Finland. The crops failed. Babies and children on our farm perished because they didn't have food. You would never want that for yourself or anyone you loved."

"At least if they died, they escaped Finland," he retorted.

Raili shook her head sadly. Eero could still remember how the two of them were in their large kitchen at that moment. Before his mother were the loose cabbage leaves she had just pulled from a quick parboil. Another bowl held the barley mixture. His mother carefully rolled the limp leaves around a ball of stuffing, folding one edge of the leaf under another so that the roll would not fall apart when placed in the sizzling lard of a hot cast-iron pan. The working girl, Berte, was in the front parlor dusting and humming some country tune. Raili continued, "Don't be so eager to escape, Eero. What would your poor mother do without you?"

"I'd take you with me," he stoutly replied.

"But why would I ever want to leave my home?" she asked in wonderment.

"I'm the only one who loves you here, and I would take care of you. Father ignores you. You know that he does. And Matti thinks only of himself."

"And what would you have me do with your sisters?" she asked. A dozen carefully crafted cabbage rolls sat on the plate between them, two for each member of the family, including Alli and Aini. His sisters were only five and seven. "Would you force your little sisters to endure that awful boat ride across the North Atlantic? Make them live in a place where no one spoke their language? They might not even make cabbage rolls in America." She laughed lightly.

"I don't want to choose between you and America," Eero said. He meant it. He wanted what he wanted, but was unwilling to give up anything he valued.

"Well, you won't have to choose," she replied. "I'll always be with you. A boy needs his mother."

Raili lied that day, and Eero never quite forgave her. Not even now, almost seventy years later. That day she already knew she had consumption, and that her best chances for survival required retreat to a German sanatorium. It was a country on the other side of the Baltic, far from their farm. While she rejected a long boat ride to America, his mother was already destined for a different dreadful journey. But in the warmth of the kitchen conversation, Eero foresaw nothing. He only thought his mother pale and subject to coughing. Not even months later, when she had a bad coughing spell and left in her lace handkerchief a bloom of blood, not even then did his young mind suspect the truth. To this day, Eero didn't understand why he failed to deduce her illness. He wasn't a tenant farmer's child. He was well schooled and well read. He had even read *Camille* by Alexandre Dumas. All he saw, all he worried about in those days, was his own life.

Focused on leaving the farm as soon as he was old enough, Eero sought to learn everything he could about emigrating. The family once vacationed at the port town of Hanko, so he knew the exact docks from which the Finnish Steamship Company boats departed for England. He recalled the seaside promenade from which the rush of people sought to board the ship that offered escape from their homeland. Even from his hotel window on that vacation, he envied the peculiar mixture of desperation and hope that fueled the emigrant crowd.

Eero hung a map of the United States in his room. He marked out strange sounding names in oddly shaped states to track where Finns headed: to the iron and copper mines of the upper peninsula of Michigan, to the docks of Seattle, to the Mesabi Iron range of Minnesota, to the cities of New York and Boston and to the farmlands of Wisconsin. Where would he go and what would he do? Eero was quite fond of stories about the American West. He heard tales that the Mesabi Iron Range was a bit like that Wild West. In his mind, he imagined himself a professional gambler traveling through forests, moving from mine town to mine town and playing cards.

But in his practicality, he determined Wisconsin would be the place to head when the time came. Eero understood only farming. While Eero didn't actually know anyone who emigrated, his mother had a cousin who long ago left for Superior, Wisconsin. Another reason to target that state. At least he would have some blood tie that could be useful.

He planned out all of the logistics. A steerage class ticket was only about $20, but he would need cash on arrival or the American officials at

Ellis Island would bar him from entering. Unlike the Nurmi family, who had nothing when they lost the tenancy on the Makinen farm, his family was one of the largest landholders between Turku and Tampere. His father could afford to stake him. He was a Makinen, even if only the second son.

Planning the details often sustained him during days of depression. A few days' sojourn in Helsinki would let him see some old friends before boarding the ship in Hanko. Then there would be three-and-a-half days sailing to Hull, England, followed by a couple of weeks across the Atlantic. He hoped he could convince the old man to give him a good amount of money, so he didn't have to travel steerage. Once in America, it was just a two-day train ride to Wisconsin. Land was cheap there, and the climate was just like Finland. That's what everyone said, and there were already thousands of Finns in the state. Times at home seemed less desperate, knowing that he could always be in Wisconsin within a month, where it would be good.

He determined to emigrate as soon as he turned eighteen, but he worried about broaching the subject with his father. He needed a financial stake from the old man, and timing was critical. Eero didn't want to risk being drafted into the Russian Army, or worse, being sent to theological school by his father. But Heineke Makinen was so clear on his distaste for the emigrants, and his hatred for the hellhole he considered America was so intense.

Eero's mother would have been on his side. But then the blood appeared in her handkerchief, and she grew weaker and thinner. A decision was made. Heineke and Raili left for Hanko to board the boat to Hamburg. In Germany, they would take a train to a sanatorium renowned for its cure. At the farm, Eero said goodbye to his mother. He held back all tears, just as he held within all the things he wanted to say. To this day, Eero reflected on how he never learned. Years later with Jaacko and Johani, and then again with Risto, he never said what should have been said.

In this case, too, it proved too late. Weeks later, his father arrived home alone. His mother's coffin followed, and her body was interred in the family graveyard. She had died within days of arriving at the sanatorium.

Bereft of his mother before he turned sixteen, saddled with a young stepmother within a year, Eero continued to plan his escape. He always wondered if Inge had been lying in wait. Had his father forced his mother into that long journey to Germany in hopes that it would kill her and free him to marry again? A horrible thought to have of one's own father, but Eero could never release that suspicion. On the farm, Inge distrusted Eero as much as Eero distrusted her. As a result, Matti's star rose even higher. He was charming to his new stepmother who was only a few years older. Eero found it all disgusting.

But in the end the change in family dynamics made it easy for Eero to leave. Without his mother, he felt no binding ties. Alli and Aini were young and would thrive without him. Matti was the golden boy. Inge detested Eero. Heineke made quite a scene when Eero first broached the topic of departing. He repeated all the familiar arguments about the weakness of those who left. But in the end, both father and son knew it would be better for Eero to be gone, and so Eero left with $500. It was more than enough funds to pay for a second-class cabin to America and allow cash to scout for good farmland in Wisconsin.

During the many days at sea, Eero often reflected on his talks with his mother. While there was no outhouse on the boat to which to escape and no sauna in which to sweat out his apprehensions, Eero found that standing alone at the railing and watching the rush of waves provided the peace to think. He replayed all that he had told his mother as well as what he had not, recalled what she advised him and what she had kept secret.

Even now, years later, such memories only convinced Eero of one thing: loss is terrifying. People require a guide through grief. But what had he done with that insight? He tried to aid Marja to deal with the deaths of Johani and Jaacko, but he did not succeed. And he failed Lempi after Marja's suicide. Let's admit it, he said to himself, he failed Lempi again when Pauline was murdered.

He blamed secrets. Everyone has secrets. Secrets from those you don't know. Secrets from those you love. Secrets even from yourself when everyone else knows the truth. But it's no easy thing to break through the binding ties of such secrets. Like Pauline's secret. His secret. Lempi's secret. Risto may have thought no one wondered why he left Finn Hall on the night of his departure party. But his father noticed. Oh, yes, Eero remembered how his son slipped out that evening. Eero thought then that a quiet moonlit night might be the perfect place and time to tell his son how proud he was of him. So Eero left to follow his son, but he stopped in the shadows of the side entrance of the hall when he saw his son strike up a conversation with the grocer's pretty daughter. He saw a hint of their happy faces as Risto lit Pauline's cigarette. Eero smiled, forgetting his mission to have a heartfelt talk with his son. As the two youngsters walked down the street and headed toward the millpond, Eero knew he should interrupt them, but Eero liked the fact that his son was a bit of a rake. He was certain that a good German girl like Pauline wouldn't let the night go beyond a kiss or two.

But a few months later Marja came home from shopping so excited. A secret talk with Mrs. Newmann had Marja bubbling in joy. She and Mrs. Newmann had concocted a ridiculous plan for a hidden adoption. Eero knew he should refuse, but he was overcome by the happiness he saw in Marja. Not only did he want her to frolic in that joy, but he also suspected that the baby in question resulted from him letting Risto and Pauline walk away in the moonlight—this was probably his own son's baby. Eero decided the adoption would be a perfect solution to make his wife happy and replace the lost Jaacko and Johani, but later he thought it was a mistake that he never told Marja what he suspected.

When Marja returned from Superior, the baby looked so much like Risto. Eero was amazed that Marja never saw it. The resemblance kept anyone in town from questioning Marja's late-in-life birth. As the years went on, and Pauline tried to ease her way into Lempi's life, Eero never opposed it. In his heart, he believed that Marja and he were really the grandparents. Why shouldn't his little Finnish girl have some exposure to her real mother?

Eero sometimes wondered whether Risto ever learned about his daughter. The few letters they received from Karelia were short and brief. Even so, Eero always read them carefully for any hint that Risto knew Lempi was more than his sister. Just in case, he once made Marja send Lempi's photo to Risto. But then the letters died. In time, Eero came to believe that Risto had been executed during one of Stalin's purges, or that his son died during World War Two. In any case, the truth about the Makinen miracle, as some in Clover called Lempi, was one more topic that Eero never discussed with a loved one.

Even today, Eero still had a chance with Lempi. He felt he should have disclosed the truth about her upbringing to Lempi when Pauline was killed in the explosion. But with the girl so upset, he couldn't bring himself to disclose the full truth. And he was troubled by conversations he and Lempi once had about clearing his land with explosives. Her interest had been strange, and he avoided thinking about it.

That damn biological urge wasn't going away. He needed to put on his jacket before heading again to the outhouse. Besides, he was making himself crazy falling into these old memories. Those days were gone. They couldn't be changed. He headed to the closet for his plaid coat. And suddenly, the urge was gone; the intestinal pain was gone.

Things were such a muddle. All these swirling memories. It was like tobogganing down a steep hill and losing complete control. One could end up anywhere, hitting a tree or getting upended in a giant snow bank. Still, reminiscing had its pleasures, just like sledding and he saw no reason to stop. One never knew when the ride would be a thrill.

Adventure always lured him, and he never looked back. When he stepped off the Wisconsin Central train in Superior, Wisconsin in 1907 to meet his mother's cousin, Eero was an eighteen-year-old raring to go—with over four hundred dollars remaining in his pocket. His father and the Finnish farm were far behind. His cousin Alvar was quick to introduce him to other Finns in the twin port towns of Superior and Duluth. The local docks were busy. Trains unloaded hopper after hopper of iron ore from the Mesabi Range. Big carriers steamed across the lake to transport the ore to foundries and mills further east. Alvar assured him that there was plenty of work to be had for any hardworking Finn in these twin cities. Local bosses trusted those from the old country.

But as Eero watched the dockworkers and the Great Lake sailors, he decided they worked too hard. On his journey west, an old Finnish saying often ran through his mind, *oma tupa, oma lupa*, or when one has his own place, one is his own boss. He might never have the family farm in Finland, but here in America, he could be a landowner. He could provide a special spot for his children.

"I want to buy a farm," he told Alvar. "I've seen land agents advertise in *Työmies* for acreage nearby."

"Don't do it," warned Alvar. "Cutover land this far north isn't good. The seasons get cold too fast, and the soil isn't rich enough. Land's cheap enough up here, and God knows the agents for the railroads and the lumber barons will be quick to convince you it's heaven on earth. But I've seen where some of my friends have landed. You could do better."

"But where?" Eero asked.

Alvar's reply was quick and confident. "South of here. In an area of Wisconsin they call the Clover Belt. It's only a hundred miles or so further south, but the weather is warmer, the snow less, and the soil is sandy, but rich. Clover and grain grow so easily, and with that you can fatten your dairy cows and get rich selling the cream. It's old cutover land from the lumbering just like up here but it costs more. Pay the price. You won't regret it. Besides, you got the money." Alvar knew how much Heineke provided his son to exile him.

So Eero found himself in the village of Clover, smack in the middle of the Clover Belt. Soon, he spent his 400 dollars for eighty acres of good soil. He had hoped to purchase a quarter section, which would have given him one hundred and sixty acres. That would still be small compared to the hectares of land on the family farm, but it would be his. He could have purchased more land in the marginal lands of northern Wisconsin. In fact, many Finns did so in small towns from Superior to Ashland to Thread. But Eero fell in love with Clover from the moment he saw the town and he never looked back on his decision to buy this smaller farm. As it was, clearing those eighty acres of slashed stumps leftover from the lumber baron days nearly killed him.

The land was his little bit of heaven. He looked out the window now and remembered how different those eighty acres looked back in 1907. Yet of all the plots he examined that year, he knew immediately that this acreage on the banks of the Black River was the right speck of land. So many of the other farms were depressingly flat, as though the fields would turn into a marsh with the lightest of storms. Trampled by icy glaciers millennia earlier, the contours of the land had largely been smoothed. But this place was different. It rose gently from the waters of the Black River, which flowed south toward the Mississippi. It offered just enough of an incline that Eero wouldn't worry about spring flooding reaching the fields near the road, where he intended to build his house and barns. The size of the remaining hardwood stumps along the river told him that the acres nearer the river held rich soil accumulated by years of spring waters dropping nutrients. In one dip of the land, a young second forest was already reemerging from the logging. He walked the entire eighty acres that first day. He imagined how the rain would fall and drain across this landscape. It was good for healthy crops.

The small rise near the rough road was exactly where he would place the homestead. From that hill, if he kept the fields clear and he planned the house right, he would be able to glimpse the river while standing in his kitchen. He was right. To this day, he could still see the river. After sixty-five years, some of the pasture he had worked so hard to clear was turning back into woodlands, but he insisted that his tenant farmer plant crops in the key fields to preserve his view. When the farmer rotated planting corn through those fields, his view of the river might be blocked for a month or so. But except for late summer when the corn was at its highest, the shimmer of the water always beckoned. In this area, the Black River ran north to south, and its banks were due west from Eero's house. In the right weather and atmosphere, the setting sun danced across the water with diamond beams of light that glinted in his windows. Such an unexpected benefit.

He bought the land from Thomas Steele, the land agent for the Oxford Lumber Company. Steele was full of promises and tried to sell his vision. Eero didn't listen to him, and even though stumps of the old cuttings blocked much of the view that day, Eero could foresee what he could create on this soil.

Fate looked on him with pleasure. After he signed the deed on a Saturday, Eero decided to attend services the next day at the local Apostolic Lutheran Church. Eero wanted to slip into the town and blend in with its people, and he figured the church would be the best place to do that. He also harbored another thought. Midsummer's Night was only a few days away, and surely the Finns would have a summer solstice party. Maybe he would see a pretty girl who he could ask to the dance.

As a result of that decision, he first laid eyes on Marja Torsonnen. He fell in love with her as quickly as he had with his recently purchased land. Marja was still a teenager and sat between two others girls her age. When Eero entered the church, he noticed their pew immediately. Clear glass windows in the church focused bright sun that enveloped the three of them in a box of light—a box that was shattered by her laughter. Eero didn't expect people to laugh in church, even if services had not yet started. But Marja did. Her excited chattering among friends displayed a warm and gregarious nature. Her blonde hair was radiant. Eero stood a second too long upon entering the church and before sitting in a pew. He didn't want to lose sight of this girl. In that moment of delay, Marja looked up. Her clear blue eyes caught his in an unexpected, but shared, glance. She smiled. He sat down, overwhelmed with an unexplainable anticipation as though he had downed an entire pot of coffee that morning at the boarding house where he spent the night. Who was she? How could he meet her?

Just thinking of that day long ago, Eero smiled. He heard nothing that the reverend preached. He lingered after the service, introducing himself to new neighbors, happy to be participating in Finnish conversations, but always keeping an eye out for the girl. Where had she gone? Of course, everyone knew everyone else. There were probably only about one hundred Finns in Clover at that time. All were very interested in meeting this new young man, and he found it challenging to keep an eye out for the girl. And then she dashed up from the church basement, ran to the minister and gaily grabbed the man's hand.

Suddenly Eero knew. This was Reverend Torsonnen's daughter. He had traveled halfway around the world to escape the life of a minister and now he found himself enamored with the daughter of one. He didn't care; he made a sudden internal pledge to marry this preacher's daughter. He was as certain of the rightness of that as he was of the fertility of his land. It might take some time to convince this girl, and maybe more time to convince her father, but he knew destiny's route.

His initial idle expectations for a Midsummers Night party now became an opportunity. He would meet her there, away from the scowl of the Lutheran Church. It proved an easy task. A typical minister's daughter, Marja was a rebellious spirit. She quickly noticed this recent emigrant's interest, and she maneuvered herself to stay in his sightlines. Eero always suspected Marja did that because her father would disapprove, but he knew better than to ever ask.

"Would you like to dance?" were his first words to her. The band was striking up a polka, and he loved the enthusiasm of the dance. In Finland, his father disapproved of all dancing. But that didn't matter now.

"Oh, speak in English," she responded. "I've lived in America almost all my life, and I'm so tired of hearing everything in Finnish. I'd be happy if I never spoke another word of Finnish. I only get into trouble when I do."

He smiled. His English was good enough to understand her, but he wasn't certain he could banter back, so he stuck to Finnish. "Well, then I will only speak Finnish, and we'll see what trouble you get into."

She smiled and replied in English, "Well, let's dance" and they twirled into the mix. But from that moment on, Marja spoke to him only in Finnish, but she left such little time for Eero to speak that it hardly mattered whether he could have answered in English. Before the dance was over, and it was long for a polka, he learned that Marja had emigrated with her parents when she was six, that her father was very strict, that they had moved frequently from Finnish community to Finnish community but had remained in Clover for the past two years, that she was about to turn sixteen, and that all she wanted out of life was to have babies—a dozen if she could!

"I need to stop," he broke in. "I can't keep dancing like this, and if you keep talking so fast, there will never be a reason for us to talk again. And I wouldn't like that!"

She lightly tapped his cheek in a mock slap. "That's fine. I have other boys to dance with. But don't worry. I'm sure we will talk again. I always talk to the handsome and clever boys."

The promise of that night still echoed in his heart, as it would until the day he died. How could he have been so certain so quickly — to know the spot on which to build a life, to recognize the woman who would make his life worth living and to persevere to ensure it all happened? Luckily, one couldn't foresee the future when one was young, or he would not have found the courage to continue. The seasons that followed proved the farm was not so perfect, and Marja was not so carefree. Her wish to be blessed with so many children would not come true.

But neither of them saw it then. Only now was it all clear. He felt an ache of loneliness in his heart. Life without his sons was hard. It proved even harder going on without his Marja. How could Lempi ever consider forcing him to give up his farm? Didn't she know what the familiarity of this place meant to him? She might be both his daughter and granddaughter, all rolled into one role that she didn't even realize, but she wasn't enough to anchor his life. The ache stayed in his throat.

It seemed unfair. Life was so long, and so many memories piled up. They shouldn't come cascading through one's mind all at once, toppling one over the other, like some madman's game of dominos. But that was what this day had become for Eero. Not that he really minded. There was something comforting in letting his memories return him to simpler, happier times. He thought just then of the fall day when he and the twins attended a rally in Clover for Senator "Fighting Bob" LaFollette. Now there was a great Wisconsin politician. Hard to believe LaFollette belonged to the same party as that scoundrel Joe McCarthy whose fanaticism destroyed so much. No, Eero wouldn't think about that senator; it would only bring on the sorrow of losing Marja. On the other hand, Fighting Bob stood for the common man. If LaFollette had had his way back in 1917, the United States would have stayed out of that European War. Who wanted America to join the fight against the Huns? Certainly, not the German immigrants who settled around Clover. Maybe, that's why so many of his German neighbors showed up for the rally in the center of town.

LaFollette was stumping for local Republican candidates and fervor was high. How his twins loved the pomp and glitter of that day! The town was awash with bunting, and the cheering was so loud at the train station that one could hardly hear the train's steam engine start up to leave. Everyone cheered on the Senator who railed against those who wanted to join the war. LaFollette was Eero's hero, and seeing the man with Jaacko and Johani was glorious. The boys were still young, but Eero was certain they appreciated the significance.

How he loved talking to those boys. Their buggy ride home that day traversed country roads basking under a glorious September afternoon, a real Indian summer day. Their top was down. The skies above were blue with only the wispiest of clouds. On such a day, even his old plow horse looked gallant pulling a buggy.

"Why were all the people cheering?" Johani asked. He was so serious. He was the boy who always sought to understand.

"Because they were seeing the great Senator LaFollette," Eero replied, smiling to himself.

"What makes him great?" piped in Jaacko. He was always the questioning twin. The two may have been identical with their blonde hair, blue eyes and wiry bodies, but their similarities were only skin deep. Their souls were so different. Surely, they should have been destined to do great things.

"LaFollette is great because he's good." Eero held up his finger to silence the boys before they could jump in with another question. The horse continued to plod toward home and hay. "The Senator watches out for the common man, people like us. He makes sure big companies, the railroads and the meatpackers don't take advantage of farmers who can't easily fight back. That helps your Ma and me. The Senator has been pushing the creation of cooperatives for us farmers, so we can work together to get better prices." The boys seemed impressed, with Eero's statements, although he realized they didn't really understand. But they liked to model themselves on him. As the three of them stood close during the rally for the sixty-one-year old senator, Eero could see that the boys sought to maintain the same expression of enthusiasm and awe that he knew described his own face. It almost made Eero laugh. At one point though, Jaacko pointed toward the Senator's big shock of a pompadour haircut and whispered to Johani, who slapped at his brother as though he were a pesky gnat.

"But aren't all people good?" Now which of the boys asked that question? Why couldn't he remember? It must have been Jaacko. Johani was shy and sensitive, quick to assume the best in anyone he met. Jaacko liked to dig deeper, never satisfied with the first answer to any question. But that afternoon, they were still little children who were naive and earnest. Maybe if he had lived, Jaacko would have taught his siblings a little skepticism. Both Risto and Lempi were always too quick to carry the torch for their beliefs, and could have used a touch of Jaacko's personality.

Eero shook his head. It wasn't good to dwell so long on the twins. It was fine when it was the rosy moments, like thinking about their buggy ride. But he needed to avoid the blacker moments. But they always came rushing back. They swirled around him now, drawing him into recalling an earlier memory of that same day at the Lucky Clover Hotel.

Eero was looking out for himself that morning. He wanted to model himself on LaFollette's courage as a prelude to seeing his hero in person, and he had a wrong to make right. When he purchased his farm years earlier, the land agent Thomas Steele and his boss, Barney Oxford, had cheated him. He loved his farm, but recently he discovered he didn't really own all of it—at least not the way he thought. Like all the land around Clover, his holdings were carved from the cutover timberlands owned by Oxford. Steele, the local Oxford land agent chartered to sell off the acreage, was a huckster at heart. In those days, Eero didn't understand English enough to know what was in the land contract. It all happened so fast; he had been too eager. Even though Eero thought he fully owned his eighty acres, he now knew that the Oxford company retained mineral rights to every farm sold in the Clover area. That made him steaming mad. It didn't matter if every neighbor was in the same boat, nor did he care that there were no valuable minerals on anyone's land. The sale was unfair and Eero was determined to get those assets returned.

Knowing Steele ate lunch every day at the Lucky Clover, he planned to corner the shifty man there. Eero marched into the hotel with his sons trailing him. For a rural town, it was a grand place. He was awed by its plushness, but determined to demand what was due him. Steele was at the table eating with two other people. One of them was the lumber magnate himself, Barney Oxford. Eero hadn't anticipated the millionaire would be in town. A young man sitting with the two seemed to be Oxford's personal secretary. Eero was not deterred. Even though he had no reason to eat in such a fancy place, he walked into the hotel dining room proudly. Linens covered the tables. Waitresses in stiffly starched aprons that went near to the floor hurried from spot to spot. As he marched up to Steele's table, Eero's twins hung back

"Listen, Mr. Steele," Eero jumped right into his purpose, "I think you cheated me." He knew his English wasn't perfect and his Finnish accent strong. The other men at the table looked up at him with some modest surprise. "I paid full cash for my land so it should be mine, clear and free. But now I find out that this Oxford company still owns part of it, that if they found copper or iron or some such thing, that they could mine it. That don't seem right." Jaacko and Johani inched in closer and he held their hands tightly. He didn't want them running off. At least that's how Eero remembered it.

Steele seemed uncomfortable being confronted before his boss. "You should have thought of that before you bought. Besides all the land around here was sold exactly the same, and the conditions were specified clearly in the deed. Mr. Oxford, who's sitting right here, sold only the land. Perfectly legal. And very common. Now I know you Finns don't have a lot of schooling, and aren't used to such things, being Mongols and such, but I can assure you there ain't nothing wrong with what we did."

Without looking up from the steak he was carving, Oxford spoke. "Mr. Steele is right, but if you want, leave your name with my secretary, Tom Ferber. He can look into it all and confirm that it's all been done properly. Tom, take down this man's name."

The young man, pulling out his fountain pen and opening a notebook, somehow managed to convey that while his colleagues' actions were legal, they weren't necessarily proper.

Eero felt bullied. "I'm not going to waste my time having you pretend to do something." The young man blushed. "There's people on the side of folks like us. Fighting Bob is in town later today. I'll go to him for help." Such a statement was mere bravado, but Eero wanted to believe it. Surely, the Senator wouldn't be on Oxford's side.

Oxford erupted, "That man is a disgrace to the United States Senate. Fights to keep us from arming our own ships, overly worried about supporting our friends in England and France. There's a reason that even Teddy Roosevelt calls him a skunk. Go to your rally and see if he can help." In a flash, the lumber baron's anger transformed. Laughing, he picked up his silverware and ignored Eero.

Steele returned to his own lunch, dismissing Eero. The young Ferber looked straight at Eero to see what he wanted to do. Eero felt foolish and humiliated in front of his boys. He bumbled into this encounter without a plan; his only option was to retreat. Even now, Eero burned in embarrassment. Sons should never see their father dismissed in such a way. They should only remember the good times.

Why did the bad memories insist on floating up? Think instead, Eero told himself, of the bunting, the campaigns bands, the applause of stump speeches and sunny buggy rides. He should have sought LaFollette's aid. Oxford cheated all the farmers and they didn't even know it. LaFollette would have been on their side.

Eero saw the Senator one more time. It was years later, and by then, Eero was resigned to knowing he didn't control the mineral rights to this land. There really wasn't any likelihood of oil or gold in the Clover Belt, so holding on to his anger served no purpose. But Eero still admired Fighting Bob. In 1924, the Senator formed the Progressive Party to run for president and he planned a campaign stop in nearby Eau Claire, Wisconsin. Eero decided to make a day trip with his son Risto. Like he did with his twins, Eero would take his one remaining son to see the great man. Eero had recently acquired a used Model T and was excited to journey fifty miles in it.

The twins were long dead by then, but their ghosts lingered on. It had been eight years since he had taken the twins to see LaFollette at the Clover rally and five years since their unexpected death. Both Marja and he remain haunted every day by the details of their short lives. Marja refused to join

Risto and his daytrip.

But it was important to take Risto on this journey. Eero knew that Marja and he were too blind to the promise of Risto. Risto was a quick and clever boy. He deserved more attention. Not surprisingly, Risto found the excitement of a political rally energizing. Eero wished Marja could have seen her remaining son in such a wonderful light, but she had changed since the twins' deaths. She no longer liked leaving the farm, and she disapproved of Eero's love of talking and politics.

On the drive home from Eau Claire, Eero discovered his young son also liked politics. Throughout the drive, they talked about topics that young boys seldom considered. They kept it all in English, as the trip was a rare chance for not using Finnish. Marja had retreated to only allowing Finnish at home after the twins' death, as though somehow they wouldn't have died if the family had only stayed more purely Finnish.

"Pa, LaFollette's on the side of all of us, isn't he?'

"Why do you say that?" Eero asked. At times during the drive, he found it difficult to pay full attention to the boy because he didn't feel in control of the automobile. It seemed to have more of a mind than his horses.

"Because he said he wanted to help the farmers by making it easier to borrow money from the banks. That's good isn't it?"

"Yes"

"And he said he wanted to outlaw children working in factories. You always said children should go to school, not jobs."

"Yes, I did"

"And don't you believe the government should own the railroads and utilities, like the Senator said, so that they serve all of us?"

"Risto, I'm impressed. You really listened to those speeches today."

"Someday, I want to be president just like Mr. LaFollette."

"Well, he isn't president yet."

"Oh, but he will be. I like him because you like him. And I want to do all the great things that you say should be done."

Eero reached out a hand to riffle his fingers through his son's sandy hair. He quickly returned both hands to the wheel. "Don't admire me too much. Think for yourself as well."

"Pa, are you a progressive like the Senator?"

"I don't know what I am exactly. Sometimes, I think I'm a socialist, sometimes a Communist, sometimes just a farmer. We're all lots of things, you know. Life can be too complicated to sum it up in one word."

"I'm going to be a progressive Communist farmer just like you."

Eero burst out laughing. The boy could be whatever he wanted to be.

Eero bent over suddenly in pain. This time it was nausea. Where did that come from? Maybe he did need to go to the outhouse, not to dump but to throw up. Maybe he ate something gone bad. Perhaps it was those canned stewed tomatoes from the lady across the road. Always bringing him jars of her old canned goods. He didn't trust her motives or her canning. He carefully inspected every lid on every Mason jar for any telltale sign of bulging. He lived too long to let botulism do him in, but maybe he hadn't been careful this time. He had been quick to dump those tomatoes in last night's stew.

Another spasm, but he decided it was all in his mind. His damned memories were trying to force him to relive the way the twins died, but he wasn't going there. Over the years, too many hours had already been given to Marja's reliving that deadly summer day. Marja never forgave him for sending the boys over to the Mueller place. He even encouraged the twins to take little Risto along. All just boys, they walked into the jaws of death. What was he thinking, letting them go off by themselves?

In the years that followed, Marja always wanted to know how he could have been so foolish. But he just wanted his sons to have fun. The Muellers had children their same age. The kids liked playing together. Besides, he had stumps to clear that day. That's the real reason why he let the boys go, but it was a reason he could never tell Marja. The truth was it was Marja's own fears that prompted him to send them off. The lads weren't afraid of his dynamiting work. They loved the explosions. It was Marja's unfounded fear. She was always convinced that he would kill them all. That was the real reason he encouraged the boys to visit the Muellers. He didn't want Marja's fears to infect them. It would have been simpler if she let Eero do the stump clearing by himself. But she always came along—as though it somehow made the whole activity safer, even though the dynamiting terrified her. If she came, then the boys came too. She wouldn't let them stay alone at the house, and so they all watched from the sidelines. But her fear was so palpable that it unnerved the boys. Eero knew that if he sent the boys to play elsewhere, Marja could fret alone. He could blast more stumps with less stress. There was the remaining ten acres to clear that summer, and he was behind schedule. So he let the boys go to the Mueller farm.

If given a choice, the boys would have opted to watch the stumps blow. They thought it was great fun. Of course, Eero knew the practice had its danger, but the work had to be done. Left after clearing the virgin hardwoods years earlier, the jagged stumps were enormous; there was no way to farm around them, so a rough pasture surrounded the remaining stumps. Cows could graze on the grass in the summer. But that was a poor use of the land; Eero needed to tap into the full potential. Over the past decade, he cleared a few more acres each year. On the northern section, where young trees were already sprouting when he bought the land, he was letting a small woods grow, keeping mostly the maples. That meant when this pasture was done, his stump-blowing days would be finished.

Dynamiting was the best way to remove the stumps. Their roots dug deep into the earth. It would take decades for them to rot away naturally. No farmer could wait for that. Everyone cleared the land the same way. Eero didn't know anyone who ever got hurt, other than one fellow up north. But he had been careless, forgetting to pay attention to his fuse length.

But Marja never saw it as safe. She nearly wept from fear with each new removal. No boy should see his mother so frightened, which is why Eero came up with the game. Inspired by a movie he saw at the Clover nickelodeon, he reimagined himself into a dastardly villain. He made a great show of biting off the fuse cord, showing a snarling face. Then after the match laid flame to the fuse, he made an exaggerated run toward safety, yipping in a fake fear that the boys found hilarious. Even Johani laughed uproariously, until the boom and geyser of debris erupted. Then the boys cheered. It was the Fourth of July each time. Seeing his boys laugh and cheer made the follow-up work of dragging away and breaking up the uprooted stump more bearable. But no matter how joyful the boys, Marja always scowled. Eero always made sure that Marja and the boys were safely distant and sheltered. He never skimped on the length of the fuse, ensuring he had plenty of time to join the family before the explosion. If anything, he cut fuses that were foolishly long. That left a danger that a fuse might peter out, and the resulting requirement to investigate why an explosion hadn't happened.

So, for this one day, he made a decision to release Marja from worrying. The boys could have fun somewhere else.

Hit by another spasm, Eero's nausea was getting worse. He decided at least to walk onto the porch for some fresh air. If vomiting overtook him, he could spew it onto the lawn. But again he wondered if his body was reacting to memories he didn't want to remember, a past he was trying to push away.

So much later, why did Lempi become so fascinated by how he cleared the stumps? Marja had always hated the past so much she never let Eero talk about the twins or Risto. After Marja did what she did, Eero broke free. He started telling Lempi stories about the early days in Clover. For Lempi, these stories were new and exciting, and of all the old stories, the dynamiting of the tree stumps was her favorite. She asked him to repeat it many times until it became their private joke. He honed his telling until he could guarantee it would make her smile. She liked hearing about the brothers she never met; she found the fears of her mother comical. By now, Eero embellished so many little bits that he didn't really know if it all happened the way he told it.

That's why it seemed so strange when a few years ago Lempi asked detailed and technical questions about his use of explosives. She wanted to know how much of a charge Eero used, where he bought the dynamite, how many seconds the fuse burned and all sorts of forgotten details.

"Why are you suddenly so interested in all of this?" he asked her.

"I just started to think it would be nice to know how things were really done on this farm, not just your funny anecdotes, but the actual details. If I don't start asking you now, how will I ever learn?" she replied.

"Okay."

"Did you have to use dynamite? Wasn't there any other way to clear the land?" she then asked.

For some reason, an answer popped into his mind. The Mueller kids down the road, who turned their father's place into the largest dairy farm around, recently excavated a pond using a different kind of explosive. After Eero asked them so many questions, one of the Mueller sons handed him a pamphlet from the state agricultural agency. It described the process.

"Nowadays there is another way. Let me go get this pamphlet about how to create explosives using fertilizer." After Eero found it in his kitchen junk drawer, he handed the brochure to his daughter.

"Thanks, Pa." she said, and never mentioned it again.

Years later, after reading the news reports of the bombing that killed Pauline, he recalled that pamphlet which described a mixture of fertilizer and fuel called ANFO. The papers said ANFO was used to destroy the Bremen College building. His memory might be fading, but Eero was certain that was the same stuff the Muellers used for their pond. Surely it was only an odd coincidence, but it worried him.

After Pauline's death, Lempi became too much like Marja, withdrawn and morose. She didn't improve when Toivo moved the family to Thread. He didn't want to think that giving Lempi an agricultural pamphlet somehow caused an anti-war bombing. But he knew he was deluding himself. Lempi was so ardent in her convictions. Pauline always worried about the people surrounding Lempi. Now Eero worried himself sick about something that almost certainly wasn't true.

Why go down this path again? If he had to wallow in past recollections, why not center on the happy ones? Like how the boys used to love picking berries. Maybe that would help him forget his pains.

Patches of berry brambles flourished among the old stumps, especially near the shade line of the emerging woods. There were all kinds: blackcaps, red raspberries and blackberries. Each type ripened to plumpness at slightly different times. Johani and Jaacko were expert pickers. Eero wished Marja's photo albums had a picture of them dressed in overalls and no shirt. Their bare feet grew hard from their tramps out to the pasture's edge with empty pails, and coming back with overflowing buckets, fingers stained from the picking and hands scratched here and there by the brambles' thorns.

Always enterprising, Jaacko suggested selling the berries in town. By themselves, the boys would walk three miles into Clover, head to the local grocer and sell their fresh berries for a quarter or two. Mr. Newmann bought whatever they had to sell, and they might use their few coins to buy some pieces of penny candy, but they saved most of their earnings to buy a birthday gift for their Ma. Eero suspected that the young grocer didn't always have buyers for these wild berries, but Mr. Newmann was fond of them. Eero wondered if a young Pauline ever watched his young boys bring in those berries.

Why was he back on Pauline? He didn't want to think about Pauline ...

or Lempi . . . or Marja. He wanted to remember the happy times with his boys and those days of promise. He was turning into Marja in his old age, refusing to see any happiness in the world and instead lingering on those dismal days best forgotten.

When the boys first became ill, the doctor made clear the reason why, and told them he would do what he could, but that it wasn't much. Marja turned to her father, seeking in the minister some hope of salvation. Whatever remained of her wild days evaporated with the doctor's diagnosis. Reverend Torsonnen, assigned to a church in Michigan's Upper Peninsula, claimed he was too far away to come down easily. He sent a telegram that said, "God will deliver." What nonsense! Eero was angry even now thinking of the old man's deluded arrogance; he would have killed his father-in-law with his own hands if the man still lived in Clover. What God would strike down two boys with a possible death sentence due to a mere whim of fate? But Marja let the uncompromising message fester in a deep hole in her heart. Every day, she lingered in the downstairs living room, where the boys had been moved to make it easier to care for them. She spooned them the watered-down whiskey to ease their pain, and with each spoonful she said another prayer to a God she once scoffed. "Deliver my babies." Eero couldn't bear to hear her whisper those words. The other word—trichinosis—was never uttered by either of them. It was too foreign and too frightening to acknowledge.

As the days passed, it became clear that Risto was recovering. For some reason, God allowed Marja's prayer to save one of the three. While parasitic worms still ate at the bodies of her other babies, the stalwart nature of her youngest defeated the invaders. Marja barely noticed, even though Risto's recovery gave Eero such joy he was almost unable to work the farm and almost prepared to believe in God. Marja chose differently. She abandoned any concern for her youngest son and focused her attentions, her entreaties, her fears and hopes on strengthening the twins.

Eero ensured the well-being of the one son the doctor said would fully recover. In fact, Eero ensured everything on the farm continued forward: the twice daily milking of the cows, the stoking each morning of the wood stove, the weeding of the vegetable garden and the harvesting of the crops. God might be stealing his sons, but He wasn't altering His seasons to delay the haying or the reaping.

Neighbors helped where they could. Nearby farmwives frequently delivered freshly baked pies or bread. As the summer wore on and local gardens were laden with tomatoes, corn and new potatoes, buckets of produce would appear mysteriously outside the back door. Eero would bring those offerings into the kitchen. But when he found a basket of fresh berries, the bright colors enlivened by bits of fresh green leaves still stuck among the fruit, the bottom of the basket stained by fresh juice, he couldn't bear to accept them. Instead, he threw the berries into the pig slop.

Marja refused to talk sensibly about the twins' condition, or how they had been stricken. "It was those Germans," she maintained, "they wanted to kill my boys, giving them bad meat, swarming with the eggs of nasty little worms."

"Marja," Eero tried to explain, "the Muellers didn't know that their pig was infected with parasites. They didn't try to kill our children. We're the ones who failed to cook the meat thoroughly."

She locked into her own paranoia. "Don't bring that up. The Germans lost the war, and now the locals are bitter. They can't stand to see happiness in the rest of us. They know what they're doing."

It depressed Eero immensely to see Marja so irrational. During World War One, both of them shared the views of their Wisconsin senator, Bob LaFollette. Lionized by the local German immigrants, the Senator tried to keep the United States out of war. He fought for the freedom of speech. For that his fellow senators vilified him. During those war years, both Eero and Marja stood up for the local German settlers—no matter how strong the anti-German fervor. After the war when the horrors of the Spanish Flu ran through the county, Marja was among the first to try to help the Muellers and their many German relatives who fell ill. Several of them never recovered, but she showed no fear of nursing. In turn, their German neighbors saw Marja's kind heart. Now his wife only saw old friends as enemies.

Then it was over. Jaacko and Johani were gone. Much of the bootleg whiskey, secured on the sly through Walther Newmann's back room, remained unopened on the basement shelf. No longer was there a need to dim the boys' monstrous reality: the slow migration of tiny worms into their hearts and muscles. No more centers of pain to kill them slowly.

Dr. Koch told Marja and Eero that if they had realized sooner how the pork was contaminated, the doctor might have successfully purged the parasites before they settled in the muscles. Some claimed it was possible to irritate the parasites while they were still in the intestinal tract. A combination of water and glycerin induced vomiting and stemmed the infection. But by the time the symptoms appeared, it was too late. Once the worms invaded the muscles, there was no treatment, only palliative methods. Dr. Koch had recommended they relieve the monstrous pain with morphine. But morphine was expensive; whiskey was cheaper. Even if the Volstead Act outlawed it, people in town knew where to buy it. Walther Newmann, always fond of the boys, sympathetically helped Eero stay supplied.

So strange about the Newmanns. Even though they were German, Marja recognized their kindness. Even as she condemned the rest of the area's Germans, she allowed the Newmanns an opening. In truth, Marja went a little crazy when death finally released the boys. She wouldn't get out of bed for a week after the funeral; she could not look at Risto for more than a few seconds; and she grew fascinated with knives. Eero worried that she would slash her wrists, or worse, walk Risto into the Black River and drown both of them.

Still he couldn't help but love her. He wanted to touch once more that joyful girl he met the night of the Midsummer festival. By the time dead leaves fell from the maple tree that rainy autumn following the twins' deaths, a bit of color returned to Marja's cheeks. A sense of energy and purpose invaded her day-to-day routines. To those who never knew her as a younger woman, or to those who didn't see her every day, she appeared to have refound her purpose in life. But Eero knew better. So did Risto; he sensed that he painfully reminded Ma of lost brothers.

Time did not heal Marja's wounds, although she became better at masking any emotional scars. Years later when Risto decided to join the Karelian Technical Aid movement, Marja said nothing to Risto when he informed them. She stared at him coldly, her lips pursed but unmoving. After Risto climbed the stairs to the attic bedroom that night, Marja turned savagely to Eero, "You made him do this."

"It was his idea," Eero protested.

"No, I don't believe it. You're always talking about politics and great men. You caused that boy to think he must make sacrifices to get your attention. He has to live up to your ideas about people like the LaFollettes and those Finns in the Communist Party. They aren't looking out for us. No one looks out for us."

"That's not true."

She would have none of it. "Oh yes it is. If Risto's train crashes going to New York, if his boat sinks going to Europe, or if he gets lost in the wilderness of Russia, will any of those people care? Will any of them show up at our door to ask forgiveness? No."

Her anguish made Eero recall the dark days after the twins' burial, only this time Marja seemed more intent and willing to speak. "Those things won't happen. Risto's a fine young man, concerned about the lot of us. He seeks to make a difference in the world. We should let him."

"You just want to kill him, the way you killed my other babies." She hurled the accusation with venom.

He didn't know what to say, so he said nothing.

"You know you did. It's your fault they ate that bad pork. It's your fault that Risto wants to leave us. It will always be your fault."

Eero stirred uncomfortably on the porch swing, looking out at the farmland that had nurtured Marja and him for over forty years of marriage. Nearly two decades now had passed since Marja's suicide. Recalling her accusation still stung. No wonder he was feeling poorly, dwelling on horrible arguments that could never be resolved. Their disputes were in the past. He should think about when Lempi entered their lives. For a while, Lempi's presence made Marja happy again.

The day Marja returned from shopping at Newmann's store, the afternoon when Mrs. Newmann invited his wife to the grocer's home for a cup of coffee, the moment when Marja realized she could be a mother again—that point in time was as happy a moment as Marja enjoyed in the remaining decades of her life. On that summer day in 1933, Eero walked into their kitchen and knew something momentous had changed. Marja was frying doughnuts. The aromas of sugar and hot oil in the air had been missing since the week Risto left home. Marja was humming and seemed twenty years younger.

"I made some fresh coffee," she said, "to go with the hot doughnuts. Sit down."

As any sensible man would have been, Eero was suspicious. But he opted not to ask questions. Let his wife tell him what made her so happy.

"Mrs. Newmann asked me to coffee today. She asked me to help her. And Pauline," she said.

"And how is that?" Eero asked.

Marja gaily laid out the entire plan, repeating every detail that Gertrude Newmann so carefully engineered: Pauline was pregnant but before anyone realized her state, she would go live with a distant cousin in Milwaukee; Marja could pretend she was ailing and travel to see a specialist in Superior, then stay for treatment; after the birth of Pauline's baby, the Milwaukee cousin would transport the infant to Superior where Marja would accept it; finally, Marja would return to Clover with a baby and an explanation that it had turned out she had not been ill, but pregnant. Who would imagine such a thing at her age?

"Ridiculous," Eero scoffed. "No one will believe it. We don't even know who the father is. The baby might not look anything like us."

When he voiced his real reaction, two things happened. The face of his beloved Marja—and he did still love her despite the craziness of the past decades—dissolved. She became once more the mournful woman who languished after the twins' funeral. In the same instant, an image popped into Eero's mind. He recalled the night before Risto departed, when his son left Finn Hall to flirt with Pauline. In the words of Marja's minister father, it was his epiphany: Eero accepted that the child was likely their grandchild and already theirs; it was their duty to raise it. The baby would solve everything.

Something on Eero's face betrayed his change of view. Marja immediately brightened. "You want to do it," she said, not asked. "I can tell Gertrude yes?"

Marja never asked what changed Eero's mind. He never told her. Only once was he tempted. It was the morning of the day Marja finally gave in to her life-long temptation of suicide.

A horrible wind storm the night before had thrashed the farm. The yard was littered with branches from the maple tree. He remembered how he had planted it on the lawn's edge back in 1913. But after the winds, it was shredded. The lawn was covered with boughs from the windbreak of evergreens that bordered the side pasture. Several shingles were ripped loose and betrayed bare spots on the roof. The storm also shrouded something else—something he didn't want to tell Marja.

Eero entered the house after the morning milking. He took off his barn clothes and left them on the side porch. He knew he would have to begin the strenuous clean up after eating. On the kitchen table, Marja laid out a large breakfast, including Finnish pancakes. She poured a steaming cup of coffee, and placed the bowl of sugar cubes close to his cup.

"Everything okay in the barn?" she asked.

He nodded yes, not willing to speak aloud. He could not risk telling her how the large word "Commie" was painted on the red walls of their barn. Sometime during the storm, local vandals had pounced. Eero was so tired of it all: tired of working the farm by himself, weary of the battle with the government and Marja's threatened deportation, infuriated by locals who looked upon them as though they were traitors. He recalled all the times he defended the local Germans back during World War One. He always pitched in during the years of the Depression to work together with his neighbors so they all could survive, regardless of background. He was a proud part of the brotherhood of Finns who created a strong farming cooperative. During all those years, Marja and he were there for the community. But Clover abandoned his wife. He would not defend them.

"I'm tired of storms," she said.

He knew Marja had more on her mind than the previous night's winds. He looked at her sadly, took her hand and pulled it closely to him. "Storms always pass," he said.

"Do they?" she asked. "All I ever wanted was a houseful of children. And I destroyed them all. What kind of mother have I been?"

"You have always been a wonderful mother."

"I killed Johani and Jaacko. You know that I did, but you have always been too kind to tell me so. I roasted that pork; I didn't cook it enough."

"No, no. That's not true."

"And I ignored Risto so much that I drove him away. What could he do but leave to find happiness elsewhere. His mother didn't love him. You know that's true. And I've tried to find him for years. But look where it's got us? Risto just wanted to do the right thing, and now he's dead, forgotten, and this town thinks his mother is a spy."

"Marja, why are you torturing yourself?" Eero asked. Ever since being released from the Federal prison, Marja moved about the house in a slow, morose trance. She almost seemed happier when still locked up. Certainly, Eero knew no way to cheer her. He thought of the accusation emblazoned on the barn's red wood. Everyone who drove down their country road would see it. He had to paint it before Marja left the house. Even if every one of their neighbors knew of the painted word, she must never see it.

Marja rambled on. "And now Lempi. So smart, so beautiful. She could have been a college girl. She should have had all her dreams come true. But no good came from our adopting her. If Pauline had kept the girl, she'd be going to college now. I destroyed that, all because I get frightened. I needed to know where Risto was. That's why I joined the Party. And when the FBI men appeared, I wanted Lempi to care for me. That's why I let my daughter tell those lies, so she would be bound to me. So many ruined lives. All my fault."

Eero pulled Marja's hands to his lips and kissed them gently, and then he stood up from the table, walked behind Marja's chair and wrapped his arms around her. He held her tight, saying nothing. Over the decades, he learned that words could not reduce her pain. He wasn't certain that anything he might do or say could achieve that.

Certainly, a hug was not enough. At least not that day.

If only Marja were still here. With her, he would happily put up with these waves of pain. Walking on the porch made him think more of his dead wife. When she was still alive, on those slow days in the fall when one could move a little bit slower because the farm wasn't as demanding, Marja and he often took their ten o'clock coffee sitting on the porch bench. Bundled up in fall jackets, they watched the occasional falling leaf be carried across the yard. Marja would hand over a cup of coffee, its saucer holding two cubes of sugar to the side. He would take one to place between his lips as he sipped the coffee. In those moments, neither said anything to the other, but found peace in the silence.

His arm felt numb, and the nausea still lingered. Maybe he should relive the old days and get a cup of coffee from inside. It might enliven him. But the sun felt so pleasant hitting him on the face. He looked up into the warmth and formed a small smile.

The heat prompted another unwanted memory. A sunny afternoon when the boys had such big smiles, a day when the boys returned from the farm, unaware that their father had been blowing up stumps. Johani and Jaacko excitedly ran up to Eero and Marja who had just returned from the clearing. Risto hung back a bit from his two older brothers. It was about three in the afternoon, and Eero hadn't yet washed up. Dynamiting always dampened Marja's enthusiasm, but she brightened considerably at the joy in the boys' voices. As though it were a prize, the twins handed over a package wrapped up in brown butcher paper.

"Open it," Risto said.

Jaacko didn't want to wait for that. "The Muellers killed a hog, Pa."

"And they let us watch," Johani added.

"They told us to give you this meat."

Marja held the wrapped package and weighed it in her hands; she stepped up onto the porch and sat on the bench. The boys crowded around her as she untied the twine and set it aside for saving. She pulled back the paper. Inside was a beautiful pork loin. Its flesh was lightly pink, with just a small amount of fat still attached. Eero thought it was unnecessarily generous of the Muellers to send over such a choice cut of their pig. They were good neighbors. He made a mental note to repay them something equally fine in the fall when he killed the pig they were fattening.

"We helped in the butchering," Jaacko bragged. The boys set off into a complete recounting of the big gathering of Mueller kin at the morning slaughter. The barn had been carefully prepared. Ropes on pulleys were in place to hoist the pig; a big vat of boiling water, buckets and tools were on hand. The boys recalled with excitement how the squealing pig was pulled from its pen. They showed no concern for the fear infecting the pig. But Eero knew his sons were accustomed to a farm's killing season.

When Eero chopped off a rooster's head for the Sunday dinner, the boys were there, prepared to pull the feathers from the bird after it was dipped into hot water. They sat by their mother's side as she quickly dressed the bird, always amused as she cut open the gizzard and cleared out its grit. When the ax targeted a laying hen, they marveled if they found a partially formed egg inside the chicken. Johani would roll any egg he found without a shell across the kitchen table as though it were a toy. Marja would retrieve such eggs—shell or not, they could be used for baking. The pig was just a larger version of the weekly chicken chopping. Still Eero wouldn't have sent the boys over to play if he had known the Muellers were about to kill a hog. Up to then, he had kept his boys from helping in the fall butchering.

But the three boys didn't seem bothered. They recounted every detail:

the way Mr. Mueller hit the hog with a large mallet to stun it into unconsciousness; how the men tied the hog's rear legs with the ropes attached to the pulleys; the way the men playfully encouraged the boys to help pull the ropes as though it took the kids' strength to yank the pig off the ground; and then the precision with which Mr. Mueller slit the pig's throat and how quickly Mrs. Mueller used her bucket to collect its blood. Eero knew she would be making blood pudding. Germans loved that dish.

Even now, decades later sitting on his porch, Eero could recite in order the process of hog butchering. As with chickens, the pig would be dipped in boiling water, in this case to soften its bristles. The men would run their hog scrapers across the pig, and then skin its hide with precision. The breakdown followed: the heavy rear legs for curing as hams in the smokehouse; the bellies sliced for side pork and bacon: the better cuts like the loin set aside for quick consumption; the head destined for boiling so that pieces of meat could be pulled for head cheese; the trotters handed over for brining into pickled pig's feet; the fat rendered down into fresh lard; the intestines cleaned and prepared as casings for sausage. The Germans always made good sausage. Truth be told, Eero would have preferred some fresh sausage in a few days to today's loin.

"Ma," he said to Marja, "we should roast this pork tonight for supper. There's no good place to keep the loin cool until tomorrow."

"We could put it in the root cellar," she said. "Not much time left before supper and milking the cows."

"There's plenty of time," he scoffed. The first mistake.

Marja frowned, but carried the meat inside the house. The boys continued to talk excitedly about the butchering. Then Risto asked a question, "What did you do while we were gone, Pa?" Johani and Jaacko looked up suspiciously, noticing for the first time the remnants of dust and debris still on Eero's clothing.

"You went blasting without us," Johani accused in a quiet way. It pierced Eero's heart.

"Yes, I did, but you know your Ma don't like you being around when I use explosives. But I tell you what. Let's walk down to that field and I'll show you what I did." Faced with the excitement of something new, they quickly forgot their disappointment at missing the actual blasts and they spent an hour trampling among the blasted ruins. Each boy found different things at which to marvel.

"Time to get home," he said, "your Ma should be setting the table for supper by now." And his three boys tramped behind all the way home, like faithful little ducklings.

"Supper ain't ready," Marja said. "The fire was nearly out in the stove, and it took a while to get it going."

"Hurry it along," Eero said. "I want to eat before milking, and the cows don't like their routines changing. It's not good to make them wait."

Marja made supper happen. Why did she listen? Normally, she had such stubbornness when it came to his demands. Why that night did she pull the roast out of the wood stove's oven when she did? Why did she carve it after it had barely rested and put all the pieces of meat on the platter? Even he could tell that the center pieces were pinker than normal. Was she exerting her independence? But he said nothing. Second mistake.

The boys were lively and hungry. Jaacko and Johani fought over who could take the first pieces of meat. Eero was amused and let his sons go first. They felt ownership that day for supper and he was willing to forego his going first. Each twin grabbed one of the center and thickest carvings—the pinkest slices. The meat was tender that night. It was actually the best pork that Eero had ever eaten, and he wondered then why Marja always overcooked it. He didn't realize pork could be so tender and juicy.

And so deadly.

Eero felt a sharp pain in his left arm. It was how he imagined his boys felt when the parasites first moved into their muscles, forming into cysts and sowing pain. Recalling the twin's faces and their unanswerable cries during the weeks that the disease went on was fruitless. There was nothing he could do then; there was nothing he could now. In the years since their loss, he avoided ever thinking about his first two sons. The past was too painful. No wonder an ache was spreading from his arm into his chest.

No salvation could be found in talking about his lost boys. His neighbors respected that. As far as Eero could recall, neither he nor Marja ever discussed the boys with Lempi. Of course, there were the few photos that Marja kept to torture herself. Lempi asked about them, but the answers were brief and designed to end the inquiry. Lempi knew little about Jaacko, Johani or Risto. To all intents and purposes, she saw herself as an only child.

On the other hand, Risto was just old enough that summer to recall his older brothers and his own brush with death. But as the years passed, his memories became a hazy story, details were slowly lost and the summer took on the aura of a family myth. Only once did Risto ask Eero about his dead brothers. It was 1928, Risto was fourteen, and Eero was about to send the boy away for the summer, not that he wanted to do such a thing, but he determined he needed to protect his son from his mother's depression. Everything around Marja was becoming contaminated. Looking each day at the calendar reminded her that Jaacko and Johani, if they had lived, would be turning eighteen. She found this observation particularly unbearable, so unbearable that she retreated into a somnambulant state. Dust built up in the house; the fire in the kitchen stove went out; and the washed sheets flapped in the wind long after they were dry. She moved slowly from task to task, often completely forgetting basic ones. When confronted, she grew agitated and broke into tears. It was too much to ask a fourteen-year-old boy to deal with the emotional breakage.

Even though he needed Risto's help with the summer harvest, Eero wanted Reverend Torsonnen to take his grandson in for the summer. His father-in-law still ministered to a small congregation in the upper peninsula town of Houghton, Michigan. The town itself was reasonably large, and even hosted a college. If things worked well between Risto and his grandfather, Eero thought Risto could stay, attend high school and then go on to college. He wouldn't be contaminated by his mother. Farming would be a challenge for Eero, but at least the boy would only have to endure the choking moods of his mother on holidays.

Eero disclosed his plan right after Memorial Day and Risto's graduation from eighth grade at the rural one-room school. He focused on the positives. Staying on the farm and going to high school in Clover would require a long walk every day. On the other hand, Reverend Torsonnen's church was just two blocks from Houghton High School. The bigger city would also have better teachers; and since there would be no need to hurry home for farm chores Risto would have time for activities like football.

Risto was outraged. The boy was growing into a man; his blonde hair was turning dark, his shoulders were widening and his anger scared Eero. "You can't send me away. I belong here with you and Ma. She needs me."

"But she's getting worse. Don't you see how she sinks so low? She barely functions, and she pays no attention to you. It's not fair to you to make you live with that every day."

"Why not?" Risto demanded.

Eero had no good response. How could he tell Risto that it was his presence that triggered Marja's depressions? Seeing the boy pushed her into wallowing in the losses suffered. She did not see how Risto was charming, quick and talented. She didn't care that he smiled easily or felt deeply for her, doing everything a young man could do to help his ailing mother. Instead, his kindness was just another lash that drew oozing memories of what might have been—Marja would never have the dozen children she gaily told Eero she wanted, and she needed no reminders of the ones already lost. A normal woman would have enjoyed what God had left her. But if Marja had been normal, Eero would surely not have fallen so deeply in love.

Risto persisted, "You can't tell me one good reason why I should stay with Grandpa and Mumu. But I can give you lots of reasons why I need to stay here. First of all, Ma and you need me to keep things going. She can't take care of the house or the summer garden by herself. And you don't have time to do it. I can weed the cabbage, pick off the potato bugs and harvest the pears. I've watched Ma enough to do it all. I could even can preserves. You won't have anything but rutabaga and cabbage to eat next winter if you don't let me stay. You'd be like the cows."

"I can hire one of the neighbor girls to help," Eero said.

"And where will you get the money for that? Things are tight. You had to go work in the timber camps last winter to help make ends meet. And while you were gone I milked and fed the cows. All the while. And still got to school on time. At least most of the time."

Eero wasn't deterred. "But you can't link your life to ours. Just because Marja isn't well doesn't mean that you're our slave."

"Pa, I thought you taught me that we're all here for one another. That the strong have to protect the weak. You don't take me seriously, Pa. You don't think I can make a difference. But I can. I like this farm, and I love you and Ma. I don't want to be somewhere else all summer. You gotta have me here when it's time to reap the grain. It's not fair to everyone else if we don't both show up for that. We're both part of the reaping team."

Eero had an answer. "Mueller's bought one of those new Massey Ferguson automated reapers. I was thinking of hiring him to do our oats."

Risto looked at him with disapproval. He seemed far older than fourteen. "More spending money you don't got, Pa. What's really going on? Why don't you want me to stay?"

The two of them were out on the front porch. Eero wanted to get away from the house because Marja couldn't hear what he was about to say. He walked into the yard, making Risto follow.

"I don't want to be harsh, son, but your Ma shouldn't see you for a while."

Risto stopped in his tracks, and his face fell. An unwanted wave of comprehension passed over his face. "What do you mean, Pa? That don't make no sense."

"It's your brothers," Eero said. "You remind your Ma too much of them. They're on her mind all the time. When she sees you, she can't help but see them. You move like them, your eyes flash like them, your voice even sounds like them. And now that you're getting older, the way you're growing so fast, the way your voice is changing, she's just reminded that she never got to see Johani and Jaacko grow up. And it curses her. She don't want it that way, but she can't help herself."

"But it ain't fair. It ain't no one's fault that they died." Risto protested. He was on the verge of crying.

If only that were true, Eero thought. But it was someone's fault. Maybe it was many people's fault. The boys carried the meat home. The Muellers raised a dirty pig. He sent the boys to play at the Muellers, and he made Marja serve the pork before it was really done—before the heat could cook the tiny worms to death. But Marja listened to him and served it. That's why he could never tell her again what to do. Because she had listened to him. And because they both knew it was really his fault.

Risto didn't look like the twins; Risto looked like Eero. And the twins resembled Marja. Seeing Risto grow was seeing a new Eero emerge, seeing a person who might make the same horrible decisions as his father. But Eero recognized that there are some truths that must never be said aloud. Some secrets deserved to remain secret. Risto would gain nothing by knowing the divisions that separated his parents. A fourteen-year-old could not comprehend such intricacies and still accept that two people could be in love.

"Your Ma just needs some time. A break in routine will help her settle. She's a good woman and she loves you. Give it a try for the summer. Forget what I said about going to high school in Houghton. Plan to come back in the fall, and go to school here. For a couple of months, I can afford a hired hand and an occasional girl in the house. You have a good summer. You graduated eighth grade. Not all the boys around here get to do that. You should be rewarded by doing something special this year. Go see part of the world, and then come back and tell your friends about it. You can tell the girls. Girls like men with experience."

Risto smiled at his father's attempt to joke, but Eero could see that this new idea was tempting his son. "You sure you can afford it? Ma won't mind?"

Eero often wondered what turned Risto's mind. Was it the thought of travel, the hope that it would help his Ma or his desire to impress girls? Already at fourteen, Risto displayed a certain prowess with females.

"But I don't want to stay with Grandpa and Mumu. They don't like me."

"Where else could I send you?" Eero asked. There were no alternatives. Marja's cousin in Superior was single, and would be incapable of caring for a boy about to be a man. But Risto had an answer.

"I can attend the Young Pioneer camp. It's up near Houghton, so Grandpa could look in on me if you're worried about that. There'll be a lot of Finnish kids there."

"Why would I send you there? Where did you get such an idea?" Reverend Torsonnen would be outraged if he learned his grandson wanted to spend the summer at a youth camp belonging to the American Communist Party. While many Finns might have a radical edge, members of the Finnish Apostolic Church were not among them.

Risto probably knew that, but was he confident in his plan. "I went to a meeting last week at the Clover Finn Hall. A bunch of people were there, all talking about making things better. They were socialists and Wobblies and Communists. This young Communist organizer named Gus Hall spoke. He wasn't much older than me, but he made so much sense. The means of production should belong to us all, not just the rich."

Eero smiled a bit at his son's earnestness. Youth could be so idealistic. It reminded him of the outrage he flung against his father back in Finland. He only wanted his own piece of land, and now his son was spouting his own approach to life.

Risto was excited. "Hall told us all about this camp they run for people my age, and the fun that kids can have there, how we can learn more about

Leninism. The Party will even pay for it. I thought about asking you if I could go, but I knew you needed me here. But now you tell me you don't. So can I go?"

Eero couldn't think of a reason to object. He didn't agree fully with Communism, thought of himself more as Progressive, much like his hero, Senator LaFollette whose children now had to carry on his legacy. There were aspects of the Communist Party that made sense to Eero, and he reasoned a young man should get exposed to a lot of ways of thinking. Eero remembered how his father was always quick to turn down Eero's idea.

"If you really want to do it, you can go," Eero said. Risto rewarded him with a huge smile and hug. Later that night, Eero told Marja he was sending Risto for the summer to a camp in northern Michigan. He didn't tell her what kind of camp, nor did she really care. He saw a brief light in her eyes and a slight smile that she quickly tried to hide. She wanted Risto out of the house, even though she would not admit it. She only replied, "Whatever you think best."

When Risto returned from the Young Pioneer Camp in August, it seemed as though his absence for two months created a double miracle. During Risto's time away, Marja snapped out of her spiraling melancholia and eagerly awaited her son's return. When he leapt off the train into her arms, she listened avidly to his excited stories. She marveled at how Risto shot up an inch or more in height over the summer and put on several pounds of muscles working and playing in the camp. Eero was impressed by a different change. Risto came back a far more articulate speaker than when he left, even if the boy was now prone to talk about Marxist theories. The summer in exile seemed quite a win.

Eero sat back against the wall of the porch. The bench beneath him had been part of the house for as long as he could remember—here on the last day he spoke to Marja, here the day the FBI agents drove up and here years earlier when he convinced Risto to spend the summer away. It most certainly had been here when the twins showed up so excited with the gift of pork. Thinking of that day, Eero felt light-headed and out of breath, a little sick to his stomach.

Back in 1920, stomach cramps were the first indication that something wasn't right with Jaacko and Johani. Their first symptoms appeared about a week after eating the pork roast. So much time had passed that no one thought to connect it back to the meal. Initially, both boys complained of bellyaches and diarrhea. Soon little Risto complained of the same pains. Eero and Marja thought their youngest was seeking the same attention as his older brothers, but then his diarrhea started. Later the next day, both Eero and Marja felt under the weather. Their first thought was that it was something they ate. But they never reflected back on the pork supper of a week earlier. On the farm, so many foods might go bad. Eero feared that it was somehow related to the Spanish Flu that swept through town two years earlier. He could imagine nothing worse than its return. He hoped it proved to be only food poisoning

Eero and Marja's discomfort soon disappeared, and a day later Risto was recovering. Whatever it was, the illness seemed short-lived. They were certain the twins would soon be back on their feet.

At first, when the boys' complaints were limited to bellyaches and the need for frequent runs to the outhouse, family life went on. Eero still milked his cows daily. He planned ahead for the oat harvesting. Marja picked the peas and beans from her large garden and proceeded to can them. Risto returned to playing or trekking to the wood's edge to pick berries.

All the while inside the boys, worms were hatching. After first being consumed in the undercooked pork, the larvae quickly molted in the body's juices, grew into adults and laid more eggs. Another generation of larvae readied an invasion. Dr. Koch later told Eero that the response system of most people would find and flush out such larvae before any damage was done. Most individuals never knew they were infected, or displayed only mild symptoms. But depending on the age and nature of the victim, sometimes the larvae flourished and their sheer numbers prevailed. They were vicious in their desire to propagate. With scissor-like mouths, the small worms would cut through the lining of the small intestine to invade the blood stream. Once there, they could swarm to every part of the body's muscles and skeleton. While Eero and Marja went about their daily routines, occasionally looking in on their sons to make certain they were okay, the parasites were conquering the bodies of the twins in a bloodless war that would leave no survivors.

Eero should have sensed much sooner that something larger was afoot. But there were always the chores: a cow wasn't giving as much milk as anticipated; a storm threatened to destroy the grain field before it could be harvested; blackbirds swarmed into the garden; fellow Finns distracted him with debates of politics; Marja worried him by falling into one of her moods. Everything masked the reality: Jaacko and Johani were not getting better.

It was about the tenth day—Marja and Eero had forgotten feeling ill and Risto seemed close to normal—when Marja called upstairs for the twins to come down for breakfast. Johani, always the more sensitive of the two, moaned that he couldn't. He complained that his muscles hurt. Jaacko didn't say anything. She climbed the narrow stairs to the small attic bedroom. She looked more closely at both. Their faces were swollen, their eyes bloodshot, and both had high fever.

She was alarmed and called down to Eero in the kitchen below. "Eero, get the doctor. Something is wrong. They're getting worse." And so Eero ran over to the Mueller farm to use their telephone to call Dr. Koch. Mrs. Mueller anxiously stood by Eero as he pleaded for Dr. Koch to drive over that morning. The doctor was well respected in town. He had stature and a brand-new Chrysler. He would know what to do.

Often, in the years that followed, Eero wondered if Mrs. Mueller ever thought back to that day in her kitchen. She was so concerned about the boys, her kitchen air redolent with the smell of frying bacon (perhaps from the very pig), and neither of them carrying the least suspicion that Mueller pork had prompted this emergency. Did she ever torture herself, as Marja and Eero both did, with a fear that it was their fault the two boys died? Probably not, Eero always decided, as the Muellers were practical people.

Dr. Koch came as promised. His shiny automobile was a rarity in the farms around Clover, but Eero saw it as a sign that all would be well. The doctor walked into the house with his heavy black bag. Marja was already in a state of great anxiety, but Eero felt strangely calmed by seeing this graying man carefully dressed in professional clothes. He was a symbol of order and knowledge. His presence was an assurance that things would work out. It was the twentieth century after all.

"Let's see what we got," Dr. Koch said. He walked into the front room. After returning from the Muellers, Eero had carried the boys down to a sick room setting he and Marja quickly set up in the front room. The doctor looked at the twins kindly, but Eero thought he seemed shaken by their appearance.

"When did you first begin feeling this way?" he asked each boy. "Have you felt this way continuously, or have your symptoms changed recently?"

The boys were timid in their answers, but Eero quickly spoke for them. He added to their brief replies whenever he felt a need to amplify the response. The doctor needed to know every detail if things were to be made right once more. Certainly, some medicine in that bag could help.

The doctor turned to Eero and Marja, "Have you eaten any bear lately?" Perplexed, they shook their heads negatively. There hadn't been bear in the area for years. Why would he ask such a thing? He continued, "How about pork that is rare or still pink?"

Marja and Eero looked at each other in sudden apprehension. Both of them immediately thought of the meal ten days earlier. The doctor realized he had found his answer. "When did you have the pork?" he asked.

"The Muellers gave us fresh pork, but that was ten days ago. It must be something else," Eero felt as though the room was spinning.

The doctor looked again at the boys, studied closely their red eyes and puffy faces, and retook their temperature. He stood up straight and motioned Eero and Marja to follow him into the kitchen, "I think it is quite likely that your two sons are suffering from trichinosis. The timing and symptoms are right. They are running quite a fever, and their eyes show periorbital edema. Sometimes, you see, pork is infested with these small worms and . . ."

Eero cut him off, "I know what trichinosis is."

"Yes. Well. The connection between pork, the parasites and these symptoms was only established forty years ago, back when I was in medical school. People didn't always know. So . . . once the worms have worked their way into the blood stream, as they have in the case of your sons, which we know because of the symptoms they display . . . well, once the worms are there, we can only wait. All we can do is seek to alleviate the pain.

"If we had known sooner in the first few days, we might have flushed the body with chemicals like carbolic acid or a tincture of iodine. This can irritate and accelerate the expulsion of the worms before they reproduce. We are too late for that, so we must let nature take its course. But Mr. and Mrs. Makinen, you should hold every hope for a full recovery. Although the days ahead may be painful for your boys, almost all recover fully from this infection. The body is a powerful thing. It will do all it can to flush itself of unwanted pests. All of you were probably infected, but as adults you fought it easily, and your youngest son must have a strong constitution. I am sure your other sons will prove equally strong. I remember well when Mrs. Makinen gave birth to them. They are fighters.

"But these worms are a mean piece of God's creation. They will seek to bury themselves deep into the muscles of your sons. The boys may suffer great weakness and muscle pains, as well as headaches and intolerance to light. If the pain gets too intense, I can prescribe morphine."

"What will that cost?" Eero asked, concerned because money was always tight.

"The druggist can tell you. Sometimes it's sufficient to give a youngster like these some watered-down whiskey to dull the senses. It's cheaper."

Marja broke in, "But Prohibition."

Dr. Koch looked at Eero. "There are ways of buying hard liquor. I am sure you can find someone to help."

"How long will it take for our boys to get better?" Eero asked.

"We should see a turnaround in a few days or a week. I will stop by again tomorrow."

In the years that followed, when Eero allowed himself to dwell on what Dr. Koch described, he understood the reality that infested his boys. The Mueller pig was infected with parasitical worms that could only have happened if the Mueller pigs ate some type of contaminated meat. Eero suspected one of the pigs devoured a dead rat. There were always rats around the barns, and pigs would eat anything. Its flesh on the day it was butchered contained larvae of trichinella, small parasitical roundworms. If not killed by sufficient heat, the larvae could thrive inside the small intestine.

When told the diagnosis by Dr. Koch, Eero wished aloud that he had inspected the loin, but the doctor said that would have made no difference. Then he wished that he hadn't insisted Marja serve supper on time. For that, the doctor could give no forgiving response, but he was polite enough to say that the trichinella were hardy creatures. They survived even in meat that was cured or salted.

When the doctor left, Marja and Eero went back into the living room to sit by the edge of the boys' makeshift beds. Risto stood behind them, watching and listening, as Eero explained to his sons how they had been infected with small parasites. He called them his brave soldiers and proclaimed they would succeed at kicking the little things out. "I have faith in you boys. You're strong ones, and these little worms can't fight your power. Try to rest. I am going into town to buy some medicine to help you feel better."

Eero hitched up his buggy, drove into town and relived the pork dinner over and over in his head on the ride. He tied up the rig in front of Newmann's General Merchandise. He still couldn't accept the doctor's judgment, but he reckoned he needed to act on the man's advice. Some of his friends gossiped that Walther sold Canadian whisky from his back room. Eero walked into the store, pulled Walther aside and told him about his sons. The grocer was quite willing to help. Soon Eero was headed back to his farm with several bottles of whisky.

Eero made one more stop. He felt a duty to warn Mr. Mueller about the pork. His neighbor listened, pinched together his lips and then muttered an apology. He thanked Eero for the alert and said he would destroy the meat curing in the smokehouse as a precaution. Something in the man's demeanor, however, suggested he didn't appreciate Eero's visit. Eero didn't care. His responsibility to the neighbors was fulfilled; now he needed to help his sons recover.

Sitting on the porch, reliving a past he wanted to forget, Eero felt such a sense of doom. Pondering old memories and everything left unsaid was doing him no good. He should go for a walk. That always helped to focus his mind. He started down the front steps and turned the corner of the house. In the distance to the west, across the fields, he could see the waters of the Black River. A covey of ducks flew low to land on the river. He should make his way down to the riverbank. Now that he leased the land, he seldom walked its familiar contours. At times, the land didn't feel like his anymore, even though no one could have a higher claim to these acres. He removed the stumps, his plow turned the soil for the first time and his hands dropped the seeds for the first crops. Without him, this farm and all that came with it would not exist.

Over the years, there had been so many walks on this land. Funny how Eero could remember the strolls with his wife and the jaunts with his boys, but it seemed as though he and Lempi never explored the farm together.

What times did they share in all those years of her growing up? He knew he should have paid more attention to her. So many things he could have told her but didn't. Such were the regrets of his life—never saying the things that mattered to anyone in his life: his mother, his wife, or his sons.

But at least he tried once with Lempi. Earlier in the spring, he spent a week with his daughter on their place in Thread. It wasn't much of a farm, not that he could blame Toivo Lahti or his parents for that. The soil in northern Wisconsin was weak and the growing season short. There only seemed time for snow. Recognizing the limits of his parents' farm, Toivo found a job in the woods almost immediately after moving back to Thread. It was the only way to ensure food on the table for Lempi and Danny. The farm, such as it was with its few chickens and pigs, was left to Lempi's management.

Danny was already a lively year old. Eero could see a bit of Marja's spirit bubbling forth, and a hint of the same charm that Risto displayed as a baby. He hoped Lempi found time to observe her son closely.

His daughter surprised him one day by suggesting they leave Danny with her in-laws and walk into town. They started down the gravel road into Thread. Remnants of snow banks remained along the roadside, but the spring air was fresh and the pussy willows were pushing out fresh growth. "Are you happy?" he asked Lempi. It was the setting that made Eero so bold.

"What a silly thing to ask," she replied. Lempi didn't look at Eero when she said it. She just continued marching forward, her body propelled by the purposeful stride that was her trademark. It was a challenge for Eero to keep up. But she didn't fool him with her light-hearted response. He could see the twitches around the eyes and the tug at the corner of her mouth. Before arriving in Clover, Eero had given his boyhood dreams a shot with a short attempt at gambling on the Mesabi Iron Range. He became an expert at tells. He knew all of Lempi's, and what each one signified. Lempi was seeking to avoid a subject.

He little understood what motivated or excited his daughter. After all these years, he realized he kept her at arm's length. Knowing that Lempi was really his granddaughter—and keeping that truth hidden from Marja—created a barrier between Lempi and him. Eero never knew the right way to love her. That was the problem with secrets. They were corrosive and ate away at normal behavior. They remained hidden from sight, doing their damage, until one day, everything collapsed. And no one saw it coming.

So many secrets in life. Too many really. In his old age, Eero began to realize that applying a layer of truth could hinder the hidden destruction. It was like when rust began to eat away at the workings of farm machinery. You had to file away the rust, and oil the damaged spots to protect them. Otherwise, over time, the rain and snow would claim the iron as its own. Nature was a relentless foe, and, if you didn't persevere, it always won. Drive by any farm and you saw a field strewn with rusting pieces of farm machinery. Something once vital was discarded and allowed to rot away. If one wasn't careful, that could happen with people's souls.

On one hand, he knew so much about Lempi, more than she would ever know, details like the identities of her real mother and father. He also knew truths of her inner self. Lempi never admitted to the despair that overwhelmed her when entry to Bremen College was snatched away, but he knew how much she longed to attend. He even knew about that boy she met on her long-ago trip to California. Oh, the two of them, both teenagers, no doubt thought they cleverly kept their romance hidden. But the drivers of the car, Eero's neighbors and Lempi's employer for the summer, were no fools. When the family returned, the husband alerted Eero to all that he knew of Lempi's summer romance. Eero often wondered what happened to that fling. Did the boy ever think of his time with Lempi? Would she have been happier if she had married him?

Unfortunately, there were other things Eero didn't know and these situations worried him the most. Did Lempi feel guilt about Marja's suicide? Guilt could eat away at one's soul. What did his daughter have to do with the bombing at Bremen College? After that holiday explosion killed Pauline, Lempi changed. Only one reason could explain why his daughter moved to this tiny town to work this desperate farm. She was seeking an escape from something. He had met the friends she kept in Milwaukee. They were a dishonorable bunch, and he knew Lempi took his pamphlet on explosives when she had no need for such information. He hated suspecting his own daughter, and longed to lance the festering sore.

"Asking if you're happy isn't silly," Eero said. "I'm an old man, and time wears on. If I never discuss things that really matter, I'll never know whether my daughter is happy. I've spent too much of my life not saying what needs to be said."

She smiled, "Then why start now?"

He looked at her. The way her smile could light up her face was beautiful. "Because I love you. I know I never told you that. I never told any of my children that. Such a simple truth. But before you know it, it can be too late to say it. I know that all too well.

"Marja and I were so happy when she gave birth to our twin boys. They were premature, and it wasn't an easy birth. Doctor Koch was put to the test that day. But the boys were fighters, and gave such cries when they took their first breaths. We heard them and knew they would grow up to be fine young men."

"Pa, I've never heard you talk before about Jaacko and Johani."

"Keeping silent was the biggest mistake your Ma and I ever made. When the boys died, it was like we etched their names in glass and perched some precious ornament on a high shelf. It was as though we were only willing to honor their memory from afar. What did it get us?" He was nearly crying.

"Nothing. Worse than nothing, the way your brother Risto had to live. In a house of silence. That's why he went to Karelia, trying to find some life, somebody who would care about him and show it. Oh, Marja and I never talked about what mattered. We never talked about any of you kids. But that don't mean we didn't think about all of you. We thought way too much."

Eero suddenly grabbed Lempi's hand, pulled her to a stop and forced her to look at him. "We have to let them all go, including your Ma. Whatever happened, happened. We can't undo what was done."

She looked away. He spotted again her familiar tell. "I don't know what you're talking about."

"All I'm saying is that it might help to talk honestly about how we feel, instead of just keeping it bottled up."

Lempi started walking again, Eero followed, and she remained silent for several seconds. Finally, she spoke. "I thought Finns didn't get emotional." She meant it as a joke, but she couldn't even smile at her own attempt.

Their walk was taking them by Big Sapphire Lake and soon they would enter the town center. Having dared to cross a forbidden line, Eero decided not to retreat. There was one topic he really needed to cover—Pauline.

"Your mother always blamed herself for how Jaacko and Johani died, and she always felt responsible for Risto's leaving. And she thought she let you down with those FBI men, the way she allowed you to lie for her. But she didn't know how to correct it, and she never knew how to live with it. It didn't matter if any of her fears were true. She was still overtaken by her guilt until finally she could not go on living."

"Pa, don't go on this way. We don't need to talk about this."

"Yes, we do. I don't want you to go the way of your Ma. I didn't need to ask if you're happy. I can see that you're not. You haven't been the same since Pauline died. I know she was like a mother to you, always looking after you, always there for you in Milwaukee . . ."

"Pa . . . "

"Why does her death upset you so much?"

"Don't go there Pa!"

"I've often worried about those friends of yours." He nearly had it said.

"Tom," Lempi suddenly shouted. An old man was walking toward them. He was tall, one-armed and a bit unkempt. He smiled at the two of them, and Lempi ran up to him. Whoever he was, his unexpected appearance annoyed Eero.

"Pa, meet an old friend of mine. And of Pauline's. From Bremen. You can't know how happy I was when I discovered Tom lives here in Thread. Tom, we were just talking about Pauline. This is my father."

The man held out his one hand to shake. "Only Lempi still calls me Tom. Most people here think of me as Mr. Packer. Not really my name, just what they see me do."

Something was oddly familiar to Eero about this man, as though a distant memory was threatening to break through his consciousness. It bothered him, just as it bothered him that he had lost the momentum of his conversation with his daughter.

"I'm up from Clover to spend a week with Lempi," Eero explained.

"Interesting town. Clover. I've been there twice. But both times made a big impression on me."

"Why is that?" Eero asked out of politeness. He wanted to get rid of this man before it became too difficult to restart the conversation with Lempi.

Packer responded. "In a different life, or so it seems now, I wrote books. I once went to Clover to say goodbye to a young man who I had interviewed and who was heading off on a mission to Karelia. That was back in 1933."

Eero was astonished. "My son was part of that group."

"Yes, I know," Packer responded, "Pauline once told me about your son. I think it was before she first introduced me to your daughter Lempi." Something in the tone of Packer's statement made Eero immediately suspect that Pauline had told this old man everything about herself and Lempi. The look that Packer gave him was quick but telling, and Eero also became certain that Packer wanted him to know that he protected these family truths. So strange that Eero had never considered what secrets others might carry. How imperfectly he played at life, Eero thought, always thinking ahead of his options, but never considering possible moves of others.

Lempi noticed none of this, but instead asked a question to keep Packer with them a few moments longer. "You said you were in Clover twice, Tom. When was the other time?"

Packer looked directly at Eero when he answered. "Much earlier. It was after World War One commenced, but before the United States entered the fray. I worked then as a secretary to a lumber baron named Barney Oxford. I traveled with him as he met with his agents across the state. In Clover, a routine meeting became unexpectedly interesting when this remarkable farmer appeared. He had twin boys with him; they were quite charming, so blonde and shy. The farmer, though, was indignant, and sought to right a wrong. The law was not on his side, although perhaps God was. In any case, my employer didn't care one bit. But something in that day's confrontation made me see Oxford in a new light. I realized I was wasting my time on earth working for such a man. Within a week, I quit and joined the American volunteer ambulance corps, traveled to France, lost my arm to an explosion during the war and, all in all, traveled a quite different path."

The troubling sense of recognition broke through. Eero remembered a day in the Clover hotel. Eero looked at this man, seeing in his weathered face remnants of the young man who once stared back with compassion at him, Johani and Jaacko. So many decades earlier. He had often thought of that day, always thinking of what he should have said to Oxford and Steele, never considering who else had listened in.

"You never know," Packer said, "the things that might touch and transform another person's life."

Eero wondered if their encounter so many years ago really did transform Packer's life. Surely, the young man was privy to more than enough of his rich boss' behavior to be disillusioned without Eero's help. At most, Eero's appearance that day might have been the straw that broke the camel's back. Lives didn't get changed so easily.

Eero groaned. Another surge of pain pressed down on his chest. It felt like one of the cows kicked him and continued to shove its hooves against his body. The pain spread through his shoulders and down his arms. Maybe his heart was going, and he should call an ambulance. He didn't care. If it was his time, he wanted his last moments to be in his fields.

Hearts were not to be trusted. They gave out too easily. It was the heart that did in Jaacko. Dr. Koch warned him that the worms could reach the heart. Oh, how Eero hated the daily appearance of that man's ruby red Chrysler. Its shiny appearance, suggesting a world of prosperity and good health, became a harbinger of increasingly bad news. If Eero could have stayed in the barns or the fields and let Marja deal with doctor's increasingly somber face, he would have made that choice. But Marja didn't have the courage to face disaster alone. Eero needed to be at her side, and so he always dropped whatever he was doing, went into the house, faced the doctor and heard the most recent complication.

"The larvae have lodged in Jaacko's heart," said the doctor, standing with the two of them in their kitchen. "His body is fighting valiantly, trying to dispel the invaders. But I am afraid that this has resulted in myocarditis."

"What is that?" asked Eero, even though he did not want to know. He once studied Latin while a schoolboy in Finland. His father thought it was useful knowledge for a future minister. To this day, Eero distrusted anything that sounded too much like the dreaded words heard in those schoolboy lessons. Nearly ever medical term met that test.

"It's an inflammation of the myocardium," the doctor explained. "That's the thick muscular layer of your heart wall. It's why your son still has such a high fever and so much trouble breathing. And have you noticed the color of his skin?"

"It looks blue," Marja ventured.

The doctor nodded. "That's an indication his heart is not working as it should. It is slowly dying. His ventricular beat has become erratic."

"But he will recover, won't he? You said people didn't die from trichinosis." Eero threw the doctor's consoling words back at him. Old hopes were a talisman to cure his son. He wanted no counter argument, but the doctor ignored his wants.

"The parasites caused a new and more serious problem. It has emerged into something more than the original trichinosis. All we can do is ensure Jaacko gets plenty of rest. Let his heart seek to recover. Keep him calm, and if he complains of pain continue to give him the watered-down whisky. He can still recover."

"And what about Johani?" Marja asked, and then added hopefully, "his skin doesn't look blue."

The doctor's look remained grave. "When did Johani start vomiting and complaining of headaches?"

"It began yesterday evening," Eero replied.

"I am worried that in Johani's case the larvae have damaged the membranes around his brain and the spinal cord. He is showing symptoms of meningitis. In rare cases, trichinosis can trigger a range of other much more serious problems."

"So we just need to let him rest too?" Marja pleaded, but Eero could tell by the doctor's face that this answer would be different.

"Mrs. Makinen, if your son does indeed have meningitis, there will be little we can do for him. There are no effective treatments. You should be prepared: the illness can run its course rapidly."

Marja realized what Dr. Koch was saying, but she would have none of it. "But that can't be. How can the boys have different diseases? They both ate the same meat. We all ate the same meat. Why would it kill my Johani? Why?"

Marja lost all hope that day. Eero saw it fade from her eyes and never return.

But the doctor proved an imperfect seer. Jaacko—the lively boy always quick to play a joke, the inventor of the most fanciful games, the ardent negotiator when selling berries to Mr. Newmann and the energetic heart of the house—his Jaacko faded quickly during that very evening. His little heart was losing to the worms.

Eero and Marja sat by the two beds in the front room, watching their children. Risto, as was increasingly the case, fled to the attic bedroom to escape. For each of the twins, the spasms of pain came in different ways at different times. Eero sat on the left edge of Jaacko's bed, seeking to be the closest to his son's heart, and held his boy's hand. Jaacko seemed to grow paler in the dim light of the kerosene lamp, and his breath became more and more shallow.

"Papa," he cried out. Had he ever called him "papa" before the that night, "Papa, I can't see anything. Hold my hand. Where's Mama?"

Marja was on the right side of the bed, situated between the two beds. She grabbed hold of Jaacko's other hand. With her other hand, she caressed Johani's forehead, burning with a high fever. Both parents sat on their separate edges of the bed, not daring to look at each other, daring only to focus on their child.

"Now, it's so bright," Jaacko said. There seemed a joy in his voice not heard in days. "I think the sun is coming up."

Eero looked up at the mantel clock, which showed a few minutes before midnight. He wanted to jump and stop the movement of its hands before the clock could ring twelve tones. He didn't want Jaacko to know how late and dark it truly was. But he wouldn't release his son's hand.

"Can I go out to play?" Jaacko asked in an unexpected bright tone.

And then he was gone.

Eero looked up at his wife in the dimness of the flickering light. Each had felt life slip out from between their fingers. But Eero couldn't let go of his son's hand to reach over to grasp Marja's hand.

Johani stirred in his bed, turning his head to look at them, his eyes lost. "Where did Jaacko go?" he murmured. "It hurts so much. Can I go too?"

Marja dropped her dead son's hand and turned fully to the living son's bed, "Don't say that, Johani. You're not ready to go anywhere. Stay with your mother. She needs you."

Was Packer right when he claimed one small act could change another's life? If so, why hadn't Eero seen a way to impact Marja's? Surely, something could have changed her life for the better. He tried so many times. From their first dance in Clover, he sought to give her constant happiness. He wooed not only her but her entire family, until finally her parents agreed to their marriage. He worked hard to clear a few acres and build the first small cabin to provide a decent home. He loved her and the twins with a passion that no other father could have met. He lost as much as she did that summer, but he never let her know it.

He gave her the freedom to mourn as long and as deeply as she wanted. When the world became too much for her, he made it less distracting by exiling Risto. When she wanted to be a mother once more, he let her adopt Lempi. He stood by her side at every step of the relentless government witch hunt. It was never enough. Maybe he needed to accept that. Regardless of what he might have done, her life story remained the same. Marja was prone to moments of great happiness and joy, and was equally destined to fall into great depressions. Eero was no more the cause of them than he was the instigator of the seasons. He could only hold her grounded when she tried to fly too high and keep her head aloft when she was in danger of going under. And one could only do either of those things so long.

Eero was now in his field, but his land wasn't making him feel better. The pain was extending deep into his stomach, seeking to conquer his entire body. Deep down, he knew it was his heart, but he wasn't going back to the house to dial the ambulance. That call would only buy him a soulless bed in the Clover hospital. His spirit belonged here, tramping across his land. His life was in this soil, in these clearings, in the trees that he allowed to grow and in the giant stump he never removed, keeping it a reminder of what the land once was. Only now after seventy years was that severed remnant of the virgin forest slowly rotting away.

During the morning, the sky had turned deeply blue; it was unmarred by clouds. It had been a similar day when they buried Johani and Jaacko. Their funeral was a joint event. Johani lived only a day longer than his twin brother. It was as though they determined to leave together, just as they came into the world.

The whole town mourned their loss. The brief service was outdoors, and the small Finnish cemetery overflowed with well-wishers. Finns from throughout the county, some three hundred of them, arrived to pay their respects. Most came by horse and buggy, a few by Model T. German neighbors from nearby farms also appeared in their Sunday best. Perhaps some came out of a shared guilt because they knew tainted meat from one of their countrymen caused the illness; Eero preferred to believe they came as payment for the kindness Marja and Eero showed the German community during the war. All the children, as well as the teacher, from the local one-room school were on hand. Many of the merchants in town, including their children, were in the crowd. Only with the passing of the twins did Eero learn how many knew and loved them. The tow-headed twins had been a lively presence in a small town.

Hundreds stood in an imperfect semi-circle around the two small coffins. Marja, Risto and Eero were next to the open graves. Marja's parents had arrived by train the day before, and her father led the service.

Many in the gathering could not follow Reverend Torsonnen's remarks. Some were too far away to hear his soft voice. Germans had trouble understanding the man's thick Finnish accent. Some Finns knew too little English to keep up with a service in English. But Eero and Marja heard every word.

"God has a plan for each of us," the reverend began. "We may not always know what that plan is. Sometimes from our limited perspective, we may even perceive it as a foolhardy map. But it is not up to us to judge what God has designed. We are here to fulfill and accept His destiny.

"An old minister like me did not expect to have to bury his two grandsons. It is a great sadness to do so. But the memories of Johani and Jaacko Makinen are also a beacon of hope. To everyone who knew them, their brief lives provided joy. Each boy was his own shining light, illuminating different parts of what makes this world so wonderful.

"We may feel the poorer for having lost the glow they brought to the things around us, but imagine how they light up heaven today, bringing joy to the multitudes who have preceded us. Perhaps that was God's intent for my grandsons all along. Or perhaps, He loaned us these two bright spirits so that we would know what we should strive to achieve. We must always seek to do the best that we can. We can be a light in our own lives, providing clarity and hope to those around us. Let us each strive to do that for Johani and Jaacko."

Torsonnen's words flowed over the hundreds of mourners, but in Eero's mind, it seemed his father-in-law intended them only for his daughter. And in Eero's estimation, Marja did not listen.

Eero felt hot beneath the cloudless sky. Under the intensity of the sun's bright light, his eyes shuttered between darkness and sight. As he stumbled forward, he could see the one remaining stump at the wood's edge. He realized now where he was heading, and he was nearly there. He would not let pain keep him from reaching his goal. He could make it to that stump.

The light grew brighter. In his mind he heard the soft whisper of Johani's voice. And then he heard the exuberance of Jaacko's. Their spirits were bright and clear—the memories of their happiness echoed in his mind. But now those remnants of the past escaped into the light because he could see his twins. They were with him; he could almost touch them.

"Papa," Johani yelled out, "let's go dynamite the stump."

And Eero saw the one remaining stump bathed in the light. Eero realized that he had left this stump untouched all these years just for this moment, until a time he could be with his boys once more and clear the final edge of his land. His sons urged him on. And they were no longer alone. Between them appeared his Marja. She was as beautiful and happy as that midsummer night when they had their first polka. She smiled like she smiled then, and her eyes danced as they danced that night.

"Let's do it," Marja said. "Let's get rid of that stump." She smiled and held out her hand. The boys shouted with excitement and joy.

In the distance where the woods met the river, rushing waters glinted in the bright sunshine and cast diamond beams of reflection upward. The day's brilliance illuminated all, finally making everything clear to Eero.

It was time to blow that stump heaven-high.

And it was done.

Danny set down the old photo. How could it interest him? He did not know the family. The only piece left in the folder was a heavy envelope. He opened it and withdrew a multi-page, hand-written letter. But the text was in a foreign language, and he could not read it. He thought it was Finnish. On the front sheet in the upper right corner was a date. The year was 1983, and the letter's salutation had his mother's name. Who did she know that would still write in Finnish?

The handwriting was small and precise, but for some reason appeared masculine. He saw a few words that he recognized: Milwaukee, Clover, Pauline. But the meaning beyond those words remained a complete mystery.

LEMPI
1983
THREAD, WISCONSIN

The doorbell rang. Lempi Lahti was in no mood to answer it. The fat in her large cast-iron pot was nearing the perfect temperature for frying her just cut dough. On Fridays, she always made fresh crullers, long johns and raised doughnuts for Toivo and Danny. She never liked to disappoint them. Besides she found something comforting in kneading the yeast dough, waiting for the pliable white lump to rise beneath its dampened towel, rolling out the dough until it was the right thickness for using the old doughnut cutter that had been her mother's, dropping the raw circles of dough into the sizzling oil, filling the farm kitchen with sweet aroma, then rolling the cooked doughnuts in granulated sugar and finally setting them on a rack to cool. Each step was a prerequisite to the final afternoon pleasure of Danny rushing in from school to munch happily on the sweet pastries. It was a pleasure only increased when Toivo returned from the woods to do the same. By evening, her husband and son would always have eaten too many, but Lempi would smile with satisfaction. At least, there was one thing that she could do right.

There was that doorbell again. Who could it be, and why were they at the front door? Any sensible person in Thread knew to use the kitchen door off the side yard. That's how things worked in small towns. If this visitor took the time to walk a few feet around the corner and knock at the kitchen screen door, then Lempi could see who it was. It would be simpler to ask the person to step inside her tidy kitchen, and at the same time drop her dough into the kettle without worrying about the fat overheating, or turning down the flame and letting the oil cool while she dealt with an unwanted interloper. Whoever was at the door didn't know Thread and didn't know that Lempi just wanted time to make her doughnuts.

Why would someone bother her on such a beautiful September morning? By dawn, the previous night's temperatures had dipped near freezing. The trees surrounding the house were well on their way to full color. The maple at the corner was ablaze with red foliage. The beeches in the distant woods were turning yellow. Outside the kitchen window overlooking her large farm garden, the dried out corn stalks and the random bursts of pumpkin orange on the ground added fall color. The sky was bright blue, the air was still and the heat of Indian summer was beginning to invade the yard. Maybe before the boys came home, Lempi would find a moment to sit on the swing seat suspended from the maple, have an afternoon cup of coffee and eat one of her doughnuts.

Another ring of the doorbell. Whoever it was wasn't giving up. Why hadn't she heard a car drive up the gravel driveway? Why would someone surprise her anyway? Suddenly, she grew worried. Even though she knew her worries were unjustified, Lempi was superstitious. She believed that in some ways the future came to her early. A thought about Toivo working in the woods flickered through her mind. Could an accident have happened? He was such a careful and meticulous man, and he loved logging the second-growth woods. She knew she should be happy that Toivo found a way of life so comfortable for him. But sometimes she resented his happiness. When he touched her at night with those massive strong hands, the fingers grown thick from his hard labor in the forest, she sometimes repressed a shudder. His touch only reminded her of all she had given up in Milwaukee a decade ago—the career she once had, along with her aspirations to do good. Toivo loved her deeply, and they both lived for their son Danny. But that was not enough—even though it was far more than she deserved.

But what if a timber company manager was on the porch to inform her of an accident? A tree could have fallen or a chainsaw might have bucked; in the woods, a disaster always lurked. She repressed a small thrill of anticipation; a horrid fantasy of having Danny all to herself threatened to burst forth. She suppressed it, knowing she could not live with herself if something were to happen to Toivo. He saved her from her worst instincts.

A fourth ring. "I'm coming," she yelled out, still not knowing who was at the door. What if the person at the front door was a school official? Nothing could be worse than if something had happened to Danny. She worried about him all the time. He could have fallen trying to climb to the top of the ropes hanging from the gym rafters. He wasn't strong or athletic, and that physical education teacher at the Thread school was a bully. He pushed Danny too hard. Or, maybe, one of the other boys picked a fight with Danny. Adolescents tended toward the mean, and Danny was too gentle a spirit.

Surely, the proper authorities would have called if something had happen to either Danny or Toivo. They wouldn't make a personal visit. Unless something truly dreadful had happened. She still remembered the day when Tuzzi, the FBI agent, entered their Milwaukee apartment to disclose Pauline's death. Over the years, she often thought about Tuzzi's anguish that morning. While suffering his own loss of Pauline, he was forced to inform them.

Lempi felt ridiculous. She was letting a doorbell derail her into fantasy. It was probably a door-to-door salesman peddling some wares, maybe an Avon lady or the Fuller Brush man. She just needed to deal with it. She took a longing look at her deep-fry kettle and turned the heat low. She would come back to it later. She picked up one of her dish towels, this one embroidered with a scene of cleaning and part of a set of towels from Pauline's trunk. Each towel documented a different day's chore based on a household schedule that never matched Lempi's. She wiped flecks of flour from her hands, walked out the kitchen, through the living room and reached the front door.

The small window of the door framed the face of a woman Lempi didn't know. Thread was a small town; she knew everyone that might come by. It certainly wasn't anyone from the school or the timber company. And it wasn't a police officer either. As usual, she had overreacted. Nothing was wrong. The woman saw Lempi approaching and smiled. Lempi decided she was a door-to-door salesperson, maybe someone new to town or an ambitious Timberton agent trying to add Thread to her territory. Well, Lempi was in no mood to buy anything.

Still she opened the door widely, even as she held no intent to invite the interloper in. The woman was in her fifties, well-dressed, and adorned with quite lovely jewelry—not the kind of pieces normally found on a woman going door-to-door. A large car was parked halfway up the gravel driveway. That explained why Lempi hadn't heard the car. The visitor didn't drive all the way in. The four-door sedan was the latest model of a Mercedes Benz. Lempi felt confused. No one in Thread drove such an expensive foreign car; the woman must be a tourist from out of the area. If so, she had definitely taken a wrong turn, as the Lahti farm wasn't anywhere near the fancy resorts or the big summer camps.

The woman smiled more broadly. "Are you Lempi Lahti, maiden

name Makinen?" she asked.

For a moment Lempi was stumped on how to answer, and she felt foolish. This elegant woman was obviously not lost. She was seeking Lempi by name. Finally Lempi found her voice, "Yes."

The woman's smile shifted slightly, as though she recognized something was amiss. "Oh good. I'm sorry to bother you, Mrs. Lahti. Or, can I call you Lempi? I feel as though I already know you."

Lempi found it odd, even a little disturbing, that this woman knew her birth name, but she gave a slight nod of assent.

"Lempi, this is really quite extraordinary. You see I have a package to deliver to you. I've carried it all the way from Russia, and the man who gave it to me made me promise that I would track you down so I could hand it over in person. The man was really quite insistent."

"What?"

"Oh, I should explain better. I'm making such a jumble of everything," she went on. "First let me tell you my name. I'm Joan Anderson and I live in Duluth. Earlier this year, I participated in a special tour to the Soviet Union, including a visit to an area called Karelia. That's where I met him." The woman fluttered her hands. "Oh, I know I'm not making any sense. There are just so many things to say, and it's hard to know where to begin. Let me try again. I encountered this man in Karelia named Risto Makinen. He told me that while you never met him, you would know he was your older brother."

Joan Anderson watched for Lempi's reaction. She remained silent for a moment, appearing to want confirmation that the man's story checked out.

Lempi was stunned. This was impossible. A woman she never met before was uttering the name of her long lost brother—a name that even her parents seldom mentioned while they were alive. Of course Lempi knew the name. She recalled a photo that had hung on the living room wall and a small boy clustered with his parents and two brothers. As a young girl she stared at that family, wishing those brothers could be with her, protecting her, making life with her mother a little bit more bearable. But two of them died as small boys, and the third named Risto vanished before Lempi was even born.

"But Risto's dead. He disappeared during World War Two. I don't understand." Then not knowing what else to say, Lempi's good manners took over. She asked, "Would you like to come in and have some coffee. I was just about to fry some doughnuts."

Joan smiled broadly. "I would love that. Because I really need to tell you everything, and not just hand over this envelope." For the first time, Lempi noticed that Joan was carrying a large, bulky manila envelope.

Lempi guided Joan back to her kitchen, ratcheted up the heat on the frying oil, poured fresh coffee for the two of them and proceeded to fry doughnuts. Her unexpected visitor described how she came to possess an envelope from Lempi's missing brother.

"As I said, I live in Duluth," Joan said. "My husband owns a department store there. Last year, one of my friends at the University told us about a large group of youth who left this area nearly fifty years ago to settle in Karelia. The whole adventure was rather like a private Peace Corps for Communists."

"Yes, I know," Lempi responded. "My father told me about Risto leaving."

'Well, we found the whole idea quite romantic, and for some reason, my friends and I dreamed up this idea to track them down in the Soviet Union. Truthfully, I just wanted to see the art treasures of the Hermitage, and this wild goose chase was an excuse. But some of my friends really wanted to dig into this forgotten story. At any rate, we sought permission for an excursion to see where these people went.

"You can't imagine the red tape we had to navigate. The Soviet Union isn't that friendly to Americans. Who knows what went on behind the scenes before we received group permission to take a train to Petrozavodsk, which is the capital of Karelia. I don't know what we expected, but certainly not what happened. News of our visit had circulated in the town. Imagine our surprise when the train pulled in . . . there was this excited group of people on the platform waiting for us. And they all spoke English. They were the remaining members of the Karelian Technical Aid. There was still was a colony of Americans in the middle of Russia! Can you imagine?

"And your brother was among them. When he discovered I was from Duluth, he begged me to do a favor. He said he had a sister in northern Wisconsin who didn't know what happened to him, and asked me to hand carry some mementos to her. I'm such a romantic; of course, I agreed. He returned to my hotel the next day with this package. Some of my friends say I was foolish to try to take something out of the country without permission. But how could I say no?" Joan looked triumphant as she finished this tale.

"How did Risto know where I lived," Lempi wondered aloud. "And why didn't he write sooner. It's been over forty years since he disappeared. My father lived on the very same farm where Risto grew up. Pa lived there until the day he died of a heart attack. Risto could have written at any time. My parents died never knowing what happened to their son. They would have wanted to know." She imagined how she would feel if Danny disappeared into the unknown.

Joan touched Lempi's hand. "I don't know how he knew you lived in Thread, but he gave me the address. And I did ask him why he never wrote. Your brother was somewhat evasive, but from talking to him and some of the others, I believe many of them were sent to work camps during the Stalin years. When they were freed to return to Karelia, the war was over. America and Russia were enemies. Risto did say he was afraid that if he ever wrote, it would create problems for his mother and father. So he stayed silent."

Lempi said nothing. She thought about when the U.S. Government jailed her mother Marja in the Fifties. If a letter from the Soviet Union had appeared in those days, her mother probably would have been deported.

Joan continued, but her tone suggested she thought Lempi's silence showed disapproval. "But Risto wanted to correct things, which is why he entrusted me with this package. He told me there's a letter inside that explain everything."

Joan suddenly looked worried, "But can you read Finnish? He said the letter was in Finnish, because he felt his English had grown too rusty. If you don't read the language, I'm sure I could find someone in Duluth to help. There's still a big Finnish community there."

"Don't worry. I'll be able to read it." Lempi placed her hand on the envelope and pulled it across the table toward her. Even though Joan's face was clear that she hoped Lempi would open and read the letter at that moment, Lempi was too selfish. She would hold it for when she was alone.

The envelope remained unopened on the kitchen table all morning and early into the afternoon. Lempi found many tasks to delay opening it. As the day wore on, the dull manila of the envelope began to fuse in her mind with the light varnish of the maple table, almost as though the Russian package was vanishing before her eyes.

She couldn't explain her reluctance to open it. It just seemed forbidden.

Earlier that morning, Joan Anderson was clearly frustrated when Lempi didn't immediately strew the contents across the table, and Lempi thought that Joan took an unnaturally long time to finish her cup of coffee and sugared doughnut. Finally, Lempi thanked Joan once again for making the trip from Duluth and promised to stay in touch; and Joan offered someday to revisit and bring along her scrapbooks which included a photo of Risto. She regretted that she hadn't thought to bring it. Amazing, said Joan, the way Lempi resembled her older brother—someday Lempi should travel to Europe to meet her brother. Lempi would have to take the trip, because it was most unlikely that Risto would ever be allowed to travel to the West. Russia was Russia, after all.

After a time, Joan's voice simply droned on in Lempi's mind, like insects flitting about the ear on a hot summer afternoon. The sound insulated Lempi from reality and suspended her in some newfound realm. The world she always knew had acquired an unexpected center of gravity, and she hadn't yet learned to stay balanced. Her brother was alive, he knew about her and yet he never came to help. Life could never be quite right again.

As a young girl, Lempi used to daydream that her big brother was still alive. She imagined Risto a prince that somehow fled Russia with both friends and incredible wealth. This intrepid group founded a small kingdom in the mountains of Europe, established Risto as their ruler, and dwelled in a beautiful castle surrounded by a golden meadow. From the keep's ramparts, one could bask in the warmth of a golden sun while always admiring the white peaks of snow-capped mountains. The youthful Lempi longed for this imaginary kingdom, certain that her brother was safe within it, and that someday he would whisk her away from her demanding parents. He would convey her to the place she truly belonged. With Risto, Lempi needed no imaginary friends. Her vision of an imagined land helped her fall asleep at night. It strengthened her to withstand the taunts of neighbor girls. It shielded her against her mother's moods. Risto was her knight in shining armor.

As with so much in her life, she learned to leave behind such childish longings. Now she felt betrayed. Risto had been there all along, living out his life in some cabin in the Russian woods, carrying knowledge of where she was and never coming to save her. Her brother failed her.

"Perhaps I should be going," Joan said. She stood up to dust a few flakes of errant sugar off her expensive dress. The large diamond ring on her finger flashed in the morning sunlight. Some of the doughnut sugar landed on the unopened envelope. "I'm driving all the way through to Milwaukee, and I'd like to get most of the way before dark. I'm sure you want some time for yourself to look at what's in the envelope." She motioned toward the table. Lempi didn't acknowledge the gesture.

Lempi stood. "I hope I don't seemed rude. It's just such a surprise to discover that my brother is still alive. It was so good of you to travel all this way to find me."

They walked through the living room together. Lempi stood in the front door and watched Joan enter her expensive car, start the engine and back down the driveway onto the county road. It was a long drive to Milwaukee from Thread, so Lempi gave her visitor an encouraging wave and smile. She stared out as the car headed west toward State Highway 17. Then Lempi closed the door and frowned.

She walked past the tattered davenport in the living room and stopped at the doorway to the kitchen. The scene inside was so familiar: the white painted cabinets, the Formica counter tops, the vinyl flooring sporting a red-brick pattern and the wooden kitchen table at which Toivo, Danny and she ate every day. The used coffee cups remained on the table, as well as the fancy cut glass plate on which she had placed a small stack of still hot doughnuts. Everything seemed familiar, but the envelope was alien. She wanted it gone.

What could it tell her that she needed to know? Certainly nothing that was of immediate concern. She returned to the doughnuts she had fried at the beginning of Joan's visit. They sat on the newspaper where she had placed them, after pulling them one by one from the fat. These had grown too cold to glaze, with no internal heat to melt the sugar and create that crinkling layer that Danny so love. She would have to frost them, and Danny would be disappointed. She mixed some milk in powdered sugar to create a simple frosting and applied it with more care than normal. She searched her cupboards for the bag of dried coconut so she could dip a few into the white strands. Wanting to do more, she pulled out her nut grinder and a package of walnuts. She ground the nuts into a fine mince to sprinkle over the remaining frosted doughnuts. It created a satisfactory display, almost as grand a selection as at a bakery. Danny might not notice that the glazed ones were missing.

Lempi looked up at the clock. Not yet noon. No possible diversions remained with the doughnuts. She strained the grease to store in the refrigerator for the next Friday. She washed and wiped the dishes. Barely past noon. Still the envelope remained on the kitchen table. Lempi's sixth sense told her no good would come from undoing that flap. Lempi dreaded seeing what her brother had sent.

What had Joan said about Risto? That he had written her a letter in Finnish. How blithely Lempi claimed an ability to read the old tongue. Her language skills were rusty at best. Since her father died a decade earlier, she seldom used Finnish. Sometimes for fun, she would look at the books in the Timberton shop that catered to the old Finns. She could make her way through the children's stories, but with more serious books, she wasn't so certain about her accuracy.

She began to think of various words from growing up: Mother, *äita.* Father, *isä.* Brother, *veli.* Home, *koti.* Recalling the old sounds somehow soothed her. She was a Finnish girl after all. What did Finns like to say they all had? *Sisu.* What a concept. A mixture of pride and determination, grit and fortitude, all carried out with a stoic face. Perhaps, Lempi hadn't always lived up to that ideal, but there was no time like the present to begin. She sat down at the table, and pulled the envelope close to her. It was time to face the truth.

The flap opened easily. The envelope seemed a slightly different size than was customary, and the paper had a cheaper quality. This package had traveled such a distance and under a strange set of circumstances. She lifted the packet up to release the contents onto the table. She fanned the few items across the table: some old photos and newspaper clippings . . . and an envelope with the multi-page letter that Joan referenced. She had expected more.

She pressed the sheets of the letter against the table to straighten the folds. Without trying to decipher the foreign words, she first took in the strong sense of personality conveyed by the handwriting. She was reminded of Pa. The penmanship was tight, straight-forward and clear: the descenders and ascenders fully formed and the diacritical marks placed with precision. The blue ink against the slightly yellowed paper was both enticing and frightening.

Rakas Lempi, rakkani, it began. "Dear Lempi, my dearest love." Did she interpret that right? Why would he say such a thing? This was a brother who had never seen her, never touched her, not even as a baby. Maybe it was a play with words, since the name Lempi meant "love." It couldn't be as sentimental as it seemed.

She continued reading, finding she needed to time to navigate the vocabulary, grateful that her brother's handwriting was so clear, and even happier that the sentences made sense. Or at least, at first, she thought she understood it all.

"Dear Lempi, my dearest love,

"Surely, it must be a shock to receive this letter. After all, I last wrote to Ma and Pa in the Thirties, and you probably think of me only as an old family memory, if you think of me at all.

"But when I learned that the United States allowed a group of Americans to visit Petrozavodsk and that these visitors were from Minnesota, I recognized this was my chance to return some artifacts that I have long treasured. I feel they rightfully belong to you.

"That decision was the easy part. My challenge was deciding what to disclose after all these years. After all, I have no idea what part of my life you actually know. It may be that you don't even know fully your own life. I decided truth was the only way to go—and that the best way to tell you our shared truth was through a story. So bear with me a little while.

"Let me write you a story which I often told my two sons as they grew up. These beautiful boys were born to my wife Irene while we labored in a mountain camp in the Urals during the Great War. Even after we returned to Karelia, they loved to have me repeat this tale. Over the years, I added more details. They loved it because it was a magical story about their beautiful sister. Here is our tale.

"Once, long ago, in a faraway land called Wisconsin, there was a handsome and smart young man (that's me) who chose to take on a noble deed. He crossed the oceans to tame the wild lands of Karelia and have many adventures.

"On the night before he was to leave, he met a beautiful maiden (her name was Pauline) with whom he fell deeply in love. She presented him with magical memories to take on his quest, and he left with her a more precious gift. They created a baby girl (her name was Lempi) who took the best of each of them and merged them into one perfect

little being."

Lempi was confused; no, she was deeply troubled. This story was no tale to tell children. This letter made no sense. She must be translating it incorrectly. Why would her brother make up such a fairy tale?

She continued reading.

"The handsome man (remember, that's me) proved his mettle in many a battle taming the wild forests of Karelia. He persevered and helped to build a better world. But one thing always troubled him: he could never go back to that far away land of Wisconsin. He knew he would never see his daughter Lempi and could not help guard her.

"Back in Wisconsin, Pauline, being a wise woman, found a way to protect her daughter. She created an enchantment that hid Lempi with the grandparents. Her magic spell ensured that no one, including Lempi, would ever doubt that the she was the true daughter of the old couple raising her. The identities of her true parents, Pauline and Risto, would always be a secret.

"But Pauline became a fairy godmother to her daughter, never straying far from her, always finding ways to help Lempi achieve her dreams. Over the years, Pauline also found ways to send news of Lempi to the handsome man in Karelia, so that he too could know about his daughter's triumphs and share that joy with Lempi's secret family in Karelia.

"And so this beautiful girl grew up, guided by loving parents, both those she knew and those who stayed hidden. One day, she found her own handsome man (he was called Toivo), they were married and together they had a strong, strapping son (this boy Daniel, according to Pauline's last letter, looked very much like the handsome Risto.) And all lived happily ever after. Or so my story ended.

"My sons loved knowing they had an older sister in America. Often, we would look at the few pictures saved from my former life, most of which had been sent by Pauline. From Pauline's rare letters, my wife and I knew that Ma and Pa never told you that you were adopted. According to Pauline, they also never learned that I was actually your father. They only knew that Pauline had borne a child out of wedlock.

"From this distance and time, I do not know if you ever suspected any of what I just told you. If my Irene were still alive, she would have talked me out of writing this letter. She was always the practical one. She would say 'Let sleeping dogs lie.' But my life has had its challenges, and I have come to believe that it is always better to know the truth. I felt you deserved the truth.

"I hope that life with Ma and Pa was good for you. Pa taught me so much about what I should aspire to in life, but I know Ma could be moody and difficult. After my

brothers died from the pig disease, it was not easy in our house. But there were many good memories over the years: the way Jaacko, Johani and I would watch Pa blow up the stumps on the farm; how we picked berries in the woods and swam in the Black River; the good times with our neighbors who were always ready to lend a helping hand; and even the Fourth of July celebrations in Clover. Oh, how my boys laugh, when I recount the fireworks and eating the "hot dogs." I sometimes wonder if I have made up the name of those sausages.

*"So many wonderful memories. But there remains an aching hole in my heart because there are no memories of seeing you grow up and be happy. But I want you to know that Pauline was not your only fairy godparent. Even though I was never there to grant your wishes or guide your path, please know that you always held a place in my dreams. I wish you, Toivo and Danny all the best in your life. And I return to you the few pieces of my life that intersected with yours. I hope that they serve as proof th*at *someone who never met you could still love you.*

"I truly pray that you accept this letter with all the love that is intended."

Lempi looked at the clippings, photographs and letter before her. The sun was bright outside and she could hear migrating geese overhead. Why had her brother (she still couldn't think of Risto as her father) burdened her with these bits of ephemera?

She fingered the most yellowed of the artifacts. It was a 1933 clipping from *Työmies*. She remembered her how father used to read the Finnish-language paper. Her parents maintained a subscription until the anti-Communist fever grew so strong after the Second World War. The clipping as it faced her displayed articles cut in half, so she realized she had the wrong side facing her. She turned it over to show a photo of a group of young men. Reading the caption, she realized these were the Clover youths who joined the Karelian Technical Aid. One of them was her brother. Just as Risto claimed in his letter, she found elements of resemblance between the man in the photo and her fourteen-year-old son. But that didn't mean Risto was Danny's grandfather.

The letter's story was ridiculous. It made a mockery of her family history. How could any of it possibly be true? It would have been better if the packet had never been delivered. Sitting in her kitchen with this envelope, Lempi felt as awful as that day she received the unwanted envelope with the Bremen College crest.

She remembered that day. On first seeing the Bremen letter, Lempi was so excited, certain it was a confirmation of consideration for the

Shindler Grant. The scholarship would transform her life. She never doubted that she would be the winner. Not another student at Clover High School was as bright as she. The school principal was fond of saying that there had never been another young scholar in Clover with such promise.

In those days, Lempi expected a lot from life. She had every expectation of completely fulfilling her ambitions. And she held so many. In America, one could go as far as one's talents led. No one questioned her intelligence or personality; she knew she would be a star at Bremen. Her giddy high school days held promise of so many possibilities: teacher, journalist, even a politician. Margaret Chase Smith, the Maine Congresswoman, was newly elected to the Senate back in 1952. Why couldn't Lempi do the same? Why couldn't she put her talents into improving the world? Even her good friend Pauline Newmann was proof positive that a professional woman could play a role in government.

But that didn't happen and neither did the story in this letter. Lempi shook her head, trying to cast out the lies within Risto's letter. No way was Pauline ever her mother. Why would Risto write such an outrageous confabulation and then arrange its delivery after so many years of hiding away? Lempi found it suspicious. Something else was going on. For some reason she thought again of Pauline's FBI boyfriend, John Tuzzi. Maybe that old man was behind this. She never trusted him. Hadn't he tried to deport her mother years ago, and then he had been there when Pauline died? Tuzzi held a personal animus toward her, and he might still believe in a duty to battle the Cold War. For all she knew, he still thought Marja a spy, considered the whole Makinen family traitors, and only sought to lay a trap.

She stopped herself before she became too deeply mired in such thoughts of conspiracy. It would get her nowhere. But still, why would anyone claim that Eero was not her father, or that Marja was not her mother? What a horrible thing to suggest. Marja raised her and did everything for her. Only a mother would have put up with Lempi's tantrums and adolescent moods. She never once indicated that Lempi was anything less than the direct result of her and Pa's love. She thought back to her mother's many mood swings, her depths of depression and occasional outbursts of anger. If Ma held a secret about Lempi, there was no way she would have kept it buried during her horrible blues. Flinging it in Lempi's face would have been too tempting, a lifesaver that would have popped Marja out of her moody waves. Ma wouldn't have cared if that truth threatened to drag Lempi down.

Lempi was certain her mother would never have killed herself if she still held that sharp barb to shoot Lempi's way. Ma never really loved her. Lempi was just a reminder to the old woman of the children she had lost—the children she had really loved, the children that were hers. No matter what she did, Lempi was the disappointment.

That was why Lempi hated visiting Marja in the Milwaukee jail. Her presence only pained them both. After all, it was Lempi's brash behavior at the FBI's visit that at least partially led to her mother's looming deportation. Lempi's lie was a silly fabrication in an attempt to help her mother out. But her mother didn't need to stay quiet about that simple lie when she was on trial. If she had exposed the truth, maybe it would have helped. It would only have embarrassed Lempi a bit. Despite all that, she forced herself to visit that jail each and every day.

In a way, what did that matter? What could Lempi still lose in those days? Lempi was tarred as disloyal and un-American. Bremen already denied her admission. Without college, Lempi had no path to reach her planned greatness. Staying away from that government jail, staying away from the gaze of her mother, would not have protected her in any way.

Pauline was so angry with Lempi in those days. "Marja is your mother. You must visit her," she said, acting as though she held motherly control over Lempi.

Lempi pouted, "No, I don't want to. She doesn't want to see me, and my being there only makes her unhappier. It would be better if I didn't go."

Pauline looked at her sadly, "No mother would ever be made unhappy by seeing her daughter."

Did Pauline really say that? Was it possible that Pauline was talking about herself? If so, Pauline was so wrong. No one wanted to see Lempi. Even Pauline learned over time that she didn't want to see her.

This letter from Risto was a fake. His story was a fabrication. Maybe the FBI wasn't involved. Lempi was paranoid to think they would go to such lengths to entrap her after all these decades. But that didn't mean Risto's story was true. He might have other reasons for spinning such a web. Perhaps he thought that if Lempi were his daughter, there was a chance she could sponsor him to return to the United States. Hadn't she read about Jews leaving the Soviet Union? Maybe there was a similar opening for old American transplants.

No doubt, Risto was quite clever. It was possible. She found this rational explanation calming. Her brother knew she existed. He learned, somehow, that both his parents and Pauline were dead. Who could deny his concocted story? Lempi rather liked him for imagining such a pretense. She might even help him. There was a part of her spirit that wouldn't mind putting one over on the government.

Then she looked once more at the photos and clippings. Risto must have protected them for years, and they weren't things one kept unless they were significant. They must be real. She was back at square one. If only Toivo were home from the woods, she could discuss what it all meant with him.

Unless he knew already. The thought chilled Lempi. Other people must know the truth about her. They probably laughed behind her back. Her entire life played out on a stage where everyone but her recognized the backdrop as fake. All the times she walked into town to buy a Popsicle at the Newmann's General Store, the old couple knew Pauline was her real mother. No wonder they were so kind and refused to let her pay for the penny candy. Finally, she had an explanation for why Marja was so angry about those visits.

Surely, Pauline's brother Galen also knew. Lempi remembered when he delivered Pauline's hope chest with its treasures accumulated for a wedding Pauline never had. Did Galen look on her as his niece that day? Or simply as the horrible mistake of his sister's?

Pauline had always been on hand for advice, willing to aid the family after the FBI visit, offering Lempi a place to stay during the trial, helping Lempi land a job at Bremen, playing at matchmaking with Toivo and even hiding the truth about buying the apartment building in Milwaukee. Pauline did so much to ensure Lempi and Toivo could have a better life. It all made sense if Pauline were really her mother.

It felt wrong to give in so easily. Surely, Pa would not keep such secrets from his daughter. Something nagged at Lempi. She recalled walking into town with Pa on his last visit to Thread, just a few months before his fatal heart attack. He wanted to talk about Pauline but Lempi wouldn't let him. She feared where the talk might lead, and she slammed the door closed. Maybe Pa would have told her that day.

She picked up Risto's letter again and held it between her fingers. She was barely able to see the handwriting for the tears that were beginning to cloud her eyes. It didn't matter. She wasn't going to read the letter a second time. Perhaps this was a lie or some odd sort of political trap. Risto might be trying to mislead her. No doubt there were other possibilities that might occur to her to explain it away. But her denials seemed a dead end. Other childhood memories eked in: she always felt some people in town whispered behind her back; her parents were so nervous when Pauline visited; and Ma and Pa were way older than the parents of all her friends.

How could she have been so blind? The clues were in front of her eyes the entire time. She dropped the letter next to the Finnish newspaper clipping and picked up another clipping in this mess. She recognized it—a front-page photo from *The Milwaukee Sentinel.* How did a man in Russia get a fifteen-year old Wisconsin newspaper if someone hadn't sent it to him? And why would Pauline have sent it?

She straightened out the clipping from the Sixties to read the headline: "Area of Riot Tense, Sniper Fire Goes On." She never expected to meet her future husband that evening, or to find her photo on the front page of the morning newspaper. She had been so angry. No one was supposed to know that she went to Milwaukee's North Side that evening. Suddenly, the whole city could see that she was there.

She stroked her finger across the image of Toivo and her. He looked so protective, the way he held her hand and seemed to pull her away from the threat of flames. He looked so young. In the starkness of black and white, he also seemed heroic. No wonder the editors chose this photo to illustrate their front page. The image mixed it all together: romance and danger, intrigue and fear, good and evil. Some speculated that the photo would win the paper a Pulitzer Prize. But Lempi remembered the entry that did win for 1967. A photographer for the AP took that honor for his shot of the shooting of a civil rights activist in Mississippi named James Meredith. Lempi always thought the Pulitzer Committee honored the right cause. In 1967, the oppression of black men in America needed far more recognition than white girls with doting admirers.

Pauline had been so excited that morning when the paper with its photo appeared. She immediately phoned Lempi to ask if she was having a secret romance, more interested in the possibility of a husband for Lempi than in why the girl had been on the north side of town. Pauline immediately recognized the man in the photo as the gardener who worked the college lawns, and she was so certain the two were there together.

Lempi snapped at Pauline for acting like a foolish teenager. But Lempi quickly went next door to borrow her neighbor's copy of the morning paper (Lempi had always preferred the more liberal afternoon paper, *The Milwaukee Journal*). Seeing the actual photo increased her annoyance with Pauline, her life, everything.

It still did. If she could, Lempi would still snap at Pauline. How could this woman be at her side for so many years, watch over her, protect her and yet never inform her of the truth? Lempi was humiliated at being duped and never knowing the woman was her true mother. She could never forgive Pauline for hiding that.

It wasn't that Lempi disapproved of all secrets. Some facts needed to be kept quiet. Among those was the reason that she ventured to the North Side that summer night. All these years and she had yet to tell a soul. Of course, it was easy to keep something under cover when no one thought to ask the relevant question. Everyone who originally saw the photo was so excited by their hope that Lempi was carrying on a romance with Toivo that they never asked what she was doing at the St. Francis Center on a Sunday night. Lempi supposed that if anyone did wonder they blamed her fascination with Negro music. The truth was quite different.

She went to the St. Francis Center that night to meet someone, but it wasn't Toivo. It was Richard Epstein, the younger brother of Peter Epstein, the first man she ever loved. After Peter was killed in the Korean War, Lempi wrote to his family in a forlorn attempt to keep alive at least a flicker of the hope found in her summer romance. Richard, who was just turning twelve that year, was the only family member who wrote back. He too needed to retain the memory of his brother. Apparently, he thought he might do this with the girlfriend left behind. Lempi was amused by the boy's adolescent ardor for doing right. Their exchange was the first in a continuing string of letters. Perhaps, Lempi saw in Richard a bit of the fervor that motivated her. As he grew up, went to college and started an activist career, they never lost touch. He wrote about traveling south with other New Yorkers to fight for civil rights. As the Vietnam War grew more ugly, he took up the anti-war banner. His letters described ties with the Students for a Democratic Society and other radical groups. Now for the first time Richard was in Milwaukee to work with a local civil rights leader named Father Groppi. The Catholic agitator. Richard was the one who suggested Lempi meet him that night at the St. Francis Center. He said that after sharing letters for so many years it was time for a true face-to-face.

The riot kept them from meeting, at least for that night. Instead Lempi was whisked to safety by the guiding hand of Toivo. What a mistaken path that started. Maybe if she'd seen the face of Richard that night, the flames would have disclosed the dangerous man he proved to be. She could have walked away before he pulled her in so deeply.

If the timing had only been slightly different, there would have been no opportunity for Toivo to pull her to safety, no catalyst for Pauline to try to ignite a romance between Toivo and Lempi and none of the life that followed. Why did Pauline latch on to Toivo anyway? A decade earlier, she never encouraged Lempi to pursue Peter. Pauline could hardly have made her disdain for Peter more obvious than that one night they dined at Karl Ratsch's. Maybe, Pauline thought Lempi needed to have a Finnish husband, a Finnish boy for a Finnish girl. Or maybe by 1967 Pauline just thought time was running out. It was ridiculous how she went overboard in matchmaking once Toivo appeared.

After the riots when Pauline noticed Toivo mowing the lawns, she dragged Lempi from Shindler Hall. That started the elaborate charade. Pauline stopped in front of the young man and pretended to just then realize that he was the same person as the hero of the photo. Lempi put on a show of being sullen, but actually she didn't mind. She hadn't dated anyone in years, and she shared Pauline's fear that she would end up an old maid. Not that she didn't admire the success that Pauline had achieved in life. It wasn't easy being a successful professional woman in a sexist America. But Lempi would prefer to share her life with someone. That afternoon, Toivo did exude a certain charm, the way he bashfully stood there, his upper torso bared and blushing through a sweaty sheen. The bright sunshine required them all to shield their eyes a bit, but it was so clear that Toivo found Lempi attractive. It gave her a little thrill, which she hadn't felt in quite some time. But she didn't let anyone see that. She wouldn't give Pauline the satisfaction, nor let Toivo know he had an edge.

Later, when the two women sat down to lunch, Pauline mentioned Toivo. "I think he's quite good looking, don't you? He seems quite strong, yet lean. You like men who look that way, don't you?"

Lempi replied, "I am not going to talk about a gardener."

"Don't be silly. You can't hide anything with me. I've never seen a boy look at you with such adoration. And don't pretend that you didn't notice.

He may not have detected the way you perked up, but I saw right through you."

"I told you he's just a groundskeeper," Lempi protested.

"When did you you become an elitist? Where's all that talk about everyone being equal, and the sanctity of hard labor? You're too serious. You spend too much time thinking about how to make things better for society, and not how to improve things for yourself. You're a part of this world. It's all right if you're happy."

"Maybe." Lempi did have to admit that she liked Toivo's strong hands, and wondered idly what they might feel like against her bare skin. She suspected his palms would be both rough and warm when pressed against her body. She quickly shut down the thought. If she weren't careful, she would blush.

Lempi looked up to see that Pauline observing her. Her friend smiled. Lempi couldn't help but laugh. Pauline smiled, "My work is done."

Lempi met Richard Epstein the first time a week later. He reminded her so much of his dead brother Peter. Already older than his brother had been when Lempi met Peter, Richard was dark with wiry, curly hair that was long and unkempt. His bell-bottom jeans needed a washing, and Richard didn't showcase the artistic, playful spirit that Lempi had found so attractive in Peter. Rather, Richard was intense and focused. His dark eyes danced with energy, but seemed a bit beady.

"I'm staying in the Midwest," he said. "I can help organize local campuses for the anti-war movement. A lot of these farm boys at the university in Madison know this war is wrong. They just need a guide to help them do something about it."

"Do they really care? The rich kids at Bremen seem quite complacent," Lempi replied.

"I don't think so. And even if they are, we know better. Find the right catalyst, and, boom, everything changes."

"I suppose," she replied.

"You know I'm right. This may be the first time we've met, but we share something. Not just my brother either. I hardly remember him. Your letters showed me the way you think. We're both on the right side of history. We can be heroes."

Richard's admiration startled Lempi. She almost expected to find some sexual longing in his eyes, because she couldn't quite believe that someone admired her convictions. But all she saw in Richard's eyes was the burning fire of a shared cause.

Where was Pauline that day? Why didn't she step in to interfere as she did in every other aspect of Lempi's life? Life would have been so much better if Lempi had walked away from that meeting. But the afternoon encounter exuded a lingering scent of a life she once wanted. Seeing someone so similar in looks and movement to Peter was beguiling. Richard flicked the ashes off the end of his cigarette in the same way that Peter did. And unlike Peter, Richard saw Lempi as an intelligent, willful adult.

Pauline would never have approved of her befriending this brother of a one-time romance. She would claim he was unsavory, and think the age difference suspicious. So Lempi didn't tell her. Months later, Pauline and Lempi walked by an anti-war meeting on campus. Richard was among the group and he ran over when he noticed Lempi. She was forced to introduce him, but she didn't tell Pauline that he was Peter's younger brother. Pauline clearly compared this unkempt firebrand unfavorably to the shy and down-to-earth Toivo, and found him lacking.

Perhaps some unexpected energy passed between Lempi and Richard. When they were alone, Pauline grilled Lempi. "Who was that young man?"

"An organizer for one of the student movements. I've talked to him before."

"He looks too old to be a student. Is he enrolled at Bremen?"

"No."

"Then why is he spending time with our students? I don't like it. You should avoid him." Suddenly, Pauline switched subjects. "I'm going to invite Toivo to dinner when your father is in town."

"Wait a minute."

Pauline gave Lempi a don't-argue-with-me look. "You aren't paying enough attention to that young man. He adores you. You know it, and frankly I think you quite like basking in it. But there has to be a two-way street. Without some encouragement, he will just disappear and you will regret it. I know Eero will like him. You're both coming to dinner."

That's how Pauline was. Neither Toivo nor Lempi could tell her "no." Prompted by Pauline, Lempi fell into a romance with a man just because he adored her. Those who should have watched out for Lempi's best interests failed her—the woman who was her mother but never told her as well as the man who claimed to be her father but wasn't. All these years, Lempi had been angry for letting herself be trapped into a marriage with Toivo. But she should be angry with Pauline and Pa. How could anyone be clear about one's own life when it was nothing but lies?

Among the papers from the envelope, Lempi noticed the mimeographed graduation program from her high school class. That night Lempi felt on the top of the world. Her future seemed so secure. She was valedictorian of Clover High, about to attend one of the country's finest private schools and ready to make a name for herself. But the moment proved to be merely a sham.

Lempi wondered if this program was the one Pauline held that evening. She remembered Pauline sitting near the back of the gymnasium. It never seemed odd that an older woman who lived in Milwaukee was in a small town like Clover on a Thursday night. She assumed Pauline was there because her brother Galen was the president of the district's school board. Truth was, she didn't really think much about it all. Pauline was always around. It would have been stranger not to see the woman.

How blind she was that night. Not to recognize that Pauline was her mother. Not to foresee the maelstrom that would soon pull Lempi into its depths. And if she had foreseen it, what would she have done differently? Throughout her life, she tried bargaining with fate. It never worked.

Lempi felt an urge to caress the commencement program as though a mere touch could restore the sense of calm she once had. She had been so certain of herself in her valedictory speech, daring the town to do more and to fight for those oppressed. How certain she was in those days of what was right and what was wrong. How little she knew. But that confidence attracted her to all things and people that shared her certainty. That's why she had found Peter so alluring the day her neighbors picked up the hitchhiker en route to the West Coast. From the beginning, Peter was full of youthful wisdom. The husband and wife in the front seat probably rolled their eyes at Peter's naiveté, but Lempi was enthralled. No one in Clover exhibited such passion. After the nasty blow of Bremen's withdrawal letter, she was ready to flout the limited worldview that dared to try to hold her back. This brash and young New Yorker was the solution. Within an hour of Peter being in the car, Lempi determined they would fall in love. She didn't need a fussy old school like Bremen. If she found a boyfriend on this trip west, then all would be right.

Lempi always made mental bargains, imagining some tit for every tat, expecting the universe to repay her if she undertook some daring action that she didn't really find all that appealing. Each second with Peter made him more attractive and intelligent. Soon, he was the person she always wanted.

As Lempi sat in her kitchen outside Thread, with Risto's hodgepodge of memorabilia, she thought about all the ways that people had failed her. Given all that, maybe the unexpected truth of her past didn't matter. If she only thought long and hard enough, she would determine some way to make up for her past mistakes. She would blaze some new path to erase her failures. It would be as though the letter had never been written, never carried across the ocean and never delivered by some do-gooder rich man's wife from Duluth.

Lempi deeply believed in creating her own reality, even if her world had never demonstrated a working model. She thought working with Richard would make good on Peter's senseless death at the end of the Korean War. Richard could be a way to transform her menial life that resulted from Red fears keeping her out of college. Richard would help her pay society back for the Communist witch hunt that unfairly cast her mother in prison and prompted her suicide. Working with Richard was the way forward.

Lempi always sought meaning. She couldn't abide thinking that it all didn't matter. Sometimes links were hard to see, but that didn't mean they weren't there. Life could not be meaningless. If not for the great Red Scare, Professor Tom Ferber would never have abandoned teaching at Bremen. If he hadn't done that, then he would never have retreated to Thread and she would not have the security of her only real friend in this dismal town. Every action had meaning and consequence.

Richard taught her that. He used Milwaukee as his base to organize students in the upper Midwest. He could easily travel west to Madison, south to Chicago and connect with students in the schools around Milwaukee. There were great colleges in town, institutions like Bremen and Marquette University, which offered fertile ground for his seeds of discontent.

Lempi saw Richard once or twice a month, but she never told Pauline about these visits. She was certain Pauline wouldn't approve. She never whispered of Richard to Toivo either. When she and Toivo first began dating, her other friends seemed unimportant. As time went on, her clandestine relationship with Richard began to feel disloyal, even though she had nothing to hide.

In the fall of 1968, with the election between Nixon and Humphrey near, Richard met Lempi for coffee. When she arrived at the coffeehouse, he was staring at the headlines of *The New York Times*. It was so much like Richard to buy an expensive out-of-town newspaper, always a day old and therefore always out of date compared to the *Sentinel* or *Journal*. But he didn't trust anything Midwestern.

"It looks like Nixon will win," he said. "And you know he will only continue the war, and who knows what else. All your campaigning for Senator McCarthy. Just wasted effort."

Lempi actually felt much the same way, but she was loath to admit it. "I don't think so," she replied. "We proved that there are people who care about the war. We forced Johnson not to run again, and now both Humphrey and Nixon claim they're for peace. At least we changed the conversation."

Richard smiled in his smug way that so often drove Lempi crazy. "Did we really?"

"Yes, we did," she stated strongly. "Whoever wins, the country won't let the war continue. We won't keep sending our young men to be slaughtered in the jungle."

"Lempi, you know you don't believe that. Don't get me wrong. It was great that you campaigned for McCarthy, fantastic that you were part of the establishment. But in Chicago, you were on the wrong side of the police line."

She broke in, "Don't forget the police stormed McCarthy's campaign offices."

"That's not what I mean, and you know it. The people who will make a difference were in the Park that night. It's the protesters, the students, the Yippies who matter. You can't beat the establishment fighting within the establishment. You just disappear in the ordinary, and the old guard stomps all over you."

"I don't agree."

"Really? If anyone should know better, it's you. Look at how the power class destroyed your family—kept you from college and hounded your mother to the grave. They took away the only man you loved—my brother— in a senseless war; and they're still doing it."

"But now I have Toivo. He loves me," Lempi protested.

"From what you tell me, I think Toivo only loves the idea of you. But what does it matter? Do you love him? Tell me that." Richard looked at her with an air of superiority, like a man who just disclosed a royal flush to her two of a kind.

"I don't know if I can love anyone," she replied. "That's the truth. I've always been alone. My parents were so much older, and were never interested in my life. Ma was stuck in her memories. And you know I had no siblings at home. Never really had friends at school. I guess I'm proof that Finns aren't emotional people."

Richard would have none of it. "What about those letters you wrote me when Peter was killed? You said you loved him. A lot of emotion was packed into those envelopes. It kept me going. So don't tell me you can't love. Here's the truth. It wasn't just Peter who died on the battlefront. Some part of you was also killed that day. Wars do that. Their destruction just spreads and spreads. Don't you want to stop that?"

Lempi was quiet. She supposed Richard could be correct on one level. But on another, she was certain he was wrong. She knew so little of life or love when she met Peter. The two of them never spent more than a few days together. Only her romantic nature made that time define her life. For some reason, she thought of Toivo's friend Jeremy. Toivo and Jeremy only picked cherries together for one summer, but they had a bond. Maybe Richard was right in his observation. Emotional ties arrived in many forms and many ways; some were often easy and quick. Yet Lempi felt separate and alone at every turn. Even Pauline often remained just a co-worker at the college. Her father was an old farmer in a small Wisconsin town, and not a beloved parent. Was Toivo more than a gardener with no ambitions? Had her ability to love and care been blown up by the war a decade earlier?

Richard watched Lempi closely. He sensed her acceptance of what he said. His tone changed. "We can make a difference. I have a plan. You can help."

***

Even now, Lempi chilled thinking back on Richard's strange hold over her. She was foolish then. Living a normal life ever since was her bargain for forgiveness. Bending her will to Toivo's and moving to Thread was supposed to make the difference. Her hopes of atonement were here in this repressive small town.

She drifted into the simple existence of a farmwife. Routine defined all. She even abandoned her love of the movies, although that had been the first real bond between her and Toivo. But the Thread Theater was closed, and it was a long drive to Timberton's old moviehouse. The only television station with a signal strong enough to reach them never aired interesting films

What took the place of the cinema were the chickens, the garden, the chores and, of course, Danny. Lempi vowed to always be there for her son, making his favorite foods for breakfast, teaching him ice skating and exploring the woods together. The world held so much for him, and she wanted him to make those discoveries with her at his side. She would never let him face the bleakness of her own life.

And she determined to be a good wife to Toivo. However rotten she knew she was within, she never allowed that to infect him. If he wanted to walk each evening, hand in hand, toward Highway 17, then she would do it. Over time, such routine created its own reality. Repetition reinforced feigned emotions until they became true. Maybe love discovered some secret redoubt in her heart, guarding a love for a husband, for a son and for a life hidden away. Sometimes, bargains worked out.

Lempi found an unexpected photo among the material. It was a picture of Pauline, Lempi and Danny—grandmother, mother and son. In it, Lempi stood next to Pauline, who in turn held the small baby. Lempi remembered the afternoon the photo was taken, even though she had never seen the actual snapshot. By the time Pauline developed the film, the two of them seldom talked.

It was the day of Lempi's first dinner party in the new apartment. The event was planned to honor Pauline and her boyfriend John Tuzzi. If Pauline hadn't purchased the building, Lempi and Toivo would still be stuck trying to raise a newborn in too small of a space. Back then, she didn't understand why Pauline had acquired the fourplex or how much it cost her. It was just a wonderful coincidence of interest—Pauline needing an investment and an apartment manager. Toivo and Lempi were in the right place at the right time.

Inviting Pauline and her FBI friend was the least Lempi could do in thanks. Reflecting back, Lempi could see how grandiose it was to call the Sunday afternoon meal a dinner party. After all, just four adults and a baby would sit around the small round oak table in a Norman Rockwell scene

As Lempi prepared the meal, afternoon sunlight flooded the kitchen. A pot roast was in the heavy Dutch oven. She stood at the sink peeling potatoes. Pauline walked into the room. Danny lay smiling in her arms. He was almost asleep.

"He's a beautiful baby," said Pauline.

Her old friend was so content holding the infant. Lempi wondered whether Pauline regretted never marrying or being a mother. She wanted to ask, but she was afraid such a question would in some way hurt the older woman. Instead, she said, "It looks like Danny belongs to you."

Pauline smiled so beautifully in response. At the same time, Lempi feared Pauline was about to cry. Lempi didn't understand why her words had such an effect, but she said nothing more.

The threat of tears quickly vanished, and Pauline continued to smile. Danny's eyes closed completely. Pauline looked up, "It must be the Clover blood," she said, "somehow even a baby knows we all belong together. And he sleeps so contented among us."

Small town bonds were powerful, Lempi agreed. They did belong together, and she vowed to stop snapping at Pauline's innocent comments. Lempi shouldn't begrudge Pauline's happiness in her new relationship with the FBI man. She should just accept Pauline's decisions. Lempi dropped her potato peelings among the scraps in the sink. She walked over to look at her baby. "You'll be his Clover grandmother," she said, tugging ever so gently at Danny's blanket. "And he'll be a lucky boy to have you."

For a moment, the tensions of the past year seemed forgotten history. Tuzzi stepped into the kitchen. He looked at the three generations standing next to one another. "This is too perfect to ignore," he said. "Let me get my camera." He was back in a moment with his Instamatic and snapped their photo. "What a Kodak moment."

Nothing in Lempi's life had ever been a Kodak moment, so she laughed out loud. Danny woke. But he didn't cry. He just opened his eyes and looked at the two women. Pauline continued her gentle rocking, and the boy's eyes closed once more. Feeling pleased, Lempi walked back to the sink. She needed to get the kettle of potatoes on the stove and serve this meal on time.

"Things have turned out, pretty well, haven't they?" said Pauline. "Sometimes it takes a while, but eventually, everything falls into place. You and Toivo. The baby. This apartment. My meeting John. Lempi, are you happy?"

"Of course," she replied quickly, unwilling to stop and think about her answer. Everyone always wanted her to be happy. Who even knew what happiness was?

"I couldn't bear it if you weren't," said Pauline.

"Well, you would have to," said Lempi, but then, embarrassed that her usual snappishness would destroy this shimmering moment, she added. "But don't worry. I am happy."

In that moment, as Lempi voiced a statement she hadn't even thought out, she realized that she was indeed happier than she had any right to be. Perhaps Pauline pushed hard to make Toivo part of Lempi's life, but he proved to be a kind and gentle man. Perhaps he wasn't ambitious, yet he had a spirit of generosity that Lempi found wonderful. And she knew that Toivo loved her as much as she loved their son. She glanced into the living room and saw that Toivo was watching them. Tuzzi still played with his camera, as though tempted to take another shot.

"If you have nothing better to do than watch us, maybe you fellows should come in here and help us with the cooking," joked Lempi in a voice intended to reach the living room.

Tuzzi made a stage whisper reply, "I don't think you'd like the results."

Toivo on the other hand started walking toward them. "Maybe I will. If only to let me be close to my son. Can't let you two women smother him."

That moment should have been the first of many such happy afternoons. In another world, the four of them would have watched Danny grow into a young man. Lempi would have returned to interesting work in the city after Danny started school. Toivo would have remained in Milwaukee. And Pauline would be alive and happily married to Tuzzi. The Norman Rockwell paintings would have continued to be painted, one stroke after another in a predictable and comfortable progression.

It wasn't to be. Lempi had to live with that every day, and sometimes she wondered why she bothered. Recalling the few happy moments helped.

The men gallantly volunteered to take care of the dishes on that dinner party afternoon. They made a great show of running a sink full of suds, clanking the pots and clinking the glasses. Lempi and Pauline retreated to the living room to chat, while Toivo and Tuzzi joked by the sink. The scent of cinnamon from her handmade apple pie lingered in the air. Lempi judged the afternoon a success.

"Well, we're done," said Toivo. He sat down on the sofa next to Pauline.

"Where's John?" asked Pauline.

"He stepped out on the back landing to take a smoke."

Lempi stood up. "Stay a while longer. I'll go ask him if you have time to watch *Disney's Wonderful World of Color* with us." Lempi and Toivo had just purchased a color television. Inviting John to stay would be a good sign.

Lempi found John on the small wooden landing, cigarette in hand, staring across the alley. Daylight Saving Time was over, so it was already dark. Lempi could see the red tip of his cigarette glowing. John looked over as Lempi stepped out the door. She leaned against the back railing to spot the moon.

"Still warm for so late in the fall," said Lempi. She hoped John would agree to stay. She didn't want the day to end.

"I have a question I want to ask," he said a bit abruptly.

"Sure"

"Do you know a Richard Epstein?"

The glow of the afternoon vanished like that. Lempi was crushed. Always an FBI man, she thought. Here Tuzzi was destroying a perfect day. Pauline and she had fallen into the old familiar groove; Lempi had forgotten how comfortable that felt and how much she wanted it. Tuzzi was snatching it away. She didn't know how or why, but his simple question was like a bomb.

And she didn't know how to answer. The situation with Richard was too complicated to explain easily. Tuzzi knew nothing of her teenage romance with Richard's brother. She never told Toivo and Pauline about her occasional meetings with Richard. And Lempi preferred to ignore Richard's radical friends, even though she let them meet at the apartment, and she sat in on some of their meetings.

Tuzzi took the moment of silence as Lempi's unwillingness to answer. "You don't need to tell me, because I already know you know the kid," he said. "I just want to give you a friendly warning. Richard and his ilk are a bad seed. You mean a lot to Pauline, and I don't want to see you get caught up in the wrong crowd."

Whenever caught in a lie or misunderstanding, Lempi grew furious. "You have never done anything in your life that was in my interest. Do you think I've forgotten your role in Ma's death? It all started with your FBI visit to our farm. I never wanted to see you again. Yet here you are. In my house."

"Don't fly off on a handle, Lempi. I'm not the enemy."

"Everyone's an enemy. At least to people like you." She stormed back into the house, letting the rear door slam hard. In the living room, Toivo and Pauline looked up.

"I'm going to bed," Lempi declared. "I have a headache." She didn't allow anyone to protest. Behind the closed door, Lempi cried. The day held such promise and she let it fall apart.

Now, decades later, seeing the snapshot with its proof of that happy day, seeing the three of them together, after all these years knowing that this sole picture showed true grandmother, mother and son—aware of all this, Lempi still couldn't explain why she reacted so strongly that day. Sure, she was foolish and temperamental, but maybe it was also guilt. Tuzzi was right to warn her about Richard. But no one's warning ever stopped her.

She wouldn't look at that snapshot one moment longer. Lempi cast it down and picked up another that showed her as a little girl standing outside the Clover farmhouse. After Toivo and she left the hospital where Pa had been pronounced dead on arrival, they went to his house and found Pa's photo album opened to this same photo. It had been a horrible day: The call that her father had a heart attack. The two-hour drive from Thread to Clover. Confirming the body's identity. Painful conversations with the doctor and a counselor. Both Lempi and Toivo were exhausted, but felt they needed to return to Pa's house, close it up and get some sleep.

Lempi wasn't sure what she expected when she walked into the cold house. Her father always seemed so neat, so she was a bit surprised to find the photo albums out of the bookcase. Pa must have been looking at them that day. She wondered if he had been thinking of her.

As an adult, Lempi never liked the photo of her as a toddler. She supposed people found her a charming enough child, but the camera captured something about her she didn't like to acknowledge. Such an air of seriousness for a young girl, as though she carried the weight of the world. Even as a child, she cared too much.

Pa always said her solemn disposition made it seem as though she were planning to save the world. She never saw what was wrong with that, but Pa thought otherwise. He sought to make her laugh; she seldom gave in. Even though his comic faces and silly quips amused her, she didn't want him to know.

Pa helped her accept the world the way it was, and that was no easy task to accomplish. She wished he were with her now. When she was a child, he was always there to support her. He would know what to make of this pile of trash from Russia. She remembered an August day in 1945 when the evil of the world seemed so depressing. While others celebrated, she brooded. The devastation in Japan seemed so wrong.

The previous day she sat with Ma and Pa as they listened attentively to the radio announce how President Truman ordered the dropping of a massive new type of bomb on Hiroshima. The city's name seemed unfamiliar and hard to remember, but her parents were clearly excited. They thought it meant the end of World War Two, but all Lempi could picture were thousands and thousands of dead bodies. Throughout the war, newspapers haunted her. Pictures from bombings in Germany gave her nightmares. She was only twelve, but she believed in a better world. And she didn't trust the radio. She set aside anything that came out of its speakers as make believe. On that day, she chose to not believe in a magical new type of bomb.

Still, she didn't sleep well that night. She awaited but dreaded the arrival the next morning of the daily newspaper. If the bombing were in the paper, she couldn't deny it. A paper's ink rubbed onto one's fingers. It was real.

No paperboy served the Makinen farm out in the country. Instead, the U.S. Mail usually delivered the paper to the white mailbox at the end of the driveway just before lunch. Pa left early that morning to help neighbors with their threshing. Ma must have been in the kitchen preparing the noon time dinner. Lempi sat in the living room listening for the mailman's car.

She could have sat on the front porch bench and more easily kept tabs on it all, but Lempi didn't want to explain her anxiety about the paper.

There was the sound of tires and loose pebbles. She willed herself to stick to the sofa for a few minutes. When she was sure the mailman was on his way to the Muellers, she raced to the mailbox and grabbed the paper—the only thing delivered that day. She rushed back into the living room, unfolded the paper and laid the twelve-page *Chippewa Herald* in front of her. The headlines were large and black. America rained destruction on Hiroshima. The bomb seemed horrific beyond anything of the previous four years of war coverage. Lempi read every word of the story and then each of the sidebars. Clearly the officials quoted thought this atomic bomb would hasten reaching peace with the Japanese. But Lempi pictured dead babies. She looked up at the photo of her three brothers: Jaacko, Johani and Risto. They were all strangers to her, gone before she was born. They meant no more to her than any of the dead Japanese children she imagined. But the Japanese dead seemed more real.

Pa walked through the back door, home for noon dinner. She heard Ma greet him. Lempi hurriedly refolded the paper. She knew Pa would want to read it after eating.

"Lempi, come into the kitchen. It's dinner time," Ma said. Pa was sweaty and dirty, but happy. He reporting the threshing was done, and he wouldn't need to go back. All through the meal—pork chops, new potatoes and fresh sliced tomatoes—Lempi was quiet and felt Pa watching her. Finally, he spoke.

"Something bothering you, pumpkin?" he asked. He liked to give her names of different vegetables. She wished he had used "kohlrabi" because that word always made her laugh. Maybe that would dislodge her image of dead children. She remembered a schoolbook picture of corpses covered in ash at Pompeii. Life could be frozen in an instant for no good reason.

She shook her head no.

Pa would have none of it. He knew Lempi's moods, and he didn't like her to sink into them the way that Ma did.

"Is it the war again?" he asked. "It's almost over now." She forgot that he already knew about the bomb from last night's radio.

"But why do we have to kill so many people?" She really wanted to know, and a part of her thought Pa could answer. He was wiser than other men in town.

"That's what wars do."

"We shouldn't keep making more and more horrible ways to fight them," Lempi proclaimed. "I read in the paper all about this new bomb. The president says it uses the basic power of the universe, the same power as the sun."

"Is that what he says?"

Lempi couldn't figure out what Pa was thinking when he said this, but she was quick to respond. "Yes, that's what he says. But the sun makes things grow. That's a good thing. This new weapon sounds awful. And aren't we awful too if we use it? War don't make any sense to me. It should disappear forever."

Ma looked at Lempi in dismay. Maybe it was even disgust. Lempi never knew what her mother was thinking. For a woman who could be so moody herself, she had little sympathy for her daughter's passions. Pa rose from the table and gestured to Lempi to follow. "Let's go outside, Lempi. We should talk about this more. It's a wonderful thing that you care so deeply. But if you care too much, you'll only hurt yourself."

He put his arm around her, drew her close to his side and together they walked out the back door. He let the screen door close with a thud, which Lempi knew would make Ma mad, but she didn't care. Pentu, their farm dog, ran from the barn toward them. Lempi reflexively reached out to pat the collie's head. Eero stopped in the middle of the yard, not far from their largest apple tree.

"The sun is good," he said to Lempi, "but everything good comes with its own dangers. Feel the sun's heat. It feels good, doesn't it? But you know if you stayed out here all day, your skin would burn. Even though the sun is millions of miles away, it can burn you. Just like you can't look directly into its brightness, or it would blind you."

Lempi protested, "We know how to keep those things from happening. We don't have to burn or go blind. We can avoid what's bad."

Pa acknowledged this. "Still, sometimes when you know a big storm is looming, you continue to work all day in the sun getting burned, because it's the only way to save your harvest."

"Pa, that's not the same as a war."

Eero looked fondly at her. "Oh, Lempi, you've grown so tall. I remember the day I first saw you. Your Ma walked off the train with you, and you were just the littlest of things. You needed so much protection.

And now, soon, you'll be a woman. All the men will need protection from you."

Lempi was annoyed that Pa was seeking a way to distract her. "Don't, Pa. How come you're not upset? Didn't you come to America so you wouldn't have to fight in the Czar's wars? You tell people that all the time."

"I tell you what, little turnip. Let's walk down to the river, watch the ducks and I'll tell you all my thoughts about men and war, all about good and bad as I see it. You can decide what to do with it all."

That afternoon was the best memory of Lempi's childhood. The two of them never made it to the riverbank, but stopped in the farm's uncleared pasture. Pa lifted her up to perch on the one remaining stump of the old forest. He hoisted himself to sit beside her. From their vantage point they could see the river and be cooled by the breeze crossing the fields. Their dairy cows were in the rough grasses surrounding them, and Pentu chased his tail in a circle until he was satisfied to lie at the stump's base.

Her father picked up Lempi's small hand with his big paw. "Lempi, you see the world as white and black, but one day you will learn it has many shades of grey. What is good at one time might well be evil at another. We must be discerning.

"It is true I left Finland because I did not want to go in the Russian Army. I have always thought our rulers are too eager to fight. It was true of the Czar back then and it is just as true of our American presidents. But I also came to this country for other reasons. I wanted to define my own life, to own a farm that was mine, to raise a family that I loved . . . and to have you."

"But you hate war," Lempi countered. She wasn't going to let him change the subject.

"Yes, you know me well. When the last European war started, your mother and I thought America should stay out of it. We believed in Fighting Bob LaFollette, who was our great senator from Wisconsin. He didn't want this country to fight in what he saw as Europe's war. The Germans around here loved him, but most of the country hated him, just like many of our neighbors hated the local Germans."

Lempi thought that proved her point. "Wasn't the Senator right? That war didn't change anything. We're fighting another one."

"Maybe so, but people try to make a difference. Like your brother Risto. He went all the way over to Russia because he believe he could build a better world." Eero looked away sadly. "I hoped it turned out well for him. The Karpela family went over, but they came back after only a year. It turned out not to be such a good life in the woods of Russia. But I like to think that Risto rose above all that. Somehow, I'm sure he made a difference."

Lempi stayed mum. She didn't need to tell Pa about her fantasy that Risto long ago left Russia to become a rich industrialist or novelist or someone powerful in a safe place like South America. Even at twelve, she still imagined one day Risto would come to take her away. That's what big brothers did—looked after their little sisters.

"I don't understand, Pa," Lempi said. "War is wrong. We need to do what we think is right. Otherwise, we're all just evil."

Eero looked out toward the river. Its water were placid, a gentle flow south toward the St. Croix and the Mississippi. "Life is like the water flowing below. It can be calm and inviting. But storms come along, and it rises rapidly, floods the land and carries away those not prepared. You have to be prepared to fight the floods. Sometimes you have to fight for what's yours."

"But how do you know when it's worth fighting for?"

"Ma's father, your grandpa, would say you can find the answer in the Bible, but you know I don't believe that. Some in town would say it's whatever our President says. I don't think it's that simple either. Ultimately, we all must carry the weight of that decision. We each have to decide what we think is right and what is wrong. And you can never stop listening, because when you stop hearing what the other side says, you just follow the crowd. And that's where the real danger lies."

Lempi let those thoughts sink in. She knew her father believed in many things, like the need to look out for one another and the power of working together, but she didn't feel like his advice made all that much sense. She wondered if he was happy with his life.

"Are you glad you left Finland?" she asked.

"Of course I am," he replied. "If I hadn't made my move, I would never have grown my own beautiful kohlrabi."

Lempi smiled, "Well, I know that war and killing people is wrong. I will always believe that, whatever happens. And I will make a difference."

***

Lempi sighed. She supposed the mixture of clippings and photos before her displayed a life story of some sort. She accepted the truth of Risto's letter. Nothing in her past contradicted it.

It was hard to absorb, but she must. During her entire life, the two people who she thought were her mother and father were actually grandparents. What difference would it have made if she had known sooner? Would Marja's moods have been easier to handle? Would Lempi have paid less attention to Eero? It would not have changed one thing.

But Pauline was another matter. Risto's letter made Lempi lose her mother twice. First, Marja through suicide, and now Pauline. Lempi didn't want to think about the anti-war bombing.

Which left the matter of Risto. Whether brother or father, he was still a man she never met. What did it matter if he continued to think of her from his Russian perch? None of these facts changed anything in her life.

It just was. It helped to explain a few things, such as why Pauline's will named Lempi her heir. But Lempi decided she wouldn't even bother to tell Toivo about this revelation. No good would come of it, and Lempi would certainly not inform Danny. Frail as he was, he didn't need to rethink his family history.

A week passed. Lempi had told no one her astonishing news. But she found it difficult not to lift the lid and stir the pot. She slept fitfully each night, not sure whether it was insomnia prompted by lifelong troublesome lies or a need to reconsider her interactions with two mothers.

After one too many groggy mornings, Lempi made a decision. She would tell Tom Ferber. Everyone in town might call him Mr. Packer but Lempi had known him for nearly thirty years and he had been the stabilizing force to her life in Thread.

She found him walking past the boarded-up Thread Tavern. That was Ferber—always walking. She parked and exited her car just as he turned the corner near the train station and old theater. She called out "Tom." He stopped in front of the fading poster for *Cabaret*, never taken down after the Thread Theater closed its doors a decade earlier. The train depot was also closed. Occasionally, a freight train still rumbled through the town, but Amtrak long ago stopped running the daily train that once connected Thread to Milwaukee. They were alone.

The old man turned and smiled. She thought his long beard more unkempt than usual. Ferber looked like an old coot. "Lempi, how nice to see you," he said. "Were you looking for me?"

She nodded yes. Ferber motioned toward the wooden benches near the train tracks—symbols of another era. So much had happened since the days Lempi took her train to Milwaukee. The Kennedy assassinations, Vietnam, men on the moon, Watergate, gas shortages and an actor becoming president. All that time and she never knew who she was.

Ferber sat down. "You appear as though you need to talk," he observed. Lempi realized he was her only friend in town. After ten years here, how could it be that no one else felt worthy of her trust? She didn't even have a short list.

Ferber was special, a friend forged by time and circumstance. He was Pauline's friend. He represented Bremen College and the life she once sought. He was smart and well-read. An outsider, like her, he was someone that the town didn't understand and didn't care to know. They simply dismissed him as an old coot nicknamed Mr. Packer.

She jumped into it, "I've heard from my brother in Russia. After all these years, it turns out he's still alive. He sent me a letter."

"Really?" Ferber didn't seem at all surprised.

Lempi didn't know what to say next. Telling Ferber the details would bare her soul and leave her with no secrets. But she needed this confessional. "Risto wrote things I can hardly believe. Everything I know; it's all gone topsy-turvy."

"Yes?" Ferber's face seemed kind and understanding, the way Lempi imagined a priest's should be.

"Risto says that I was adopted, and that he was my real father. He claims Pauline was my mother. Everything in my life is a delusion."

Ferber didn't seem shocked. "How would this discovery make a lie of all the love you've received over the years from so many people?"

Lempi looked up at him in shock. "You knew, didn't you? You knew that Pauline was my mother." She felt betrayed and angry.

"I suspected. Pauline never actually told me, but I knew her so well. I was aware that she occasionally wrote to Risto, and I long ago guessed a teenage pregnancy delayed her college years. Then I heard her talk about you. I met you. The details all matched. But I never asked Pauline for confirmation. It was her secret to keep." He paused. "But back to the point,

Lempi. What does this change? All the same people were still there for you."

Lempi looked across the square in a bargain for time to find the right response. On the far side, the horrendous modern facade of the Piggly Wiggly grocery store faced the square. Like her, the building didn't belong. A few tourists walked the streets. They represented a world she once wanted: a life of affluence and urban sophistication, a life to which visitors returned when their north woods holiday ended. Anchored to a husband and son, she was robbed of that life. Lies sent her down this path. Deception led her to this tiny town.

"I just know it makes a difference," she said. "If I had known Marja was my grandmother, maybe I wouldn't have feared her moods. I might have treated her better; maybe she wouldn't have burned herself alive. And if I knew Pauline was my mother . . . well, I wouldn't have let my mother stay away on Christmas Eve. I could have kept her from working in Shindler Hall when it was bombed. I could have kept her alive."

In her mind, Lempi thought of still more: the lives of Eero, Toivo and even Danny were stunted because of her. She never treated any of them as they deserved. How could you do the right thing when you didn't even know who you were?

"Lempi, you know I love you, but I won't let you delude yourself," Ferber looked unusually stern. "You aren't responsible for Marja's decisions. You didn't place the bomb at Bremen College. Nor can you take the responsibility for anyone else's life. Not Toivo's. Not Danny's."

Ferber grabbed both of Lempi's hands and forced her to look directly in his eyes. She tried to resist. He didn't know everything, and she would never let him know everything.

"But Lempi, you chose your life, and you must take responsibility for that. You are who you are because of the actions you took. No other reason. No other person's fault."

Lempi pulled her hands loose. The driver in a car going around the square looked curiously at the two of them. Suddenly, she wanted to be in that car, fleeing to anyplace other than Thread.

Lempi looked down at her hands and kept her eyes from connecting with Ferber. "I've never been in control. Bremen College took away my chance, all because they thought we were Communists. And, guess what, my real father was, but they didn't even need to know that. And Pauline forced me into a romance with Toivo. This world doesn't care about any of us. It likes to fight its wars and grind people like us into the dirt. Even now, we have a president who doesn't care a thing about the common person. Why else would he invade a little country like Grenada?" Lempi still hated war, however minor the conflict might be.

Ferber's voice took on an edge. "Lempi, you are in charge of your own life. Stop evading responsibility. Yes, the great fear of the Fifties stole your chance to attend Bremen. But only for that point in time. You could have still attended college, maybe a different college, maybe at a later time. But you chose otherwise. You took the easy way out. Like here in Thread. You wither away in boredom. You fence yourself onto that small farm. You do that. With your work experience, you could have found a job. There aren't that many clever and talented people in this neck of the woods.

"You know you could have done more. But you closed yourself off. Just answer this: do you have any friends in this town other than me?"

Lempi didn't respond.

"And don't degrade your marraige. Toivo clearly loves you, and quite frankly, I am pretty certain you love him back. Maybe Pauline engineered the beginning. Maybe, Toivo hasn't been the romance you imagined as a teenager. But the two of you depend on each another. You take comfort in each other's presence. I see it in the way you walk along the highway each night, hand in hand. The whole town would testify that you're deeply in love. Can you truly say you're not?"

Lempi scoffed. "What do they know? They can't even remember all that you've done. And you can hardly lecture me on personal decisions. You've hidden yourself away in this tiny place. You've abandoned everything you once accomplished."

Ferber smiled. "So they call me Mr. Packer. And maybe I did retreat and hide. But I am much older than you. I accomplished what I wanted in my life, and I like to think there may still be some tricks ahead. Whatever I've done or not done, it doesn't change your options. My life and my decisions are not the role model for your happiness.

"Accept Risto's letter for what it is. It can be your spur to rethink your life. If you're not happy with the way you treated Marja or Pauline, then behave differently with Toivo and Danny. Break the chains of yesterday and live for tomorrow. You can change. It is up to you."

***

Toivo, Danny and Lempi sat at the kitchen table. Her family, at least all that was left of it, was in one place eating. Not quite all, she corrected herself. Her real father was out there somewhere. She tried to imagine the frozen lakes of Karelia. After talking with Ferber, she stopped in Thread to find Karelia in the library's massive atlas. She located the page for the western Soviet Union. Her finger outlined the block of land north of Leningrad and east of Helsinki. The map showed many lakes and no mountains. Like Thread, it was a region that was far north, cold and prone to snow. But in Thread, remnants of the ancient Penokee mountain range rose in waves between the town and the shores of Lake Superior. On the other hand, their farmland itself was flat and prone to swamps. Lempi imagined Karelia was much like their farm. Her fingertips felt the texture of the printed page, but that didn't bring her real father any closer to her. His letter spoke of love and a desire for closeness, but it was an impossible dream. She wanted nothing to do with Risto.

At the table, she felt Danny watching her. She was reluctant to meet his eyes; she never liked looking directly into them. God, she hoped he didn't realize that. His eyes held a sorrow deeply buried, a blackness of despair so contradictory to his clear blue irises. He was a handsome child. His skin was beautifully fair, and she hoped it stayed that way. His voice was just starting to change, and she feared the hormones of puberty would soon wreak havoc. He was turning into an adult. She saw the stains on his underwear when she washed. Maybe he had wet dreams, but he often locked himself in their one bathroom. Toivo tolerated it, but she wanted to knock on the door and disrupt him. How long would it be before Danny no longer needed her?

"You look a million miles away, Mom," Danny said. "Something going on with you?"

Toivo looked up, startled. Once he had paid attention to every emotional sign that she emitted. Now, they were just two sleds slipping down a powdery hill. They might be next to one another, sharing the frosty snow flung up, but they never touched on their private journeys downhill. If one of them were to hit a rock, fly high in the air and crash in the path of the other, what would happen then? Lempi couldn't say, and didn't want to know.

"Everything okay, honey?" Toivo asked. Maybe he wasn't as far away as Lempi tended to think. Maybe they were really on the same two-person toboggan, skimming recklessly across the banks, riding their way to some safe end.

"Of course," she replied. "I was just thinking about supper."

Toivo and Danny looked at one another as though she were daft. Supper was supper, even when it involved favorite items. She chose the night's menu as a way to celebrate the arrival of another Friday. Danny wouldn't have to return to his middle school classes until Monday, and she could watch him relax as Friday night unwound. She knew her son didn't get along with the other boys in town. She didn't understand why. She didn't think she should ask.

For Toivo, the weekend didn't matter as much. Truth was he probably loved his job more than he loved her. Lempi talked to Toivo's boss once, who claimed that Toivo understood trees. He treated every limb and tree trunk as though it were a conscious, feeling thing. Lempi saw the way Toivo walked around their own farm, touching the trees like some farmers did with their cows, treating them as pets. Toivo probably wished he could go to work every day.

Still, today started the weekend. She needed to demarcate the days for herself as much as for them. Toivo had his work. Danny had his studies. She was left to her thoughts wrapped in housework and cooking—and they were insufficient to distract her from the enormity of her past. She should listen to Ferber and choose the kind of life she wanted.

So Swiss steak, mashed potatoes and creamed corn were a surrogate for celebration. You took what victories you could. Danny ate heartily, as boys turning into teenagers normally did. This was after downing at least four raised doughnuts earlier in the afternoon. More sweets lay ahead, including caramel rolls made earlier in the day. Both her men loved them.

"Supper is really good, Mom."

She took another bite of the Swiss steak. The heartily pounded and slowly braised beef melted in her mouth. She loved this homey dish probably more than either her husband or son. "So tell me what's new at school, Danny. I need to hear about something other than TV soap operas."

The boy clammed up. He grabbed a piece of bread and buttered it. Lempi knew she shouldn't have asked. Danny didn't fit in. Earlier in the semester, the school asked her to come in for a talk. Danny was a smart kid. There wasn't a problem with that. But he stayed to himself, and some of the older boys picked on him. Danny never fought back. He ate alone in a corner of the cafeteria. He avoided the middle school sports teams. He had no friends for the ride on the school bus. He stood near the corner of the school during the breaks, rocking from foot to foot, awkward in his recent growth spurt. He deflected any attempts by the girls or boys in his class to talk. Lempi didn't understand why her son was so insecure. She knew the girls in his class thought him cute. In small towns, mothers talked. If he only tried, Danny could have many friends.

Lempi blamed herself. She was a bad role model. What kind of mother locks herself away, spends her life on a farm looking after a few chickens, growing vegetables and picking fruit? She filled a basement with canned provisions just to avoid going mad. The shelves in the basement held more filled Mason jars than the three of them would ever eat.

But she had a reason for being a recluse. Danny did not. She lived a life before going into hiding. Danny was just about to begin his. She made so many mistakes, and she needed to keep him from making a single one. She needed to help him scale the mountains ahead, not get bogged down in her swamp.

Now Toivo watched her face. She knew she could never mask her true feelings from him. He stopped eating. "Has something happened?" he asked. "You've been distracted and edgy for days."

He looked at her the same way on the day they learned of Pauline's death. He knew then, and she guessed he knew now, that there were things she would not tell him. Toivo was decent and hardworking. He deserved someone better than her.

Lempi was too quick to let him take over when she was overwhelmed. It was as though she had depleted her own sense of self in those political years of the late Sixties. Championing Eugene McCarthy. Fighting against the war. It all came tumbling down around her, and she retained no energy to begin anew.

Toivo alone arranged their move to Thread. He worked out the deal with his parents to take over the family farm. He packed up everything that they moved, and sat in the hot sun holding a garage sale to rid them of the rest. He even helped Galen close out Pauline's estate and maximize what little money remained. Once in Thread, he was the person who found a new doctor for Danny.

All she did was sit in the car, hold Danny in her arms for the seven-hour drive from Milwaukee to Thread and listened quietly as Toivo sang the lullaby that calmed Danny into a sound sleep.

That trip was the map to the life that followed. She barely participated. She knew where they banked, but nothing about the balances in the accounts or whether they had trouble paying the bills. For over a dozen years, she kept to a mindless routine: she got up in the morning, made her husband breakfast, saw that Danny stepped onto the school bus, cleaned the house, took care of the garden, fed the chickens, gathered the eggs, drowned herself in television soaps and an occasional book from the library, made supper and washed the dishes, retired to bed, made love to her husband if he wanted and woke up each morning to do it all again.

Such was her life. Until forced to confront its reality by a brown envelope filled with old photos and clippings, she hadn't evaluated its emptiness. Now scraps of papers, a letter from a man she'd never met and old photos called everything into question.

Maybe she found these relics of the past safer than becoming involved with the real world. The patchy signals from the NBC station in Rhinelander were enough to torment her with the nightly news. The *Timberton Daily World* was a constant reminder of the world's unfairness. She knew what was going on. She didn't simply flee the wider world when the bomb went off at Bremen. She knew that Nixon proved to be the crook she always thought he was, and she cheered when he resigned. She watched the last of the troops flee Saigon on their helicopters. She paid attention as Hmong refugees fled from the mountains of Southeast Asia to a cold refuge in Central Wisconsin, more victims cursed by a war she tried to end. The country, in a growing malaise, turned to another man she despised, Ronald Reagan. She endured it all, never able to make a difference.

Maybe her father abandoned America to try to build a better world in Russia and maybe it worked out for Risto, or maybe it didn't. But she never felt the world was getting better here in America. Nobody cared about one another. Everyone was willing to take advantage of the weaker, like that bully who tormented her son. Lempi sighed.

"Something is wrong," Toivo insisted.

Lempi looked at her husband. His face was kind, but she felt she hardly knew him. He was a better person than her. He looked so worried; so did Danny. They bore a strong resemblance, she realized, but her son also reminded her of a photograph she had seen of Risto.

Tears began to stream from her eyes, but she said nothing.

The father looked at the son. Neither said anything. They had seen this sort of thing too many times.

Lempi settled into an odd sort of calm. Facts were what they were. There were other things to consider. Winter was coming. Once the snows started in this far northern part of the state, the snow would not relent until the late days of March. She needed to get the house ready for the cold days ahead. Taking advantage of unexpected warm days, she rushed to complete a thorough fall cleaning. She washed the walls, replaced the paper in all the kitchen cabinets, rummaged through the closets to identify clothing ready for the rag pile, straightened out the garage and rearranged the canned goods on the basement shelves. Her energy never lagged.

She didn't let herself spend one second thinking about Risto's letter and his collection of clippings. The envelope and all it contained went to the bottom of Pauline's trunk. It could stay there, out of sight, out of mind.

There was a comfort in the piney smell of her clean kitchen and the orderly nature of every nook and cranny in the house. The list of chores was running low, but she was wondering what to tackle next when she heard the crunch of tires against gravel. She could tell it wasn't Toivo's car, as it drove past the front entry and proceeded down the driveway toward the kitchen door. Maybe it was someone she knew.

The vehicle stopped. The heavy slam of the car door echoed into the leafless woods. Someone was coming to the back door. At least, Lempi thought, it wasn't the lady from Duluth again. She couldn't deal with another revelation.

Because the kitchen door lacked a window, Lempi couldn't see who was outside. Expecting it would be someone she knew, she opened the door without waiting for a knock. Outside, a tall man's raised arm was about to rap the door. He stepped back in surprise. Lempi recognized her visitor immediately. He was older and grayer than she remembered, but she knew it was the FBI agent who haunted her life. It was John Tuzzi,

Pauline's boyfriend. She hadn't seen him since their Milwaukee days. His appearance had settled into a more rugged, yet somehow frailer, version of the man she once knew. She pushed a bit on the door, as though tempted to slam it shut.

"Hello, Lempi," he said. "It's been a while."

"What are you doing here?" she demanded. As though she had risen out of her body, Lempi felt she was looking down on two people she hardly knew. She pictured a middle-aged woman in a faded house dress and poorly tied apron inside the kitchen; outside in the yard, an old man stood ramrod stiff, his morning shadow crossing the fallen leaves of autumn.

"Can I come in?" Tuzzi asked.

"Tell me why you're here." Lempi's cold fear pulled her senses back to earth. Past truths were rushing toward her all at once, demanding that she play out the role she had taken on in life.

Tuzzi took a moment to glance around the small farm. In his scan, he took it all in: the fading paint of the small white farmhouse, the crumbling shingles on the bowing roof of the barn, the broken rails on the wooden fence, the fallow fields that lay beyond, the cackle of chickens in the distant coop, and the bare tree branches silhouetted in the unforgiving sunlight. "It would better if we sat down inside. Where it's warm," he said.

"Are you still an FBI agent?" she asked. "Can I see your badge?"

He shrugged. "I'm retired. This is something personal involving you and me. And Pauline." There was a weakness to Tuzzi that Lempi had not initially seen. He must be nearing seventy by now. A pallor clung to his skin.

"Okay," she said. She held the door open to permit him to walk into the kitchen. "I'll make some coffee. Why don't you sit at the table?"

Lempi could never say 'no' to people. It had been like that with Richard. In those days when they first met for coffee, he begged her to help him with the antiwar cause. He relentlessly reminded her of the horrors consuming the world. Each day, he recited how many more American boys had died needlessly in the jungle. He identified the corporations making money off the war: The airplane factories in California. The chemical company formulating napalm on the east coast. The uniform makers in the south. Across the nation, companies fed at the trough of death. Sharing a moment with Richard was like enlisting in a crusade. And that crusade targeted all her old enemies—the country that kept her from attending

Bremen, those false patriots who hounded her mother into suicide and the capitalists who flung the country into such a great depression that Risto fled to Russia. In a small coffee house at the end of the Sixties, a drink with Richard was flavored with all of that.

The coffee she was about to share with Tuzzi would not be the same. He pulled out the wooden dinette chair. "Coffee would be great."

Her electric percolator was still plugged in. By now, the coffee might be a bit burnt, but it would do. She poured a cup for each of them, plucked some cookies from the jar, placed them on a plate and set it all on the table. "I still don't know why you're here," Lempi said. "After all these years, what do you want with me?"

"I've never given up on the Bremen bombing," he said. Tuzzi seemed a bit ill at ease. "My bosses lost interest in it years ago, even before I retired. But the case has never been closed, at least not officially. We know Richard Epstein was the ringleader, and he is still on the wanted list. He disappeared after the bombing. At first, we thought he fled to Canada. That's where we found two of his gang. But there's never been a sign of him there. Not in Toronto. Not in Vancouver. Maybe he went underground in the U.S. But I have never doubted that he remains alive. I've vowed that I will hunt him until the day I die. He killed the only woman I ever loved."

And that bombing killed my mother, Lempi thought, but I don't care where Richard is. She wondered if Tuzzi was aware that Pauline was her mother. Who knew the secrets shared on bedroom pillows?

Tuzzi continued, "And I think you may know where Epstein is. If you do, I want you to tell me."

Lempi was startled. Richard had never communicated with her. Not once had he tried to reach her to apologize for the damage he done.

"Why would you think I know anything?"

"Because I have friends who still help me keep an eye out on those I find interesting, and because of that, I know you recently received a shipment from someone in the Soviet Union. I think it may have been a communication from Epstein. The two of you were close. Sometimes I wonder how close."

Now Lempi was shocked. How could Tuzzi know about the envelope? Was the FBI spying on her? She chose to remain silent.

"What was in that package, Lempi? Don't think we don't track what happens when Americans visit the Soviet Union. Who they visit. What they bring back. An agent alerted me that a Joan Anderson of Duluth was given a package in Karelia to deliver back to you. Was it a message from Epstein?"

The plan started innocently enough. One day while Toivo was working, Richard and his friends sat in her living room. One kid said the group should create a stir to demonstrate their cause was serious.

"And what would create that stir?" Richard asked. He was more interested in helping draft dodgers reach Canada than in public protests.

"Create a symbolic blow against the establishment," Lempi piped in. "Do something visible and big, something so outrageous that the media can't ignore it. Show them we mean business about stopping this war."

Richard looked at her as though she were a fool, but the others grew excited. Their ideas bubbled over. One person suggested a giant sit-in to shut down Milwaukee traffic during rush hour. Another wanted to cover the front of the city hall with pig's blood. The more timid just wanted to march in the streets.

"It's all been done before," declared Richard. "None of those things have any impact. The best way to end the war is to cut off the supply of soldiers. We need to get everyone to resist the draft. That's how we make a difference."

"But what if we give people something to rally around? Something that reinforces their spine? Symbols matter. Remember the Boston Tea Party, the sinking of the Maine, Davy Crockett fighting at the Alamo?" Lempi felt high just saying it aloud.

Richard found her amusing. "And do you have such a symbol? Here in Milwaukee?" he asked.

"What about the Army Computing Center at Bremen College? What if you bombed it?"

"Lempi, I'll ask again? Has Epstein been back in touch with you?" Tuzzi's air of triumph angered her. It was as though Tuzzi thought he already knew the answer.

"No, he has not," Lempi snapped. "I've not talked to Richard since Pauline died."

"Then who sent you a package from within the Soviet Union?"

Lempi looked at this aging Don Quixote in her kitchen; he was just some old man on a quest to avenge Pauline's death, and she despised him. Why couldn't he give up and face reality? What did it matter to him who sent her what? "It was from Risto Makinen. You know . . . the Communist son of Eero and Marja Makinen. Remember Marja, the woman you and your FBI harassed until she lit herself on fire? Still searching for the person who caused that death?"

"Lempi, I was just doing my job," Tuzzi started, and then stopped himself. "Wait a minute. You want me to believe that your brother reappeared after forty years?"

Lempi looked at him disdainfully. "It should be easy enough to check. He lives north of Leningrad in the Karelia district. Why didn't you interview the woman who was asked to carry his letter? She could have told you. Save yourself a trip in the future, and avoid reminding me of everything you took from me. Funny thing is, maybe the U.S. government was right about my family. Maybe one of my parents was a Communist." Lempi stopped herself. She wasn't going to tell this man the details of Risto's letter.

"Why did he get in touch with you after all these years?"

"I guess he saw an opportunity to reconnect and he took it."

"Can I see his letter?"

"I burned it," she lied. "I was afraid the FBI might show up again and try to deport me as a Communist. But I guess I'm just a cog in your chain to entrap a radical terrorist."

Tuzzi stood and straightened his pants. His hands fidgeted as though he felt compelled to put on a hat, although he didn't have one with him. "Lempi, I'm sorry if I bothered you. But Pauline was murdered. Even after all these years, I can't let it go unpunished. I would think you would care just as much. You know she loved you."

Richard's eyes lit up at the idea of bombing the computing center. "You're right on one thing. The center deserves to be bombed," he said. "Their research is all about improving bombing efficiency. Their mathematics kill."

"And the center is at the heart of the campus," Lempi pointed out. "And remember that it occupies two floors of a building named for Shindler. That right wing brewer is profiting from this war as much as any of your other criminals. It would be justified to blow up his building. The whole nation would pay attention."

One of the girls first raised the concern about casualties. "But there's always people in that hall. You'll kill someone if you bomb it." The girl, a comely sophomore at Bremen, was Richard's latest admirer. Richard paused. He wasn't like some of the more radical SDS members who were eager to spark some revolution.

"Not if you plan it for a holiday like Christmas or New Year's," Lempi rejoined. "I know. I spend a lot of time in that building. The halls and offices are as empty as can be on a holiday. There're no guards. And no custodian after eleven."

Lempi could see the idea was exciting the gang, but Richard remained skeptical. "Where we would get the dynamite. Isn't it controlled? None of us know anything about explosives. We'd probably kill ourselves trying to light the fuse."

"I have an idea," Lempi said. She spoke slowly, trying to pull from her memory both the tales Eero used to tell of blowing stumps and a recent conversation about how his next door neighbors used an explosive created from fertilizer. "I think we could get the right recipe for an explosive from the state agricultural bureau. And we wouldn't need to buy any dynamite."

It had all been her idea. She set the plan in motion. Richard was a city boy. She pushed him over the edge. And, even at the time, she knew creating an antiwar symbol didn't motivate her. She wanted revenge against Bremen, against Shindler and his scholarship, against the U.S. government with their FBI goons and everyone else who had blocked her success.

After the horrific Christmas Eve, Richard and the others fled. But Lempi had to stay and live with Pauline's murder.

The cookies she set out for Tuzzi were uneaten. His sludge-like coffee was half-drunk. Tuzzi was clearly eager to leave now that he realized there was no smoking gun.

"I am sorry if I upset you, Lempi," he apologized, "but I will never stop looking. Someday, somewhere, I am going to ensure everyone involved with Pauline's death faces justice. I'm not leaving it to God."

"You're on a fool's errand. Too much time has passed."

"Maybe not. Besides I have nothing but time to keep slogging away. The Federal Government isn't interested, but state laws were broken as well. I have some paperwork ready to go to the Wisconsin state attorney . . . as soon as I figure out a few more pieces. He could officially reopen the case for the state." Tuzzi looked directly into Lempi's eyes, and held them an unnatural length of time.

"It was a long shot to think that your envelope came from Epstein. But I've always thought you know more about that night than you've told me, so I took a chance.

"The truth is that I think Richard is hiding in California. Got some real clues about a potential ID there, and if the state authorizes reopening the investigation, I'll have the resources to flush him out. I'll get the bastard, bring him back to Wisconsin and sweat out of him every last fact about what went down that day. I tell you, Lempi, everyone's going to pay. I won't give up as long as I still have a breath in me."

Lempi wasn't interested. She walked toward the door and held it open, "I'm sorry you drove all the way to northern Wisconsin to find out nothing. Like I said, you could have just called."

"I needed to see your face when I asked. You never played poker well."

She said nothing. Tuzzi gave her another penetrating stare.

"But I can tell you're not lying about the packet coming from your brother." Tuzzi touched the brow of his head as though saluting. "Give my regards to Toivo." Lempi thought to herself that telling Toivo any of this was just about the last thing she would ever do.

It was over. Everything sent by Risto was now at the bottom of the old hope chest. It seemed appropriate since Lempi suspected Pauline had originally sent most of the clippings. Time for them to return to the trunk of memories.

In the end, everything would no doubt rise to the surface. No matter how hard the attempt, truth does not sink into the dark water of memory.

Secrets stew with a life of their own and bubble forth with a buoyancy generated by their own heat. All Lempi could seek to do was to weigh it down and sink it a little deeper. Perhaps that would give Danny a chance.

That morning, Toivo left for work the same way he departed every day. He put on his lumbering clothes, checked that his thermos was filled with hot coffee, grabbed his black metal lunch box and leaned in toward Lempi for a quick kiss. Just a brushing of lips, really, a brush of warmth from lips chapped by cold weather. But it meant something. She knew that. It was his promise that he would be careful in the woods. It was his commitment to return. It was Toivo saying that he loved her despite all her failings.

Toivo might suspect, but he could never know how deep her flaws were. That knowledge would destroy for him every kiss and every holding of hands during their years together. She couldn't let him lose that. After all these years, she owed him at least that.

Departing the house, Danny was more subdued than usual. He walked slowly toward the spot at the end of the driveway where the school bus would stop. Maybe he was being bullied again. She waited to watch for the old yellow bus to arrive promptly at 7:55 am, as it did every school day. For eight years, Jack Manny, the bus driver, promptly appeared to transport her son safely to and fro. School provided Danny with a normalcy in his life. This small town was good for him. Too fragile to deal with city bullies, Danny would drown in the turmoil of a large urban school. Maybe in the dowdy hallways of the Thread school, he was picked upon, but he was also protected. Everyone knew everyone. Townsfolk cared for one another. No one would let anything go too far. They would accept Danny for who he was.

But even for this place, some acts were unforgiveable. She needed to shelter Danny from those. Her one legacy. Someday her horrible secret might bubble up from the muck. Tuzzi might finally find Richard and determine the truth. When that happened in some future time, let the shame fall on a fading memory of a woman who once lived—and not on the men who loved her.

Lempi was alone in the house. Dirty breakfast dishes reminded her of life's mundane needs. She lifted up the egg-smeared plates to carry them to the sink. She scraped crumbs from the toasted homemade bread into the trash. She rinsed orange pulp from the small juice glasses. She considered saving the layer of congealed bacon fat in the old cast iron pan, but decided that Toivo wouldn't know what to do with it, and so she wiped it clean with a paper towel.

With her big farm sink filled with hot sudsy water, she washed the dishes. The warm water was a small pleasure and Lempi realized how cold the house was. Toivo left without lighting a fire in their wood furnace. She should get a good fire going so the house would be warm when Danny returned that afternoon. Maybe later.

She threw coarse salt into the cast iron pan and scoured it clean. She gave it a quick rinse, then set it on a burners with the flame turned high for a fast dry. She didn't want it to rust for her men. The hot iron smell lingered as she placed the wiped dishes in their proper spot. Her dishtowel was embroidered with a baking bear for Friday. Danny would expect fresh doughnuts when he got home. But the kitchen was so clean. She couldn't bear to dirty it. She folded the towel on the sink rack.

Lempi walked room to room. She let her hand glide across the furniture that defined their lives. Most of the wooden pieces originally belonged to Toivo's parents. When she escaped Milwaukee, she assumed their life. All in all, life in Thread proved not much different than the Finnish immigrant routines of her youth. If the small farmhouse had been her self-imposed prison, it always felt familiar.

She wandered into Danny's room, seeking tasks to fill the remaining hours. For no good reason she had a timeline, but the minutes ahead seemed unnecessarily long. She opened Danny's sock and underwear drawer, and marveled at the jumble. She refolded the underwear onto one side of the drawer, and lined up rolls of socks on the other. Would he ever notice what she had done? She opened his closet door and similarly ordered his shirts and pants. It didn't take long. They never had a lot of money to buy Danny a big wardrobe. He didn't seem to mind, but then Lempi was never certain what went on behind those big eyes.

Danny had his pleasures. That she knew. He liked to roam the fields and pastures of the farm, and was fond of bringing home private treasures—a walking stick, a monarch butterfly chrysalis, an odd-shaped piece of quartz. For a few days, they would mesmerize him until he would discard them from boredom. There was no pattern to what caught his attention. Maybe it was the novelty, the uniqueness or just the serendipity of a moment. But in those invested beats of time, his beauty was intensified by the animation of his interest. She would miss seeing those moments. But they would continue—with or without her.

It was only ten o'clock in the morning. Lempi decided to walk the route of her evening stroll without Toivo. The air outside smelled fresh and big. The light breeze enveloped her with the crispness of bright leaves falling. As she headed toward the main road, she could see there was little traffic on Highway 17. Not many people drove this far north so late in the season. Still, for safety, she walked against traffic and stayed on the edge of the ditch. The sun warmed her. In the illuminating sunlight, this walk felt so different than in the evenings with Toivo. Details popped that she never noticed in the pale twilight.

Such walks were always a moment of peace. They were important to Toivo too, she knew, but they meant something else to him, and who could ever know what was in another's mind. But for her, rhythm released her. The regular motion of step after step, the light crunch of the shoe hitting the edge between grass and gravel, a regularity to life, a predictability in which one could find comfort and release.

Toivo liked to hold her hand on these walks. He had the warmest hands and they fed her energy. For the first time ever, she wondered if she returned some type of life source. What had he gained from these walks over the years? What would he do without her? If there were a God, maybe he would let her spirit return one day to take a final walk with her husband.

By the time Lempi returned from her walk, she felt light-headed, but she was certain of her next step. Too often in her life, she failed to think through her actions. She simply flowed along whatever stream she encountered. No wonder she ended up in such treacherous waters.

She returned to Danny's room and sat on the edge of his bed. Its chenille bedspread was worn. She took a final look. A large poster for the TV show *The Dukes of Hazzard* decorated one wall. She wondered if Danny had a crush on the Daisy Duke character, although she found the actor John Schneider quite handsome. On the other wall, Danny had pinned a large poster of Christopher Reeve as Superman. If only there were some caped hero who could fly in to make everything right. But there was only her.

Finally, Lempi stood up. She entered the single bathroom and pulled from the wall cabinet a prescription bottle of sleeping pills. The container was nearly full. She seldom used them, perhaps because she sensed that one day she would need them for another purpose. Lempi wasn't as reckless or foolhardy as to take Marja's approach to death. Funny, how she could no longer think of the woman who raised her as Ma. Risto had taken that away from her.

She held the bottle in her hand and weighed it, but really she was evaluating the future. Which way led to the greatest happiness for Danny and Toivo? She knew the answer. She really had no choice.

It was eleven o'clock.

It was her time.

She would set things right.

And it was done.

EPILOGUE
1983
THREAD, WISCONSIN

An eagle flew high over the landscape of Thread. For a moment, the bird eyed the smoke that rose from the farmhouse chimney. Cinder grey bits floated aimlessly upward. The trajectory of smoke shifted, buffeted by a chilled northern breeze.

Uninterested by smoke, the eagle flew higher. The bird circled back around the house in a broader and broader path. From the air, the eagle saw no signs of life in the house. But deep in the basement, Danny, as hidden as a mouse in its burrow or a rabbit in its warren, was feeding the fire. The eagle circled still wider, unaware and uninterested in the boy in the basement with his collection of past lives.

The wind shifted. Particles of smoke wandered into new directions, dispersed into smaller and smaller elements. Change was in the air. A storm might be coming.

In the basement, Danny stoked the fire with the last of the pieces of paper he had found. Why keep any of it? These photos and clippings were meaningless, and he was angry that his dead mother left them behind. The smoke grew darker. Old newsprint. An ancient photo. Remnants of lives lived and gone.

Danny paused. Only one item remained. He looked at it and decided to set it aside. He burned the rest.

Above, the eagle ka-kawed and flew north to seek more promising grounds. Perhaps it followed the bits of smoke, the remaining atoms of memories and hopes, transgressions and sins. Purged by the fire, everything returned to its beginning: the bits of silver halide embedded in the old photos, the carbon in the ink, the dextrose of the paper—rendered by flame into ash and smoke. The smoke fled into the stormy winds of polar air rushing south from Canada

The eagle flew higher and higher, surveying a broader universe of woods and lakes. It had no memory of the smoking chimney. It cared nothing about the crying boy beside an opened trunk, a boy who desperately wanted to find answers, but only uncovered mute photos and clippings.

The fire died down. The remaining smoke merged with the cold wet wind crossing the ridges of the Penokee range north of Thread. Moisture-laden air was forced to move upward. It compressed, the water attached itself to the seeds of smoke and began to drop as flakes of snow. As the snow grew heavier, the eagle retreated to its nesting tree. The sun set, the night cold deepened and snow blanketed the fall earth with a wintry cover.

The world moved on, as it always does. One sick pig infected a child. One lost child begat another. One act of idealism failed to deliver. The boy knew none of it.

In far off Russia, Yuri Andropov, recently named premier of the Soviet Union, gave no thought to a young idealist he sent to the Urals in 1939. In Minnesota, Eugene McCarthy, a civil Don Quixote planning yet another run for president, did not recall volunteers from his 1968 Wisconsin primary. Former Milwaukee mayor Frank Zeidler, hoping to revitalize the Socialist party with a 1984 run for U.S. president, did not mourn an old assistant. An aged Gus Hall, never thinking about a long ago speech in Clover, conferred with activist Angela Davis about a potential run as U.S. Communist Party candidates.

In Madison, Fighting Bob LaFollette's grandson, Bronson LaFollette, the attorney general of Wisconsin, set aside John Tuzzi's proposed investigation into the Bremen bombing. He judged it unworkable. These decisions would not impact Danny's future in Thread; their past actions had already changed his life.

In the morning, the rays of dawn skipped across the glittering crystals of the new-fallen snow. No smoke marred the crisp blue sky. The eagle soared again.

The eagle did not think of Danny in the basement. It did not worry that the boy fell asleep beside the cinders of the furnace, beside his mother's trunk. It did not know that Toivo, when he returned from work and found his son asleep, lovingly carried the adolescent boy up the two flights of stairs to his bed without awakening him. It could not ponder if Toivo was surprised to find a forgotten photo of Pauline, Lempi and Danny clutched in his sleeping son's hand, nor could it care what the father and son discussed when both awoke to a new day covered in snow. Only they could know.

In the morning, it is a new day. The eagle circles lower to the ground. Already, the unblemished snow has been touched. Small mouse tracks lead straight ahead, the scampering feet of a fresh morning. The eagle swoops in.

It is not yet done.

Life continues.

AUTHOR'S NOTES

The Finnish Girl is inspired by a few incidents within my own family. A neighboring woman left my mother a steamer trunk filled with hand-crafted items, and my mother often wondered why. My mother's brother was a volunteer in the Karelian Technical Aid, and no contact occurred between him and my family from the late Thirties until the early Seventies when it was discovered he was alive and well in Karelia. Several of my father's relatives died of trichinosis in 1913 from an infected pig. However, the rest of my family's story is far less lively than that found in *The Finnish Girl*.

The Finnish Girl is based on a very specific historical era, and many of the novel's incidents occur within actual events. This includes the emigration of Finns to the Midwest, the ill-fated Karelian Technical Aid movement, the rule of Milwaukee by Socialist Party mayors, the deportation of elderly immigrants during the Red Scare, the importance of Wisconsin to Senator Eugene McCarthy's 1968 campaign, and a similar bombing to my fictional one at the Army Math Research Center at the University of Wisconsin-Madison. Yuri Andropov, Gus Hall, Robert LaFollette, Eugene McCarthy, and Frank Zeidler are all real historical characters (although I accelerated the posting of Andropov to Karelia by a year for the sake of the story.)

For those readers interested in knowing more of the details behind these periods, I'd suggest the following books:

Bates, Tom. *Rads: The 1970 Bombing of the Army Math Research Center at the University of Wisconsin and Its Aftermath*. New York: HarperCollins Pubishers, 1992.

Caute, David. *The Great Fear: The Anti-Communist Purge Under Truman and Eisenhower*. New York: Simon and Shuster, 1978.

Engle, Eloise. *Finns in North America.* Annapolis, MD: Leeward Publications, Inc., 1975.

Halberstam, David. *The Fifties.* New York: Open Road, 2013.

Knipping, Mark. *Finns in Wisconsin.* Madison: The State Historical Society of Wisconsin, 1977.

Kolehmainen, John, I., and Hill, George W. *Haven in the Woods: The Story of the Finns in Wisconsin.* New York: Arno Press, 1979.

Larson, Olaf. F. *When Horses Pulled the Plow: Life of a Wisconsin Farm Boy 1910-1929.* Madison: The University of Wisconsin Press, 2011.

Minehan, Thomas. *Boy and Girl Tramps of America.* New York: Farrar and Rinehart, 1934.

Schrecker, Ellen. *Many Are the Crimes: McCarthyism in America.* Princeton: Princeton University Press, 1998.

Sevander, Mayme, with Hertzel, Laurie. *They Took My Father: Finnish Americans in Stalin's Russia.* Minneapolis: University of Minnesota Press, 1992.

White, Theodore H. *The Making of the President 1968.* New York: Anthenum Publishers, 1969.

Zeidler, Frank P. *A Liberal in City Government: My Experiences as Mayor of Milwaukee.* Milwaukee: Milwaukee Publishers LLC, 2005.

I am also indebted to two unpublished memoirs written by members of the Karelian Technical Aid. The first is "My Life" written by my uncle Armas Siikarla, a volunteer who lived out his life in Karelia. The other, written by a member of my mother's neighboring family (who returned from Karelia after a year as volunteers) is titled "Is Number 13 Lucky or Unlucky: An Autobiography" by Oliver Karpela.

My deepest thanks to my husband Robert for his ongoing encouragement and insights. Thanks also to Dr. Betsy Tieman and Dr. John Tieman for reviewing my description of trichinosis. My appreciation to all those who reviewed my first novel on GoodReads and Amazon; your feedback helped me grow as a writer.

Finally, for those interested in knowing more about what happens to Danny Lahti, Toivo Lahti, or Tom Ferber, aka Mr. Packer, look for my first novel, *Tales from the Loon Town Cafe.*

ABOUT THE AUTHOR

Dennis Frahmann grew up in Wisconsin, trained in journalism and spent most of his adult life in New York, Minneapolis and Los Angeles. Today he resides with his husband, Robert Tieman, in the seaside village of Cambria, California.

Made in the USA
Lexington, KY
22 August 2015